The Accidental Mother

Rowan Coleman

W F HOWES LTD

This large print edition published in 2009 by
W F Howes Ltd
Unit 4, Rearsby Business Park, Gaddesby Lane,
Rearsby, Leicester LE7 4YH

1 3 5 7 9 10 8 6 4 2

First published in the United Kingdom in 2005
by Century

A CIP catalogue record for this book is available
from the British Library

ISBN 978 1 40743 290 8

Typeset by Palimpsest Book Production Limited,
Grangemouth, Stirlingshire
Printed and bound in Great Britain
by MPG Books Ltd, Bodmin, Cornwall

FSC
Mixed Sources
Product group from well-managed
forests and other controlled sources
Cert no. SGS-COC-2953
www.fsc.org
© 1996 Forest Stewardship Council

**'But what will we do then?
If we can't stay here?'**

Six-year-old Bella looked at Sophie, her dry eyes burning.

There had to be a moment like this, Sophie thought, in everyone's life, when the very next thing you say might change you and the world as you knew it forever. She felt her stomach dip and churn as if she had just run headlong at a cliff edge and brought herself to a stop at its very brink.

'Then we'll work out what's best,' she answered, feeling like a coward.

'What's best?' Bella said dimly, staring down at her feet again. Then she sat up a little and lifted her chin. 'Okay,' she said with a look of weary resignation that should never have visited her young face.

There had to be something, Sophie thought, some promise she could make to Bella and Izzy that she absolutely knew she could keep. Some promise that could give the children something solid to rely on.

'A funny, touching story—and another unputdownable read.'
—*Company* magazine

'A charming tale . . . sophisticated.'
—*Heat* magazine

ALSO BY ROWAN COLEMAN
FROM CLIPPER LARGE PRINT

The Accidental Wife
The Baby Group

For Mike
1971–2005

ACKNOWLEDGEMENTS

Thank you so much to the amazingly creative and always supportive Kate Elton and Georgina Hawtrey-Woore, both of whom make the editorial process such a pleasure. And to all the team at Arrow and Random House for the hard work and dedication they put in every day with unfailing enthusiasm.

Thank you to Lizzy Kremer, the world's most dedicated agent, always on the end of the phone, even during maternity leave!

To Maggie Crawford and the fantastic team at Simon & Schuster and Pocket Books, thank you for believing in me and my book.

And to my dear friends who keep me going, Jenny Matthews, Rosie Wooley, Sarah Boswell (and her mum, Mrs Darby), Clare Winter (and her mum, Mrs Smith), and Cathy Carter (and her mum, Mrs Bell). You all give me so much encouragement.

Finally, thank you to my wonderful husband, Erol, whose love and faith never waver, and to my daughter, Lily, who is so clever, beautiful, funny, and kind that I can scarcely believe I'm her mother!

The Accidental Mother

CHAPTER 1

Sophie considered the question Jake Flynn had just asked her.

It wasn't a difficult question. It didn't require a degree in anything to understand it, or any special knowledge of semantics. No, it was much more tricky than that. Jake Flynn had just asked her out to lunch, but that wasn't really the question. The question was – what *kind* of lunch?

As Jake waited for her reply on the other end of the line Sophie sat back in her chair and swivelled it so that she could see out of her office window and down onto the Plaza below, and watched the wind gust and sweep an errant piece of brightly coloured litter in whirls and swoops across the near-empty expanse. One of Sophie's main difficulties in life (not a problem – she refused to admit that she had a problem despite her PA Cal constantly assuring her otherwise) was knowing when men were attracted to her. Other women and most of her friends – OK, all of her friends – seemed to have the sort of intuition that kicked in at least a month before Sophie's did. Whilst her friends had frequently planned short engagements and long marriages based solely on thirty seconds' worth of eye contact in a nightclub, Sophie was far too afraid of getting it wrong to wait for anything less than large bouquets of flowers delivered to her desk and an invitation to a romantic break in Venice as a sign that a man was interested in her. And as only one man had done this in the last decade – Sophie's ex-boyfriend Alex – her relationship experience was limited to him and a handful of hopefuls that friends and colleagues had lined up for her. All of whom admitted defeat at the first obstacle.

The first obstacle being Sophie herself.

Sophie's confusion about Jake Flynn's lunch invitation arose from the fact that he was a client, her newest and most important client in some weeks. He was the one she hoped was going to give her the edge she needed to secure a hotly contested promotion. She would wow her boss Gillian with the lucrative long-term contract she was planning to negotiate with the Madison Corporation, Jake's company.

Cal had declared after the very first meeting almost three months ago that Jake fancied her.

'He does not,' Sophie had told him. 'He's just being friendly and, you know – American. Americans are very friendly.'

'Not that friendly,' Cal had retorted. 'Not unless they want a lawsuit slapped on them.'

Sophie had shot him one of her best silencing glances and told him that the most important

2

thing was to persuade Jake Flynn that McCarthy Hughes was the best corporate events company to organise his organisation's first UK event. And to show him that her ideas, plans and budgets knocked all the competition into a cocked hoop, as her mother would say.

And Sophie had triumphed.

'I've never met a party planner quite as serious as you,' Jake had told her as he left their first meeting. 'You could be a general in the army!'

Sophie had laughed politely and shaken his hand (wondering if his comment had anything to do with her forgetting to wax her top lip the previous evening), and walked him to the lift.

'*That* was called flirting,' Cal had informed her as she got back to her desk.

'Cal,' Sophie had warned him, 'he wasn't flirting, and even if he was – which he wasn't – I wouldn't date him because he's my client.'

'You're a party planner, not a lawyer,' Cal had said. 'I don't think it's against the rules.'

'It's against my rules,' Sophie had said.

'Everything's against your rules,' Cal had replied.

Since Sophie was so hopeless at working out if a man was attracted to her, mostly she avoided thinking about it. But now she couldn't stop speculating about whether or not Cal was right about Jake. It was like part of a crossword puzzle that she couldn't solve.

She couldn't help but dwell on the fact that

Jake Flynn was very handsome in a proper square-jawed sort of way. And he was dreadfully polite and, Sophie noticed, had very fresh breath. It would be disastrous to mistake good manners and good dental hygiene for attraction – she would never live it down. But Jake really was out of bounds, which made him all the more intriguing. Not because Sophie was the kind of woman to throw caution to the wind and embark on an ill-advised affair with reckless abandon, but because she preferred her love interests to be off limits. It was much safer and far less time-consuming.

A good five seconds had passed since Jake had asked her out to lunch, and Sophie did a split-second review of the available facts.

The party was planned, the date was set and all the arrangements were made. There was no real reason for Jake Flynn to be in touch with Sophie until just before the party itself, and that wasn't for nearly a month. Still Sophie couldn't decide what kind of lunch Jake had in mind, but she realised in a moment of clarity she was going to have to say 'yes' – he *was* her most important client, after all.

'Sorry, Jake,' Sophie said, efficiently covering the pause. 'I was just looking at my diary and there's nothing in at twelve so . . . Oh hang on, what's this?' The initials 'TA' had been penned into the twelve o'clock slot in purple ink. That wasn't Cal, he was far too organised to deface her diary in such a slapdash way. That was her executive trainee, Lisa. Sophie sighed. There were no other details, just the letters TA, written in round girlish letters. How many times did she have to remind Lisa to ask Cal to put any new entries in her diary? The trouble was that Lisa was scared of Cal, and even though technically he was her PA too she would rather gouge out her own eyes with rusty nails than ask him to do anything for her.

'Well, whatever it is it can be moved,' Sophie said, feeling uncharacteristically capricious for a second before her stomach muscles clenched with worry. It couldn't be that important, she told herself. If it was, then even Lisa would have brought it to her attention.

'Great!' Jake said the word on an exhaled breath. 'OK I'll swing by and pick you up, shall I, at twelve?'

'Oh well, you don't have to do that, Jake . . .' Sophie began, before pausing for a moment to consider the ambiguity of their meeting. 'But you can if you want,' she finished a little awkwardly.

'I want,' Jake said, with a laugh. 'I'll see you at twelve.'

'Super,' Sophie said.

Jake hung up.

Sophie looked at the receiver and decided that now was not the time to think about the fact she hadn't had sex for over a year and worry that if she ever ended up in bed with someone again, she would be really terrible at it.

Seeing she had five minutes until her next

meeting with Deutche Bank, she glanced at the pointed toes of her new pink suede boots and smiled. It had taken a good ten minutes longer to get into work this morning simply because she'd had to be extra careful as she picked her way through the puddles and remnants of last night's dirty half-hearted snow, in a bid to keep the suede pristine. And then of course there were the heels. It was tricky and probably even risky to run down a wet and crowded escalator in high heels but still, as Sophie lifted her right foot and then her left in turn, she felt it had been worth the risk. Of course, she could have put her new boots in a bag and worn trainers to work, changing them under the desk the moment she got in, but she didn't have any, and anyway trainer-changing was for wimps. Besides, Sophie felt the best thing about her new boots was actually wearing them, come hell or high puddles. Sophie might not have been the world's most adventurous or spontaneous person but she was very hard core about her shoes – all forty-eight pairs.

Cal said once that her flamboyant love of footwear demonstrated the inner diva in her struggling to break free from her puritanical, sexually repressed exterior.

Sophie pointed out that she frequently wore skirts above the knee and so was neither puritanical nor sexually repressed, thank you very much. Cal had snorted in derision and said if there was a closet for straight people she would be in it.

He said she wore flash shoes to cover up her total lack of sexuality. Sophie told him that he was quite wrong. It was just shoes. Shoes and boots and mules and pumps. She loved shoes in all colours, shapes and sizes – her reaction to seeing a new pair in *Vogue* or *Glamour* was almost visceral. It was a gut-wrenching longing that didn't abate until those particular shoes were safely nestled in their box and swinging from her wrist in an expensive waxed paper bag. And then there was a moment of perfect bliss and satisfaction followed by the anticipation of winning that day's shoe-off with her office rival and general all-round nemesis, Eve McQueen.

Cal often said that there were specialist websites for people like her, but Sophie shrugged off his comments and told him that actually it was because her mum made her wear clunky Clarks shoes to school until she was fourteen, even though her friends were wearing grey patent leather with an ankle strap and a maroon bow on the side.

She told him her shoe collection was the little part of her that could be free and creative. Her shoes were what made her stand out from all the other women in grey or black business suits.

Cal said it wasn't her shoes that did that, and Sophie decided not to ask him what he meant.

It might even be, Sophie thought, biting her lip as she straightened her calf and stretched her toes to a point, that her shoes were what made Jake

Flynn ask her out to lunch – if indeed it turned out that he was asking her out to a *lunch* lunch and not a lunch *lunch*.

She frowned. She had succeeded in confusing herself again. Luckily Cal snapped her out of the moment.

'The Germans are coming,' he said, opening her door without knocking. Sophie surreptitiously tucked her booted leg back down behind her desk and sat up. 'They're in the lobby on the way up – do you want to meet them at the lift?'

'I want,' Sophie said, allowing herself a tiny smile as she heard herself echo Jake. 'Let's practise German on the way.'

'*Guten Tag Herr Manners*,' Cal said slowly and carefully. The fact that he was multilingual made him a real asset, as he never tired of reminding her.

'*Guten Tag Herr Manners*.' When Sophie said it she sounded like her cat Artemis coughing up a hairball.

'Mmmm,' Cal said. 'Once more with feeling.'

'*Guten Tag,* oh bollocks.' Sophie hated it when she couldn't get a thing absolutely right and she especially hated the fact that she was no good at languages. It wasn't the actual words so much – although she didn't really know any besides the ones Cal told her – it was the accent. She just couldn't let herself go enough to get the accent right.

'I don't think our German cousins use that

phrase,' Cal told her flatly. 'Maybe just stick to English. Germans speak very good English. Most nations speak very good English and, while I approve of your attempts to be transglobal, I think in this case you should take advantage of that.'

'I think you're right,' Sophie said. 'I just like to pay . . .'

'. . . attention to detail.' Cal mimicked her mantra with eerie accuracy.

Sophie laughed. She was really very fond of Cal. They had been together for almost five years, it was Sophie's longest relationship with a man and she knew she could rely on him absolutely. He was the best PA on the floor. In the early part of their relationship she had once spent nearly three months being in love with him and wishing that he was straight. But then she realised that if he was straight she probably wouldn't like him at all, because who likes a straight man who spends that much time reading girls' magazines? Since then they had gradually become closer and closer friends, and Sophie had fallen in love with an anonymous risk assessor in the building over the road instead.

She had had frequent late-night, slightly slurred discussions with friends or Cal about whether her long-distance admirations were actually 'love', in the purest sense of the word. Sophie maintained that they were exactly that, pure love, an updated version of the medieval kind when lovers weren't necessarily required to talk to each other. This meant no false promises were made, nobody got lied to, no-one got left and no person, in particular Sophie, had to spend several months pretending she wasn't in the least bit sad or hurt.

'Sounds like stalking to me,' Cal had said.

Sophie focused her attention back on the Germans.

'Anyway, where's Lisa? She knows we've got a meeting at eleven.' Sophie scanned the office looking for her trainee, the third and supposedly vital member of her team, although Cal cheerfully referred to her as 'the Dead Weight'.

'She's got all the costings for this meeting and they'll be here any minute – if she's crying in the toilets again I swear to God I'm going to . . .'

'Be nice to her and tell her it doesn't matter?' Cal snapped. He wasn't afraid of sharing his opinions as to how useful Lisa was. 'You should just bin her, she's rubbish.'

'It's her first job,' Sophie said. 'Everyone's crap at their first job. She just needs a bit of time to get into it.'

'She's had eight months.'

'Just get her, OK?' Sophie said in her boss voice.

Cal saluted her and headed purposefully towards the ladies'.

Sophie watched the numbers on the lift creep up, and sighed. She had been training Lisa for the best part of a year now. She really liked her, she could see she had potential, but Lisa just couldn't seem to separate her head from her heart. It was as if the two organs had been fused into one tumultuous mass. Lisa had such a dramatic love life that the average romance writer would have rejected it as too unbelievable. Sophie had tried to give her pep talks over the months, and the last time her trainee had had a crisis during office hours, Sophie had even wiped Lisa's eyes and gently suggested that she might want to try to cut down on the number of men she dated or maybe even stop seeing men altogether for a while – especially as it didn't seem to be working out for her.

'Give them up completely like you, you mean?' Lisa had asked her with the typical wide-eyed tact of a 21-year-old. 'But what about sex? Don't you miss shagging?'

Sophie remembered feeling her cheeks begin to colour and she had decided against confiding in Lisa that in the eighteen months since her boyfriend Alex had left her via e-mail she hadn't had sex once. It wasn't that she didn't miss it, she did in a sort of abstract, romanticised way. But she didn't miss it with anybody in particular. Not even with Alex – and she had nearly been in love with him – did the earth move for her. She suspected that the earth didn't move for any woman and that the whole thing was a massive conspiracy made up by women's magazines and men to make all women feel insecure. But then people like Lisa did sort of throw that theory out of the window. Lisa, it was clear, really enjoyed having sex even if it inevitably ended in emotional disappointment.

'I haven't given men up,' Sophie had told her. 'I'm just choosing to put my job first at the moment and I think you should do the same. Now is an important time for us. If Gillian really does decide to give up work then someone will need to take over her job. Opportunities are opening up. I want the best out of my career and so should you. I'm giving you a big chance here, Lisa, it's time for you to grasp it with both hands. Don't let me down.'

'I will, I will,' Lisa had promised her obliquely. But she had fallen in love with the water-cooler-refill man on the way back to her desk, and when he dumped her two weeks later she was back to square one.

The lift had paused on the floor below Sophie's.

'She's here.' Cal almost shoved Lisa at Sophie, who looked at her trainee with a critical eye. She had reapplied her make-up but her eyes were red and puffy and her nose swollen. She'd been crying again.

'Dave chucked you?' Sophie asked her in the final few moments as the lift reached their floor.

Lisa's tender eyes widened with distress. 'All I did was ask him to meet my mum. Is that too clingy?'

Sophie sighed. It had to be said that if Lisa was a superhero she would probably be known as Cling Film Girl, but now was certainly not the time to bring that up.

'We'll talk about this later,' she said. 'Just stay focused and remember what you're here for.'

And the lift doors slid open.

When Sophie and Lisa returned from the meeting, Sophie was feeling very pleased with herself. It had gone exceptionally well, and Lisa had made it back to her desk without becoming engaged. Things were looking up. She even had time before lunch with Jake to catch up on her paperwork. Or maybe she'd swing by Eve's office and tell her about her new contract, show off her new boots and generally try to piss her off.

'You don't have to tell me it went well,' Cal said, peering at her over the top of a copy of *OK!* 'I can tell it did just by looking at you, you've got that triumphant Boudicca look again. Sophie Mills Warrior Queen Party Planner.'

Sophie stopped dead in front of his desk and took the magazine from his hands. 'Do some work,' she said. 'I've got some free time now so I'm going to catch up on some . . .'

'. . . celebrity gossip?' Cal said, looking miserably at his magazine.

'Filing,' Sophie lied.

She had barely made it to the exclusive celebrity-wedding pics when Cal interrupted her.

'Slight problem with you catching up on your filing,' he said, glancing over his shoulder with a fastidious look. He lowered his voice. 'Of the unscheduled variety. Elasticated waistband.

Headscarf.' Sophie blinked at him. 'There's a "lady" here to see you!' he exclaimed as if his previous description had been more than sufficient. 'It must be your twelve o'clock – TA? Or Tess Andrew, I should say.'

Sophie blinked at him and thought about Jake, who might even at that very moment be about to 'swing by', and a part of her was relieved by this obstacle that had presented itself.

'Can you cancel her? Tell her my diary's double-booked or something?' Sophie asked him with the justifiable conviction that Cal could get most people to do most things.

Cal stepped into her office and closed the door behind him, standing close enough for Sophie to be able to smell Chanel Allure. She wasn't sure if it was *pour homme* or *pour femme*.

He held out a greying and dog-eared business card. 'She gave me this. She said could she have it back please as she's only got one. Budget cuts or something.'

Sophie took the card and read it. 'Tess Andrew, Highbury and Islington Social Services'.

'But we only deal with private companies,' Sophie said, looking confused.

Cal shrugged. 'I told her that. But she says it's personal. She says she's got to see you – now.' Cal paused for a beat. 'Look, Sophie, I'm sorry but she means it and she is in the diary after all. She says she phoned this morning and a nice young lady fitted her in and said it would be no trouble at all. She says it's really urgent.' Any trace of Cal's habitual humour or sarcasm was gone.

'Urgent?' Sophie said uncertainly. What could a social worker want with her? Oh God, she groaned inwardly. She hoped it wasn't the neighbours complaining about her mother's dogs again, not that she could blame them if it was. It didn't do much for house prices, living next door to a kennel. However, Sophie was not her mother's keeper. She couldn't stop her breeding dogs if she wanted to – they were all looked after and RSPCA-checked. Sophie could vouch for that. She grew up in dog-related chaos and she frequently felt the dogs took precedence over her. After her dad had died sixteen years ago Mum had begun not only to breed dogs but to take in waifs and strays. She needed a farm in Surrey really, not a Victorian terrace in Highbury. Sophie couldn't think of another reason for a social worker to be here and she could do without all that again, but if Cal couldn't persuade this Tess Andrew to leave then nobody could.

'OK, if I must,' she said, briskly managing the moment with her usual aplomb. 'Maybe I can get her in and out before Jake gets here.'

'Jake's coming here to pick up you up?' Cal said, raising an interested eyebrow. 'He so loves you.'

Sophie found Tess Andrew sitting in Cal's chair anxiously clutching a large sequinned bag.

15

'Miss Andrew.' Sophie smiled at the pleasant-looking woman who was probably in her fifties, amply proportioned and with an inherent air of disarray, set off nicely by her gypsy look. 'How can I help you? Because I have to say when it comes to my mum and her dogs – there's no logic there. She sees their "little faces" and all sense goes out of the window. I don't get it myself, I'm a cat person.'

'I'm sorry, Miss Mills? It's not about dogs. Or . . . er . . . cats.' The woman followed Sophie into her office.

'Sophie – call me Sophie. If it's not dogs, what is it? Drains?' Sophie speculated out of left field. She wasn't exactly sure what it was social workers did and the downstairs drains were a bit iffy.

'Thank you so much for seeing me at such short notice,' Tess Andrew said. 'It must be odd. Me just turning up out of the blue, but . . .' she paused, '. . . I'm afraid I've got some bad news.' Sophie felt her stomach swell and buckle. Those were the words her headmistress had used on the day that her dad had died of a heart attack. A cold fear drenched her. Was it Mum after all? Was Mum ill or . . . ?

'OK,' she said, steeling herself. 'Go on.'

'I'm very sorry to tell you that your friend Caroline Gregory is dead,' Tess Andrew said.

Sophie stared at her. She felt a bubble of relief burst in her chest and she laughed.

Tess Andrew looked startled and Sophie realised how callous she must seem.

16

'Oh – I'm sorry, Ms Andrew – but there's been some kind of a mix-up. I don't know anyone called Caroline Gregory. I thought you'd come to tell me my mum was ill.' Sophie took a breath and composed herself. 'I'm sorry but I think you've wasted your time. I think you've got the wrong Sophie Mills.'

Tess Andrew seemed puzzled and closed her eyes for a moment as she furrowed her brow.

'Oh no,' she said, looking awkward and uncomfortable. 'Oh look, I'm so sorry, I forgot. Of course she didn't use her married name, did she?' Sophie gave her a blank look and watched as Tess Andrew composed her face again into its bad news mode. 'I'm sorry, Sophie. I meant to say Carrie, Carrie Stiles of St Ives in Cornwall. She was killed in a car accident, outright. Carrie Stiles is dead.'

In an instant, Sophie flashed back to laughing with Carrie Stiles in the girls' toilets of Our Lady Catholic High School for Girls, as they folded the waistbands of their grey pleated skirts over and over until the hems gradually lifted above their knees. Then they would stand on the toilets, smoking Silk Cuts out of the open windows.

Carrie Stiles was dead. Carrie who had once been her best friend. Her surrogate sister and ally for a long time until the friendship had eventually ebbed, as old friendships sometimes do, and dwindled to a phone call once a year or so, with Christmas cards and presents for Carrie's kids, her godchildren. But if someone had asked her,

17

just out of interest, who her best friend was, she would have instantly answered Carrie Stiles. Sophie struggled to remember how old the children were. Young, possibly even less than six, she thought. Cal always organised the birthday presents – he would know. She looked at Tess Andrew, who was watching her closely, holding a packet of tissues at the ready.

'I'm sorry – it *is* a shock,' Sophie said, still not able to register the information. 'We were close once. But thank you. Thank you for letting me know. I didn't realise that Social Services did this sort of thing. I thought you were too understaffed and overworked. So, when's the funeral do you know?' Sophie was aware that her voice sounded all wrong. As if she were making an appointment for a routine meeting, not a funeral. Not Carrie Stiles's funeral. Carrie had been alive somewhere else for so long that it seemed impossible that she was not still there, leading her life as usual, just out of view.

Tess squeezed the packet of tissues and twisted it in her hands. She looked more upset and uncomfortable than Sophie did. Sophie supposed that the shock was making Carrie's death seem unreal. Not like the day Dad died. That was real from the moment she had known. The truth was that whilst Sophie still thought about her dad every single day, she hadn't thought of Carrie in ages. She tried to remember signing the last Christmas card she'd sent her just a couple of weeks ago, but couldn't.

Cal wrote out all her cards, including the few personal ones that she sent. Sophie just signed them one after another – her name and then three kisses, XXX.

'I'm afraid,' Tess said uneasily, 'that the funeral was some time ago. A little over six months actually. From what I understand it was quite an affair. Carrie had a lot of friends in the area. They organised it for her. Her mum went down, she was a bit fitter then. She said it was exactly how Carrie would have wanted it, "pagan" I think was the word she used. They scattered her ashes in the sea, at a favourite spot of hers and the children's.'

Sophie tried to picture a group of people she didn't know scattering Carrie Stiles's ashes in the sea. It didn't make sense to her. It was like a dream.

'Oh,' she said. It was strange to know that Carrie had not been in the world for six whole months now and that her Christmas card would have gone unopened. She was unjustly hurt that she had missed Carrie's funeral, but not surprised. She didn't know any of Carrie's St Ives friends and she'd hardly known Carrie's husband. Sophie took a deep breath and tried to bring the real world back into focus.

She had to get on, to go to lunch with Jake. She had to do something that was normal and that she could control and understand. She couldn't understand Carrie being dead. She just couldn't think about it.

'Well.' Sophie glanced at the business card she was still holding, before handing it back as requested. 'Tess, thank you for letting me know. You're right, it was a shock but I think the best thing is to get on with life as normal – so if that's all?'

Tess Andrew looked taken aback and shook her head.

'Oh dear,' she said apologetically. 'That's not the only reason why I'm here, Miss Mills. Sophie. I didn't just come to tell you Carrie was dead. Oh dear.' She took a deep breath. 'It's the children. Carrie's children. Bella is six and Izzy is just three and a bit.'

'Of course,' Sophie said, shaking her head grimly. 'It's terrible for them. Just terrible.' She didn't understand what Tess wanted from her.

'Good, I'm glad you appreciate how difficult it's been for the poor little mites. That'll make everything so much easier for them.'

Sophie was confused. 'Make what so much easier?' she asked politely.

'For the girls to come and live with you.' Tess studied Sophie's blank page of a face. 'You've forgotten, haven't you? I was afraid that you might – people never take these things seriously.' She could see that Sophie wanted her to get to the point. 'Carrie named you in her will, but we only just found it, you see, a couple of days ago. Her neighbour had volunteered to sort through her things before they got cleared out – to save anything special and important for the girls. They found it in the bottom of a box of paints, can you believe?' Tess Andrew switched her smile back on. 'She named you as the girls' legal guardian, Miss Mills. She wants you to look after them.'

CHAPTER 2

Sophie *had* forgotten. Of course she had – why would she remember a half-drunk promise she had made three years ago? Carrie was never supposed to actually die.

It had been after the girls' christening. Carrie's mum had arranged the whole thing in the same Highbury church in which Carrie had been christened and confirmed. It was just after her first stroke, a mild one that she recovered from quickly, but she'd suddenly got a sense of her own mortality and a renewed religious fervour that meant she had to see her grandchildren christened before she died, she simply had to, or so she'd told Carrie.

'Of course it's emotional blackmail,' Carrie had told Sophie on the phone, sounding strung out and stressed, two conditions invariably caused by her mother. 'I don't want them christened. But Mum's really turned the screws so I'm coming up with both of them. It's either that or living purgatory for the foreseeable future.'

Sophie felt a lot of sympathy for Carrie. She too knew what it was like to have a twilight-zone mother. In fact a lot of women her age had similar experiences with their mothers. It seemed to Sophie that immediately after becoming mothers, women began a long and degenerative process that slowly transformed them from bright and interesting to dotty and eccentric. It was one reason amongst many why Sophie decided she never wanted to have children, mainly because she never wanted to become *her* mother, let alone anyone else's.

And Sophie's mum was only crazy about dogs. Carrie's mum, on the other hand, was a leader in the field when it came to bitter recrimination and emotional blackmail.

'What about Louis?' she remembered asking Carrie. 'I bet he doesn't want it. You could say he's put his foot down and blame him, couldn't you?'

Carrie hadn't answered for a moment and Sophie could hear the new baby gurgle and cough down the line.

'Oh well, no . . . I just . . . Well, no, it doesn't matter, I've said yes now.' Carrie's laugh had seemed a little thin. 'Poor Bella, God knows what she'll make of it, getting water chucked over her head by a bloke in a dress at three years old! Mum's even sorted out godparents, dreadfully pious cousins from Tottenham. But I put my foot down. I said I'd have at least one friend that I chose. You will do it won't you, Soph? I don't think I can face the whole eternal guilt-trip thing all on my own. You are a product of Our Lady's too – at least you understand.

23

And anyway, you'd make a good godmother, set the girls a good example and all that.'

'Of course I'll do it,' Sophie had said, looking forward to the prospect of mulling over old times with Carrie. 'But you won't be alone will you – Louis will be there, won't he? He'll stop your mum checking you into a nunnery!' Sophie tried to remember if Carrie had laughed at the rather feeble joke, but couldn't.

'Louis can't come,' Carrie had told her, her voice wavering a little. 'It's work. I told him not to worry about it. This whole thing is for Mum anyway. It's her show.' Sophie thought of the one time she had met Louis at Carrie's registry office wedding. Carrie had been eight months pregnant in a white crocheted smock with wild flowers entwined in her brown curls, looking like a pagan earth goddess. Mrs Stiles had managed to over-shadow the whole event by not being present. Sophie had barely spoken to Louis. He seemed slightly drunk even during the ceremony and she thought the very least he could have done was to have combed his hair and shaved off his near-full beard of dark stubble. He was personable enough and friendly, but secretly Sophie disapproved of the whole relationship, it was just too impulsive.

Carrie had met Louis while she was on a long-planned painting holiday in St Ives. He was into surfing and photography. They both shared a love of art and the sea. 'Met most marvellous hunk,' Carrie had written on the postcard she'd sent to Sophie. 'Am going to keep him.' She was pregnant three months later and they were married eight months after that. Sophie had privately given it six months, as she made her excuses and slipped out of the pub wedding reception. She had felt out of place in her lilac suit and matching shoes, her long blonde hair ironed straight over her shoulders. Everyone else had been hyper-casual in jeans and tie-dyed tops. Carrie had asked her to stay longer but she explained she had to drive back up to London that night. She'd been working towards a promotion even then. The marriage *had* lasted longer than six months and Sophie had been proved wrong – a new baby proved her wrong conclusively, she supposed. And she had agreed to be the girls' godmother.

The christening had gone exactly as Sophie expected. It was long, the church was cold and no-one understood what the charming but heavily accented Dominican priest was saying. The baby screamed relentlessly for the duration of the service and the toddler – Bella – had the sort of thick cold that made Sophie feel like she had a temperature and sore throat just by looking at her. Sophie had had to hold the baby at one point and it had looked up at her. Two huge, blank, black eyes peered out of a wrinkled, pinkish face devoid of any recognisable emotion, and Sophie hadn't got it. She didn't understand why Carrie was so crazy about the baby. About both her children, actually. It had to be more complicated than just

25

hormones duping all new mothers into eternal slavery. How could anybody be so in love with a leaden lump of alien life-form that looked like it had no humanity in it whatsoever, just an un-remitting, single-minded will to suck mankind dry of everything that it had to offer? No, Sophie hadn't taken to the baby at all, but at least Bella could talk and seemed quite sensible.

'I like your shoes,' Bella had told her as they stood by the font. 'And your pretty, beautiful clothes. Like Barbie.' She had reached for Sophie's hand and Sophie had held it for twenty minutes even though she feared the slight stickiness of Bella's palm was not caused by excitement alone.

Later that night she had sat up with Carrie long after everyone else had gone home or gone to bed. They had stockpiled three of the bottles of Blue Nun that Mrs Stiles had got in for the occasion, and were two thirds of the way through the second bottle.

'Oh my God,' Carrie had said with the practised hushed giggle of a mother. 'What about that time we got caught in the boys' changing room at St Peter's! I so thought we were for the chop then. My God. I thought Mum would literally kill me. She didn't though – she just looked at me and told me she was disappointed in me and so was Jesus.'

Sophie remembered the occasion – they had only narrowly avoided suspension. Her own mother had been too busy worrying about a new litter of puppies to be that cross. 'Silly girl,' she had said to Sophie when she heard. 'If that Carrie told you to jump off a cliff you would. Just don't do it again love, OK?'

'It was a fifth-form dare wasn't it? Who could get Toby Barnes's boxers out of St Peter's. What were we thinking? It just goes to show what clueless virgins we were. If we'd had any sense at all we would have stayed well clear of Toby Barnes's boxers.'

'Yes,' Carrie had remembered. 'Unlike Ursula Goodman. She got far too close to them. Pregnant at fifteen. Exiled to Welwyn Garden City. Nightmare.'

Sophie had poured out the last of the Blue Nun. 'Well, you're a young mother and you seem to love it,' she had said. 'But then again I suppose it's different when you've got someone to share it with it.'

Carrie had nodded and drained her glass in one gulp. 'God this stuff is rough,' she had laughed. She had paused and Sophie had waited, sensing that she wanted to say something.

'You know we bought the house after the wedding?' Sophie had nodded. 'Well, mortgages and kids make you think about stuff. We made wills and even got life insurance!'

Sophie had nodded again, approvingly. She'd made a will soon after she'd bought her flat, and arranged a policy to cover her mortgage in case she got knocked down by a bus. It was just sensible. Tidy. She was impressed that Carrie and Louis were even thinking that far ahead. Perhaps Louis was good for Carrie after all.

'Recently I've been thinking that my will doesn't do enough,' Carrie continued. 'I have to make provision for the girls in case anything happens to me, to both of us I mean. Name a guardian, you know.' Carrie had smiled at Sophie. 'Someone who's not my mother. So I was wondering, Soph – would you do it? Would you be the girls' guardian? You're the only person I know with a proper job.'

Sophie had laughed. 'Oh I'm flattered!' she'd said.

'You know what I mean. You're the only person I think I'd trust with them.'

'Really? You must have some very irresponsible friends.'

'Well, yes I have,' Carrie had said, only semi-joking.

The two women had laughed and Sophie had felt a rush of their old comradeship flood back. She had been touched and warmed by the request. It showed that they were still close, even all those miles apart. She had been flattered. Sophie didn't know if it was the Blue Nun, the nostalgia or echoes of a hundred promises that they had made unthinkingly to each other over the years, but in that moment she was uncharacteristically impulsive and accepted what she assumed was a kind of token gesture of commitment from Carrie. A gesture to reaffirm this friendship.

'Of course!' she had said without hesitation.

'Of course I will. If anything ever happens to you and Louis, which it won't, I'm your girl.'

Sophie shook her head. Her patience with Tess Andrew was draining away rapidly. It was bad enough to find out that Carrie was gone, but worse still for the news to be mangled by so much ill planning and incompetence.

'Miss Andrew,' Sophie said scathingly. 'Obviously I do remember that agreement. But that was in the event of *both* parents dying. You didn't mention Louis. He wasn't in the crash, I presume? He is the children's guardian. He's their father. I would have thought that was obvious.'

Tess puffed out her chest at Sophie's tone and suddenly looked a lot more formidable. 'Yes, technically that is correct and we're doing our best to track him down, but—'

Sophie cut across her. 'Track him down? What do you mean track him down?' She asked incredulously.

Tess pushed the chair she was sitting in a couple of inches away from Sophie's desk and took a breath. 'Louis Gregory left the family home some time ago. We can't trace him. We think he's overseas.'

Sophie rubbed her temples with her thumb and forefinger. 'Carrie was on her own?' she asked, trying to force her mind to absorb all the information that was being thrown at her.

'Yes, since the little one was a baby apparently,' Tess Andrew said, looking slightly thrown. 'I thought you would have known.'

Sophie thought of all the Christmas cards with Louis's name on that she had sent, and the cards she had received. To be honest, she probably never read them that closely, but now she thought about it she was fairly sure that Carrie always signed any cards or letters either just from herself or sometimes 'from us all'. She had spoken to Carrie a few weeks after the christening and then a few months after that. Neither time did Carrie mention that Louis had left her, and it wasn't exactly the sort of thing one asked in a casual conversation. After that they hadn't spoken. Sophie just always assumed, like Carrie probably did, that they would speak at some point. But neither one of them had got round to making that call and Carrie, her life and her family had slipped further away from Sophie's life until they were almost entirely separated. Until now.

Louis must have left her alone with a new baby. Sophie had known from the first moment she set eyes on him that he wasn't the kind of guy to settle into marriage and fatherhood. She thought that she had been proved wrong – but she hadn't.

Even so, it still didn't make her the children's guardian.

'Their grandmother surely –' Sophie began, staring at the second hand of her watch escaping from her. She wondered if Jake was outside now, talking to Cal and Lisa.

'Oh yes,' Tess nodded. 'Mrs Stiles brought them home with her right after the funeral. They're here in London. But two small children are a lot for an old lady to cope with: they can't seem to settle. Bella has missed a lot of school, and Mrs Stiles is very frail you know. High blood pressure, angina. She tried her best but there came a point when she had to call us in to help her. We've only been on board for the last few weeks. Anyway, the council's moving her into sheltered accommodation. A place came up just before Christmas and she has to take it now or she'll lose it. And even if she *could* cope with the girls, you can't take children there. She feels awful about it, as you can imagine – but to be honest I think the girls would be better off somewhere that wasn't so . . . gloomy.'

Sophie tried to take in all the information that Tess Andrew was imparting.

'Carrie had a lot of family,' she said. 'No brothers or sisters admittedly, but tons of cousins – she was Catholic!'

'Yes, well. Most of them have moved away or have families of their own. There's no-one willing to take the kids on, and besides,' Tess looked at Sophie with renewed determination, 'Carrie named you. You agreed to it. Surely you must have thought about what it would mean when you agreed to be their guardian?'

Suddenly Sophie felt the walls of her office close in on her and the air seemed to leak out of the room. She stood up abruptly.

'I have to go, Miss Andrew,' she said. 'I have a lunch.'

31

Tess stood up too.

'Lunch?' she said, looking bewildered. 'Look, I know it's a lot to take in, a lot to ask – but Carrie must have thought she could ask it of you or else she wouldn't have put you in her will. And we're thinking of what's best for the girls in the short term. There aren't very many options, Sophie. Until Carrie's will was found there was only one – foster care or a home until we could find their dad. We're not asking you to have them for ever, we're asking you to have them until then. On a short-term basis.'

Sophie stopped by the door. 'Short-term basis?' She repeated the three words as a question.

'As you pointed out, the girls do have a father. We're looking for him and I'm sure that when he knows what has happened he'll want to come back and look after them. It would just be until we find Louis Gregory and let him know what's happened.' Tess coughed into her hand as she finished the sentence.

Sophie thought for a moment about two bereaved children she hardly knew living in her flat. There were a lot of things that Sophie was very good at. Pushing the envelope, thinking outside the box, making lists about lists and pie charts. She was extremely good at pie charts. But she'd always said that when she discovered her limitations she'd be happy to admit them. That time had come.

'I'm sorry, Tess,' she said. 'I really am. But I

32

don't know anything about children. I hardly even know Bella and Isobel. It would be wrong of me to say yes. Wrong for them. They need someone who knows how to help them.'

Tess's face remained impassive.

'Perhaps you're right, Sophie. In an ideal world that would be best. But do you know how many children need foster care in London tonight? Hundreds. Do you know how many foster parents we have? Nowhere *near* enough. If they don't come to you I have no choice but to place them under a care order. They'll be going to a home, if not tonight then tomorrow at the latest. They will stay in a local authority home until a foster place comes up or their dad comes back. They try their best at the homes, but trust me, they are always a last, last resort. It could be weeks, months even, until we find them a foster home. I might even have to put them in separate homes. I still haven't been able to find them a place together.' Tess looked intently at Sophie. 'If you agreed to take them you wouldn't be on your own. I'd be able to apply for a supervision order and I'd be assigned to you as your support worker, with you all the way. They're missing their mum, Sophie. If they could be with someone familiar it would really help them. Please at least take a moment to think about it. You are their only hope right now.'

Sophie hesitated for a moment. She thought again of the day that her dad had died. After her headmistress had sent her home, Carrie must have seen her out of the classroom window, stumbling across the playing field in tears. She'd put her hand up, told the teacher she needed the toilet and had walked right out of school and run after Sophie.

'Don't tell me you've finally got yourself expelled,' she'd said to Sophie when she caught up with her. Sophie had dissolved into more tears and told her what had happened. She remembered the feeling of Carrie's arm around her shoulders for the rest of the walk back to Sophie's house until she stopped at last outside the front door. The dogs started barking.

'I could come in,' Carrie had offered. Sophie had shaken her head.

'No, I think I have to go in on my own,' she had said, wishing she didn't have to. 'But thanks.'

'Look,' Carrie had said. 'I know it's not the same, I know you love your dad and that I hate mine and that your dad is dead and mine ran off with the neighbour and made my mum go mental but . . . well, I do sort of understand a bit. I know what it feels like losing your dad. Even though mine's a bastard and yours was great.' She had paused for a moment. 'You realise that now there are two fatherless children at a Catholic school. I'm not the weirdest one any more!' Incredibly, Carrie's stumbled attempt at words of comfort had made Sophie almost smile. Where, in the weeks that followed, other people would stifle her with sympathy and sensitivity,

Carrie had done the one thing that had made life bearable. She had made her laugh and let her forget for a few minutes every now and then that her dad had dropped dead of a heart attack at a petrol station without any warning at all. Carrie let Sophie be angry, let her cry, let her talk about boys, batwing tops and legwarmers and cry again if she wanted to.

'I'm glad I've got you, Carrie,' Sophie had said as her mum had opened the front door. The girls had hugged each other for a long time until eventually Sophie knew she had to go in.

'I'm here for you,' Carrie had said. 'Always, for ever, whatever.'

'I know. Me too. Always, for ever, whatever.'

Sophie hadn't thought of that moment for years, but now that she did she could remember exactly how it had felt and exactly how much strength the unwavering friendship of a thirteen-year-old girl had given her. 'Always, for ever, whatever.' It was something the girls had said to each other daily, until they'd almost stopped thinking about what it really meant. But when it had mattered Carrie had been there for Sophie, supporting her through the very worst time of her life. Sophie had been waiting a long time to return the favour. Self-assured, stubborn Carrie, tired and embarrassed by all the handouts she and her mother had received from well-meaning church members after her dad left, prided herself on never asking anyone for help. She'd never needed help – until now.

'How long?' Sophie said, not quite believing what she was thinking of agreeing to.

'Pardon?' Tess said, clearly having expected a flat refusal.

'How long until you get hold of the father?' Sophie asked her.

Sensing fragile progress, Tess pursed her lips and made a professional judgement. It was important she didn't lose Sophie now.

'Well, like I say, Social Services have only been involved for a few weeks. But I don't think it will be long. A week maybe – two at the most?'

Sophie considered the information. 'Two weeks – OK then. For Carrie. She would have done it for me. I wouldn't let the girls get split up, I couldn't. So I'll take them for two weeks, as long as you promise to move heaven and earth to make more suitable arrangements at the end of that time.'

'I will,' Tess said, lifting her chin a little.

Absently Sophie touched the cool back of her hand to her blazing cheek. Her complexion was always the first part, actually the only part, of her to show visible signs of stress. She could hide it with concealer but she always resented the fact that she couldn't control it. She took a deep breath.

'Right, well, let me know dates and times and things, and get back to me later in the week.'

'Pardon?' Tess said.

'I have a lunch,' Sophie repeated with some frustration.

Tess looked at her.

'Actually, Sophie, I was rather hoping you could come with me now to pick up the girls. I brought all the paperwork with me for you to sign.' She reached into her glittering bag and produced several forms which she waved at Sophie as proof.

'You mean now, right now? You want me to have them right now?' Sophie repeated herself incredulously.

'That is the idea,' Tess said with a tight smile. 'After all, the girls need your help *now*. Not when you have a window in your diary.'

Sophie wondered how all these events had managed to erupt and tumble down on her head at this precise moment without her even noticing they were coming. She looked down at the pink toes of her new boots and knew she just had to accept that her day wasn't going to go the way she had planned, because nobody knew better than she did that sometimes your life turns itself on its head without waiting to ask you for permission. She looked up at Tess and gestured to the visitor's chair.

'OK,' Sophie said simply. 'If you'll excuse me for a few minutes I just have to rearrange some appointments.'

At last she opened the door to her office and stepped back into the normal world where things were happening just as they had before she got dragged into the alternative reality presented by Tess Andrew. For a split second

Sophie considered making a run for it and then she knew she couldn't. She just wasn't the sort of person to walk away from a problem without solving it. Even if she wanted to her pride wouldn't let her.

Jake Flynn was sitting on the edge of Cal's desk. He turned and smiled at her as she emerged and behind his back Cal swooned in his chair.

'Are you ready?' Jake asked her.

Sophie looked at him.

'No, I'm not ready,' she said, feeling every word.

Jake's face fell.

'Look, Jake, I'm really sorry but I . . . I just found out that a close friend of mine died and I . . .' Sophie could not put the last part of the sentence together but it seemed like she didn't have to.

'Oh Sophie,' he said gently, 'I'm sorry. Well, of course you aren't ready. Don't worry about lunch.' He paused for a moment as if assessing what he should say next. 'Work can wait – I only wanted to go over a few last-minute details you've probably already sorted out. Don't worry about it at all. And I'm really sorry for your loss.'

Sophie nodded, not knowing whether to feel relieved or disappointed that Jake had been taking her out for a business lunch after all. She looked at Cal.

'I'm going to be out of the office for the rest of the day,' she said. 'Cancel everything and ask Gillian if she's got five minutes, OK?'

Cal nodded and looked from Jake to Sophie and back again.

'Will you be OK?' Jake said, reaching out and holding her elbow. It was such a strange, mannered gesture that Sophie found it rather touching.

'I will,' she said. 'It's . . . complicated, Jake.'

Jake nodded and his hand dropped back to his side. 'I'll call you,' he said.

'I'm not sure when I'll be back in the office but Cal and Lisa have everything under control so you don't have to worry . . .'

'I'm not worried and I'll call *you*,' he said.

Cal watched him heading for the lift.

'Mmm,' he mused, more or less to himself. 'Now even I'm confused.' He looked up at Sophie. 'What else can I do?'

Sophie smiled at him.

'Right now? Nothing. In the next couple of weeks – probably everything.' And she told him as quickly as she could everything that Tess had told her.

'Bloody hell,' Cal said, wide-eyed by the time she had finished.

'I know,' Sophie said.

She turned around and looked at her office door. Then she took a deep breath and went back in.

CHAPTER 3

For twenty minutes Sophie sat and listened to Tess talking about procedures, in phrases she had never dreamed would be relevant to her life. Tess explained that she would be granted an interim residency order immediately and with it full parental responsibility.

'Technically,' she told Sophie, 'you have it anyway as legal guardian, but because of the unusual circumstances of this case I think it's important to keep you and the girls under supervision. You'll have me for guidance and support until things are firmed up.'

Sophie narrowed her eyes at Tess imperceptibly. 'Yes, but it's only a temporary arrangement, isn't it?' she reminded her. 'This all seems a bit over the top for a couple of weeks.'

'Not at all,' Tess said. 'It's standard procedure with a supervision order – a one-size-fits-all policy I'm afraid, but generally it works very well.' She beamed at Sophie. 'Now, we have got the girls down for counselling but—'

'Counselling?' Sophie picked up on one of the stream of words. 'Are they – I mean, are the girls traumatised in a – you know – bad way?'

Tess raised an eyebrow. 'As opposed to a good way?' she said, looking slightly perplexed.

'There's no need to look at me like that!' Sophie retorted. 'Look, I don't have much – any – experience of children, except for my own childhood and that was . . . unusual. My mother didn't raise me, a chocolate Labrador called Muffin did.' Tess raised an eyebrow again. 'OK so that's a bit of an exaggeration, but in any case I don't have much to go on. I have no idea what to say to happy normal children let alone ones whose mum has died and whose dad has deserted them!' Sophie caught her rising tone and lowered her voice. 'What I'm saying is if they need *expert* help I'm not the one to give it.'

Tess paused for a moment just to check that Sophie had nothing further to add. 'Counselling is a standard procedure that is available to the children if need be.' She thought for a moment. 'I have only known them for a little while but I can tell you that Bella is a very self-contained, mature little girl. She never talks about Carrie at all. I think it's a coping strategy. I think she feels she has to hold it together for Izzy's sake. And Izzy? Well, she is a typical three-year-old, although obviously the crash has left her rather unsure of cars. She prefers not to travel in one. And in any event, as you are only having them temporarily I don't think you have to worry about their deeper issues. Just a familiar face, someone who knew their mum, will help them. Someone to take their minds off things – that would mean a lot right now.'

'But I'm not a familiar face,' Sophie said. 'I haven't seen them in years.'

Tess smiled. 'But they've seen you. Carrie kept a photo of you and her together – at your sixth-form leaver party, Bella told me. You've got different hair, different clothes – but apart from that you look the same.' Tess slotted in the compliment with professional discretion. 'The girls brought it with them from the house. They know who you are. They talk about you. Apparently you always get them the best presents.'

Sophie looked out of her window over Broadgate Circus and watched a woman more or less her age walk across the concourse wrapped up against the cold in swathes of cashmere. Suddenly she wished she could swap lives with the wonderfully free woman and in the same moment remembered with pressing urgency that she had been trying to find time to make a trip to the ladies' all morning. Now she *really* needed to go.

'OK,' Sophie said briskly, as she stood up. 'Well, I have to sort things out with my boss. The rest of the day off, you know . . .'

'Two weeks off, you mean,' Tess said.

'If need be,' Sophie mumbled, hurrying to the door.

'Well, you can't leave them home alone . . .'

'I realise that, but –' Sophie opened the door and found herself jiggling on her toes. She felt like a naughty child trying to escape class.

'So you'll need to take time off,' Tess reaffirmed.

'Fine. I'll take the week off.' Sophie snapped. 'I can always work from home. Now, if you'll excuse me, I really do need to sort things out.' She closed the door on Tess with a good deal more firmness than was strictly required.

'I'll make her another tea, shall I?' Cal said as Sophie marched past.

'Don't bother,' Sophie said shortly.

'Sanctimonious, self-righteous, pompous . . .' Sophie grumbled under her breath as she headed for the ladies'. As she passed Eve's office, Eve fell in line with her and four metal-tipped heels clicked along the tiled floor in purposeful union.

'In-ter-est-ing,' Eve said, carefully pronouncing each syllable of the word as she observed Sophie. 'What do we have here? Sour looks and bitterness.' She cocked her head sweetly at Sophie. 'You didn't nail the Germans, did you?'

Sophie lifted her chin. 'Signed sealed and delivered. Three conferences, summer party, Christmas party, staff. All corporate entertaining. For two years.'

If Eve was impressed she hid it well.

'Yeah well, I think they were ripe for a change. I reckon even Lisa could have landed them.'

Sophie ignored the jibe and stopped outside the ladies'.

'Are you smoking this morning?' Eve asked her, slipping the top of her packet of Marlboros out of her trouser pocket as if they were contraband, which in a smoke-free office they more or less were. It wasn't that smoking was banned entirely, it was allowed outside, but hardly anyone smoked any more, except for Eve, and Sophie sort of – she didn't consider herself to be an actual smoker because she only smoked three cigarettes a day and never indoors – and their shared involvement with nicotine was possibly the only thing they had in common. It also provided an opportunity for them to size each other up and see how the competition was doing.

Tess Andrew could wait ten more minutes.

'Yes I am smoking,' Sophie said with conviction, pushing open the toilet door.

'I'll wait for you,' Eve said.

Five minutes later and feeling considerably re-freshed, Sophie found herself lighting a second cigarette from the butt of the one she had just smoked, glad that the chill of the morning was providing a cooling antidote to the heat of her cheeks.

'So, considering you've done so well,' Eve said, looking Sophie up and down as she channelled a plume of smoke through her pursed lips, 'why are you so stressed? And don't deny it, your face looks like it's in the early stages of leprosy. You haven't even flaunted your new boots – are you ill?'

Like Sophie, Eve wasn't wearing a coat, but the cold didn't seem to affect her, probably because she was already cold-blooded. Sophie wound her arms around herself, glanced at Eve and appraised the situation. Eve couldn't in any way be described as a friend because it was hard to be pally with your mortal enemy, even if they did throw you the occasional Marlboro Light. But Sophie and Eve inevitably spent a lot of time together during office hours and had developed a mutual, resentful respect that had evolved into a relationship of a kind. After all, they were the only two of their breed. Gillian was at the top of the tree and Eve and Sophie were two of the three managers beneath her. The other one was Graham Hughes, but he was so incompetent that nobody really counted him; he only had the job because of his second name. Eve was the only other person at McCarthy Hughes who knew exactly what it was like to be Sophie, and how much she wanted to move into Gillian's job, if and when Gillian stepped down from the office in order to spend more time with her family. Sophie had been working for ten years towards this moment, and she wouldn't let her chance to sit in Gillian's chair go without fighting for it tooth and nail.

Outside the office Sophie wouldn't have gone near Eve with a six-foot barge pole. But sensing that this was one of those times it paid to keep your enemy closest, Sophie decided to tell her everything.

'I just found out an old friend of mine died,' she said flatly.

There was no other way to put it. So far her feelings about the news seemed entirely two-dimensional, as if she had read the words off a page but hadn't really felt what they meant yet. Carrie's death didn't seem real. Sophie supposed that would change when she met the children, and that thought terrified her. Not feeling anything would be much easier, she decided, and also much worse.

'Really,' Eve said, keeping her voice even as she stubbed out the butt of her cigarette with the black pointed toe of her Prada shoe. Sophie abstractedly decided that that day's silent shoe-off was a draw. Eve had the label, but her shoes were over a year old. Sophie's boots were high street but they were copies hot off the catwalk. 'Carrie is dead and you're thinking about shoes,' a part of Sophie's mind told her. She ignored it and looked closely at her gorgeously shod toes.

'So, were you close to this friend?' Eve asked her.

Sophie considered the question. 'We were once, you know, at school,' she said. 'And for a while after she went to university and I started working here. We kept in touch – met up in the holidays – but we both changed. She got married pretty soon after she graduated and moved away.' Sophie considered the length of time and distance that had grown between her and Carrie. 'So we weren't so close any more, no – but well, you know . . .'

Eve tipped her face back to a glimpse of the sun that a passing cloud had temporarily revealed, and Sophie guessed that probably she didn't know.

'So it's not all doom and gloom then,' Eve said lightly. 'You won't be having weeks and weeks off for compassionate leave?' She couldn't help but sound hopeful.

Sophie squinted at her and thought anxiously

about the time she would inevitably be out of the office in the next few days.

'Not at all,' she said. A significant part of her – the part of her that knew Eve was a natural predator – didn't want to tell Eve the rest of the story. But she also knew that if she didn't it would look like weakness, and Sophie was scared of showing Eve any sign of that.

'There is another slight complication that has arisen, though,' Sophie said carefully, considering the best way to play the situation. Let Eve think that her rival's position was being compromised, and then when Sophie showed Gillian she could cope so well with a crisis and still be on top of her job she'd be a stronger contender than ever.

'Did she leave you loads of money?' Eve asked her.

Sophie shook her head and paused for effect. 'No – she left me her kids.'

For the first time ever Sophie witnessed Eve lost for words, if only for a second. And then she found two that Sophie considered extremely apt.

'Fucking Nora,' Eve said.

Gillian had two children of her own: eight-year-old Jack and four-year-old Matilda. Sophie knew their names and ages because of the many photos and drawings that adorned Gillian's office walls, and their occasional visits to the office.

They were the reason, Sophie supposed, that as she relayed the events of the morning tears welled up in Gillian's eyes. A vital and extremely attractive woman in her early forties, Gillian Hughes was Sophie's inspiration and role model. She had cut a swathe to the very top when other women were still complaining about glass ceilings, and had become a partner in the firm by the time she was thirty-five. She openly encouraged her younger staff to try for promotion and to achieve the dizzy heights she had reached. With her as your boss you felt that anything was possible, everything was achievable. Sophie had learned everything from her and she didn't mind admitting that she wanted to be Gillian when she grew up. She wanted Gillian's job, her sense of presence, her innate authority and also her really great wrinkle-free skin. She was so tightly in control of every strand of the business that Sophie had been taken aback by her unprecedented display of emotion. The plight of the children touched her instantly.

'Oh my God,' Gillian said softly, shaking her head and staring out of the window. 'It's your worst nightmare, your worst nightmare ever. The thought of leaving your children alone in the world. Every mother's deepest fear.' She looked at Sophie. 'Your friend must have trusted you very much, Sophie. You should be proud.'

Sophie felt a little guilty. Proud was the very last thing she had been feeling. Beholden, embattled, terrified and shocked – all of those things had registered – but pride had yet to make an entry in her top five chart of whirlwind emotions.

'Of course I do,' Sophie lied so as not to

disappoint Gillian. 'And, well, I'm afraid I will need some time out of the office while the children are staying with me. The social worker says . . .'

'Of course,' Gillian said generously, before leaning forward a little in her seat. 'How long exactly?'

'Not long at all,' Sophie said hurriedly, sensing that already Gillian was trying to find out precisely how much all this would impact on her business. Her boss might be compassionate but she was also a level-headed businesswoman. 'I won't need long . . . it's just for a week or two, until they find their dad, you see.'

'So you'll want two weeks off straight away then?' Gillian asked her, suddenly sounding less generous. 'To spend time with your godchildren.'

'No I won't –' Sophie began, not wanting to irritate her. 'What I mean is that of course I *do* want to spend time with them, the poor darlings, but I won't just walk out on my responsibilities to McCarthy Hughes. You're being extremely kind – but I don't want to take advantage of that kindness. I'll have to be at home mainly, but I'm sure I can still supervise Lisa and Cal, and I'll be in at least twice a week. Three times maybe. Maybe I'll pop in every day. I'll get a nanny or something.'

'For two weeks?' Gillian said with amusement. Obviously Sophie had said something funny but she wasn't exactly sure what.

'Yeah, you know, from an agency or something,' Sophie said uncertainly.

'It seems a little extreme, Sophie, for such a

short time. If that's all it's really going to be, we'll manage for a few days without you, you know.'

The comment could not have stung Sophie more if Gillian had leapt over her solid oak desk and whacked her smartly about the face.

'I know!' Sophie said with a brittle laugh and just a hint of a whine. 'But I'm in the middle of some important projects right now, especially the ship party. That's coming up really soon and there's heaps left to do, even though we're completely on top of it of course . . .'

'Of course,' Gillian said, smiling wryly.

'So, I mean, I will take it as holiday but I'll just keep working too if that's OK.'

Gillian seemed to mull the proposition over and Sophie wondered, not for the first time, how it was that Gillian managed to wear chic little chiffon neck scarves loosely tied at her shoulder without them constantly coming undone or flopping down like Sophie's did whenever she had tried it. Perhaps she glues them on, Sophie thought.

'Look,' Gillian said at last. 'I appreciate your dedication, Sophie. It doesn't go unnoticed. But I wonder if you realise what you are taking on? Let's play it by ear – if things change or you find it too much to do both then Eve can always step in—'

'No!' Sophie interrupted her and then instantly regretted it. It was like interrupting the Queen. 'Sorry, Gillian, I just meant that I can handle it. No-one needs to step in. It's not for very long. How hard can it possibly be?'

CHAPTER 4

For the first ten minutes of the taxi ride to Mrs Stiles's house, Sophie and Tess did not speak to each other.

Sophie was too busy fretting about the looks on Lisa's and Cal's faces when she told them what was happening, and wondering what the implications of those looks were. They were like a theatrical mask. Lisa's face had been the tragic one, and Cal was pure comedy, neatly glossing over the whole dead-mother-of-two element to see the funny side and to give Sophie a rundown of all the hilariously calamitous events that were bound to befall them.

'Look . . .' Tess said, breaking the silence as the cab turned onto Upper Street. 'I think you are doing a incredible thing here, I really do, and I want you to know I'll be there to help you. It's not as if you're on your own.'

Sophie half-smiled at her. 'Thanks,' she said, tucking a strand of hair behind her ear and looking out of the cab window. The record shop where she and Carrie had spent so much time peeping at boys over the tops of Stone Roses LPs had had

51

long since been replaced by a mobile-phone shop. 'I want to help, I really do. It was just the surprise of it all; it happened so quickly, for me anyway.'

'I know,' Tess said, studying her profile. 'That was my fault, I did bungle it a bit. It's not like me at all, but I've never worked on a case like this before.' She held out a hand to Sophie, who turned and looked at it. 'Let's try and work together to do something good for these children – OK?'

Sophie nodded and shook her hand.

'OK,' she said. 'I'll give it my best shot.'

Mrs Stiles's house, her life and a large part of Sophie's past had already been packed away. There were several crates in the hallway, marked 'Storage', and a host of cardboard boxes stacked against any available wall space, all marked S.H. The house in which Sophie had spent so many hours, laughing and plotting and dreaming with Carrie, had been swept away, leaving only faint shadows and outlines to prove that it had ever been there. Even Mrs Stiles herself had faded to the point where she was almost translucent.

When Sophie had seen her at the christening she had been looking older and tired, but the last three years seemed to have shrunk her away almost to nothing. She was inches shorter and her skin was papery-thin and grey.

'Mrs Stiles,' Sophie said. 'I just couldn't believe it when I heard. I'm so sorry.'

Mrs Stiles nodded and gestured for Sophie to

sit down on the beige velour sofa that she and Carrie had giggled on the night of the christening and countless times before that as girls.

'We tried so long for Caroline, her dad and I,' Mrs Stiles said. 'When she came I was so un-prepared that I thought it was the change! She was my miracle. My gift.' Mrs Stiles's smile faded. 'I don't know why loving her so much wasn't enough. I don't know why she went away, why she let that . . . *man*,' she spat out the word, 'ruin her life just like her father ruined mine.' She coughed and gagged as if she might choke on her bitterness. 'And now the lives of those poor chil-dren too. Everything that's happened to them has happened because of *him*. If he'd been at home like he should have been, supporting his family, Carrie wouldn't have been driving that death trap.' She stopped talking abruptly and caught her breath. 'I just feel so angry and all of this, *all* of this is his fault.'

Sophie did not know quite what to say so she said nothing and listened to the house, perfectly silent except for the ticking of a clock.

'Where *are* the children?' she asked eventually.

'Upstairs,' Mrs Stiles said. 'I told them to wait there and not a peep until we were ready for them. They're no trouble as long as they know who's boss. They've packed all their bits – they don't have too much with them, just one big suitcase, every-thing else is still in Carrie's house. The neighbour's been good, keeping an eye on it – but there's so much that needs doing. I didn't think I would have to do it.' She reached out and took Sophie's hand in hers. Her skin felt dry and rough.

'I just can't do it,' she said, and Sophie knew she was talking about the children.

'I know.'

'Well,' Mrs Stiles said with a sharp edge to her voice. 'I always told Carrie that you were the sensible one. And now look.'

Sophie sat back in her chair and withdrew her fingers from Mrs Stiles. She had expected her to be upset but not angry.

'Ms Andrew, call the girls down will you?' Mrs Stiles said.

Sophie swallowed hard and counted the last seconds of her foreseeable freedom away as the sound of footsteps thundered down the stairs, the living-room door flew open and a small child flung herself into Sophie's lap with some considerable impetus, winding her momentarily.

'Goodness, child, slow down,' Mrs Stiles said, but the child in question ignored her and flung her arms around Sophie's neck. At first Sophie thought it was Bella, but then she saw Bella standing in the door frame and realised that this must be Izzy in her lap, resplendent in a lilac fairy costume complete with wings and a glittery net skirt. The child kissed Sophie wetly on the cheek and patted her head fondly.

'My mummy's car is broken,' she said. 'There was a BANG and a man in a van and it's broken now, it's in the garage. I don't like cars, do I? Have you got any chocolate birthday cake? Are you three or seven today?'

Sophie looked at her. 'Um,' she said.

Bella crossed the room and gave Izzy a sisterly look of disapproval. Sophie thought she saw a trace of Carrie in the expression – just a trace amongst the dark good looks they must have inherited from their father. Carrie had been fair-skinned with light brown hair. These girls had huge black eyes and olive skin.

'Shut up, Izzy,' Bella said. 'She's much older than seven, idiot.' Bella held out her hand and Sophie took it, still struggling to find something appropriate to say.

'I like your boots,' Bella said. 'I like pink, it's my favourite colour.'

Sophie smiled at them both. 'Me too,' she said.

'Me too!' shouted Izzy, causing Mrs Stiles to wince. A passion for chocolate and an eye for shoes. Maybe Sophie did have something in common with the girls after all. A shame then, she thought as she smiled fixedly at them, that she felt as if she were having her very life pulled inside out by an overwhelming vacuum of fear.

'Right then,' Tess said a couple of hours later, gathering up the reams of papers she had laid out across Sophie's blond ash coffee table. 'I'll be off. See you tomorrow, girls.'

'Bye, Tess,' both girls sang absently, mesmerised

by something Tess had found for them to watch on TV involving huge, brightly coloured puppets and a lot of shouting.

'Off?' Sophie said anxiously. 'Off where?' Her small, neat flat had already been transformed into a jumble sale of dirty, multicoloured clothes. Tess had suggested that when she had time Sophie might clear the girls a drawer, but in the meantime she helped them sort out what was clean and what wasn't, refolded what she could neatly into the suitcase and loaded the rest into Sophie's washing machine. Sophie, who was more of a dry-clean-only sort of girl, rarely used her washing machine. When it juddered and shook its way into a final spin she had jumped out of her skin.

'Where do you have to go *now*?' Sophie repeated her anxious question.

'Oh, you know, work. It's almost four, Sophie. I have to get all this signed, sealed and, er, delivered tonight.'

'But so soon? I mean, do you think I'm ready? You said before in the cab that you'd help me, that I wasn't alone!' Sophie said tremulously.

'I know,' Tess replied as she dumped a sheaf of papers into her sequinned patchwork tote bag. 'And I meant it, but I can't move in. There are other people who need me out there, plus a load of paperwork that needs doing. The law makes a special provision for cases like yours. I'll be at a night court until late arranging your residency order.' Tess looked around the flat, the first floor

56

of a converted Georgian town house, and tucked one chin into another as she smiled at Sophie. 'Look, you have a nice flat. Obviously a little too small for an adult and two children, what with only having one bedroom and no garden, but on the whole I'm satisfied. It will do for now.'

'Hang on a minute,' Sophie said as a thought occurred to her. 'If you've only just decided that my flat is "satisfactory", how did you know I'd be OK to have the girls? I could have been a drug dealer or a high-class prostitute. I could be anyone.'

Tess raised a sceptical eyebrow as she looked Sophie over. 'Highly unlikely,' she said. 'But I *have* checked you out. You don't have a criminal record, you hold down a good job and pay a mortgage. Besides, you're not "anyone". You're the woman the children's mother named as guardian – that is quite some recommendation. And the girls seem to have settled in OK. I think they're getting used to moving around, poor mites. You'll be fine.'

Sophie looked at the girls. What Tess said was right – she had expected them to be Dickensian waifs, thin and pale and red-eyed. But they seemed to be handling this with much more presence of mind than she was, and they *had* been very manageable since they left Mrs Stiles.

Sophie had thought there would be tears when they said goodbye to their grandmother, but they hadn't seemed too sorry to leave her. Mrs Stiles had told them she would see them soon and to

57

keep their chins up and both of them did, literally in Izzy's case, causing her to walk into the gatepost at the bottom of the garden path. If there had been any hint of tears it might have been from Mrs Stiles, who had pressed her lips so firmly together as she watched the girls leave that her mouth had turned pale and bloodless. She had shut the front door before they had closed the garden gate behind them.

Miraculously, Sophie had seen a black cab turn into the street and had stepped out onto the kerb to hail it, but just as the cabbie caught her eye Tess pulled her back onto the pavement and waved the driver on.

'What's the problem?' Sophie asked Tess. 'Was it money because I was going to pay – my place is a long walk from here, you know. I didn't think these two could walk that far. Short legs and all that.' Sophie looked at the battered and brimming suitcase at her feet. 'And this is heavy.'

Tess shook her head.

'Oh look girls!' she exclaimed. 'Ants!' Astonishingly, the discovery seemed to delight both children, who crouched over the crack in the pavement and watched the busy insects track and bustle across the stone slab.

Sophie raised a questioning eyebrow at Tess. 'I didn't think we'd be stopping for a natural history lesson,' she said.

Tess took a step closer to Sophie and lowered her voice.

'I told you Izzy is still a bit iffy about cars,' she said. 'After the crash.'

'Oh.' Sophie had forgotten that piece of information. 'When you say iffy what do you mean exactly?'

Tess chewed her lip. 'Izzy was in the car on the way to nursery when Carrie was killed. A van hit them side-on at a junction, doing fifty. Izzy was in a car seat. She was protected. Frightened and alone for almost ten minutes until help came, but physically unhurt. Carrie's seat belt was faulty. Apparently she knew it was, she just hadn't got round to getting it fixed. She was killed outright. Thrown from the car. So Izzy's a bit iffy about getting in cars, including cabs, I'm afraid.'

Sophie looked down the length of the tree-lined road that she and Carrie had walked along so many times together over the years, talking incessantly, making plans, creating dreams for themselves. Carrie was going to be a painter, of course, and a fashion designer. She was going to live right by the sea in a tower and marry a fisherman. Sophie was going to become a vet and run a cat sanctuary. She was going to marry Jason Donovan. It was funny how Carrie's dream never changed and how she had made it more or less come true. Sophie's plans always changed from year to year – different occupation, different celebrity husband – until her dreams and fantasies had faded away into real solid ambition, into her life as it stood now. Even knowing exactly what she wanted and exactly where she was going, Sophie assumed she had enough time left on earth to make it happen. But Carrie had never planned to be thrown from a car and killed taking her daughter to nursery. Neither one of them had ever dreamed they'd die. Not now, not ever.

'Does she understand what happened then?' Sophie asked. To be perfectly honest, she had no idea what a three-year-old could or could not understand. If she'd ever thought about it before, she would have guessed that age group had about the same amount of reasoning power as the average dog – maybe a collie or a German shepherd – and much less than a cat.

Tess shrugged. 'She understands that it was very frightening and that she hasn't seen her mummy since. I'm not sure what else she understands, I haven't really had time to talk to either of them properly. I don't think anyone has. Like I mentioned before, I've got both the girls down for counselling but, well – there's a waiting list.'

For a second Sophie did not know what to say and she felt the weight of the children's terrible loss nudging at her edges. She blinked hard and chased the feeling away. There was no time for that now, she told herself. Right now she needed to stay focused on the project in hand.

'There's a bus stop at the end of the road,' she said at last, hefting the suitcase off the ground. 'We'll get the bus.'

★　★　★

60

'Anyway,' Tess said as she checked her mobile. 'I'll pop back in the morning, see how you're getting on, OK?'

Sophie nodded. 'Right,' she said to Tess, desperately trying to fight the wave of panic that was surging in her chest. 'What do I do with them?' she hissed. 'They're OK now, but what if they start crying or something?'

'Then give them a hug,' Tess told her.

'A hug?' Sophie looked dubious.

'Yes, but in the meantime just give them some tea,' Tess added, looking at her watch.

'Tea? Really? OK. If you say so.'

Tess gave Sophie a slightly quizzical look as she accompanied her downstairs and opened the main entrance. As Tess walked out, Sophie's cat, Artemis, walked in, shouldering her way past Sophie's legs without the faintest of greetings. Sophie wasn't offended, that was just Artemis. It took her a long time to establish complete trust with a human. Sophie wasn't sure exactly how long, but it was definitely longer than the three years since Sophie had rescued her from the cat home where she had been the least popular and most solitary inmate. For some reason, though, Sophie had been drawn to her and had slavishly adored her from the moment she brought her home. An emotion that was definitely not reciprocated.

Normally when Artemis came in this way she'd shoot straight up the stairs and into the kitchen looking for her dinner. But today she stopped at the foot of the stairs and stared up them.

'Ah yes,' Sophie said to the cat. 'There's something I've got to tell you.' She scooped Artemis up in her arms. The cat went rigid in her embrace and tightened her claws on Sophie's sleeve just enough to make holding her uncomfortable. Sophie took this as a good sign. If Artemis had been really pissed off she would have drawn blood and twisted her way to an escape by now. 'The thing is, Artemis – we've got guests. Children. Now, I know you hate noise and mess and people invading your space and touching all your things, but it's only for a week, OK? So try to be nice. At least try not to be violent. I mean, you never know, you might really like them, couple of kids to play with.' Artemis did not look convinced and neither was Sophie. After all, the only other creatures that her cat had ever happily played with to date were a disembowelled mouse and a not quite dead starling chick. Still, no need to tell the girls *that*. Sophie carried a horrified Artemis into the living room and presented her to the children.

'Bella, Izzy,' she said. 'This is my cat Artemis . . .'

'Catty!' Izzy shrieked with delight and bounded over the arm of the cream leather sofa in one fluid moment. Artemis shot out of Sophie's arms with a yowl and disappeared into the bedroom.

'Um, that was my cat Artemis,' Sophie said. 'She's a bit . . .' Sophie was going to say antisocial but thought better of it. 'She's a bit shy. I got her from a cats' shelter. Her last owners weren't very kind to her so people aren't her favourite thing. No-one else wanted her because she was so . . . shy. We get along OK though. I love her and she ignores me. It works pretty well.'

Izzy had dropped to the floor and was peering under the sofa.

'Catty? Catty where are you?' she enquired. 'Come back, catty. *Izzy's going to cuddle you up!*'

'The thing is, Izzy,' Sophie said to the child's bottom, 'it's probably best that while you're staying here you leave her alone. OK?'

'OK,' Izzy said cheerfully. 'Cat-teeeeeeeeeeeeeeeeee? Whereareyouoooooooooo?' She peeped around the living-room door and looked each way down the short hallway before advancing towards the bedroom. Evidently, Izzy's definition of OK was different from Sophie's. Well, looking for Artemis would keep her occupied for a few minutes, Sophie reasoned. There was no way Izzy would find Artemis on top of the wardrobe, her favourite bolthole, so they would both probably be quite safe for the time being.

'So,' she said to Bella, who remained sitting, her hands primly on her knees. 'Tess said to give you tea. How do you like it? Milk, sugar? Earl Grey? I think I've got Darjeeling somewhere . . .'

Bella blinked her brown eyes at Sophie from under her thick black and slightly too long fringe.

'I think she meant *food* tea, Aunty Sophie,' she said slowly, as if English wasn't Sophie's first language. 'Like *dinner*?'

Sophie sat down on the sofa next to her. 'Obviously I knew that!' she lied. 'I was joking! Ha ha. Get it?'

Bella shook her head. 'No,' she said deadpan. 'It wasn't funny.'

For a moment Sophie was reminded of a film she'd once seen where the world was taken over by evil aliens disguised as kids. She forced the thought to the back of her mind. She was the adult, they were the children. She was in charge. It wasn't like, for example *The Omen*. These were Carrie's children. Not the Antichrist's – although she really hardly knew Louis, so she couldn't rule that out entirely.

'So, tea!' Sophie said with renewed vigour. 'Let's go and see what's in the fridge, shall we, Bella?'

There was nothing in the fridge except for half a pint of skimmed milk, three shrivelled spring onions, low-fat margarine and two Marks & Spencer's low-fat ready meals: Thai Green Chicken Curry and Seafood Pasta. That would have to do.

Sophie took the two meals out of the fridge, forked their film covering with enthusiastic aggression and shoved them in the microwave.

Bella watched Sophie display the extent of her culinary skills, her eyes just about reaching over the rim of the worktop. 'What *is* that?' she asked her.

'It's seafood pasta and chicken curry,' Sophie said. 'Yum yum.'

Bella said nothing but eyed the microwave warily for a moment. She looked around the narrow galley kitchen. 'Your kitchen is very small,' she said. 'Where do you eat?' It was a valid question.

'On the sofa usually,' Sophie said. 'Is that OK?'

Bella looked sceptical. 'Well, it's OK for me but . . .'

'Excellent, that's settled then.'

Just at the moment that the microwave beeped there was a crash from the bedroom and the screech of a furious cat followed closely by the cries of a distraught child. Sophie and Bella ran into the bedroom. Izzy was lying sprawled on Sophie's bed, with Sophie's old-style umbrella in one hand and half of one leg trapped underneath Sophie's empty and thankfully lightweight suitcase.

'Catty!' Izzy sobbed, waving the umbrella wildly at the open window. 'Catty, come back!'

Sophie looked out of the small window that she always left open for Artemis to come and go as she pleased. She must have scooted across the balconette and onto the downstairs extension roof and off into the evening in double quick time. Sophie didn't think she'd be coming back anytime soon and she felt a pang of helpless anxiety, although she didn't know why she worried about Artemis. Artemis was a pretty tough cat. Some poor rodent was really in for it tonight.

Bella climbed onto the bed and pushed the suitcase off the still miserable Izzy and onto the floor
with a thud. She put her arms around Izzy and
pulled her into a sitting position. Kissing the
younger girl's thick black hair, Bella patted her
firmly on the back three times.

'There. There. There,' she said with each pat.
Sophie wasn't sure what she was supposed to do.
Perhaps she was supposed to hug Izzy and do a
bit of patting too, but she didn't quite know how
to go about the whole hugging and patting thing.
She left it to Bella and sat on the edge of the bed
instead.

'What happened, Izzy?' Sophie asked her.

'Catty was stuck, I was helping catty, like when
Bob the Builder helped Pilchard,' Izzy sobbed.
'But she ran away! I wanted to cuddle her up!'

Sophie guessed that Izzy had spotted Artemis
on top of the wardrobe and, unable to reach her,
had climbed onto the bed with Sophie's hook-
handled umbrella and tried to hook the cat down.
That would have horrified poor old Artemis. Still,
that proved that Izzy had at least as much
reasoning power as a border collie, after all. Sophie
ventured out a hand, patted Izzy's knee, then
quickly withdrew it.

'Don't worry,' she said. 'Artemis will be back.
Probably best not to cuddle her up next time she
comes home, though – she's not a big fan of the
cuddle as a concept.'

'OK,' Izzy sniffed.

Sophie wasn't sure whether or not to take that as agreement. The microwave beeped again. 'Tea's ready!' she said brightly and both girls did look more cheerful. They must be really hungry, poor kids.

In preparation, Sophie positioned them both on the sofa and gave them a piece of kitchen roll each to prevent spillage. She gave them a knife and fork and looked through her practically medieval five channels only for something they could watch, settling in the end for *Richard & Judy*.

'Oooh a knife,' Izzy said, inspecting the implement as if it were a lethal weapon.

In the kitchen Sophie tipped each ready meal out onto a separate plate. She thought for a moment and then tipped the seafood pasta onto the Thai green curry plate and mixed it round until it was a slightly lighter shade of green. Then she split the mixture into two and slid one half back onto the second plate. That way there'd be no arguments about who was having what, she thought, feeling pleased with herself. Foresight: that was what she had displayed there. A key problem-solving skill was to solve the problem before it even occurred.

She took the plates through to the living room, where Izzy was endeavouring to cut open the sofa with the serrated edge of her knife.

'Um.' Sophie made especially sure that she did not raise her voice. 'Izzy, don't do that, OK?' she asked her, wondering if the exorbitant cost of the sofa would mean anything to Izzy. Probably not.

'OK!' Izzy said, sawing away regardless.

'Here's tea now anyway.' Sophie handed the girls a plate each. 'Enjoy. I've just got to make a couple of quick calls so I'll be back in a minute, OK?'

'OK!' Izzy said, transferring her sawing attentions onto the food.

Bella looked at her meal suspiciously and poked it with her fork. 'OK,' she said with much less enthusiasm.

Sophie picked up the phone in her bedroom and phoned Cal first.

'How's it going?' he asked, unable to keep the amusement out of his voice.

'Fine, it's fine actually.' Sophie wondered if her voice sounded as high down the other end of the phone line as it did in her head. She made a conscious effort to lower it a half-octave. 'I've given them their tea, then I expect they'll go to bed after,' she said confidently.

'What, at five o'clock?' Cal did not sound so confident.

'Never mind that,' Sophie said, brushing his doubts aside. 'Did the contracts from the bank come through?' Cal confirmed that they had. He gave her a rundown of the rest of the day's events and the inside scoop on how Lisa had handled all of her new duties.

'Pretty well, actually,' Cal said. 'She hasn't cried for the whole afternoon. Barely even a sniffle. Well, maybe the occasional sob – but mainly I think you being out of the office is good for her. She's too scared of me to mess *me* around.'

Sophie ignored the last comment. 'Good. Listen, I want you to come round in the morning. Bring my laptop – I didn't have time to pick it up when we went. Bring all the stuff we talked about today and our schedule for the week. I want to sort out exactly who's doing what, when.'

'Yes, sir,' Cal said. 'Should we synchronise our watches?'

Sophie did not laugh. She didn't like it when Cal called her sir.

'Any other calls?' she asked.

'Jake called to see if we'd heard from you. He asked me for your home number and I said it was against company policy and all that, but he said what about your mobile number and I said I supposed that would be OK if it was really important, and he said he needed to talk to you about the party. So I offered to see if I could help him but he said he'd just give you a ring and see how you were doing, so he clearly fancies you even though you've just recently become a single mother. I think you should marry him. He's a keeper.'

Sophie gave a short hysterical laugh.

'Look, Cal, I need to get my head round this. Carrie's gone and her children are in my front room. I can't think about any of that stuff – so please, for my sake, just give it a rest will you?'

There was a short pause.

'I'm sorry, Soph.' Cal's voice softened. 'You know me, the more complicated and emotional things get, the bigger and more stupid my mouth gets. Look, if I can help you with anything you know I will, don't you?

Sophie smiled. 'I know,' she said. 'You're a mate. Just come over tomorrow – at lunchtime, OK?'

'Yes, sir,' Cal said, resuming normal service. 'Over and out, sir!' And for once Sophie didn't mind.

She listened for any sound of disturbance from the living room. All was quiet on the western front except for the faint jangle of the *Richard & Judy* theme tune. She dialled her mother's number. As usual it rang only twice before she heard the receiver clatter to the floor and the sound of dogs baying and yapping. Her slightly hard-of-hearing mother had trained her Great Dane cross, Scooby, to answer the phone when it rang. Unfortunately she had not trained it to take messages, or perhaps more vitally to go and fetch her and let her know that someone was waiting on the end of the line.

'Mum!' Sophie yelled down the phone. 'Mum! Mum! Mum!' It was a bit of a lottery as to whether or not her mum would work out that someone was on the phone. But the more Sophie yelled the more the dogs barked, which meant it was more likely her mum would come and see what they were barking at, which in turn usually resulted in a conversation.

Finally there was a clank and the sound of her mother's voice conversing with the dogs.

'Get down, poochies – get *down*! Hello?' Her mother spoke into the receiver at last. She always sounded surprised when she answered the phone, as if she'd forgotten each time that it had been invented.

'Mum, it's me,' Sophie said.

'Hello, dear.' Her mum's voice warmed. 'Oh, I am glad I called you. I've got a lot to tell you. Felicity's got to go back to the vet again – same dicky tummy, I don't know what it can be but there's been poo every—'

'Mum!' Sophie finally succeeded in stopping her mother's download of dog-related information. 'Look, I'm sorry but I've got something to tell you.' And she told her about Carrie and the children.

'Oh dear,' her mum said after a long pause. 'How terrible. How terrible.'

Sophie agreed once again that it was, she knew it was terrible but she worried that she was secretly thinking so for all the wrong, selfish reasons.

'The thing is, Mum, I don't really know what I'm doing. I thought maybe you could come over? Give me some tips? Please, Mum?'

Her mum hesitated as Sophie knew she would. 'Tonight, dear, do you mean?' she said uncertainly.

'Well, it is sort of an emergency.' Sophie was disappointed at her mum's reluctance even though she knew that prising her away from her dogs was near impossible, especially in recent years. Sophie did think, though, that under the circumstances she might have made an effort.

'Please, Mum,' Sophie said, resenting having to ask twice. 'I need you.'

'All right,' her mum said, with slow reluctance. 'But I won't be able to stay for long. Mitzy's expecting, you know – it could be any minute.'

Sophie said goodbye and looked at her reflection in her dressing-table mirror. She looked exactly the same as she always did. Neat and efficient. Calm and in control – so why did she feel as if she'd suddenly been sent into a war zone, thrown in amongst bloody chaos without the faintest clue what to do, not even any basic training? She made herself take a deep breath. Managing children was no different to managing any other project. All it required was a broad depth of knowledge, a cool head and brilliant negotiating skills. That and twenty-four Diazepam and a large bottle of whisky. Sophie smiled at herself in the mirror. Things were not quite *that* bad. Yet.

'It's just two weeks,' she told herself. 'You'll be fine.'

The bedroom door opened a crack and Bella's fringe peered round the corner.

'Um, Aunty Sophie,' she said ominously. 'I think you'd better come and see this.'

Sophie instinctively steeled herself as she followed Bella back down the hallway to the living room, imagining the very worst that could have happened. She did not imagine hard enough.

'My sofa!' Sophie cried, ignoring the child who

was covered from head to foot in Thai-curry-seafood-pasta. 'Oh my God! My sofa! My . . . sofa.'

Half of her cream leather sofa was now a greenish colour and so were her two faux fur cushions, their once strokeable softness now converted into punk-like sticky spikes.

Izzy grinned at her. 'Tea was all bleugh and yuk,' she said reasonably, by way of explanation. 'So I made a painting with it on the sofa!' Izzy clearly thought that the artwork was something that should impress and not depress Sophie. 'Is there any ice cream please?' she asked.

Sophie resisted the urge to weep. She ran through all the legal and moral reasons why it was not a good idea to throw a child out of the window, until she was sure she had stopped herself from screaming. She took a deep breath and counted backwards from ten just to be on the safe side.

'What have you done to my sofa?' Sophie said with much more control than she felt. 'Why have you . . . *ruined* my sofa?' She turned to Bella. 'Couldn't you have stopped her? Couldn't you have come and got me? I mean, you're the responsible one.'

'I'm only six and a half,' Bella said, looking irritated. 'And anyway, you were on the phone and you said it was OK for us to eat on the sofa and I didn't know that she was going to do that, did I? I just went in the kitchen to get some more water and when I came back she'd tipped it everywhere and . . .' Bella stopped talking and

Sophie was worried that she had made her cry. But when she looked up at Sophie her eyes were dry.

'Really,' Bella said, giving Sophie a look of pure recrimination, 'Izzy needs *adult* supervision.'

'All right, I appreciate that it's not your fault,' Sophie said. She looked at Izzy, narrowed her eyes and tried a phrase her mum used on her frequently as a child. 'What have you got to say for yourself, young lady?'

Izzy giggled and clapped her hands over her mouth. 'Oops,' she said. 'I done a wee-wee in my pants!' The child giggled again and pointed at a trickle of liquid running over the edge of the sofa and dripping onto the sheepskin rug. Sophie wanted to break down and cry over her sofa, she wanted to weep for her rug, she wanted desperately to mourn her faux fur cushions but she could not, she told herself. She could not be crying over rugs, or cushions or sofas when so far she had witnessed neither one of these children crying over the loss of their mother. Whichever way you looked at it, they had the moral high ground. And children were more important than sofas or cushions. Apparently.

OK, so she had misjudged the situation. Sophie hastily demoted Izzy's intelligence to that of a slightly brain-damaged cocker spaniel. As the only adult present she had to accept responsibility for the incident and take it on the chin. Now she had to manage the damage limitation.

Izzy seemed happy enough covered in food and in wet pants – she could wait. The sofa could not.

Gingerly Sophie picked up Izzy and held her at arm's length. This was harder than she imagined. Izzy was pretty heavy and very ticklish. She giggled and kicked her legs, sending a fine spray of goo all over Sophie's dry-clean-only skirt. Sophie gritted her teeth and thanked God that she'd removed her new boots and locked them safely away in her wardrobe.

'I'm just putting you in the kitchen for a minute, Izzy,' Sophie told her. 'Just while I clear up the mess, OK?'

'OK!' Izzy said.

Sophie was not reassured. She set her down on the lino by the window and cast an eye about for any more potential disasters. There were no sharp objects in view, no toxic substances and no box of matches. Everything should be fine.

'Let's play statues. You stand very VERY still for as long as you can and don't move. OK?'

Izzy nodded.

Twenty minutes, two rolls of Bounty, three bowls of warm soapy water later and Sophie and Bella had made quite a good job of cleaning the sofa, although Sophie suspected there was no hope for the cushions, consigning them regretfully to a bin bag that she put outside in the communal hallway.

'Thank God,' Sophie told Bella sincerely, 'that Marks & Spencer don't use artificial colouring.'

'Thank God,' Bella agreed.

Sophie noticed her food also uneaten but mercifully still congealing on the plate. Now Sophie had a moment to reflect, it *did* look like something one of her mum's dogs might produce from either end.

'You didn't like it either, did you?' she said.

'It *was* rather disgusting.' Bella wrinkled her nose.

Sophie suppressed a smile. For a small child Bella did have a large vocabulary.

'I'm sorry, Bella,' she said. 'This is all new to me. I am a bit crap at it, aren't I?'

'Yes, but you're trying.'

Sophie somehow found the energy to get off her knees and stand up again, and held out a hand to help Bella up.

'Aunty Sophie?' Bella said, still holding onto Sophie's fingers. 'I love Grandma and everything but I'm glad we've come to stay with you.'

Sophie felt herself smile and her resolve strengthened. 'Really?' she replied, warmly deciding to fish a bit further. 'Why's that?'

Bella shrugged. 'Grandma doesn't have a telly.'

Sophie nodded and glanced at the TV, where the end credits for *Richard & Judy* were rolling.

'Fair enough,' she said. 'Well, I suppose we'd better go and clean up your sister.'

'Yes, before she starts eating the cat food,' Bella said.

Sophie laughed. 'You're joking, right?'

Bella wasn't joking.

Sophie gave her mum a cup of tea and her very best resentful look. Iris looked offended.

'I got here as soon as I could, dear,' she said.

'Mum, it's twenty to ten! I was hoping you'd be round before they went to sleep. That's when I needed help the most.'

But oblivious to Sophie's trials, Iris was unrepentant.

It was shortly after Sophie had discovered Izzy snacking on the Kitekat that she made what would later prove to be a critical discovery. When a three-year-old girl is determined to do something she really, *really* means it.

In this case, Izzy had refused point-blank to remove her fancy dress, even for a much-needed bath. At first Sophie had tried reason and logic to persuade the child out of the dress. But then as Izzy's screams had grown to eardrum-perforating levels, and Sophie had clutched at all the available straws, she had turned in desperation to Bella.

'What do I do?' she had asked Bella, who was watching with detached interest, her hands clapped over her ears.

'Let her keep the dress on?' Bella had suggested casually. Simple, brilliant and entirely effective.

A few minutes later Sophie had washed child and dress in her bath, tipping in large amounts of Chanel bubble bath in an attempt to mask the smell, too fraught to resent the sacrifice.

'She's always happy if you let her get her own way,' Bella had observed, sitting on the loo.

'I'm not letting her get her own way,' Sophie had said with determination. 'I'm multitasking.'

'I would have been here earlier, Sophie,' her mum said now, 'but Oedipus Rex started having one of his turns and I had to stay with him until he settled down. I don't want the neighbours complaining again, do I?'

Sophie shook her head. 'You should move, Mum. You should sell that house and move to the country. You'd get somewhere much bigger for your money and it wouldn't matter so much that you have the canine version of the Von Trapp family.'

Iris sniffed. 'I don't know anyone in the country,' she said, looking a little hurt.

'You don't know anyone here any more,' Sophie reminded her. 'No-one wants to come round in case they catch rabies.'

Iris sighed. 'I want to live near you, anyway,' she said wistfully. Sophie covered her surprise. Her mum loved her dogs so much that Sophie sometimes forgot that she was probably also fairly fond of her daughter too.

'So what do you think about the cat-food thing, then?' Sophie said, deciding to change the subject before they somehow got embroiled in one of their long, consistently unsatisfactory and ultimately draining conversations about what it meant to be a good daughter.

Her mum considered the question for a moment. 'I think it will be fine,' she said. 'There was an article about an old lady who couldn't pay her gas bill in the *Express* last week. She'd been living off cat food, the poor old dear, even though when the neighbours broke in they found thousands of pounds in cash under her bed.'

'Why did the neighbours break in?' Sophie asked her.

'Because she was dead, dear,' her mum said as if it were a stupid question.

'Dead!' Sophie panicked momentarily as she wondered what the maximum sentence was for involuntary manslaughter.

'Oh no, no,' Iris said quickly. 'She didn't die of cat food, she died of hypothermia. All alone in the world you see – her children had abandoned her.'

'Oh thank God,' Sophie said with relief. Her mother raised an eyebrow at her. 'Well, you know what I mean.' Sophie sighed and drew her legs up under her. She wrinkled her nose. The sofa still smelt decidedly spicy. 'The thing is, Mum, I have no idea what I'm doing. I know I'm only having them for a week or so but right now that feels like a week or so too long. I'm useless.'

Her mum reached into her bag and pulled out a book. She tossed it to Sophie, who was expecting something useful on childcare. She should have known better.

'*Dr Robert's Complete Dog Training and Care Manual*?' Sophie read out the title in disbelief. 'Mum! They're children, they're humans – or at least that's what I've been told! How's this –' she wagged the book at her mum – 'going to help?'

Her mum pursed her lips. 'You'd be surprised, actually. The principles are more or less the same. Sit, stay, come, etcetera. House-training. A spot of doggie psychology. It could work wonders, I expect. I wish I'd known all that when I had you. That's the trouble with you cat people. No imagination.'

Sophie tossed the book onto the floor in disgust. 'You must know something about looking after children, Mum. You brought me up after all – more or less.'

Iris nodded and looked slightly abashed. 'I know darling, I know, but I've – well, I've forgotten how I did it. It sounds silly but it was rather a long time ago and I don't know – it's just gone out of my head. The only thing I do remember is feeling like I was always getting it wrong. I can't have done too much of a bad job though – look at you. Successful, independent. Can't get a husband but that will come . . .'

Sophie sipped her tea and felt it warming the back of her throat. 'Don't want a husband, Mum. Don't *want* one,' She said irritably. 'There is a difference.' Sophie's mother looked sceptical. Sophie thought about Jake. 'And even if I did, I never exactly know when one wants me.'

'That's the easy bit, dear,' Iris chuckled, thinking that Sophie must be joking. 'It's what to do with them after you're married that's the hard part.'

'You and Dad never had any trouble,' Sophie said.

'Yes, well.' Iris smiled fondly. 'Your father and I always had incredible sexual chemistry. I can't tell you how I've miss—'

'Mum!'

'All I'm saying is that a woman has needs, I know since your father passed . . .'

'Mum!' Sophie hissed at her mother, afraid to raise her voice. 'I don't want to talk to *you* about "needs", mine, yours or anyone's – OK? I need your help with these children!'

Iris shrugged. 'Alex was a nice young man,' she said, wilfully ignoring her daughter's attempt to force her off the rails of the current conversation. 'He seemed to really care about you and he brought me some lovely flowers.'

Sophie felt the muscles tighten in her chest with anxiety and frustration. She had told her mum time and time again why things hadn't worked out with Alex.

In the end Alex had told her he was tired of going out with her. Tired of the amount of effort it took to get her to leave her job alone for even a few minutes and spend some time with him. He had said he jumped through hoop after hoop to get her attention but nothing seemed to work. So he had tried a last-ditch attention-grabber.

He had asked her to marry him.

Crucially, Sophie had hesitated. Not for a few minutes or days but for nearly three weeks. And she didn't just hesitate when he'd left her that evening, with a ring in a box on her coffee table

– it was the last time she talked to him face to face. She just didn't know what to say so she didn't say anything.

Eventually Alex had sent her an e-mail telling her he assumed her silence was a no – unless she wanted to tell him otherwise. Sophie had never replied to that either, except to have Cal courier the ring back to him without even including a note. She'd let the biggest and potentially most important relationship in her adult life slip away simply because she didn't know how to be in it. No, it was worse than mere negligence. She hadn't just let it slip away. She had deleted it.

And although her friends, especially Cal, told her she was crazy to let him go, she told them she couldn't keep him, because she wasn't absolutely certain she *wanted* to.

Sometimes, though, she did miss him. Well, not him exactly, more the warmth he left in bed in the morning. Sophie shook her head. Her mum was managing to railroad her again.

'Can we just for one moment try to think about the most immediate problem?' Iris looked rather vague. 'The kids!' Sophie reminded her.

'I'm sorry I'm not more of an expert on mother-hood,' Iris said, the slight sharpness in her tone going over Sophie's head. 'But, well, I think you just have to trust your instincts. Listen to your intuition and you won't go wrong.'

'I think that's the problem,' Sophie said glumly, wishing she hadn't smoked all five of her remaining cigarettes shortly after the girls had gone to bed.

'What is, dear?' her mum said. Sophie looked up at her blankly. 'What's the problem?' Iris pressed her.

'Well, most women have intuition built in, don't they?' Sophie said. 'Give 'em a kid and they know what to do with it instantly – at least that's what we're all led to believe. But obviously I have that particular gene missing . . . I never get any intuition about anything, Mum. I mean, how do I know what to do for the best unless I have all the available facts in front of me – in black and white? This intuition business sounds like total nonsense to me – like reflexology or astrology.'

Iris smiled. 'Your stars did say you were facing great upheaval,' she said.

'Really?' Sophie looked interested for a moment, until she realised her mum was teasing her. 'Anyway. I don't think intuition really exists. I think it's a myth.'

'It isn't,' Iris said.

'You would say that – and anyway, how do you know?' Sophie challenged her mother.

'I just do, the same way I know that you have it, Sophie,' Iris said, pausing to find a way to talk to her prickly daughter without offending her. 'Sometimes I think with all this work and career and promotions that you've forgotten yourself. You're always working towards something, but I wonder if you even know what for?'

Sophie rolled her eyes. 'Mum, things are different now. I know what I want from my life. I want to get to the top. I don't need a man or children to be happy or fulfilled. I *want* to be successful.'

'But *why*?' her mum asked her, stressing the last word. Sophie looked at her and wondered how it was they shared the same language, as Iris never seemed to understand what she was going on about.

'I want to be the best I can,' Sophie said, frustrated that the conversation had somehow drifted onto her mother's favourite subject yet again – Things That Are Wrong With Sophie.

'And anyway, this isn't about me,' she said irritably. 'It's about now and the next couple of weeks. I've got to come up with a coping strategy and I thought you could help me – I should have known better.'

Iris dipped her face and looked at her tea, and immediately Sophie felt sorry. 'I'm not saying you're not a great mum, I mean you are great and you are my mum and I love you – but you were never exactly conventional, were you?'

Her mum shrugged. 'Possibly not,' she said. 'It was the Seventies, dear. Nothing was.'

'I know – all I'm saying is that I don't have it. I don't have that way you're supposed to have with kids. I understand Artemis better than I understand children and Artemis is not an easy cat to understand. She's got issues.'

Iris finished her tea and set the mug down on the coffee table. 'I don't think anybody would expect you to instantly turn into an expert under these circumstances, Sophie. I'm sure Carrie wouldn't. In fact, if I remember Carrie correctly she'd think the whole thing was pretty funny.'

Sophie felt the corners of her mouth creep into a smile. Carrie *would* be seriously tickled by everything that had happened this evening.

'I'm sure you'll pick it up eventually, a capable girl like you,' Iris reassured her.

'Eventually, maybe,' Sophie conceded. 'But not in two weeks.'

CHAPTER 5

'Aunty Sophie!' Sophie opened one reluctant eye and looked at Izzy. She felt like she had only been asleep for a total of forty-seven minutes. 'Psssssst, Aunty Sophie,' Izzy whispered at the top of her voice. 'Wake up, wake up. I want breakfast. I want Cheerios *and* Shreddies *and* Krispies *and* Coco Pops *and* milk!' Izzy's eyes widened in clear anticipation of the delights that her cereal fest would bring. She was out of luck, though. Sophie did not eat breakfast. She didn't even have any bread any more, they'd finished it all last night. On realising that she had to feed the children something, Sophie had made the piles of toast which they had eaten on the kitchen floor – just to be on the safe side.

Sitting up, Sophie rubbed her eyes and looked at her watch. It was just before six a.m. It turned out that she *had* only been asleep for a total of forty-seven minutes.

Her mother had left just after eleven and Sophie had been sitting on the edge of the sofa wondering exactly how she had come to this point in her life, when she'd heard a loud buzzing. For a few moments she thought the day was being topped off nicely with an invasion of giant killer wasps, then she realised it was her mobile phone vibrating on the coffee table. Nobody ever called on it out of office hours. Its loud thrum against the blond ash was rather disconcerting. Sophie picked it up and looked at the display: it said number with-held. Unable to leave a phone unanswered, she had pressed the call button.

'Hello?' she had said uncertainly.

'Sophie?' It was Jake Flynn's voice. Sophie had looked at her watch. Jake at this hour?

'Look, I know it's late and I've been wondering about calling you all night,' Jake had said quickly. 'I wanted to see how you were. I nearly didn't ring but then I thought if I were you I'd be sitting up all night worrying.' He had paused. 'Tell me to go away if you like, but I thought you might want someone to talk to.'

Sophie had chewed her lip. 'Um no – thanks for calling. It's very . . . nice of you,' She'd said. She would have to ring Cal in the morning and ask him to verify, but she was fairly sure that phone calls at this hour were quite a good indicator of Jake being interested in her on more than just a business level.

But what if he *did* like her? Appreciating his good looks when he was just her most important client was one thing. A man who phoned her late at night to ask her how she was was completely different. If he did like her like that, what did it mean? How would she feel about him then – a real, three-dimensional, fleshy version of him who would want her in the real world instead of when she was daydreaming in the bath?

Sophie's laboured thought processes had crashed and she had shut her eyes for a moment to reboot. He still might not fancy her. He could just be being American again. Americans are famous for not being very good at observing boundaries.

'So how are you coping?' Jake had continued, and Sophie had realised that he was the first person to ask her that.

'I don't really know, Jake, there's so much to take in. I mean, Carrie's gone . . .' Sophie had paused to listen to those words out loud again. She still could not make sense of them. 'It's a bit surreal,' she'd finished after a moment.

'You know you're not alone, don't you?' Jake had asked her.

'I know. I've got this Tess woman, the social worker, and Cal and Lisa will handle everything in the office until I can get back in – you don't have to worry, Jake, I won't let anything get in the way of . . .'

'That's not what I meant.' Sophie had heard him breathe out. 'Look, Sophie, I really like you and just in case you were in any doubt about what I mean by like you, I mean I like you in a non-business, personal kind of way. I am very attracted to you.'

'Oh.' That cleared that up then.

'I know you've got a lot on and maybe I should be stepping back and letting you get on with things but, like I said, I really like you. I don't want to let this go before it's had a chance to become something. Something that might be really great. I understand that right now you just can't think about anything like that, so in the meantime I want to be your friend. I guess that's why I'm calling you at this hour of the night, to let you know I like you and that if you need me I'm here for you.' Jake had laughed. 'I'm hoping you'll be so impressed by my chivalry you'll fall for me and let me take you out on a date once all the dust has settled.' There had been a short pause in which Sophie had realised that Jake had been asking her a question.

'Of course,' she had said automatically.

'And I was thinking I could come by and take you all out one day. To the zoo or something? I have all this leave owing to me and after all I'm the boss – I'm sure I can give myself a day off at short notice.'

'That would be lovely,' Sophie had said, her mind still on the fact that Jake Flynn definitely 'liked' her, which left just one question – did she definitely like him?

'So – it's OK if I call you on a non-business footing?' Jake had asked her again.

'It is,' Sophie had said, painfully aware of her stilted responses.

'Then goodnight, Sophie.' That time Jake had said her name it sounded different.

Sophie had sat on the edge of the sofa with the phone in her hand and wondered about how different her day might have been if Tess Andrew hadn't turned up. She wondered if Jake would have been so open and upfront at their lunch date. If so, she wondered if they might have met that evening for dinner, and he might have escorted her home. She had closed her eyes and tried to imagine him kissing her, and then opened them quickly again. It wasn't that she wasn't attracted to Jake, but she was glad in a way that this obstacle had thrown itself up between them. Speculating on what might or might not happen with Jake was far too complicated to be fitted into her present worrying schedule. She had so many other things to worry about: abandoned children, absent fathers, dead best friends. Sophie's stomach had clenched as she ran down the list.

She had decided to worry about her cat instead. It was far less worrying.

And so she had lain awake on the slightly too short and rather smelly sofa for most of the night, worrying about Artemis. Artemis liked her routine, she did not like disruption of any kind, it seriously freaked her out. For all the tough and together front she put on, all the girl-about-town swaggering that she did, she was a bit of a scaredy-cat when it came down to it. Sophie had worried that she wouldn't come back, and she didn't want

Artemis to leave her. Despite being the world's most unfriendly pet, Sophie would miss her sitting on what had become her very own armchair, casting Sophie the occasional imperious glance.

Fortunately Artemis had come back just before five a.m., which Sophie had considered something of a step forward in their relationship as Artemis must have thought of the flat as a home worth coming back to, even with two fighting children in situ. After eating what was left of her food and having a drink of water, she had stalked into the living room and regarded Sophie with a look of pure recrimination before leaping onto the armchair and curling up on its cushion with her back turned on Sophie, who was somehow comforted by the snub.

Sophie had looked at the ceiling and for the first time in the last twenty-four hours allowed herself to think about Carrie. Closing her eyes, she had pictured her the last time she had seen her, three years ago. Small but curvy, with dark honey curls and hazel eyes that glittered when she laughed – and she was always laughing. She'd tied her hair up in a bandanna and wore a pair of paint-splattered dungarees over a vest top. She'd teased Sophie for fretting about the upholstery on her beloved car as she drove her and her sticky children to the station to catch the train back to Cornwall.

'Call me if you need me,' Sophie had told Carrie as she helped her onto the platform with her luggage. 'Call me anyway, but call if me you need me, too – any time, OK?'

Carrie had laughed as she threw her bag onto the train with no regard for whom or what it might hit.

'Always, for ever, whatever – right?' she had said, hugging Sophie as she reminded her of their ancient pact.

'Exactly,' Sophie had said, not quite able to say it back to her for fear of sounding a bit cheesy.

'Let's see each other really soon, OK? I mean, I know your life is one constant social whirl but I'm sure you can find time to see us somewhere.' Sophie knew that Carrie was trying to make a gentle point, because although her job did guarantee at least three parties a month, her life outside the office had dwindled almost to nothing.

And Carrie had been right, Sophie was letting her social life slip away. It wasn't that she didn't have friends out there who wanted to see her and whom she wanted to see. It was just that something always came up at work to prevent it happening, and nine times out of ten she would have to cancel at the last minute. With Carrie there was the excuse that she lived a couple of hundred miles away, but Sophie was just as bad at keeping up with other friends. Christina and Sue who both lived in Islington, for example. She hadn't seen either of them in months and they were practically neighbours. And she was supposed to meet the McCarthy Hughes old girls for a drink on every fourth Thursday but the last time she had made it, it was just after last orders and all she could do was kiss her friends on the cheek as she exchanged hurried news in the queue for a taxi.

'You have to let your hair down more,' her recently engaged friend and former colleague Angie had told her. 'Don't let McCarthy Hughes run your life. You don't want to turn into Gillian!'

Sophie had laughed, but secretly thought that actually that *was* what she wanted.

Still, Sophie remembered thinking as she had said goodbye, Carrie was different. Carrie was her best friend and as much a part of her life as her mum was – if not more. No-one knew her like Carrie did. She had to make more of an effort.

'Let's not let another two or three years go by again,' Sophie had said sincerely. 'I never remember how much I miss you until I see you.'

'I'm going to take that as a compliment,' Carrie had said, with a grin. As the train had pulled out of the station Bella and Carrie had pressed their noses against the window and crossed their eyes as Sophie waved them goodbye. Sophie had never seen Carrie again.

'I'm sorry, mate,' Sophie had whispered, 'I really am remembering how much I miss you now, believe me.' And then twenty-three hours of drama overcame her and she finally fell asleep.

That had been forty-eight minutes ago. Right now Izzy was repeating her breakfast order with increasing urgency. Sophie looked over at the armchair. Artemis was no longer in it, lucky cat.

'OK, OK,' she said, holding the palm of her hand in front of Izzy's face. 'Shush.'

Izzy did shush. Her eyes filled with tears and her lips quivered perilously.

'No!' Sophie said quickly in conciliatory tones, fearing the wailing and screaming and holding of breath that had preceded last night's bath. 'No, no, no, no, – don't cry, Izzy! Aunty Sophie wasn't telling you off, no! Because you are a lovely good girl, aren't you?' Izzy nodded and sniffed in a deep, damp breath. 'Yes, yes you are – super-duper good excellent good grown-up girl who isn't going to cry.' Sophie nodded at the child encouragingly and, returning her nod, Izzy climbed without invitation onto Sophie's lap and wound her arms around Sophie's neck.

'I'll be a good girl for you, Aunty Sophie,' Izzy said, picking up a thick strand of Sophie's hair and winding it around her fist. 'I'll be your friend and we will all be happy and you won't be cross, OK?'

Sophie nodded. She knew that any normal woman would be charmed and delighted by the statement – so why did Sophie feel like it was a Mafioso-style threat?

'It's a deal,' she said, uncertainly.

'I'll kiss you now, OK?' Izzy said, and without waiting for consent she pressed her slimy face onto Sophie's tensed cheek, leaving a damp nose print just under one of Sophie's twitching eyes. 'Then breakfast. I want Cheerios and . . .' As Sophie contemplated how to break the no-breakfast news to Izzy, she noticed a walking pile of laundry approaching though the living-room door. Bella dropped the sheets onto the rug.

'Izzy wet the bed,' she said, a little anxiously. 'It wasn't me.'

Sophie felt the damp of the fairy-dress skirt begin to seep through her pyjama bottoms, and took a deep breath. She wasn't going to get stressed about it. It was just wee on her leg. It wouldn't kill her. It probably wouldn't kill her although she might have to look that up on the Internet to make sure. She'd just have to get changed, put these pyjamas in the bin and buy a new bed after they'd gone, that was all. And new bedclothes and a new sofa and new cushions and new rugs. She wondered if the presence of a dead friend's children was an acceptable risk on her contents insurance. If it wasn't, it should be.

Sophie lifted Izzy off her lap and sat her on the fragrant pile of sheets where she could do the least damage.

'OK,' she said to both girls. 'Only thirteen days to go.' Both children stared blankly at her. 'What I mean is, I have no food in the house. We'll have to go out for breakfast – to the twenty-four-hour Sainsbury's at Manor House. We'll get dressed, and we'll go there, OK?'

'OK!' both girls said.

'I'm hungry,' Izzy said, glumly. 'I'm *starving*.'

'I know. Which is why we have to get ready extra quickly. And why we have to do *everything* that Aunty Sophie says, OK?' Sophie stared at both the girls as if she could hypnotically implant obedience into them. They stared back at her. She formulated a plan.

Of course Sophie's plan, which was to empty Izzy's treacherous bladder completely and get everyone out of the flat before malnutrition set in, did not work.

This was what happened instead.

Sophie sat Izzy on the toilet and told her not to move until she came back. Then she returned to her bedroom to dress, where she found Bella holding one of the Manolos in one hand and balancing precariously on the other with one foot. Sophie regarded the scene as if she had just come across Bella with her finger in the pin of a live grenade.

'Nooooo!' Sophie had shouted commando-style and, in her head at least, in slow motion.

Bella's face fell and she slumped on the bed face first, letting the shoe drop to the floor. Sophie scooped it up and cradled it momentarily before realising that potentially she had things a *little* out of perspective. She had been about to offer Bella a go of her M&S standards when a clatter and a scream sounded from the bathroom. The Manolo was abandoned once again as Sophie realised her

96

rookie error of leaving Izzy alone in the bathroom for longer than a nanosecond. She found her jammed securely in the loo, her calf sticking out at right angles from the seat and wriggling furiously, her face and upper torso caked in Sophie's expensive make-up collection.

Which had meant another bath. And which Sophie was sure would mean another tantrum.

In the event, though, Izzy was amazingly contrite and even allowed Sophie to remove the offending fairy dress, which was now beyond all help, as long as Sophie replaced it with an identical one. Sophie chose not to worry about the logistics of that promise, concentrating only on the results it got.

Eventually she dressed in the bedroom alongside both girls. Bella had selected a pair of red leggings with yellow dots on, an electric blue T-shirt, a lime green cardigan and a pink cotton ra-ra skirt to finish the outfit off. And robbed of her fairy dress, Izzy carefully picked out items of clothing that were entirely yellow.

In the meantime Sophie struggled to find clothes that were suitable for taking two small children to the supermarket. Sensible clothes were not her strong point. Almost everything she bought was chosen to wear to the office or a function. And she bought everything with a particular pair of shoes in mind. A pair of shoes that came in every colour and style and would invariably have improbably high heels attached to them, because Sophie put shoes first. In her experience shoes were like fashion magnets. The right clothes would simply be drawn to them. Subsequently she was limited as to casual wear, principally because she didn't do much casual wearing.

Eventually she found a pair of jeans that she had forgotten about, and only possessed because she had felt compelled to help her mum redecorate the house last year with washable stainproof paint. After some rooting about in the back of her drawers she also found an old pink Calvin Klein T-shirt with the logo spelt out in diamanté, which she pulled reluctantly over her head.

Then she looked at her shoe rack, which was neatly attached to the inside of her wardrobe door, and scanned her shoes for a practical option. The most sensible and expendable pair she had were from River Island, low kitten heels in magenta pink with pointed toes and a thin strap that crossed each toe horizontally, ending in a tiny bow.

Once, only yesterday in fact – although it seemed like a dim memory now – it had amused her no end that such a pair of shoes were her most sensible ones. Now it dismayed her. Not because she wished she were better prepared for all scenarios, but because she wished that her life was back to normal. She wished that she still had a life in which she did not need to be prepared to ferry two kids round a supermarket.

When the threesome finally emerged from the flat Sophie felt curiously triumphant, as if she had survived an apocalypse.

'The thing is,' she decided, squinting slightly in the glare of the bright winter sun, 'to keep your nerve. If I can just do that it'll be a breeze.'

The trouble was, Sophie wasn't sure how long she could keep her nerve. It felt like she was embarking on a difficult and dangerous journey, one that, because no end was in sight, seemed never-ending.

Sophie was not the sort of person who liked to surrender any control over any small part of life and she realised the biggest source of her anxiety was not the children themselves (although they were especially scary), it was the thought that her fate, as well as the girls', rested solely in the hands of Tess Andrew and Social Services. And it would take them for ever to find the girls' father. The thought of that made Sophie's blood run icy cold. The only sensible thing to do was to regain control of her fate. She would have to find Louis Gregory herself, because the sooner she did, the sooner she would get her life back.

CHAPTER 6

Cal was not nearly as enthusiastic about Sophie's plans to turn bounty hunter as she was. Especially when she asked him to look Louis Gregory up on the Internet – as if the man and his whereabouts would be handily listed by Google in an A–Z directory of Missing Feckless Fathers.

'This is not the telly, Sophie,' Cal told her impatiently over the phone the morning after she decided to find Louis Gregory herself, mainly by getting Cal to do it. 'You don't type a name into the Internet and then suddenly *schum-schum-schum* there's their current location, address and a satellite image of their every movement. I told you this when I came over yesterday. Didn't you hear me? Do you know what I got when I typed in Louis Gregory? Three hundred and eight-two thousand matches. And is your Louis Gregory *the* Louis Gregory? New Zealand's greatest living sheep-shearer Louis Gregory? Not unless he's sixty-two and a Maori he's not.'

Sophie had tapped her chipped nails on the edge of her bed. She was nervous about being in the bedroom when the girls were not but she didn't want them to know she was looking for their dad. She wasn't even sure they knew they had a dad. They hadn't mentioned him since they'd arrived. She wasn't sure what sort of a reaction that news might trigger, but if it was anything on a par with their reaction to the news that she did not have the CBeebies channel on her TV she didn't want to risk it.

'Oh come on, Cal,' she begged. 'I need you here. It's an emergency.'

'Why don't you do it?' he snapped. 'You're the one on holiday after all.'

Sophie paused. She thought about telling him in detail about the inevitable demise of her laptop after he had left yesterday, involving a tube of John Frieda Sheer Blonde hair serum, the residue from an empty box of Coco Pops and a pair of nail scissors, but she decided against it. She couldn't stand the ridicule again; she could still hear the hysterical laughter of the IT support man ringing in her ears.

'My laptop's bust,' she said. 'I'm not getting a replacement until next week. And anyway, if this were a holiday it'd be an all-inclusive trip to the Siberian salt mines of the former Soviet Union. Cal, you're my personal assistant – assist!'

Cal tutted. 'I think you're taking the personal bit a bit too literally,' he muttered.

Sophie paused. She never stopped to think about the nature of their relationship too closely but she had made the assumption that the occasional weekend shopping trips, the odd after-work cocktails in the city and their rare but virtuoso rendition of the karaoke duet 'Love Lifts Us Up Where We Belong' meant that it was more than just a professional one. Perhaps she *was* asking too much of him. Perhaps she was straying into 'things you can ask your boyfriend to do on the grounds that you let him have sex with you' territory.

'I'm sorry,' she said stiffly. 'I didn't mean to impose on you.'

Cal huffed again. 'Oh for Christ's sake, don't pull the martyr act on me, love, I'm immune. Besides, I've got the answer to all our problems.' Cal lowered his voice. 'I know someone who can help.'

'Who?' Sophie asked, touched and reassured by Cal's reclassification of her problems as 'ours'.

'Maria Costello,' Cal said proudly. 'Private detective. She's not cheap but she's good – she *always* gets her man. We've got a lot in common in that respect.'

For a moment Sophie didn't know what to say. She associated Cal's friends and acquaintances with a number of professions from drag queen to car mechanic, but she would never have guessed he'd know a private detective.

'A private detective?' she asked. 'How do you know a private detective?'

Cal's voice was rich with drama. 'Oh, you know. I've done a little – let's call it – "freelance" work for her.'

'Freelance work? What sort of freelance work?'

'Well,' Cal whispered. 'Have you ever heard of "the honey trap"?'

'Yes?' Sophie said uneasily.

'Well, honey, I was the honey in the trap!' Cal giggled.

'You're lying!' Sophie cried, utterly scandalised. 'Please tell me you're lying – if this ever got out . . . you have to be lying,' she repeated.

Cal sighed. 'Yes, all right I am lying – spoilsport. Her offices are in the shop underneath my flat but that's just boring. Anyway she *is* very good and I've told her all about you and she says she can find him, no problem. She says it will be, quote unquote, a piece of piss. Do you want to see her?'

'How much would it cost . . . ?' Sophie began uncertainly, before she and Cal reached the same conclusion at exactly the same moment.

'Actually – I don't care how much it costs,' Sophie said.

'Trust me – you don't care how much it costs,' Cal said simultaneously. 'And besides,' Cal continued, 'you have nothing better to spend all your money on.'

Sophie had to agree that right at that moment in time she did not.

'All right, ask her to come to the flat today. We'll be here for the rest of the day. I've worked out that if we don't actually leave the flat, we've got an eighty per cent better chance of survival. But don't tell Gillian that.'

'Righty ho,' Cal said jauntily. 'Now, if you don't mind I think I'd better get back to my real job.'

'Is everything OK there?' Sophie asked anxiously, thinking about *her* real job. After all, she'd been out of the office for nearly forty-eight hours.

'Everything is fine. Nobody misses you at all,' Cal said, specifically to irritate her. 'Except possibly your new boyfriend, Jakey.'

'He's not my boyfriend,' Sophie said wearily.

'Of course he's not, because you only like men when you're not sure if they like you. Now Jake's actually come out and said he wants to be in your life, you'll get cold feet and run away and do spreadsheets or something . . .'

'Cal!' Sophie interrupted impatiently. 'Why are we talking about this now?'

'Because Jake is too good to run away from.' Cal pressed on regardless. 'If you want to keep him you have to get over your fear of intimacy and stop acting like you're a closet lesbian. Or a frigid closet lesbian.'

'Now I think you're taking the "personal" part of PA too literally,' Sophie said, her impatience for the conversation to be over tempered by wanting to hear what Cal had to say.

'I'm just saying, don't make the mistake you made with Mr Luscious Loss Adjuster.'

'What mistake?' Sophie asked him. 'I only ever saw him from a distance. I never even spoke to him.'

'And that,' Cal finished matter-of-factly, 'was the mistake!'

'Yes, well.' Sophie wanted to come back with a snappy rejoinder, but as usual nothing come to mind. 'Just make sure you keep me updated, OK?'

'Like talking to a brick wall,' Cal said and he hung up the phone.

Maria Costello arrived at ten minutes past ten that same night. It was a night that had followed a day that was, Sophie's exhausted brain reasoned, as stress-free as a day was ever likely to get as long as the children were invading her flat. This was largely because she had worked out a fairly efficient containment system involving food and television. She drew the curtains to exclude any unwanted foray of daylight onto the TV screen and she watched daytime television all day with the girls sitting either side of her, occasionally rising from the sofa to bring them another snack. Fortunately they had been so starved of TV at Mrs Stiles's house that they were prepared to watch anything with gormless awe, like a couple of cave girls who had just been brought forward in time fifty thousand years or so to marvel at the modern world inventions. And as for Sophie, she didn't care what she watched as long as it wasn't another of her precious possessions being executed.

'You are very old to have blonde hair,' Bella told Maria Costello as Sophie showed her into the blanket-and-clothes-strewn living room.

The detective wrinkled up her slightly hooked nose as she looked around the room and then down at Bella.

'And you are very young to be up this late,' she said, with a slightly stern high-end Liverpudlian accent. Sophie put her hand on Bella's shoulder and drew the child closer to her, suddenly sensing how very small the little girl was in comparison to the large and rather solidly bosomed Ms Costello. Sophie didn't know exactly what she expected from a private dick, as Cal had begun to refer to her, but it hadn't been a Day-Glo orange tan and jewellery almost as brassy as her hair.

Maria Costello must have guessed exactly what she was thinking. 'You don't need to blend in these days, love,' she said. 'I can do almost all of my work from the office.' She winked at Bella. 'Mind you, I'm a master of disguise when I need to be.'

'Who are you and what do you want from us?' Bella asked her, quoting verbatim a line she'd heard on *Neighbours* earlier in the day.

'Maria is here to see me, Bella,' Sophie said. 'It's just about work, nothing to do with you. Now, you've got your glass of water, haven't you? Run along and get into bed because tomorrow we're . . .' Sophie stopped dead in her tracks. She had nothing planned for the girls the following day except watching TV, eating dry cereal on the sofa and chicken nuggets and chips on the kitchen floor (ketchup required extra safety measures), '. . . going to be awake again,' she finished lamely.

'Can I finish telling you the story about the flying fairy pony?' Bella asked her. She had begun this story – seemingly one she made up herself – the previous night. It was surprisingly quite gripping, but tempting as her offer was, now was not the time for chapter three.

'No, let's save it for tomorrow – so that Izzy can hear it too. Go on, off you go.'

Bella eyed Maria Costello suspiciously before finally padding into the bedroom. Sophie smiled nervously at the formidable-looking woman and suddenly felt quite small herself. She had expected Maria for most of the day, finally giving up on her making an appearance after nine p.m. Sophie was not prepared. She did not have *her* formidable-woman clothes on. She had her Snoopy jim-jams on – her one concession to casual wear – and they didn't have quite the same impact.

'Um, do you want a drink?' She offered, thinking of tea, coffee or hot chocolate.

'Got any whisky?' Maria said hopefully. Sophie hadn't got any whisky. She had two thirds of a bottle of Baileys that Lisa had given to her at Christmas after drinking the first third sitting on Sophie's office floor weeping about some bloke who hadn't kissed her under the mistletoe. Sophie had thought about the bottle of Baileys a lot in the last couple of days but so far she had not succumbed to it. Now she was not alone it was acceptable.

'I've got Baileys?' she suggested.

'Make it a double,' Maria said and Sophie obligingly filled two mugs with the coffee-coloured liquor. Of course she did have glasses, but for some reason mugs seemed far more appropriate. Private detectives always drank whisky (or Baileys) from cracked mugs on TV.

'So.' Maria settled onto the sofa, crossing her gold heels neatly. 'Did you know your sofa smells of—'

'Yes,' Sophie said. 'So can you find him?'

Maria nodded and took a large mouthful of the Baileys, holding it over her tongue for a few seconds.

'Let me get this straight. The guy leaves his pregnant wife in the lurch and runs off to God knows where to find himself and shag a load of tarts – am I right?'

Sophie would have dropped her Baileys in surprise if she hadn't been treasuring it so very much.

'Well, yes, in principle.'

It seemed Cal had told Maria the details of the case in his own no-nonsense style.

Sophie quickly filled Maria in on the real situation. Maria's face softened and she bit her glossed lips.

'Oh the poor little darlings,' she said gently.

Sophie just managed not to roll her eyes and say, 'Yes, yes, blah, blah, blah – and what about poor little me?'

'Yes, I know,' she said briskly instead. 'Terrible. And you see, I can only have them temporarily and after that they are going into care so it is rather urgent . . .'

'Why?' Maria asked.

Sophie looked taken aback. '*Well*, because obviously the less time they spend in care the better,' she said, feeling that that was rather obvious.

'No, I mean why can you only have them temporarily?'

Sophie chose her words carefully. 'I'm just not a person who can . . . who is very good with children, it's not fair on them.'

Maria scrutinised her as she knocked back the rest of her Baileys.

'Trust me, you have to be a seriously shite person to be a worse option than some of the care homes I've seen. And besides, you looked like you were doing all right to me.'

Sophie held Maria's gaze but said nothing, choosing to skim lightly over the issue what kind of person she might or might not be. Maria was just one more person in a long line of people who wanted to know exactly what it was that made her tick. Her mother's constant mantra whenever they met was why, why, why? Cal speculated daily on the various personality defects she had, even inventing new ones to fit her apparent weirdness. Even Jake was probably wondering if her ice-queen reputation was one that could be melted with diligence. And now this woman wanted to know if she was the kind of person who would let two small children go into care rather than risk her own sanity.

Sophie was tired of being scrutinised. Tired of people trying to work her out. At least in this case she was the customer and the customer was always right.

Maria finally shrugged. 'All right, you'd better tell me all you can about this Louis Gregory and I'd better track him down,' she said.

'Are you sure you'll be able to?' Sophie asked her. 'When the police and social services haven't had any luck?'

'Amateurs, the lot of them.' Maria lit up a cigarette and, seeing the look of longing in Sophie's eyes, handed her one. 'I'll find him, and quick too,' she said, blowing smoke out along with her words. 'Don't you worry about that, darling. I have *ways*.'

After Maria had gone Sophie sat on the sofa and stared at the blank TV screen. It was amazing, she considered, how quickly humans adjusted to unusual situations. This was only the third night the girls had been sleeping in her bed and she had been lying awake on her sofa, yet this period of quiet reflection and despair had become almost routine.

At least she was doing something that would help all of them, even if it was costing her £55 an hour plus VAT and expenses. Once they had found Louis and brought him back to the UK then the girls would no longer be her responsibility. She would have done the right thing by Carrie and the right thing by them and the right thing all round and she could go back to work in a nice new pair of shoes and everybody would be happy, especially Gillian. Except of course she'd be handing the girls over to a man they hardly knew, who had walked out on them without so much as a second thought.

'My God I love him so much!' Carrie had said the night she rang Sophie to tell her that not only was she pregnant but she was getting married too. 'He just looks at me with these incredible brown eyes and – I'm not joking – he makes my knickers fizz!'

Sophie remembered that description exactly because fizzing knickers was not something she had ever had first-hand experience of at that point in her life, and probably – if she was entirely honest – never had since.

'You're sure this is love are you, and not just plain old lust?' Sophie had said with typical caution. 'I mean, are you sure you want to marry him? You hardly know him.'

Carrie had laughed. 'Oh Soph, how would you know the difference anyway? You've only ever lusted after people you can't have. Besides, I know everything I need to know about him. He's bloody gorgeous and he makes me laugh. And – I'm having his baby, I'm six weeks gone. When I told him I was really worried that he'd walk out on me and that would be the end of us but he really wants us to have it, Soph. It was a risk but somehow I knew he would. He grew up without a proper family, and he really wants to give that to his children. It's going to be wonderful. We are going to be wonderful. Trust me.'

Sophie did trust Carrie because for all her impulsiveness and recklessness she had an incredible determination to be happy, and Sophie had never heard her sound happier than in that moment.

'If you're sure, I'm happy for you, Carrie, I really am,' Sophie had said and she had meant it.

'He's a good man, Soph. Once you get to know him you're going to really love him too, I promise.'

Except of course Sophie had never got to know Louis, she'd barely even met him before he'd left his wife and kids and run away to the other side of the world.

'Why didn't you tell me, Carrie?' Sophie said quietly into the half light. 'I would have been there for you, you know. Always, for ever, whatever.' The words sounded corny in the empty room and Sophie felt the fragility of a friendship that had fallen apart without her even noticing, as if it were a spider's web disintegrating in her hands.

Sophie wondered where Carrie was now. Not whether she was in Heaven or Hell, or even now reintegrating in the marine ecosystem somewhere off the Cornish coast. She wondered where Carrie was inside her, because still three days later she had not cried for Carrie, she had hardly had time to feel sad, but even when she did, like now, the sadness was negligible. It wasn't as if she had blocked it out with some grave and protective outer shell. It was more like if there was any sadness inside her at all there were so many other layers between Sophie and the core of her missing and loving Carrie that she could barely touch them.

Sophie closed her eyes for a moment and tried hard to feel the grief. She willed herself to cry but no tears came. Perhaps all her feelings were muffled by layer after layer of insulation, because she could not remember the last time she had really felt anything. Except that wasn't exactly true, she admitted to herself. She could remember the last time. It was the day they cremated her dad.

Sophie shook her head to clear it. She didn't want to think about her dad now. She needed to stay focused. When all the practicalities were sorted, that was when she'd start to feel Carrie's death. She knew it was.

The edge of her bare foot touched something cold poking out from beneath the sofa. Using her toes to slide the object out, Sophie reached down and picked up a book, *Dr Robert's Complete Dog Training and Care Manual*. Sophie looked at the picture of a soppy red setter grinning ludicrously on the front cover and smiled. Only her mum would give her a dog manual to read for helpful child-rearing hints and tips. With nothing better to do she flicked through the pages until she stopped at the chapter entitled Puppy Psychology; a subtitle that read 'Puppies and Car Travel' caught her eye.

Sophie shrugged. It was late, and she wasn't going to sleep any time soon. Maybe a page of two or puppy psychology was worth a go.

She was on paragraph two, wondering if you could buy worming tablets for children, when Artemis appeared from the kitchen window and strolled over. She took one look at the cover of the book and, Sophie could have sworn, wrinkled her pink nose up in disgust before stalking out again in the general direction of the bedroom. Sophie smiled to herself. Amazingly, Artemis had seemed to adjust to the girls being in there far more quickly than she had. She had even caught Artemis sitting only three feet away from Bella that morning as Bella studiously attempted to draw her ear. The cat was sitting perfectly still as if she were trying to be extra helpful. Perhaps it was because all three females – Artemis, Izzy and Bella – had something in common. They were all at least half-feral.

'Cats and dogs and kids,' Sophie muttered to herself as she settled back down on the sofa. 'Basically the same principle.'

She turned to the chapter on antisocial behaviour.

CHAPTER 7

Friday morning began with Lisa sobbing down the phone, saying, 'I'm sorry, I'm sorry Sophie. But you've got to come in, it's Eve – I can't stop her. You won't believe what she called me.' Sophie would believe it. She pretty much believed Eve capable of anything, although she hadn't expected her go in for the kill quite so soon.

'Where's Cal, pass me to Cal,' Sophie told Lisa, who put her through with a snuffle.

'What's the deal, Cal?' Sophie asked him.

'Eve is in your office right now,' he said. 'She's got your leads file, your Rolodex and somehow she's got your PC password –' Sophie opened her mouth to holler, but hearing her sharp intake of breath Cal cut her off before she could utter a word. 'Don't shout at me, I don't know how she got it – because it definitely wouldn't have been anything obvious like – oh I don't know – "*Sophie*", would it?'

Sophie, who did suffer from a lack of imagination when it came to passwords, clamped her mouth shut.

'Anyway,' Cal continued quickly, 'she says that Gillian has asked her to help you out by keeping on top of things while you're away being all noble and saintly. I tried to stop her but she said if I had a problem to speak to Gillian. What could I do? If Gillian says it's OK for her to be in there then it's OK, right?'

'No, she's using that as an excuse to raid my clients list and take credit for all my ideas,' Sophie said matter-of-factly. She wouldn't have done the same thing in Eve's position, but only because she didn't have the balls and total lack of conscience.

'Probably. Lisa did try to stop her going in but she called Lisa a . . . let me see, oh yes – a "fat blubbering pointless rusty old bike" and Lisa started to cry and, well – you can guess the rest.' Cal paused. 'I think you'd better come down.'

'I'm on my way,' Sophie said and hung up the phone. She looked round at the girls, who had taken up their habitual position on the sofa in their pyjamas, watching repeats of *Trisha* with an expression of fascinated horror.

'Right, spit spot, come on girls – double quick, we're going out.' Their heads jerked in her direction as if she had told them it was time for walkies.

'Out! Out! Out!' Izzy hopped off the sofa with joy. 'Oooh good. Am I going to wear my fairy dress?'

Sophie shook her head; the fairy dress had gone in the bin and was probably even now being buried in a concrete container in the middle of the North Sea.

'I know,' Sophie said, remembering something the dog book had said about using distraction. 'Let's have a race. We'll go and look in your suitcase and whoever gets dressed the quickest wins a fabulous prize!' Both girls leapt up in anticipation as if Sophie was about to throw a stick for them to fetch. 'Ready, steady, GO!' she shouted.

And that was how twenty-seven minutes later the three girls emerged from the flat blinking in the daylight: one dressed in jeans and a slightly grubby pink Calvin Klein T-shirt and fleece jacket (Sophie); one dressed in a ballerina/pirate fusion complete with eyepatch and musical wand and topped off with a jumper and a poncho (Izzy), and one wearing a rainbow-striped hand-knitted jumper that was at least ten sizes too big for her, falling off one shoulder to reveal the greying lace of an aged vest, and coming down to just below her knees where her Angelina Ballerina wellington boots began. All topped off with a lurid pink puffa jacket.

'Are those wellies comfortable to walk in?' Sophie asked Bella, wondering what the chances were of a bus coming any time within the next four hours.

Bella furrowed her brow. 'I wasn't thinking about comfort, Aunty Sophie. I was thinking about speed. I wanted to win the prize. And I did!'

'You didn't win, I won!' Izzy shouted as they boarded the 149 bus.

'I won!' Bella shouted back.

'I won!' Izzy yelled.

'I won!' Bella repeated.

'I won!' Sophie shouted them both down so that they, the bus driver and the six or so passengers already on the bottom deck of the bus stopped talking and looked at her. Sophie dropped some pound coins into the driver's change tray and ripped the tickets off the machine. 'I won,' she repeated as the bus lurched away from the stop and more or less threw all three of them into an empty seat. 'I was dressed before either of you so actually I'm the winner.' She squeezed both the girls next to the window and jammed herself onto the end of the seat.

'But you can't be the winner,' Bella protested. 'You're the grown-up and anyway you already had your clothes on when you set the competition so that doesn't count.'

''S'not fair!' Izzy joined in. 'Not fair, not fair!'

Sophie looked at both girls and bit her lip. She wanted to tell them that life wasn't fair and that it was about time they realised that, but it sounded exactly like the sort of thing that Mrs Stiles used to say to Carrie on a regular basis, and she knew that Carrie would hate it being said to her children even if at this moment Sophie thought that Mrs Stiles might have been right. But she wasn't heartless, just rather tired, so she said, 'OK, we'll call it a three-way tie. We all win, OK? After I've sorted out work we'll go and get a prize.'

Izzy and Bella exchanged suspicious looks.

''Spose,' Izzy said.

'I won,' Bella said but very quietly and mostly to herself, folding her arms across her chest, her shoulders slumping.

'Er, I think you'll find I won,' Sophie couldn't resist repeating, before she caught a woman looking scathingly at her, realised exactly what she was doing, and she shut up.

Sophie stopped the girls in front of the office building where McCarthy Hughes occupied the seventh and eighth floors. The children looked upward, open-mouthed.

'A giant's house,' Izzy breathed, awestruck.

'It's a skyscraper, thicko,' Bella said. 'Giants' houses are much bigger.'

Sophie thought about the chapter on puppy psychology she'd read last night. Body language, it was all in the body language. If you believed that you were in control and in charge *they* believed that you were in control and in charge – or something like that. Show no fear, that was what the manual said, because they can feel it through the lead. So perhaps it was fortunate after all that it was probably illegal to make children wear leads. She crouched down on the steps of the building and, putting a hand on each of the girls' shoulders, looked them directly in the eye.

'Now listen,' she said. 'This is where I work. This is my job. It is very, *very* important that whilst you are in this building you do exactly what

I tell you. You don't scream or run away or cause a flood or . . .' Sophie narrowed her eyes at Izzy '. . . attempt to fix anything just like Bob the Dentist . . .'

'Bob the Builder!' Izzy said, with a giggle.

'Whatever. Do you understand?' Sophie looked back at Bella, whose attention had drifted skywards once again, and pressed her palm gently down on the top of her head until she was looking in her eyes again. 'You don't run about, you don't touch anything, you don't talk to anyone because this is Aunty Sophie's job and it is a very VERY important job.'

Bella screwed up her mouth into a sideways knot. It was an expression that Sophie was beginning to learn usually preceded an impudent and often hard to answer question. She braced herself.

'What do you do, Aunty Sophie?' Bella asked. 'Are you a doctor, or a vet or a . . .' Bella searched for an occupation that could be appropriately described as very important. 'Are you an astronaut?'

Sophie sighed – there were a lot of people in the world who thought her job wasn't very important, comparatively speaking, and couldn't see why she allowed it to occupy ninety per cent of her life, but she hadn't expected a six-year-old to jump on the bandwagon.

'I plan parties,' she said quickly and half under her breath, before adding, 'really, really important ones.'

On the way up in the lift Sophie planned several different types of camouflage to get the children into the office unnoticed. Perhaps she could hide them under her coat or maybe stick photocopying-paper boxes on their heads and edge them along in the shadows. Or they could belly crawl along the orange carpet tiles . . . She stopped herself. She didn't have to sneak the girls into the office. Children, like smoking, weren't absolutely banned. Gillian's nanny brought her two in every now and then, during half-term holidays for example, and everyone would smile at them and ask them how school was and look nervous in case anybody made one of them cry, like John Baker in Marketing did shortly before he abruptly left McCarthy Hughes after an apparently unrelated incident. But Izzy and Bella weren't like Gillian's children. Compared to Gillian's neatly combed and surprisingly sedate offspring they were like half-wild savages that had previously been raised by wolves.

Miraculously though, the open-plan part of the office was completely empty and Sophie guessed that everybody would be in Gillian's huge office going over the week's events. Despite her conviction that she wasn't doing anything wrong, Sophie hurried the girls towards her office at high speed, and once she had more or less thrown them safely through the door she slammed it behind her and adjusted the venetian blinds on the interior windows so that no-one could see in or out.

'Are you being chased by the Feds?' Cal asked, twirling in her chair and looking her up and down. 'You look terrible, by the way.'

Sophie glanced around the office.

'Where's Lisa?' she said.

'In the meeting,' Cal replied. 'She said she couldn't go in because everyone would know that she had been crying, and I said everyone was used to that by now and she had to go in anyway as it's her job and you can't just back down from every challenge life throws at you otherwise you'll never get anywhere: look at Liza Minnelli.' Cal smiled at the girls and winked. Both girls giggled. 'And off she went like a trouper. I lent her your emergency mascara, which she put on over her old mascara, so ironically she actually does look quite a lot like Liza Minnelli now.'

Sophie had to admit that Cal's inability ever to answer even a simple question without turning his response into a lengthy monologue did slightly impact on her affection for him, especially when time was of the essence.

'So what's the damage?' she said, walking around her desk and opening the drawers until she found some spare notepads. She took out a couple, two biros and a set of highlighter pens, and gave them to Bella. 'Sit here in the corner and do me some lovely pictures, OK?'

Bella took the pens and sat reluctantly on the carpet tiles. 'What of?' she asked as Izzy plonked herself down next to her.

'Anything,' Sophie said impatiently. 'Draw the view.'

Bella looked around her, assessing the view of desk legs, the bottom half of two filing cabinets and a wastepaper bin, a deep frown slotted between her brows.

'*I'm* drawing mermaids,' she said to Izzy, who shook her head.

'I'm drawing Arsey-miss,' Izzy said, and it took a moment for Sophie to realise she meant her cat and was not planning a self-portrait. She returned her attention to Cal, who reluctantly vacated her seat.

'Well?' she asked.

'Same as before – Eve has your Rolodex, your leads book and your diary,' Cal repeated in a sing-song voice, his eyes skyward. 'She said Gillian told her to take them. Lisa could hardly contradict her and she couldn't go marching into Gillian's office asking what she thought she was playing at, so after the briefest of struggles we let her take them. What else could we do?' He gave a little shrug and examined his nails.

'Right.' Sophie walked back to the internal office window and, prising open one of the blind slats, peered through it. Her colleagues were gradually filing back to their desks. She spotted Eve standing by Gillian's office door, talking and laughing with their boss as if they were best friends. 'The meeting's out. Lisa will be here in a minute. I want you and her to keep an eye on those two. Don't let them out of your sight, OK?'

123

Cal didn't have time to answer before Lisa opened the door.

'Thank fuck that's over,' she said with feeling.

'You're not supposed to say fuck in front of us.' Bella's voice floated up from the other side of the desk.

'Fuck,' Lisa exclaimed again at the sound of the disembodied voice booming from the other side of the desk, followed a moment later by Bella's stern and reproachful gaze. 'Oh f . . . flip,' she said, staring at Bella. 'Sorry, Sophie, I didn't know you were going to bring them in.'

Sophie chewed her bottom lip. 'Not much alternative, Lisa,' she said, briefly assessing what Lisa was wearing – a pink button-down waisted shirt. Not her usual style but it would have to do. 'Anyway, never mind that now, take your top off.'

Lisa looked alarmed. 'I beg your pardon?'

'I said take your top off,' Sophie said impatiently. 'I'm not going in to see Eve and Gillian looking like this, am I? Lend me your shirt until I've sorted this out.' Sophie ignored Lisa's reluctance and peeled her T-shirt off over her head. 'You can wear this, all right? Now hurry up.'

Lisa took the less than fragrant T-shirt gingerly and draped it over the back of a chair before unbuttoning her shirt and handing it to Sophie.

'Is now a good time to tell you I lied about being gay?' Cal said. Sophie ignored him but Lisa's cheeks burned brightly as she pulled the stained T-shirt over her head. Perhaps she had a secret crush on Cal. Otherwise he'd be the only man on the planet whom she had not focused her attention on at one time or another.

Buttoning Lisa's slightly too tight shirt, Sophie untied her hair, combed her fingers through it and twisted it around into a tightly knotted bun at the back of her head before securing it with a biro. Cal handed her her emergency mascara, which she applied somewhat haphazardly in the ghostly reflection of the office window, then she took the remnants of one of her lipglosses out of her jeans pocket and rubbed a little onto her lips.

'Right,' she said, pulling the shirt down over the top of her jeans. 'How do I look?'

'You look like a slightly podgy Amazon preparing for battle,' Cal said, giving her the thumbs up.

Sophie gritted her teeth and headed for the door. 'OK. I'm going to sort this whole mess out. All you two have to do is keep the kids under control and out of Gillian's sight. Do you think you can manage that?' she asked them.

'Of course we can,' said Lisa, smiling down at the busily drawing girls. 'Easy-peasy.'

Somehow Sophie did not feel reassured.

As she opened Eve's office door she was confronted with her bony arse. Eve was in the midst of committing two cardinal sins. Not only had she opened her office window, thus threatening to send the carefully controlled climate into total disarray, she was hanging out of it smoking. Sophie watched for a moment as Eve kneeled on the seat of her chair, her elbow resting on its back, trying her best to blow the smoke out of the window but failing as a passing gust of wind blew every puff back in her face. Of course Sophie could just push her out of the window and claim it was an accident, solving all her problems in one fell swoop. But it had been hours since her last cigarette, and Eve was holding her packet in one hand. At that moment Sophie could have happily have murdered Eve, but she just couldn't bear to let the cigarettes suffer too. She contented herself with slamming the door behind her and watching Eve jump, before retreating from the window and flicking her fag onto the street below as she slid back into her chair, her face a picture of innocence.

'Sophie!' she said, reaching behind her to pull the window shut. 'What a nice surprise.'

'You're not supposed to do that,' Sophie said nodding at the door, sounding a lot more like a school prefect than she had intended.

'You're not supposed to do *that*,' Eve said breezily, looking Sophie up and down. 'Never wear a shirt that gapes in the bra area, Sophie. I thought you knew better.'

Sophie knew Eve's tactic better than anyone – she was not going to be thrown. She sat down with a thud and one of the buttons pinged off Lisa's shirt. Sophie did her best to ignore it.

'What are you playing at, Eve?' she said bluntly.

Eve shrugged. 'How do you mean?' she asked, casually.

'What are you doing in my office taking my Rolodex, my leads book and my client account info?'

Eve rolled her eyes. 'Oh that. You've raced all the way down here over that, have you?' She picked up a pen from her desk and swung it by its tip. 'Gillian asked me to keep on top of your stuff. So I did. What's the problem?' Eve looked genuinely mystified.

Sophie bristled, her inner fury stoked by the fact that she wasn't exactly sure what the problem was herself. Cal had rung her, Lisa had cried and before she knew it she was charging down here. Perhaps that *had* been a slight overreaction.

'Lisa is handling everything,' Sophie said, carefully moderating her accusatory tone. 'I'll be back in the office soon enough. Just give me back my stuff, OK? You don't need it.'

Eve sighed and dropped her chin. 'Sophie, really, I'm quite disappointed in you. I thought we were supposed to be on the same team? I don't know what you think I was up to but . . .'

At that moment Eve's assistant walked in with a pile of photocopying and Sophie's Rolodex. 'I've photocopied this like you said. I'm just about to do the book now, OK?' She caught sight of Sophie and Eve gave the poor girl a look sufficiently evil to send her scuttling out of the room without waiting for a reply.

'I knew it!' Sophie scooped the pile of photo-copying up off Eve's desk and plonked her

Rolodex on top of it. 'You're poaching my contacts, my accounts and my prospective clients.' Sophie stared at Eve, who still appeared unfazed even when caught in the act. 'Come on, Eve, don't piss me about, I know you too well to buy this butter-wouldn't-melt act. Gillian *might* have asked you to check up on Lisa but she certainly didn't ask you to go through my drawers and do this!' Sophie brandished the pile of photocopying as Exhibit A.

'OK, Miss Marple.' Eve held out the palm of her hands. 'I was. It's a fair cop.' She smirked like a schoolgirl who'd just got caught snogging behind the bike shed.

Sophie was taken aback. She hadn't expected such an easy confession. 'Well . . . right,' she said. She found the wind suddenly taken out of her sails. 'Just don't do it again, OK?' she continued uncertainly, gathering up the sheaf of paper in her arms, which had the double advantage of covering up the gaping hole the pinged-off button had revealed. And she realised that this was exactly what Eve wanted her to do – to leave without making a fuss. She sat down again and, still clutching the papers to her chest, she pulled the chair closer. Eve's face was perfectly devoid of expression.

'It's pretty shit behaviour, isn't it? To try and get one over on me when I'm not here to do anything about it?'

Eve raised her eyebrows and twiddled her pen.

128

'The best time to do it, I'd have thought,' she said glibly, suddenly switching on her death's-head smile. 'Come on, Sophie – you'd have done the same thing.'

'Actually,' Sophie said with conviction, 'I wouldn't have. Let's cut the crap here. We both know that if . . . when Gillian steps back from the office we want her job. We both know that only one of us is going to get it, and that the other one would rather slit their wrists and wear flip-flops than endure the ignominy of staying here and reporting to the other one. I understand that, I accept it. I don't have a problem with competition as long as it's fair. And shafting me whilst I'm looking after my dead friend's kids is not fair, Eve. It's evil. Seriously evil.' Sophie paused for effect. 'Gillian would be horrified,' she concluded with the hint of a threat.

'Oh yes, the dead friend's kids,' Eve said bitterly. 'How very convenient.'

Sophie opened her mouth and then closed it again – where was the usual 'poor little mites, oh how terrible' routine that she had become used to?

'I beg your pardon?' she said.

'Well, it's all very well going on about it being fair competition and all that bullshit. But it's not fair, is it? It hasn't been fair since you waltzed off to do your Mother Teresa bit. Gillian *loves* you right now! She goes on non-stop about how selfless you are and how rare it is to have the kind of guts it takes to rise to this kind of challenge and how you must have been such a good friend for wosshername thingy to trust you with her most precious legacy blah fucking blah. How is that fair? Have I got a dead friend with fatherless kids? No. Therefore it's not fair.' Eve lifted her chin slightly. 'I was just levelling the playing field,' she finished.

'I didn't ask for all this!' Sophie exclaimed, gesturing at the door as if all her problems were piled up high behind it. 'Do you think I'm happy that my best friend is dead?'

'Don't seem too depressed by it, frankly.'

'Trust me, I'm depressed!' Sophie yelled at Eve. 'I'm sorry if Gillian thinks what I'm doing is the right thing, but do you honestly believe at the end of the day that she is going to give me a job over you because of a bit of babysitting?' Oh God I hope so, Sophie thought to herself. 'She's a tough businesswoman, Eve. She'll give it to the person who's best at their job and me being out of the office is dragging me down enough without you doing your DIY sabotage on me, OK?'

Eve leaned across the desk so that the two women were just a few inches apart.

'OK!' she replied. 'But just ask yourself one question, Sophie. Why do you really want this promotion?'

Sophie shook her head. 'Why does everybody keep asking me why?' she protested. 'Why this! Why that! No-one ever asks *you* why.'

'Because we all know you've been at McCarthy

Hughes since puberty, that you've worked your way up the ladder, paid your dues in blood, sweat and tears etcetera. But seriously, why are you here, why do you *really* want this job – why does it mean so very much to you? Are you absolutely sure that you're not here now sitting in my office as a senior accounts manager at McCarthy Hughes by mistake? What if the Job Centre had sent you to a fashion magazine or, or a pet shop?'

Sophie sat back in her chair abruptly. It was a surprisingly tricky question to answer off the top of her head.

Seeing her expression, Eve laughed. 'You didn't choose this career, Sophie,' she said. 'It chose you, and never once in the last ten years have you stopped to think about whether or not it makes you truly happy. You have no idea why you want this promotion other than that it's there. It's your Everest.'

'That's not true,' Sophie said promptly. 'Obviously I want it because this is my career. Because it's what I've been working for for the best part of my life.'

'Face it, Sophie – you're so stuck in a rut you can't see past it. But ask yourself this, what are you going to do when you've got Gillian's job? Where are you going to go – what will you have left to work towards then, huh? What happened to your childhood dreams?'

Sophie rolled her eyes and thought of Jason Donovan. 'He got bald and developed a twitch – that's what happened to my dreams. Come on,

131

Eve, get real, will you. This is me you're talking to. I don't fall for all your bullshit mind games.'

'Oh Sophie, Sophie, Sophie –' Eve lamented. 'You should follow your dreams before it's too late, not joke about them to cover up your true despair.' Sincerity was etched all over her face.

'My reasons are good ones,' Sophie said, unimpressed. 'I put a lot of years into this business and I want the rewards that I deserve. The same reasons as you, I'm sure?'

Eve stood up and, coming around the desk, she sat on its edge, crossing her legs so that one of her shoes dangled from her toes, revealing a fleeting glimpse of a Dolce & Gabbana label. Sophie seethed. She still had on her now-rather-the-worse-for-wear River Island flatties with one laddered pop sock.

'Not at all,' Eve said completely seriously. 'I want this promotion because this is all I've ever dreamed about since I was a tiny girl.'

'Bollocks,' Sophie replied, and not only because she genuinely doubted that Eve was ever a tiny girl.

'Well, maybe, but I'm here now and it's every man for herself, if you know what I mean.' Without explanation Eve took a plastic bag out of her desk drawer and, standing on her chair, she reached up and secured it over the smoke alarm with an elastic band. Sitting back down, she chucked Sophie a much-longed-for cigarette across the desk, which Sophie had to force herself not to scrabble for. After lighting up, Eve paused for a tortuous moment before throwing Sophie her lighter too. A few puffs later, Eve looked Sophie in the eye and sighed. 'I'm sorry, really,' she said. 'OK?'

Sophie watched her through the haze of smoke. 'I doubt it,' she said mildly. 'But just don't think I'm a pushover, OK?'

Eve considered the question. 'OK.' She sounded unconvinced. 'You know it's nothing personal, don't you? I just get carried away a bit with the whole competition thing. I suppose I'd be quite annoyed if I had to sack you one day. Because, you know – you make me look really good.'

Sophie examined her. It was very hard to tell when Eve was joking, largely because she had a very blurred line between humour and general savagery.

'Well, you're on your own for the foreseeable future at least. God only knows when I'll spend any decent time in the office again.' Sophie instantly regretted letting that piece of information slip.

'I thought they were going back next week?' Eve said, with interest. 'If I'd known you were going to be out longer I'd have waited for a decent period before raiding your office.'

Sophie pursed her lips. 'They *are* supposed to be going back next week . . .' she said, thinking she was making the children sound like some faulty goods that needed to be returned. She thought of Maria Costello and of Gillian's approval of her angel-of-mercy mission. Of course she had said to Eve that she didn't think Gillian would be handing out promotions based on childcare abilities but maybe, just maybe, she would. And she would be much less impressed if Sophie handed them over to languish in the hands of Social Services rather than returning them to their long-lost father, even if that meant that they might go outside sometimes and eat more than three things.

Before Sophie could say anything else Eve's phone rang, and she looked at the caller display unit.

'Gillian,' she told Sophie, picking it up whilst simultaneously opening the window behind her.

'Hi Gillian, what can I do for you?' she said, hooking the phone receiver under her ear and attempting to wave the smoke out of the still-open window as she spoke, as if Gillian would be able to smell her cigarette down the phone line. 'Yep, yep, OK I'll tell her. Yep, right now.' Eve hung up the phone.

'Oh dear,' she said with a tiny sharp-toothed smile.

'Oh dear what?' Sophie said, handing the butt of her cigarette to Eve, who threw it out of her window.

'The little cherubs. It looks like they got out and went exploring.'

Sophie leapt out of her seat. 'Fuck, fuck! What did they do – what did they wreck?' She braced herself.

'Nothing, they just went for a little wander and made a new friend –' Eve savoured the moment.

'They're in Gillian's office. She'd like you to go over. Straight away please.'

But Sophie had already left.

'And then after *Neighbours*, again, we watch the news and then we watch *Bargain Hunt*, again, and then we watch *EastEnders* and then we watch . . .'

'Bella! Izzy!' Sophie forced a laugh. 'I thought you were drawing me lovely pictures!'

'We finished,' Bella said, holding up a sheet of paper covered in mermaids. 'We came to show you but we couldn't find you. So we showed this lady who is very nice and gave us a biscuit. We told her we don't eat fruit in case it makes us poo.'

Gillian smiled at Sophie and Sophie smiled back at her, trying desperately to work out if it was a genuine happy smile or an 'I'm about to rip your head off' smile. It was quite hard to tell with Gillian.

'Sit,' Gillian said. Sophie sat. 'What lovely girls your godchildren are! Izzy was telling me all about the fun she's been having at your house, including being flushed down the toilet . . . ?' Gillian raised an eyebrow.

'Ah yes, well . . .' Sophie hastily began to explain but Gillian laughed. Sophie laughed too, slightly hysterically.

'Oh they are so funny at that age, aren't they? A pure joy from the moment they wake up to the moment they go to bed.'

Sophie nodded in agreement. She supposed that

if you had a nanny and didn't see them for eight hours of the day that might be true.

'Oh yes,' she said. 'Joy. Absolutely. Pure.'

'You should have said you were coming in – if you'd rung me I'd have told you not to bother. Lisa's been doing very well with Cal's help and Eve's been keeping an eye on her.'

'Ah yes, but—'

'So, how have you been coping?' Gillian asked, fixing her with her almost unbearably penetrating gaze.

Sophie struggled to maintain eye contact, a little uncertain how to respond because Gillian had never asked that question before. Sophie always coped. No, that was wrong, Sophie had never 'coped' before because she didn't have to – she had never struggled with any challenge until now, and 'coping' had never been a requirement. Was she supposed to tell Gillian that everything was just fine, or was she supposed to confess that she was finding everything a bit difficult? Which response would make her look better and which answer would make her more promotable?

'Um,' Sophie said.

'Oh, I know,' Gillian said, treating Sophie to a conspiratorial little smile that Sophie had never seen before and which she found slightly unnerving. 'It's such a shock, isn't it?' Gillian said cosily. 'Children change your world completely. I planned for my two darlings – but I wasn't prepared for them in the least!' Gillian leaned forward slightly in the chair. 'And, you know, I think it's harder when you have them a little later in life, don't you? When you've been used to being your own person for so long and suddenly there's this little being that's . . . that's . . .' Gillian clicked her fingers as she searched for the word she wanted.

'Like a bloodsucking little leech?' Sophie offered.

Gillian's smile faded momentarily before she decided that Sophie must be joking and her rarely heard laugh chimed like broken glass.

'I was going to say, this little being is totally *dependent* on you for life,' she finished. 'But you're really showing guts here, Sophie. I applaud you.'

Sophie felt herself straighten in her chair. 'Thank you,' she said, glancing at Izzy who was sorting through the contents of Gillian's waste bin, and at Bella who was listening intently. 'They are good kids, bless 'em.' Bella probably raised an eyebrow at her but Sophie couldn't be sure due the density of her fringe. 'It's just a case of getting everything settled.' Sophie smiled at Gillian, who nodded sympathetically.

'It must be even harder for you of course, because you didn't plan it. For you it's like they've just fallen out of the sky.' Sophie realised that that was exactly how it felt and suddenly, looking into Gillian's kind face, she felt the threat of tears build up behind her eyes. But she couldn't cry, because Gillian would think she was crying for Carrie or the children and she wouldn't be. She'd be crying for herself.

'Yes,' Sophie said, making her voice stay steady. 'It does feel a bit like that.'

Gillian laced her fingers on the desk and looked at them for a moment.

'Look, Sophie, I think you and I know each other very well by now, don't you?' Sophie nodded. 'I know that you're not the sort of person to ask for help – in fact, I know that you're not the sort of person who usually needs any help. But I want to know how you think this will all pan out. Do you think you can keep up your job to sufficient standards in the midst of this upheaval?'

Sophie began nodding even before Gillian had finished asking the question. 'I can, of course I can,' she said, gesturing at the children. 'This is just temporary. Really. Work comes first for me, Gillian. You know how many years I've put into McCarthy Hughes, I've always been loyal. I won't stop now.' Sophie found she was leaning forward in her chair, desperate to impress her intentions on her boss.

Gillian observed her for a moment longer. 'The minute you think you're not handling this, the minute it all gets too much, I need to know, do you understand?'

'Yes,' Sophie said, feeling the kind of anxiety in the pit of her stomach she hadn't experienced since the first three times she failed her driving test.

'You know I really feel for you, don't you?' Gillian said, a hard edge glinting under her

138

compassionate tone. 'But this is a very important time for McCarthy Hughes. Up until this point you've been integral to our success. Don't think I haven't noticed that, Sophie, or that I haven't got plans for you.' Sophie felt simultaneously pleased and deeply uneasy. 'But business isn't what it once was for events companies. Budgets are tight; we have to be more competitive and more on the ball than we have ever been before.' Sophie got the distinct impression that when Gillian said *we* she actually meant *you*.

'I suppose what I'm trying to say is that I want to support you in this, I am full of admiration for you. But if you start to feel that you can't manage to look after the children and keep up with work I'll need to know. I'll need to make other arrangements.'

'That won't happen,' Sophie said instantly, wondering darkly about what 'other arrangements' might be.

'Good,' Gillian said. 'Look, I know you've heard all the rumours about me stepping down from the office and passing the baton on, haven't you?'

Sophie nodded dumbly. There was no point in denying it. Gillian would only know she was lying.

'Well, I'm telling you and nobody else that that is only going to happen if I feel the people I can trust to take on that responsibility are able to put one hundred per cent into this job. Do you understand what I mean?'

Sophie nodded again, wondering if she really did understand.

'Good,' Gillian said. And then she began to look through the papers on her desk, always a sure sign that your presence was no longer required. For a second Sophie was too stunned to be able to move. This morning she had had a life in total chaos, yes, but it had been a temporary chaos, under-pinned by the one constant in her life – her job. And now it seemed that Gillian was telling her extremely nicely that if she took her eye off the ball she could lose what she prized most highly. Sophie looked at the two girls and pushed the ugly, rising resentment back down into the pit of her stomach.

Gillian looked up at Sophie again and flashed her her best smile. 'Well, off you go, and take these two to the zoo or something. I'll see you next time you're in for a progress report.'

As she stood up and gestured for the girls to leave the room, Sophie looked at the top of Gillian's neatly bobbed head which was already bent over some paperwork. She knew Gillian: when she had made up her mind that something should happen, it happened. If others disagreed or thought that some further discussion was merited, Gillian would sit and listen and smile politely and seem to consider all the alternatives, and then do exactly what she had already decided in the first place. Which was why it was fortunate that she was a rather nice lady in her forties instead of some despotic dictator. But even so, Gillian had scared her. For the first time since taking on the children Sophie realised that there was a chance, if she didn't handle this very carefully, that she would never get her old life back at all.

There was, Sophie realised, only one way she could make this work. She had to accept that she was stuck with the children for as long as it took to get hold of their dad – she'd just have to make sure she covered all the bases. It would be hard and stressful but, she reminded herself, it wouldn't be for ever, just until Maria Costello found Louis. And Sophie was sure she could cope until that happened.

Praying that Maria was as good as she said she was, Sophie took the girls back to her office to brief Lisa and Cal, but they were nowhere to be seen.

'Where did Lisa and Cal go?' Sophie asked Bella.

'To the ladies', Lisa was crying,' Bella said.

'Again?' she asked herself more than Bella. 'What was it this time? A broken nail? Or did some passing stranger chuck her?'

Bella looked perplexed and shook her head. 'No, I think she was pretty upset about Izzy pouring glue in her hair.'

Izzy nodded vigorously. 'Yes because it went all sticky and white,' she said with a gurgle.

'And because Cal said she should be used to having sticky white stuff in her hair – why's that, Aunty Sophie?' Bella asked.

'Never you mind,' Sophie replied. She opened her desk drawer and took out her emergency safety pin, feeling secretly delighted that she finally had a suitable emergency for its use. She looked at the upturned faces of the girls staring at her as she closed the gap that yawned across her cleavage. 'Come on, let's go. I'll call them later and do a conference call.'

'Are we going to the zoo, zoo, zoo, you can come too, too, too, like the nice lady said?' asked Izzy, hopping from one foot to the other.

'No,' Sophie said as she led them to the lifts. 'We're going somewhere even better.'

'Where? Where?' Izzy cried.

'Back to the flat.'

As Izzy's face crumpled dangerously, Bella's eyes darkened. 'But what about our prize?' she demanded. 'You said we were getting a prize!'

Sophie paused for a moment. She'd forgotten about the prize and she'd rather hoped they had forgotten too, but as the detonator in Izzy's head was only seconds from going off, Sophie rapidly changed her plans.

'Of course!' she said with a huge smile. 'Let's go to the prize shop!'

'Hooray!' Izzy said, the tantrum abating instantly. 'Let's go. Let's go! Let's go!'

CHAPTER 8

Half an hour later, as Sophie watched Bella trying to decide between a pair of faux sheepskin boots and pink suede shoes with hearts on the front, she made a mental note that bribery seemed the most effective way of controlling the girls, especially Izzy. She had read about it in the dog book. They recommended liver treats, but Sophie thought clothes and toys were probably more appealing to small children. The moment she had told Izzy only nice quiet happy girls get fairy dresses she had transformed into a more sugary version of Shirley Temple, and now had at least three members of staff in the palm of her sticky hand.

'Oh what a darling,' one of them remarked to Sophie. 'Her daddy must be awfully good-looking.'

'Wouldn't know,' Sophie said absently as she watched Izzy, who had found her prize immediately and put it on over the top of her current clothes. It was a frou-frou little number in pink and lilac chiffon with silver trim. She twirled and twirled in it with wild abandon, and Sophie felt momentarily jealous. How lovely to be made so instantly happy so easily.

As for Bella, she had one of each shoe on either foot and was turning back and forth in front of the mirror, lifting one foot and then the other, narrowing her eyes as she looked at her reflection and then closing them tightly before opening them again, as if to get the full shoe effect.

Sophie rested her chin on the heel of her hands, and waited. If she knew anything it was that you couldn't rush buying a pair of shoes.

She smiled fondly at the expensive thick paper bag with corded handles that resided by her feet. From the moment she had seen the new season's pair of Luc Berjen tweed shoes in the shop window to the moment she had handed over her credit card her heart had beat like a drum, and now she felt elated and content. In her admittedly limited experience, shoe-shopping was so much more satisfying than sex, with the afterglow of contentment lasting much longer and leaving behind much less mess. Which was why she jumped off her stool when her mobile's polyphonic version of 'Love Lifts Us Up Where We Belong' boomed out into the store.

The girls stopped as if they were playing a reverse version of musical statues and stared at her for a moment before continuing their activities.

'Good news,' Maria Costello said in her ear. 'I've found him.'

'You've found him?' Sophie said in disbelief.

Bella looked up at her sharply and, sitting down with a bump on her behind, shushed a giggling Izzy, who had collapsed on the floor next to her.

'You found a replacement ice sculptor so soon, *Lisa* – well done – already?' Sophie said carefully.

'More or less,' Maria said. 'At least I think I've found the country he's in. I'm almost sure he's in Peru. From what I can tell he's been there for about two years, that's if he hasn't moved on since the last time my contact saw him . . .'

'Who's your contact?' Sophie asked.

There was a sharp intake of breath.

'I never reveal my contacts, love.'

Sophie rolled her eyes. She was starting to think that Maria took the whole spy thing slightly too seriously. She was secretly certain that whoever Maria's contact was it was nothing more mysterious than one of Louis's conquests, numbers of whom would no doubt be littered around the world while he lived his life of Riley.

'And so?' Sophie pressed Maria. 'Got an ETA? One day? Two? What?'

'I said I *think* he's in Peru,' Maria said sarcastically. 'It's a pretty big place. I'll try to locate him from my nerve centre but if not I might have to go out there – you'll have to foot the bill mind you, and I always go business class on flights over four hours.'

Sophie's heart sank. 'Maria, Lisa I mean – be honest with me – are you going to find . . . my ice

145

sculptor or am I throwing my money away for nothing?'

'Did you know he was in Peru before I started looking?' Maria said irritably. 'Did anyone?'

'No,' Sophie said hesitantly, wary of offending her and wrecking what might be her only hope of finding Louis. 'But are you *sure* he is?'

'Look, love, I'm a private detective. I'll find him. And I'll call you when I know more.'

'There's just one thing,' Sophie said. 'Do you know what he's doing in Peru?'

But Maria had hung up.

Sophie noticed Bella watching her intently. 'You have to go a long way to get ice sculptors these days,' she said.

What had begun as a quick trip to buy prizes had made Sophie very popular with two very happy little girls: Izzy was happy because she loved her party dress and because Sophie didn't make her take it off when they left the shop but instead persuaded the assistant to cut off all the labels and remove the security tag with Izzy still in situ. And Bella was happy because after she had regretfully put back the pink shoes in favour of the more sensible boots, Sophie had gone and bought her the shoes too.

This, Sophie had decided, was what being a godmother was all about – buying presents and being popular was definitely where it was at. Her smugness lost a little of its shine when she realised that all she had ever done as their godmother until this point was to turn up to the christening and send her PA out to buy presents three times a year. Sophie wondered: if Carrie had told her about Louis, if she had told her about being on her own with the children and evoked their old promise, *would* she have made more of an effort to see her? *Would* she have had more to do with the children as they grew up? To be perfectly honest, she didn't know. She would probably have just assumed that she and Carrie were different people now, that Carrie had her own support network down in St Ives, her own collection of new and different friends who seemed to help her get along very well without Louis until fate stepped in and fucked everything up for her. Until the girls had arrived on Sophie's doorstep and all those girlhood promises and pacts they'd made to each other suddenly seemed vitally important again.

So it was with a peculiar mix of guilt and pleasure that Sophie took her god-daughters to several other shops and bought them more clothes, and when in one shop they both stopped and picked up identical orange stuffed-cat toys and hugged them as if their little lives depended on it, she bought them those too, along with a baby doll for Izzy and a giant drawing and painting set for Bella.

There had been a slight wobble on the way home when, seeing Izzy screw her fists into her eyes and yawn, Sophie had tentatively suggested a taxi. And Izzy had been on the point of a total nervous collapse when out of nowhere, exactly like a knight in shining armour – bar the armour – Jake Flynn suddenly appeared.

'Goodness me, what a beautiful dress,' he said to Izzy, whose mouth froze mid-wail and transformed itself into a smile.

'Thank you,' she said prettily. 'I am beautiful, aren't I?'

'Jake!' Sophie exclaimed, managing to sound both grateful and surprised.

'Cal told me you'd been into the office today,' he said with slight reproach. 'I would have come and taken you out for lunch if I'd known.'

Sophie remembered his offers on the phone and realised that in the last few days she'd hardly had time to think about Jake at all. In her real life she would have been obsessing over every detail and nuance of their conversation for weeks, whilst putting off any chance to find out what it really meant in case it really did mean something. In this life, though, she didn't have time to think about it. It was an unlikely blessing.

'Who are you and what do you want with us?' Bella asked Jake darkly. Jake laughed. Bella did not.

'I'm Jake,' he said. 'I'm a friend of Sophie's. And you are . . . ?'

'Bella, and she's my sister Izzy. She's only three so she's very stupid, she'll talk to anyone.' Bella looked up at Sophie and then at Jake again. 'Are *you* her boyfriend?' she asked.

Jake paused and glanced at Sophie, who grinned stupidly and shrugged.

'Not yet,' he said with a slow smile. 'But I'm working on it.'

'Her sofa smells of curry,' Bella said helpfully. 'And she plucks the hair from her top lip.'

Jake laughed and Sophie hoped the chill of the dark afternoon would keep her skin under control.

'Well, Bella,' Jake said, gallantly choosing to ignore her revelations. 'You look like you've got plenty of booty in those bags. Are you going to get a cab home?'

'No, no, NO, NO, *NO!*' Izzy began to wind up her protests.

'Quite right too,' Jake said, quickly picking up her bags. 'Look, here's the bus now, come on guys!' He picked up three of Sophie's bags as well and swung Izzy onto the double-decker, helping Bella and then Sophie hop on board.

As they found their seats Sophie stared at him. 'You realise this isn't the right bus?' she asked him, not sure whether to be enchanted or irritated.

'Really? Well, we're off on a little detour then.'

And Sophie discovered that she was really rather pleased.

Izzy was charm personified on the journey home. She did not throw one tantrum between the bus stop and Sophie's front door and, launching into a monologue with 'Did you know trees are made of hard paint and ice cream?' chatted happily to Jake about everything in her known universe.

As they collected themselves and their bags on the pavement outside the flat, Sophie smiled gratefully at Jake.

'Thanks so much,' she said, expecting him to catch the next cab back to civilisation.

'Not a problem. Now, which number are you? I'm dying for a cuppa.'

And Sophie couldn't help but laugh because 'cuppa' sounded so funny in an American accent.

Jake stood beside Sophie in the kitchen as she made tea and poured out two glasses of milk as if it were the most natural thing in the world for him to be there.

'Am I being too much?' he asked her. 'I'll go if you like.'

Sophie considered the alternatives. 'No please, stay,' she said and Jake fixed her with a long blue-eyed look that made her feel certain he was just about ready to kiss her.

'One lump or two?' Sophie asked, holding up the sugar bowl as a shield.

Jake smiled and took a step back. 'None,' he said, wryly. 'I'm abstaining. Apparently.'

They carried the drinks back into the living room to find Izzy fast asleep more or less where she had fallen right in the middle of the floor on the now grubby rug, her arms flung above her head in abandon.

'Shhhh,' Bella said, pointing down at her sister, with her usual razor-sharp observation. 'She's asleep.'

Sophie smiled at the little girl, her mouth half-open, the half-crescent of her long eyelashes sweeping the tops of her apple cheeks. She could definitely see why people liked their children when they were asleep. Even she felt rather fond of Izzy just at that moment.

'Here, let me,' Jake said. Bending, he scooped Izzy into his arms. 'Where now?' he whispered.

Sophie led him through to her bedroom and hastily smoothed out the crumpled duvet, motioning that he should lay Izzy down. As he did so Sophie drew the quilt up over her, leaving her fully clothed and entirely unwashed.

'No pyjamas?' Jake asked her, trying not to smile.

'No,' Sophie said quite seriously. 'You see, I've discovered that if you wake her up after even a few minutes of sleep she thinks that she's been asleep for a whole night and is ready for action again. It's best not to risk it.'

The sight she saw when they came back into the living room made Sophie certain that the fragile peace was about to be shattered. Bella was sitting in Artemis's chair and so was Artemis.

'Don't move a muscle,' Sophie hissed at Jake, who stood behind her, his way into the room blocked by her outstretched arm. He surveyed Bella sitting with the big grey cat and looked puzzled. But he didn't know Artemis.

Bella sat with her feet tucked under her, hugging a cushion to her chest. The cat sat on the broad width of the chair arm, her front paws curled neatly

151

under her. She watched the interloper intently, with a fixed green-eyed stare. Sophie held her breath, certain that at any moment the defensive and highly territorial animal would pounce on Bella with the special fury she reserved for anyone who sat in her chair when she wanted to sit in it.

'Don't make any sudden movements,' Sophie said to Bella, her voice low and even. 'Just keep your hands in view and step away from the chair.'

Bella raised the palm of her left hand hesitantly as Sophie had instructed, but instead of getting off the chair she reached out very slowly and stroked Artemis just behind the ears. Sophie closed her eyes and braced herself for the screaming.

'Bloody hell,' she whispered to Jake.

But nothing happened.

She opened them again. And saw the strangest thing. Instead of ripping Bella's eyes out, Artemis didn't move except to dip her head and tip it to one side slightly, clearly indicating to Bella exactly where she wanted to be scratched. Instinctively, Bella obliged and after a beat the room was filled with a loud rattle.

Artemis was *purring*. Sophie had only ever heard her purr once before and that was with one of the helpers in the shelter, just before she brought her home. She'd been waiting three years for Artemis to purr for her but she never had, until now.

'Bloody hell!' Sophie said again, but this time her voice was filled with awe.

'What is going on?' Jake asked her, feeling slightly stupid about whispering.

'Nothing!' Sophie exclaimed in wonder.

'Yep,' Jake said, raising both his brows and crossing his arms. 'That's what I thought.'

Carefully, Sophie edged into the room and sat down on the sofa to watch the tableau of cat and girl, a tiny smile turning up the corners of her mouth.

'She likes you,' Sophie said.

'Cats do like me,' Bella said, still looking at Artemis. 'We . . . well, when we were at home we had a giant cat called Tango because he was orange but . . . but when we had to go and live with Grandma he had to go into a home because Grandma is allergic to cats and now I don't know who he lives with.' Bella turned her profile a little further away from Sophie. 'So I know that cats like me.'

Sophie slipped off the sofa and knelt on the floor in front of the chair.

'But Artemis doesn't even like *me*, Bella,' she said without jealousy. 'I'm just her landlady. For her to let you stroke her like that after only knowing you for a few days must mean that you are a very, very special person.'

'Really?' Bella looked at Sophie.

'Really.' And because she felt suddenly so grateful to Bella and because she sensed that she needed Bella too, Sophie put one arm around her shoulders and gave her a little hug. 'Thank you. Thank you for making Artemis feel safe and happy.'

She covered Bella's free hand with her own and squeezed it gently. Artemis shot out a paw and scratched the back of Sophie's hand in one fluid movement, giving her a most irritated look before hopping off the chair and running at full pelt past Jake and out into the hallway.

'Ouch,' Sophie said, looking at the four red welts that had begun to rise on the back of her hand.

'Sorry,' Bella said, looking worried. 'I'm sure she didn't mean it.'

Sophie laughed. 'Oh she meant it, but you know what? It doesn't matter. I'm just glad she's found a friend. She really needed one.'

Bella and Sophie smiled at each other, and Sophie realised it was the first time they had truly connected since Bella had arrived in her life. It was as if she had caught a fleeting glance of the little girl that was in there somewhere, hiding behind the protective outer layer. Sophie felt a curious jump in her abdomen as she watched that Bella retreat again almost before her eyes, and realised that, just for a moment, it had felt as if she had been talking to Carrie. But Bella glanced at Jake, still standing in the door frame, and any trace of Carrie was gone in an instant.

'If Artemis liking me after just a bit means I'm a special person . . . ?' Bella began slowly.

'Yes?' Sophie said with a smile, hoping to coax that other Bella out again.

'Does that mean that her not liking you after three years means you are a rubbish one?'

Sophie thought for a moment. 'Probably,' she conceded. She was getting used to Bella's blunt observations, and besides, she didn't have the energy to be offended by a six-year-old.

'Well, I love Artemis, Aunty Sophie, but I think she's wrong. I don't think you're rubbish. I like you – you *are* funny.' Bella patted Sophie's knee in commiseration. 'It's been an awfully long day – can I go to bed?'

'Absolutely,' Sophie said hastily, possibly sounding a bit too pleased.

'Should I brush my teeth?' Bella asked her.

'Better had do,' Sophie replied. 'At least once every other day is the recommended minimum.'

'Is he going home now?' Bella nodded at Jake, who had come into the room and was sitting on the arm of the sofa.

'In a little bit,' Sophie said.

'He'll probably want to kiss you, bleugh,' Bella said, wrinkling up her nose.

'I'll tell you what,' Sophie told her. 'I'll come and brush my teeth with you.'

Well, there was no harm in being prepared.

Half an hour later Sophie offered Jake a glass of warm Baileys.

'Sorry,' she said. 'It's all I've got, unless you want another "cuppa"?'

Jake smiled and took the glass from her hand, so that the tips of his fingers brushed hers.

'No, I think I need something a little stronger.'

Sophie took a bigger gulp of her Baileys than was probably ladylike.

'You know,' she said reflectively. 'Sometimes I work from eight in the morning to ten at night – later than that if we've got an event on. I don't take a break or stop for lunch, I keep going, and at the end of the day I'm tired, but not this tired. I've *never* been this tired before in my life and . . .' She demonstrated her exhaustion quite eloquently by drifting off into silence.

Jake watched her for a second or two before putting his glass down and taking hers out of her hands and setting it beside his.

'You are doing amazingly well,' he said.

Sophie looked longingly at her glass. 'Thank you.'

'I mean, from the moment I met you I got all the obvious things about you, straight away,' he told her. 'You are beautiful and clever and formidable.'

'*Formidable?*' Sophie repeated the word uncertainly.

'I like a challenge,' Jake said with a grin. 'What I'm trying to say is I like and admire you. I'm really attracted to you – but all this? Seeing you handle it all with such grace and goodwill . . .'

'Well . . .' Sophie wasn't sure about that last part, and was feeling increasingly flustered under his intense gaze.

'You've blown me away,' Jake said. 'I think I could really fall for you, Sophie Mills.'

Sophie froze. This was it. He was laying his cards on the table and she felt like a rabbit caught in the headlights. She'd had a crush on this man for weeks and now she just wanted to flee the scene.

'Oh,' she said. And then, 'Um, how nice.'

'I'm going too fast, aren't I?' Jake asked her anxiously, all bravado gone.

Sophie shook her head. 'No, no – I mean – look Jake, it's just there's so much going on in my life right now. So much I've got to keep on top of. There's work and that's so important, and the girls, of course. I've got to get their dad back otherwise they'll go into care and that would be wrong. I don't think that now is the right time to start anything . . .' Sophie gabbled, almost unable to believe what she was saying. For the last few weeks whenever she had thought about Jake she had imagined what it would be like to hear him saying those words, or something very like them. Now that he was, she suddenly felt like leaping up and opening all the windows and washing the kitchen floor. Maybe Cal was right about her. Maybe she did have intimacy issues. Maybe she did like the idea of Jake falling for her much more than she liked the reality. After all, the idea was much less time-consuming and complicated.

'I understand that,' Jake said gently. 'But can I ask you, Sophie – is it just that? If it is, I can wait until you're ready. But if you don't think you're attracted to me at all then you'll tell me, won't you?' He laughed. 'Usually I can tell what a woman

157

is thinking just by looking at her. You're not at all like that. You're a genuine enigma – I can't figure you out at all.'

Join the club, thought Sophie as she looked at Jake, at his lightly tanned face, his blue eyes and dark blond hair. He was indisputably attractive. If you looked up the word 'attractive' in the dictionary it would probably say in italics, '*See under Jake Flynn*'.

'I am attracted to you,' she said, and she was – it was impossible not to admire a man who was so aesthetically pleasing.

Suddenly Jake leaned forward and picked up her hand, pulling her closer to him.

'Well then,' he said, his voice low, 'would you mind if I kissed you? Just so I've got something to dream about while I'm doing all this waiting.'

'OK then,' Sophie squeaked.

Jake's arms snaked around her waist and pulled her body tightly against his, and he moaned in the back of his throat as he kissed her. Sophie opened her lips under his and closed her eyes. It was a nice kiss, a warm kiss, and it did feel good to be so close to another human body. She tightened her arms around his neck and he slid his hand under the hem of Lisa's shirt and . . .

'Izzy's been sick,' Bella's voice boomed in Sophie's ear. She and Jake sprang apart in one movement.

'Your cheeks have gone red,' Bella said, screwing up her mouth as she looked at Sophie. 'Anyway

Izzy's been sick in the bed. I tried to get her to do it in the bin but she couldn't wait. But at least she missed most of your shoes.'

Sophie brushed the back of her hand unconsciously across her mouth and looked at Jake.

'I'm sorry,' she said. But he just shrugged and smiled.

'No, I'm sorry,' he said. 'I *knew* there was a reason why we were waiting.' He laughed sweetly. 'Come on – I'll help you clear up.'

Later on, when bedclothes and pyjamas had been changed, baths had been had and an overwrought three-year-old had finally been cajoled back into bed, Sophie shut the door on Jake Flynn and sat on the sofa looking at the blank screen of the TV.

It *had* been a nice kiss, she concluded. And it had felt good to be in someone's arms again. Sophie had begun to wonder if that was as wonderful as kissing ever got, when exhaustion finally overtook her and she slept on the sofa sitting up, fully dressed and entirely unwashed.

CHAPTER 9

Maria Costello called Sophie again at nine a.m. exactly, on a Saturday morning almost two weeks later.

'I've nailed him,' she said.

Sophie had to pause for a beat before her brain managed to tell her who was on the other end of the phone. In the last couple of weeks she had become so locked into her strange new life of juggling the children, work and Jake that she had almost forgotten there was a prospective end in sight. A time when she might just get her ordered, quiet, peaceful life back.

'Really?' She stood up, feeling a rush of blood and adrenalin to her simultaneously overstretched and shrinking brain as she did so, and walked away from the table where she had been trying to update her month-end figures in the midst of a cats' tea party, taking the phone into the kitchen. 'And have you found out *exactly* where he is?' Sophie asked her.

'Exactly,' Maria said triumphantly. 'I've got his numbers, his address. I'll give you his inside leg measurements if you want me to.'

'The address will do,' Sophie said, scrabbling about in her pen drawer, which always seemed to contain everything except pens. Finally she found an Oxfam biro at the back and ripped off a piece of kitchen paper to write on. 'Go on.'

'Here's the phone number of the school he works at.' Maria read out the numbers and the address with brisk efficiency, spelling out the Spanish words at staccato speed. 'The bill's in the post, OK?'

'Hang on,' Sophie said, hurriedly. 'Did you say he works at a *school*? What kind of school? Can't you tell me a bit more about him? I mean, I had him down as an international drugs baron.'

Maria laughed, but she didn't sound amused. 'More of a male Mother Teresa,' she said. 'He's been working as a volunteer for a street kids charity for the last couple of years.'

Sophie processed that bit of information. That was not what she had expected to hear. A man who left his wife with a newborn baby and disappeared leaving behind all his responsibilities didn't seem the type who would go on to devote his life to a children's charity. Sophie decided it was probably the guilt, but being a coward as well as a bastard he had tried to salve that guilt a few thousand miles away, instead of facing up to what he had done at home.

'And it's definitely him?' she asked.

'Definitely,' Maria said firmly.

'Er . . . thank you, thank you, Maria.'

'I want payment by return of post.' And Maria hung up.

Sophie put the phone down and looked out of the kitchen window to see Artemis balanced on the prow of the neighbours' fence, poised to eviscerate the next passing vole or some other unfortunate mammal.

So Maria had found him and now Sophie had to think about what that was going to mean. Two weeks ago she would not have thought of anything beyond finding Louis. Now she realised his return would have consequences for everyone involved. She thought of the expression on Mrs Stiles's face when she had mentioned Louis. She thought of Carrie, alone with her children, too proud or embarrassed or maybe too distant to tell her that Louis had gone.

Sophie realised now that she hadn't considered what the consequences might be for anybody else besides herself. It was very likely that now she had found Louis, her life would improve and the burden of the children would pass from her to him, which after all was only right. But what if him coming back wasn't the best thing for the girls?

Two weeks ago she wouldn't have thought twice about dialling the number and getting Louis back here as fast as humanly possible, but in the fourteen days that had passed since Maria's first phone call something had changed. Something that Sophie could hardly have put her finger on until that moment.

She realised she had actually started to care for Bella and Izzy.

It wasn't like being in love or anything as grand as that. She hadn't suddenly felt compelled to adopt them and call them her own. After all, she hadn't even kissed or hugged either of them since they had arrived. But Sophie felt she had come to respect them, coping as bravely and as stoically as they did with all that had happened to them. She was grateful for this, as she was certain that if they had worn their grief on their sleeves she would never have been able to handle them. And besides, she had got unexpectedly used to the new rhythm of her life and having the girls in it.

In fact, Sophie reflected, the hardest obstacle to overcome had not been the children exactly, but working her job around them. Somehow she had expected it to stretch and give way like a fast-flowing river rushing past boulders. She had thought that Gillian's motherly compassion for her dead best friend's kids would be endless and that her need to keep Sophie on would be intrinsic, but Sophie had learnt something in the last two weeks that she would rather not have discovered: that as far as work was concerned she was expendable. It was a cold and sobering lesson to realise that the ten years she had devoted to McCarthy Hughes had not earned her any security to speak of, but even so it made Sophie more determined that she should not let all that she had worked for slip away.

So they had developed a routine.

Every morning Izzy would wake Sophie up just after six. The two of them would wake Bella and then all three would eat cornflakes and toast on the kitchen floor. Sophie would suck down a cup of boiling hot instant coffee in two or three gulps as if it were the elixir of life, and Bella and Izzy would neck a pint of semi-skimmed between them.

The three would then wash together in the bathroom. Sophie would fill up the sink with warm water, hand the girls a sponge each and do her best in between their splashes and soakings to get herself clean. She would look at the bath and dimly remember a time when she used to have an hour or so to lounge in it, but the best she could manage now was a swift shower after the girls were in bed. Dressing was relatively easy, mainly because Izzy only wore one thing, which worked out fine since Sophie had begun to use her washing machine regularly and then dry the fairy dress on the radiator every other night. She supposed there was some kind of unspoken rule that you should not allow a child out in public in a dress that had caked tomato ketchup encrusted down its front, but she refused on principle to wash it every single day.

Bella was even easier to manage, choosing items out of her meagre wardrobe with the kind of élan her mother would have been proud of. There had been an incident when she had helpfully put on a load of washing and succeeded in turning all Sophie's pristine white underwear a sort of brothel pink, but Sophie had been surprised to discover she didn't care. Her pants might be pink, she reasoned, but at least they were clean. Sophie herself managed to keep up an outward appearance of groomed neatness which hid the other lesser parts of personal care that she had let go, so that stubble grew on her legs and under her arms and her fair brows thickened slightly. No-one was going to know after all, she decided, and whether she realised it or not it gave her another reason to keep Jake Flynn at arm's length.

And then Sophie would take the girls to the office every morning between nine and one. The first day she did this Gillian had suggested in a kind but resolute manner that she organise some part-time childcare, as an office was no place for small children – which had convinced Sophie that she was in one of those fairy tales when the prince has to achieve three impossible tasks to win the hand of the princess – but Sophie had nodded politely and asked Cal to find the number of a childminder in her area, checked she was registered and double-checked her references. She had taken the girls round to meet Alice Hardy that very afternoon. Bella and Izzy had seemed to like Alice's friendly, sunny ground-floor flat with a playroom, and while Bella read a book to herself, seated at a mini table and chair set as Sophie talked over terms with Alice, Izzy went as far as to play shops with little boy who was spending the day there.

So it had been a bit of a blow the following morning when the girls realised Sophie was leaving them with Alice, and Bella had collapsed into tearless, inconsolable sobs. Sophie felt that Izzy's tears were more a reaction to her sister's distress, but Bella's reaction had taken her aback. She hadn't seen any kind of emotional outburst at all from the uniquely even-tempered child, and so had supposed her placid exterior was the norm. But as Sophie waved the girls goodbye, Bella's face had crumpled and she had backed away from Alice and turned into Sophie's leg, clinging onto her.

Sophie had crouched down to try to untangle Bella, and Izzy had launched herself at Sophie's back, flinging her arms round her neck. Sophie thought briefly it was like being wrestled by two man-eating crocodiles.

'Come on girls,' She had said briskly. 'Let's be reasonable.'

'Please don't leave us here,' Izzy had begged Sophie. 'Please don't leave us!'

'It's only for a couple of hours!' Sophie had said, irritated at first. 'I'm coming back!'

'*Please* don't leave us again Aunty Sophie,' Bella had cried. 'We don't know these people and please don't make us live with people we don't know – please, *please!* We'll be so quiet, we'll be so good and I won't let Izzy be naughty please, *please!*'

'I won't, I won't, I won't,' wailed Izzy right in Sophie's ear.

It took a moment for Sophie to decipher the words from the sobs, but once she had she thought she understood.

'This is just while I go to work,' she had attempted to explain. 'Like school or nursery. It's not a foster home or anything like that.' Sophie had sensed that Bella wanted further reassurance but she didn't know what else to say.

'If we're with you we know we're safe,' Bella had managed to mumble, her black eyes made liquid by the tears that threatened but did not fall.

It had been strange, the look that passed between Sophie and Bella then. Sophie realised that somehow, in just over a week, Bella had come to trust and need her, clinging onto – Sophie guessed – the one thing that seemed relatively stable. It was another hint, another glimpse of the real girl that was hidden so carefully. It was an insight that made Carrie's death suddenly seem all too real, and for a second Sophie felt the threat of tears prickle behind her eyes. She wasn't the only one who locked her emotions tightly away.

Since the moment Tess Andrew had walked into her office Sophie had barely allowed herself a moment to think about Carrie, partly because she felt she didn't have the room or time yet to grieve or to miss her, but also because she was afraid that when the dust had settled she might find out she felt nothing at all, or else not nearly enough for the death of a friend who had once meant everything to her. But in that moment Sophie felt everything that Bella was feeling and she knew that somewhere inside her feelings for Carrie must still live, because otherwise there was no way she would have responded to Bella in the way that she did. And knowing that, she felt her attachment to the children increased by one more fragile strand, because Bella was showing her a reflection of herself. A picture that made sense.

'OK,' she had said with a shrug, 'you're coming with me.'

'Children often cry like this at first,' Alice had told Sophie kindly. 'And they're nearly always putting it on. They're happy as Larry as soon as Mum's gone. They'll soon get used to it.'

Sophie had looked into the other woman's open, well-meaning face.

'You're probably right,' she had said. 'I just think that these two have got enough to cope with already.'

And the moment Sophie had walked into the office with the children that morning she had gone straight to Gillian's office and played her tactically in a way she would never have previously dreamt of.

She had told Gillian she had tried to leave the girls with a carer, and how they had reacted.

'They've just lost their mother. They're terrified of being abandoned again.' It was a direct challenge to Gillian, daring her not to show compassion for the children's plight. 'I know this is no place for kids but I'll make sure they're kept out of the way and I won't let it interfere with any of my work. The minute it does I'll think again.'

'It's not just what I think,' Gillian had said cautiously. 'There's Health and Safety and insurance and all sorts of other things to consider.'

'It's only temporary,' Sophie had pressed her. 'Their dad will be back soon.'

'Well, you'd better make sure you're only in the office for as short a time as possible. And I want to see updates on all your accounts before you go.'

Sophie had had a long talk with the girls, explaining at length why they had to be extra good. They had stared at her blankly, the connection Sophie had felt with them seemingly lost again.

And then Cal had produced a huge box of building bricks. He had unrolled a colourful rug and set it down in one corner before tipping the bricks out, and Izzy had hopped with anticipation.

'Here are crayons, and pens and paper. And here's two Barbies and a Barbie car. Now,' he had looked sternly from one the girl to the next, 'these are *my* toys and I am *very* kindly letting you play with them, so I expect you to play nicely, and share and not take them out of this office, or I will have to take them back. Do you promise?'

'Yes, Cal!' the girls had chorused before descending on the rug.

Cal had winked at Sophie. 'It's sort of like learning another language. Once you let yourself go enough to get the hang of the accent you'll be fine.'

'Well,' Sophie had said, 'thankfully I'm only on a short trip so all I need is a phrase book. Anyway where did you get all those toys from?' Sophie had been full of gratitude and admiration for her PA.

'I told you,' he had said. 'They're mine. From when I was a kid.'

And Sophie had decided she believed him.

It was in the middle of this gradual build-up of routine that Tess had arrived one evening at the flat.

Sophie had squinted at her as she held the front door open.

'I'm sure I know you,' she had said sarcastically. 'Oh yes! That's it! You're the one who told me I wasn't alone and that I could expect regular visits.'

'Well, you weren't alone,' Tess had said, bustling her way into the flat. 'I've called you every day and every day you've said that things have been going well. I've had this awful neglect case to deal with. And sometimes there aren't enough of us to go around, we have to prioritise.'

Sophie had shrugged. Tess did phone her every day, it was true, and she supposed that she only had herself to blame for the fact that her tiredness and slowly decreasing powers of communication led her to tell Tess whatever she wanted to hear in order to get her off the phone and allow her to go to sleep in front of the TV. But then again, as nearly two weeks had passed since the girls arrived and all three of them were still alive, she supposed she hadn't actually been lying. It gave her an unexpected sense of achievement and satisfaction.

'How's it really been?' Tess had asked her once she had a mug of tea in her hands.

'It's really been really hard,' Sophie had said. 'My job's been the worst part. But I think I'm on top of that mainly. I even landed a new client this week. It was quite funny because Izzy had just felt-tipped some stripes on my linen skirt but I had to go into the meeting anyway and the woman asked me where I got it – she said she thought it was fabulous! It's ruined of course. I've added it to the bill. And I suppose I haven't been sleeping well or eating the way I used to and my skin's gone . . .'

'How has it been for the girls?' Tess had interrupted her, and Sophie had remembered belatedly that she wasn't the most important person in her life any more. She had thought for a moment.

'OK,' she had said. 'I mean, I get the feeling that most of the time they're living in a sort of suspended animation, waiting for a time when they know exactly what's going to happen to them, when they can *feel* what has happened to them. I guess we're all like that.' She had realised that was the way she felt too.

'I've had them for two weeks now,' she had continued. 'Have you found Louis yet?' She had decided not to mention her own efforts to locate him.

Tess had dropped her gaze to look at her bangles. 'No,' she had said evenly. 'But we've only been looking for a month, remember. We know he went to the States right after leaving here. It's the red tape you see, dealing with government bodies overseas. It holds everything up and makes it all so slow.' She had looked back up at Sophie. 'But I know we set a time limit on this. I've found a foster home that will take them together. They could go tomorrow if you like.'

It had been a pivotal moment. A moment when Sophie could have let all her worries go and pass the buck, pass the children onto someone else. But she had remembered the look on Bella's face that morning at the childminder's too clearly, and she had remembered that flash feeling that had burned across her chest. Even though a large percentage of her still wanted to, she just couldn't do it. She couldn't abandon the girls, who had been through too much already and still had so much more to face. And although she wasn't conscious of the thought, Sophie couldn't do it to herself. Slowly the instinct and intuition that she claimed never to have had were awakening – a small sleepy part of her dimly sensed that she needed the children just as much as they needed her.

'They can stay with me,' she had said.

Tess had looked genuinely surprised. 'Really?' she had said.

'Yes. Like you said, there's still a good chance Louis might turn up and I just don't think it would be right to move them again now. We've got a routine and everything.'

'But if it's affecting your job . . .' Tess had said, uncertainly.

'I'm coping,' Sophie had said firmly. She had always liked a challenge.

And of all the distractions, obstacles and challenges that had suddenly sprung to life on a previously tranquil horizon, Jake positioned himself firmly in the middle.

He had called Sophie the morning after they had had the perfectly nice kiss.

'I've got to tell you,' he'd said. 'I couldn't stop thinking about that kiss.'

'Lovely,' Sophie had said for want of anything else to say.

'It was lovely, wasn't it?' Jake had laughed. 'That's such an English word, "lovely".'

'I think you'll find most of the words you speak are English.'

Jake had laughed again. He had a sweetly unself-conscious laugh like a delighted little boy, which didn't quite go with his suited and booted hard body. 'When can I see you again?'

'Well, we've got to meet next week to sign off the last lot of invoices for your party . . .'

'So lunch after that? I know you'll have the kids but we could all go maybe?'

'Jake, I don't know.' She didn't want any mis-understandings between them. 'Remember what I said before about waiting a while? There's so much on at the moment. I just – I can't really see you in that way. I haven't got any time or space to think about you, to really know what I'm feeling. It wouldn't be fair on you.'

Jake had paused for a moment. 'Well,' he'd said. 'I knew exactly how I felt about you before you'd even uttered one word, but I guess maybe that's the difference between us. You're an instant smash hit while I'm more of a grower. I understand how you feel, Sophie, and I respect that. I won't ask for any more kisses just yet. But you might as well know, I'm not going to give up on this. I think we could really have something.'

'Do you?' Sophie had felt hopeful that he might be right.

'I do. So how about we say no kissing for now but you let me be your friend. You need a friend right now.'

'I do,' Sophie had conceded.

'So I'll bring over some wine and a Chinese tonight. No strings.'

'OK. And, Jake, thank you. I really appreciate all this.'

'Of course you do. And that's why sooner or later, one way or another, you're going to fall in love with me.'

174

Jake had come over that night and twice again since, sitting and talking about work and children with Sophie until she had yawned extravagantly and he had taken the hint. She had enjoyed his company and the way he had looked at her, but never once had she felt the urge to throw caution out of the window and let him kiss her again.

'I will,' she kept telling herself. 'When the time is right. It's just that the time isn't right yet.'

CHAPTER 10

Clutching the piece of paper that might hold all their futures on it, Sophie walked from her bedroom to the living room to check on the girls. They were lying on the floor with the two Barbies that Cal had graciously allowed them to bring home, acting out some kind of intense drama which – from what Sophie could glean – was based on a recent episode of *Coronation Street*.

'All right?' she asked them casually.

They ignored her, which was usually a good sign – when it didn't mean they were in the midst of extreme naughtiness. This morning Sophie didn't care either way.

'I'm just going to tidy the bedroom up,' she lied. 'So don't go swallowing any choking hazards, OK?'

There was no response, except for the high-pitched chatter of Barbie Ken Barlow telling Barbie Deirdre he'd never trust her again.

Sitting on her bed, Sophie looked at the number again.

She wondered if it might be an idea to actually tidy up her bedroom before phoning, but then she made herself look her reflection right in the eye.

'You have to do this,' she said. 'There is no alternative.'

She dialled the number and heard a series of clicks on the line before the long foreign ringing tone sounded.

Sophie put down the phone.

'What am I *thinking*,' she said out loud and with some relief. 'They'll speak Spanish, or Peruvian or Inca or something. I need a phrase book at least – or . . .' An idea popped into her head. 'I'll phone Cal.'

Sophie had done the bedroom and changed the sheets by the time Cal arrived.

He looked her up and down as she opened the door, still in her pyjamas. 'You should just dread your hair and be done with it,' he said.

Sophie said nothing because she knew he was seriously pissed off with her for dragging him out of the bed of an Italian chap called Mauro, who was apparently not only drop-dead gorgeous but made the best spaghetti carbonara in the whole of London.

'You never eat food unless it comes in the form of a canapé,' Sophie had reminded him half an hour earlier as she'd tried to persuade him to give up his Saturday for her. 'You don't even like pasta.'

Cal had bitched and snipped at her via his mobile for most of his trip over, but Sophie had taken it on the chin because after all he was right. He *didn't* have to come over to her flat and help her on a Saturday morning. It *was* above and beyond the call of duty. She *would* have to grovel to him for weeks, to come and take him to lunch and sign him off for as many Friday afternoons as he wanted for a period of six months. But he was still doing it, and as he wasn't trying to get her to shag him Sophie was reassured that it was a strong evidence of his friendship.

'Hello girls,' Cal said to Bella and Izzy as he passed the living room. They were now lying in front of the TV but miraculously they didn't appear to be watching it, perhaps because the programme was some kind of sport. Bella was drawing yet another mermaid-strewn coastal scene with her new set of felt-tips, and Izzy was feeding her new baby doll.

'Come on, baby,' Izzy said, sounding rather impatient. 'Let's have some nice chips for tea on the kitchen floor and then we'll watch TV all day!'

Cal raised an eyebrow at Sophie. 'And to think they're all saying you're a natural with the kids,' he said tartly.

'Yes – well,' Sophie coughed. 'It's a learning curve. So, anyway, follow me to the bedroom.'

Cal followed her, with a derisive snort. 'That's exactly what Mauro said to me,' he said mournfully as Sophie closed the bedroom door behind her. 'So come on then, tell me what this is all about – although why you couldn't tell me on the phone I don't know.'

'Because your mobile signal wasn't very good and I didn't want to have to shout in case "walls have ears", if you know what I mean.'

'I don't,' Cal said sharply. 'So speak English. You're being annoying.'

'I know. I'm sorry. I had to call you over because of your language skills. I had to think for a moment if Spanish was one of them, but then I remembered in your interview when you told me you'd travelled all around the world that you'd worked in Barcelona for a year for a law firm and spoke fluent Spanish.'

Cal pursed his lips and looked out of the bedroom window. 'Yes, I do recollect that,' he said carefully.

'Well, Louis Gregory is in Lima, and I looked it up and they speak Spanish in Peru. So I need you to phone up and speak Spanish to whoever picks up the phone so we can get hold of him, OK?'

Cal bit his lip. 'And you don't speak Spanish at all?'

'Nope,' Sophie reaffirmed with a nod, her hands on her hips. 'You know me!'

'So you'd have no idea what the Spanish person or indeed I was saying, for example?' Cal double-checked, crossing his arms over his lucky shag shirt, a pale-blue one shot through with subtle silver pinstripes.

'Not a sausage,' Sophie said, honestly.

'OK, I'll do it.' Cal took the piece of paper with the number on from Sophie and sat on the edge of the bed looking at it.

'This is important, isn't it?' he said, with an edge of reluctance.

'Just a bit!' Sophie replied, laughing nervously. 'The lives of three people depend on its outcome!' She put a hand on his shoulder. 'That's why I really do appreciate you coming over, Cal – you're totally saving my life here even if you are pretending to be all flippant about it. You really are wonderful, you know.'

Cal nodded. 'I'm sorry, Sophie,' he said, unable to look at her. 'I lied on my CV. I lied in the interview. I didn't go round the world, I went skiing in Aspen for two weeks once and I didn't work for a year in Barcelona for a law firm. I stayed there for a month with an old boyfriend and worked in an English bar until we broke up. I can't speak fluent Spanish. I can barely speak tourist Spanish. I can't actually speak fluent anything. When you ask me to tell you what to say to overseas clients I look it up on the Internet. There's this amazing site that gives you pronunciations and everything.' Cal dropped his head and braced himself, although Sophie didn't know why. He should know by now that she was terrible at losing her temper – it required far too much abandon.

She just stared at him. She didn't know what to be more cross about, the fact that he had lied his way through his job interview, the fact that she had fallen for it or the fact that he was about as much use to her now in practical terms as he was as a lover. And then she remembered, at least he was here. He had come and he had told her

180

the truth when it mattered. He hadn't bluffed his way through a tricky situation to save himself and as far as he knew she had never accidentally offended a foreign client by asking them to have sex with donkey in a bassoon or anything like that. At least Cal covered his CV lie with good accurate research.

'Bastard,' she said, but in general rather than directed straight at Cal. 'Look, you must remember some basic phrases if you lived there for a month, surely, and we did that Spanish fashion label a couple of months back. You must remember something from then?'

Cal shrugged. 'I guess so,' he said uncertainly, before catching Sophie's look of anxiety. 'Oh what the hell, I'll do it.'

'Well, go on then.' Sophie nodded at the phone, unaware that she was twisting her fingers as she watched him.

Cal picked up the receiver and put it down again. 'But what's the time difference? There might not be anybody there?'

Sophie sighed and sat down on the edge of her bed alongside him. 'I don't know, I forgot to look that bit up. It's five hours to New York, isn't it, and it's at least as far away as that.' She looked at her watch. 'So assuming it's about the same, it's just gone eleven now here, so it's either four o'clock in the afternoon there or . . . six o'clock in the morning. I think it's six o'clock in the morning.' Sophie sighed again. 'There'll be no-one there, will there? I was really psyched up for this too.'

Cal watched her profile, her chin dropping to her chest.

'Let's do it now anyway, you never know, we might be lucky.' You need to get this sorted, Sophie – any longer cooped up in this flat eating Coco Pops and you'll have three of those chins to be depressed about, Jake will go off you and then I'll have to handle your sexual repression for ever.'

'I am not sexually repressed . . .' Sophie began her routine protest.

'Yeah, yeah, whatever.' Cal dismissed it with a wave of his hand as he dialled the number and they waited. The passing seconds seemed to stretch on for hours.

'Ah, hello . . . um *buenos días* I mean.' There was a pause during which Cal nodded at Sophie and winked. '*Arrepentido* about the, er, *hora*. It's an emergency a . . . *urgencia*?' Sophie gave him a worried look. His Spanish sounded all made up even to her, and the faint voice of the person on the other end of the line sounded less than thrilled to be talking to Cal at six o'clock in the morning. But Cal pressed on, smiling as he spoke as if his charm might somehow work long distance. 'Me *llamo* Cal, and I am trying to speak. Um, *hablar*? To Louis Gregory. LOUIS GREGORY *por favor*? URGENCIA.' Sophie heard the faint rattle of a voice on the other end of the line. '*Sí . . . Sí . . . Sí. Gracias!*'

'What are they saying?' Sophie whispered to him.

'Not the foggiest, but hopefully they've gone to get someone who can speak English. I think they got the emergency bit,' he said proudly. 'I learnt that after my boyfriend broke his ankle coming off a moped and I had to call an ambulance.' Cal listened intently to the echoes on the end of the line. 'If I'm not very much mistaken somebody in Lima likes listening to Justin Timberlake in the early hours of the morning – and who can blame them?'

They waited for what seemed like an age and then Cal looked at Sophie as he heard the clatter of the receiver being picked up.

'Oh, hello,' he said after a pause. 'Right then, hang on a moment.' He held out the receiver to Sophie, who stared at it in horror.

'But, Cal, I can't speak Spanish . . .'

'You don't have to. It's him. It's Louis Gregory.'

'So,' Cal said urgently, as Sophie put the phone down. 'What did he say, how'd he react, did he cry?'

Sophie shook her head and replayed the conversation she'd just had, because it had happened so quickly she wasn't exactly sure she'd understood it.

'Listen, babe – do you know what time it is? You've woken the whole place up! Look, before you say anything, I meant to call you, but I've just been up to my eyes in it . . .' This had thrown Sophie. She had not expected Louis to be

183

expecting a call from another Englishwoman whose male secretary put the call through with the world's worst Spanish in the early hours of the morning – or indeed from another English-speaking woman at any time, full stop. She thought that perhaps Cal had made a mistake and it wasn't Louis at all.

'This is Louis Gregory, right? Formerly of St Ives, Cornwall?' There was a short silence, and Sophie had almost physically felt Louis's senses tauten, his laid-back sleepiness drain out of his body.

'Yes?' he'd said, and he'd laughed, probably a nervous reaction Sophie had decided in retrospect, but one that had made her feel even more jumpy.

'Hello, it's Sophie, Sophie Mills? Do you remember me?' There was an echo on the line, and after Sophie had finished each word she heard it repeated again in her ear, her voice sounding thin and girlish and not at all like a voice delivering serious news. 'Sophie Mills, I was at your wedding. Carrie's friend. Carrie Stiles's friend – I was a friend of your wife.'

The echo had continued for another beat and Sophie was able to sense the change in him, thousands of miles away. She could picture him sitting up a little straighter, the smile fading from his face as moment by moment he realised what her call meant. It meant something bad had happened.

'Where are the girls, are they hurt? Is one of

them hurt? What's happened?' he had said quickly, and Sophie had found herself stumbling to re-assure him – this absentee father and wife-leaver that neither girl seemed to know existed – that both his children were OK.

'They're OK, they're here with me. They're not hurt.' She had heard him breathe out a sigh and almost felt it in the shell of her ear. He had taken a deep breath.

'What's happened, Sophie?' he had said, but somehow Sophie knew the question was a formality. He already knew the answer. So she just told him outright.

'Carrie is dead,' she'd said.

'Carrie is dead,' the line had echoed, and Sophie had breathed in sharply as if she was hearing the news for the first time too. But then her fledgling sense of intuition had faltered. She had been bracing herself for an emotional outburst, questions, tears even. But there was nothing – just silence. Sophie remembered how she had felt when she first heard, how she still felt – as if her heart was a thousand miles away – so she went on filling the void with details. 'It was a car accident, almost seven months ago.' Still Louis had said nothing. 'She was killed outright. The girls went to live with her mother and then Mrs Stiles couldn't cope and called in Social Services about a month ago. They were sorting out the house and found a will. I was in the will, as guardian. So the girls came here.' She took a breath. 'Social Services have been looking for you for the last few weeks but they had all the red tape to get through, so I hired a private detective to find you and she did.' This time it was Sophie's nervous inappropriate laughter that had echoed in her ears. 'Look, Louis, I know you haven't seen them in a long time, maybe you don't want to but . . .'

'I'll be on the next flight I can get on,' Louis had said out of the silence.

Sophie had been taken aback by the sound of his voice, hardened with urgency.

'Oh, right, OK then,' she had said slowly, supposing that she had the result she wanted. 'Let me just give you some details . . .'

She had heard him scrabbling for a pen, then he took down her address and number.

'Thank you for everything you've done,' he had said. 'But I'm coming to get them, now.'

'Do you know when . . . ?' The dialling tone had buzzed in Sophie's ear. '. . . we can expect you,' she had finished into thin air.

She had learned very little about Louis from that phone call. He had hardly reacted to the news that the mother of his children was dead, and he had just more or less assumed that he could waltz back after three years away and take the girls off to God knew where to God knew what kind of life, without so much as a by-your-leave. She experienced yet another unfamiliar sensation, a sharp protective pang in her gut, followed by a surge of unexpected fierceness. She found herself thinking, 'over my dead body,' and then she smiled to herself as she realised just how apt and inappropriate that phrase was at exactly the same time.

She looked at a bemused Cal.

'He says,' she told him, 'he's coming. Not big on details like how or when, but he's coming apparently.'

Cal rested his lightly stubbled chin in the palm of his hand.

'*And* – what's he like?'

Sophie shrugged again and felt a worm of worry begin to insinuate its way into her chest as she contemplated all the possible consequences of the chain of events she had just set in motion. She bit her lip and looked at Cal.

'I don't know,' she said. 'I just don't know.'

CHAPTER 11

The girls were delighted to see their grand-mother. Izzy twirled and pranced around the small front room of the new ground-floor apartment, bumping happily into the crowd of old furniture, and Bella, although less showy than her sister, did quite a lot of discreet toe-pointing and heel-lifting in a bid to show off her own new shoes to their maximum advantage. Unfortunately in the midst of Izzy's balletic crazi-ness only Sophie, a fellow toe-pointer, noticed, so she bent down and whispered into Bella's ear, 'Your shoes look fabulous,' which made Bella smile.

'Calm down, Izzy!' Mrs Stiles remonstrated as Izzy threw her arms around her legs and buried her face in her skirt, declaring, 'I love to see you Grandma!' at the top of her voice.

'I love to see you too, darling.' Mrs Stiles looked flustered but pleased by this sign of affection. 'But I'd also love to keep my knees in one piece; this arthritis – it'll be the death of me if the blood pressure doesn't get me first,' Mrs Stiles said, patting Izzy on the head.

'Or the cancer,' Bella reminded her.

'Oh yes, well you're right. It might be cancer, bowel probably, I've got terrible constipation,' Mrs Stiles said matter-of-factly and Sophie realised that the children must have discussed the exact nature of Mrs Stiles's demise quite often during their stay with her, which she found rather disturbing. A philandering father or a morbid grandmother – it wasn't much of a choice when it came to close relatives.

'Oh, you'll outlive us all,' Sophie said with forced joviality.

'I sincerely hope not,' Mrs Stiles said bleakly. Her face took a downward tumble as if somebody had switched the gravity back on, and Sophie realised the import of what she had just said.

'I'm sorry, I only meant . . .' She sighed. 'Oh look, I don't know what I meant,' she said with a vague gesture to back her up. 'I'm sorry.' Mrs Stiles ignored her.

'Do you two girls want some lemon barley and a French Fancy?' Mrs Stiles said. The girls nodded and Sophie followed Mrs Stiles into the small kitchen and leaned against the door frame, watching Bella and Izzy breathing hard against the living-room window, drawing faces in the mist before it faded. Then, flinging open the patio doors, they ran out into the small shared court-yard and began marching around and around the central bird table with apparently motiveless enthusiasm.

'I've just cleaned those windows,' Mrs Stiles said to Sophie, pressing her lips together. It wasn't that she didn't want the girls here, Sophie decided, it was rather that she didn't like them turning up unexpectedly. She didn't like any unannounced pebbles rippling the calm surface of her routine. Sophie didn't blame her; she supposed that two sudden if minor strokes and the death of your daughter would make you cling onto the belief that every tomorrow is much better off being exactly the same as yesterday, because at least then you knew where you stood. And Sophie was about to throw a bloody great brick into her pond, so to speak.

Once again Sophie had cause to reflect on the fact that she had been so keen to find Louis, so certain that his arrival would be the answer to everyone's problems, that she hadn't stopped to consider the implications of him turning up for anyone else. Not for Mrs Stiles, not for Tess Andrew and not for the girls. However, Louis was coming now and there was nothing she could do to stop that, so she had to tell her – and if there was one thing that Sophie had learnt over the last few days, it was that if you had to tell somebody something they didn't want to hear there was no way to dress it up.

'Louis is coming back to London. He's coming to see the girls.'

Mrs Stiles poured water into the two beakers of lemon barley she had prepared, and set the jug down on the worktop before turning to look at Sophie.

'They found him then,' she said. 'I hoped they wouldn't, I told that Tess not to bother. She more or less told me it would take months. I'd hoped for the girls' sake she was right.'

Sophie didn't know how to react to that piece of information so she said nothing but watched Mrs Stiles shake her head and twist her swollen knotted fingers, her left side slow and heavy.

'Well now he'll be happy, won't he?' she said bitterly. 'Now he'll get everything his own way, won't he? My daughter's dead, out of the way for good and he can come waltzing in like some kind of hero and drag them off to heaven knows what kind of life.' She shot Sophie a red-hot look. 'I certainly won't ever see them again, once he's got them. He won't let me.'

Sophie tucked her loose hair back behind her ear and chewed her lip for a moment. She had to be straight with her. 'It wasn't Tess who found him,' she said. 'It was me, sort of. I spoke to him earlier today.' Sophie remembered her sense of unease at the end of the conversation. 'He sounded really worried about the girls, he said he'd come straight away.' But her uncertainty sounded in her voice and Mrs Stiles looked sceptical. 'Really, I can't suddenly have two children, Mrs Stiles. As much as I . . . like the girls none of us can carry on the way we are, it's not fair on them or me, and what's the alternative? I thought that this is what Carrie would want.'

Mrs Stiles looked over Sophie's shoulder and out of the window to where the girls continued to circle, the winter sun blanching all the colour out of her skin.

'Carrie wanted you,' she told Sophie pointedly. 'That's why your name was in her will. Besides, you hardly knew her at all when she died – how would you know what she would want now? Well, I'll tell you what she didn't want. She didn't want a husband who ran out on her and her children at the first sign of trouble. And she wouldn't want him taking those two girls.' Mrs Stiles narrowed her eyes. 'Oh, he might play at being a dad for a while – but for how long, how long before the novelty wears off and he's bored again? What will happen to them then?' She took a deep, shuddering breath. 'I just *wish* I was twenty years younger and could look after them myself. If I could, I'd fight tooth and nail to keep them from him, to do *something* for Carrie at last. To be able to help her. She would never let me help her, she never wanted it. Sometimes it felt like she hated me, but I don't know why, Sophie, I don't . . . Because I loved that child *so* much. She was my *life.*'

Sophie was appalled to see a tear track its way through the powdery surface of Mrs Stiles's skin. She reached out a hand and touched her thin shoulder.

'I'm all right,' Mrs Stiles said, taking a step away from the gesture. She reached for her kettle with her right hand and filled it at the tap.

'Look,' Sophie said. 'Tess won't let him just walk off with them. I won't let him, I promise you. He can't anyway, there's all sorts of orders and things protecting them.'

She looked towards the living room as the girls marched in through the double doors, around the ancient coffee table and back out again. 'They don't even know he's coming yet.' She lowered her voice. 'Do they even know who he is?'

Mrs Stiles put two tea bags in a pot and watched the kettle boil.

'All they know is that he's never been there for them, not even when they needed him the most,' she said, picking the kettle up the moment it boiled and filling the pot to the brim. 'Carrie would never have a bad word said against him, but I told her – they should know. They should know what kind of a man he is.'

Sophie hesitated for a moment before asking Mrs Stiles the question she had really come to ask. 'Did Carrie tell *you* straight away that Louis had left her? Because, well – I didn't know.'

Mrs Stiles looked sharply at her. 'She never told you?'

Sophie shook her head.

'No,' Mrs Stiles continued. 'She didn't even tell me after the christening. I dare say she never would have told me at all if it had been up to her. But she started having money trouble. I know she didn't want to ask me for help, but she had no choice. She needed some money to keep her going with the mortgage repayments until she could start this new full-time job she'd got. Of course I asked what Louis was doing to get them out of trouble and that's when it all came out. He'd been gone nearly a year before she told me.'

Mrs Stiles gazed into the distance as she reflected on the memory. 'When she was a little girl, the age of those two out there, we were such good friends. So happy, you know. I wish . . . I wish I hadn't let everything that happened between me and her father come between us. After he went I was so hurt, so angry. Not just at him but at everything. We were never that close again. I knew I was pushing her away but I couldn't seem to stop myself. I always thought there'd be time to make things right one day. I was wrong. And now these two will be off with Louis and I won't have any time with them either.'

Sophie reached out and squeezed Mrs Stiles's arm.

'Please,' Sophie said. 'Try not to worry. Look, I'll pop out the front now and call Tess. Once I've told her, she'll know what to do, OK?'

'Don't be long,' Mrs Stiles said stiffly, pouring milk into a jug. 'Your tea will stew.'

For some reason, perhaps because Sophie had lost track of what day it was, she had assumed that social workers were on call seven days a week, but it appeared that Tess was not available on a Saturday afternoon after all. Her mobile was switched off and her work number rang off the hook. Unable to produce anything to reassure both Mrs Stiles and herself, Sophie sighed. Noticing her breath in the cold air she took a surreptitious look left and right, reached for the packet of Marlboro Lights she had managed to buy on yesterday's shopping trip at the same time as buying the girls a king-size Snickers bar each, and smoked one quickly, stubbing the butt out under the toe of her shoe and bending to scoop it up, slipping it into her pocket and taking a few more deep breaths of cold air before she went back in. Her temples throbbed as she tried to work out all the implications of what might happen next, and she felt a kind of hollow worry gnawing away at her from the inside out.

Sophie had the strangest sensation that she had felt exactly like this once before, standing in the cold watching the heat of her breath cool in the air, letting the tips of her toes freeze rather than move her body into the next moment and the moment after that when things would never be the same again. It was a sense of déjà vu that was as strong and as jolting as the memory triggered by a smell or a photo.

It didn't take long to place the memory. It had been at her father's funeral. Sophie had been standing in her best black shoes by the little pile of autumn flowers the crematorium had arranged for him in one corner of the courtyard. Friends and family had milled there for a while shaking hands and avoiding eye contact, not really knowing what to say to each other, until the modest crowd had drifted off and headed back towards the cars in preparation for the wake. That empty, worrying sensation had occurred just before Sophie finally realised what had happened. She had been standing beside a wreath of flowers with a card that read 'To Dad, miss you so much' when the pain, the shock and the horrific knowledge that loving her dad wouldn't mean anything ever again had rooted her to the spot and engulfed her.

She had been unable to move. She had stood watching everybody else leave. After a few seconds Carrie had noticed Sophie was not among the group and had come back to fetch her.

'Come on,' she had said, her cheeks rosy from the cold. 'It's freezing.'

'He's gone,' Sophie had said, staring at Carrie. 'Nothing's ever going to be the same now.'

'That's not true.' Carrie had hooked her arm through Sophie's. 'We'll stay the same, you and me. We will always stay the same, I promise. Always. For ever. Whatever. Right?'

So Sophie recognised the way she was feeling now. She knew it was exactly how she had been feeling on the day she had said goodbye to her dad just before the pain got too much and the walls came down between her and the hurt. And Sophie knew at last that Carrie had been wrong, and she had been right.

Nothing ever stays the same.

When Sophie finally went back inside she was entirely unprepared for what she saw next, but at least it lifted her from the complicated coil of her thoughts.

Actually it wasn't so much what she saw, which was Mrs Stiles sitting on the sofa flanked by the two girls, their respective heads leaning sweetly on each of her shoulders as the ensemble rocked from side to side. It was what she heard. The old lady and two small girls were singing 'Motorcycle Emptiness' by the Manic Street Preachers as if it were some kind of raucous lullaby, with Bella and Izzy filling in for the thunderous guitar solo with enthusiastic 'Nee, nee, nee-nee neeeows'.

Certainly Sophie thought she'd never live to see the day that Mrs Stiles sang hard-core political Welsh Rock, although she did change some of the more controversial lyrics for propriety's sake. Still, as unorthodox as the rendition was, it sparked an unexpectedly vivid memory which came thundering back to Sophie just as the sound of the girls' version of the guitar riff suddenly became real again in her ears.

It was summer. She and Carrie were more or less eighteen. Still so close that they felt they would always mean as much to each other as they did on that day, that it would be impossible for them to drift apart. It had been just a few weeks before Carrie was due to leave for university and it would be another week or so before Sophie would get her entry-level job at McCarthy Hughes. In reality they were about to take their first steps in completely opposite directions.

They were in the park, Sophie with her brand new portable CD player that weighed a ton. They'd just bought the new Manic Street Preachers CD from Our Price on Upper Street and they were sitting on the grass listening to it, turning up the volume on the CD player as loud as it would go – which wasn't very loud. Dressed entirely in black, they looked especially cross and sullen because that seemed the most appropriate expression for listening to the Manic Street Preachers, who were, it seemed, quite cross and sullen about most things. But when 'Motorcycle Emptiness' had come on Sophie had been unable to stop herself from humming along under her breath and tapping her bare toes against the rough grass in time to the catchy tune. Carrie had maintained her scowl as she studied the CD's sleeve.

'Yeah, too fucking right, Sylvia,' she had said aloud.

'Sorry, who?' Sophie had said looking over her shoulder, a little slow because just at that moment she had been wondering what the chances were of her getting James Dean Bradfield to sleep with her and if he did what the chances were of him being cheered up by it and if he was would she still fancy him so much as his sullen good looks were at least half of his appeal.

'Sylvia Plath, dummy.' Carrie had rolled her

eyes. 'On the cover under the title of "Motorcycle Emptiness" there's a line of her poetry, about God. About there being no God, to be precise.' Carrie had read Sophie the line which she couldn't quite remember now, but which she knew she hadn't really 'got'. Sophie had blinked at her friend from behind her shades.

'You are such a pleb,' Carrie had said. 'And anyway James Dean Bradfield wouldn't sleep with you, you're too middle class.'

Carrie had sighed and flopped back onto the grass. 'There is no God, Soph. There is no order or truth, nothing in the world is fair or just. You have to fight for everything you want in this world because no-one will give it to you. Not even God. Especially not God.'

Sophie had sat up and looked closely at Carrie. She realised that her usually effortlessly cheerful friend wasn't feigning anger. She was genuinely furious.

'What's up?' Sophie had said simply.

'It's Mum, isn't it? It's always Mum. Nothing I do is good enough for her. She's never just proud of me. She's never just happy for me. And now this course I've got onto – even that's not good enough. Never mind it's one of the most com-petitive art courses in the country. She wants me to change to something more academic, like history. She's my mum but she doesn't even know me. She knows nothing about me – why can't she just support me for once instead of throwing flipping God in my face every five minutes and trying to control everything I do? I just want to be me. I can't wait until I can get as far away from her as possible and have my *own* life, a normal happy family life and be free of her for good.' Carrie had shaken her head as if an angry wasp had somehow got inside it.

'She's not that bad,' Sophie had said. 'I think she's going to miss you. She's just scared about you going.'

'I know. So why is she doing her best to make me so keen to leave?'

Sophie had shrugged. 'I don't know, Carrie. Your mum is even weirder than mine.'

'Well, I'll tell you one thing,' Carrie had said. 'From this moment on I'm never doing anything I don't want to do. I'm never going to miss another chance, another experience or feeling. I'm going to take everything I can out of life and whenever I forget or feel like I can't be bothered or look like I might be turning into Mum – God forbid – I'm going to play this song to remind me. A song about living life to the full.'

They'd both paused and listened to the exhilarating guitar riff once again.

'Actually I think it's about political apathy and oppression,' Sophie had said.

'Yeah, I know,' Carrie had said, winking at her. 'But it's got a rocking good chorus.'

★   ★   ★

It took a few more seconds for the trio to repeat to fade but when they had finished, and Izzy had covered her face and giggled and Bella had kissed her grandma's cheek with no-nonsense firmness, Mrs Stiles did seem to be a little happier and more calm.

'You should be on TV,' Sophie said, applauding gently.

'It was Carrie's favourite song,' Mrs Stiles said. 'A load of old rubbish of course, but she and the girls sang it all the time.'

'Not all the time,' Bella corrected her, with her usual passion for total accuracy. 'It's our cheering-up song. I don't really know what it means but . . .'

'It's got a rocking good chorus?' Sophie said. Bella nodded and smiled.

Sophie felt more or less in control as she walked the girls to the bus stop, her equilibrium restored after the gathering tide of feeling that had threatened to breach her defences at Mrs Stiles's house. She felt as if she knew how to deal with Louis now, as if somehow Carrie had told her. She knew she couldn't shut the door on him, because she had been the one to open it. She had to let him in for the girls' sake, and that what was best for them was the most important thing. This might be their only chance to know their father; she couldn't stand in the way of that. But she also knew that they needed someone to support them as they got to know him and as the possibilities of a future with him opened up. They'd need someone if, as Mrs Stiles predicted, fatherhood got too much for him and he decided he couldn't take the children on after all. They needed another option.

Ever since Sophie had spoken to Louis on the phone she had felt doubly angry with him. She was angry with him for going, she was angry with him for coming back. It was an impossible way to feel but somehow she couldn't let it go. None of this should have been her responsibility. If he had been at home looking after his family, then maybe *none* of this would have happened. Maybe Carrie would still be alive two hundred miles away, just a phone call out of reach.

When Sophie tried to imagine what effect Louis's return would have there were all sorts of obstacles, all sorts of corners that she couldn't see round, but she knew one thing. Their atheist mother had made her their godmother for a reason, to stand by them in times of need, and Sophie was going to do it. Not because she had to, she discovered as they waited at the bus stop, but because she wanted to. And she wanted to not only for the children, whom she had gradually started to admire and even like, but for Carrie, whom she was slowly beginning to miss from the outside in, like a spring thaw. Sophie was missing her friend – fierce, strong and independent Carrie, who had been her best friend once, on that sunny afternoon in Highbury lying on the grass, playing the air guitar.

Carrie, who was more alive to her now than she had been for years.

It was almost dark when they got back to the flat. The pale winter sun had sunk beneath the bare branches of the tree tops that laced the horizon, leaving the cold grey sky with a faint amber glow. Sophie stopped by her much-missed black Golf with cream leather interior and patted it fondly. And then she had an idea. She thought about the dog book and the chapter she had read on puppy carsickness. She thought about her CD collection which was spread over the footwell of the passenger seat and which contained the Manic Street Preachers' greatest hits.

'This is my car,' she said to Izzy.

Izzy looked at the car.

'She's got a name – can you guess what it is?'

Izzy blinked at the car. 'Car?' she said after a moment.

Sophie shook her head. 'It's Phoebe.' Of course the car hadn't ever had a name in its life. Sophie only loved her Golf because it did a ton down the M25 and still felt like it was cruising. 'She told me last night that she's lonely and she knows you don't want to go for a ride in her or anything like that, but she wondered if you fancied just sitting in her for a bit because it would really cheer her up.'

Izzy's face became deadly serious. 'No thank you, Phoebe,' she said.

The main difference between three-year-olds and

dogs, Sophie realised, was that three-years-olds talk back. 'Never give up until you've cleared that first hurdle,' the dog book said, so Sophie persisted, seriously worried that she had made a rod for her own back. She opened Phoebe's rear passenger door and nodded at Bella to get in. 'Well, how about if Bella sits in the back and I sit in the passenger seat here, like this' – Sophie opened the front passenger door and perched on the seat sideways – 'with my feet on the pavement and you sit on my lap? That would cheer Phoebe up no end.'

'That's a good idea,' Bella said, climbing in and sitting on the edge of the seat, her legs dangling over the side.

Izzy remained motionless, standing on the pavement and, although she was less than a foot away, she suddenly seemed almost out of reach.

'I was in the car with Mummy,' she said in a low voice. 'And there was a big bang and I was a bit shaken up, wasn't I?'

Sophie bit her lip. 'I know,' she said.

'And Mummy went out of the car.' And she hasn't come back yet. Is she coming back?'

Sophie felt the waters close over her head and suddenly realised what the term 'out of your depth' really meant. She had been prepared for crying and tantrums and holding of breath, but she hadn't been prepared for this. She looked over her shoulder at Bella, who sat perfectly still, her mouth and chin tucked into the neck of her coat, her eyes downcast.

'No, Izzy,' Sophie said after a moment, because there was no other answer. 'Mummy isn't coming back. Not because she doesn't love you or Bella or want to be with you but because she's gone now to be in the sky and the stars—' Sophie stopped, because she realised that as Izzy took everything she said quite literally, she was now squinting up at the sky looking for stars that had been blotted out by the city's orange glow.

'But I know one thing,' Sophie said, regaining Izzy's attention. 'Mummy wouldn't want you to be scared of anything because you are such a very brave girl and I know you don't want Phoebe to be sad, do you? So why don't you come and sit on my lap and we'll sing "Motorcycle Emptiness", OK?'

Izzy looked confused.

'She means "The Little Car" song,' Bella said out of the half-dark. 'We used to sing it a lot in the morning in our Mini on the way to school.'

'"The Little Car" song,' Sophie repeated.

Izzy took a step forward and climbed awkwardly onto Sophie's knees, winding her fist into Sophie's hair for support. She looked around the interior of the car. 'Ready, Phoebe?' she asked the car.

'Vroom, vroom, ready,' Sophie said in a gravelly voice.

Izzy started humming first and then Bella, who was the only one who knew all the words – or at least Carrie's version of the words – chimed in. Awkwardly at first, Sophie joined in here and there.

Gradually the mumbles and humming grew louder and louder until they finished the song on a rowdy crescendo.

'Yay!' Sophie said, applauding with her arms still around Izzy's middle.

Izzy smiled. 'Did you like that, Phoebe?' she said. 'Do you feel all better now, car?'

'Vrooom, yes I do,' Sophie said in her new-found car voice. And to think only last week she was chairing meetings of international import in boardrooms. Still, needs must. 'Do you want to come for a ride with me next time? Um . . . vrooom?'

Izzy climbed off Sophie's lap and hopped back onto the pavement. 'No thank you, Phoebe,' she said. 'But I will come and see you again soon. I promise.'

Sophie's downstairs neighbour emerged from the communal front door and walked briskly down the steps just as Izzy squeaked, 'Please let us go in now, we are ever so cold,' with Dickensian feebleness. The neighbour cast Sophie a chilly look over her shoulder and headed off to her Saturday night yoga class.

Izzy was already in bed waiting for Bella to tell her the next part of her story when Bella came into the kitchen for some fresh water. Sophie refilled her glass.

'That was a good idea today, Aunty Sophie. With the car I mean. I think you helped Izzy a bit.' Bella said.

Sophie looked at her and, with a surge of new-found confidence concerning child/dog psychology, asked her a question. 'Listen – are you OK? Because you know if you wanted to talk about your mum . . . or your dad even . . .'

'I'm fine,' Bella said. She took the glass carefully out of Sophie's hand, her expression completely neutral.

'Look, Bella,' Sophie began. 'All I'm saying is that . . .'

'I'm fine, Aunty Sophie,' Bella said, smiling just to prove it, a wide, teeth-revealing, mirthless grin. 'Come on, it's the pen-ult-i-mate part of my story tonight.' She used the word she had heard the BBC continuity announcer say earlier with consider-able care.

'OK,' Sophie said. 'That sounds exciting.'

About half an hour later, thrilled and relieved that Blossom the fairy pony looked like she would make it back to her home with the mermaids by the sea after all, Sophie went back into the living room and fished the dog book out from under-neath some cushions. Artemis came out of the kitchen and gave her a passing glance before curling up on her chair, turning her back on Sophie just to ensure she didn't make any more reckless stroking attempts.

'What do you reckon, Artemis?' Sophie asked the cat's back as she flicked aimlessly through the pages. 'Do you think there's anything in here about telling your abandoned puppy that Daddy's coming back?'

Of course there wasn't, so Sophie threw the book on the floor and stared up at the ceiling. He was coming, so she had to tell them. But how? Then Sophie had, in her opinion, a quite brilliant idea.

Tess could tell them.

With that settled, she began the chapter on nutrition. It told her that chocolate can be fatal to dogs.

'Thank Christ we're not dogs, hey, Artemis?' Sophie said.

Artemis did not dignify the comment with a response.

CHAPTER 12

Tess sighed and looked out of the window. Sophie, who usually enjoyed the winter because it was much more sensible than the summer and gave a girl scope for much better clothes, was not enjoying the end of January because the sun persisted in shining in crisp blue skies day after day. Sophie was not a fan of sunshine. It seemed to give people an excuse to wear far fewer clothes than suited them, turn up late for work, take weeks and weeks off at a time and dawdle about being wistful over some romantic liaison or another. She had hoped for a typical wet and gloomy English winter. But no, the sun kept shining, interfering with people's moods and, worse still, their daytime TV viewing. She was glad she had blackout curtains because she didn't know what she would have done without the TV in the last few weeks. TV, Sophie had decided in the small dark hours of the night, was the world's greatest invention, topping out the wheel, antibiotics and, yes, even the peep-toed sandal.

Tess sighed again.

'You seem a bit pissed off to be here, actually,' Sophie said with an edge of recrimination.

Tess pursed her lips at her. 'Well,' she said with a slow blink, 'it is Sunday. A day recognised in many cultures to be one of rest. But as the many messages you left me were so adamant that you had to see me – here I am. At your service.' Tess was making no attempt to hide the irritation in her voice, which Sophie felt was frankly rather unprofessional.

'Yes, well, you want to try having two kids in your house. Rest? What's rest? There are no days of rest round here,' she said, raising a now rather bushy eyebrow. She beckoned Tess into the kitchen and pushed the door to.

'So you'll want to know why I've asked you here today,' Sophie said.

'I can hardly bear the tension,' Tess replied dourly. 'Look, if you want to tell me you've changed your mind about keeping the girls until we get Louis then just tell me. That foster place has gone now so I'll need all the notice I can to . . .'

'How long did you say it would take your lot to find Louis?' Sophie asked, regretting the absence of a spotlight to shine in Tess's eyes.

'Well, you know.' Tess looked uncomfortable. 'A couple of weeks – three or four at the most.'

'Yes, that is what you told me,' Sophie said. 'Funny that, because you told Mrs Stiles it would take *months*.'

Tess was momentarily flustered. 'Ah well, yes. Because that was what *she* wanted to hear. I promise you, we have done our best,' she protested feebly. 'As much as resources and time will allow. And you know . . .' she faltered under Sophie's stony glare, 'I can assure you that every possible undertaking has been . . . er . . . undertaken to—'

'So,' Sophie cut across her. 'You're in the business of telling people what they want to hear rather than the truth are you, Tess? You tell Mrs Stiles it will take months so she doesn't have to worry about Louis stealing her grandchildren away, and me that it's a matter of days so that I'll be your free babysitter. How is that ethical?'

'Look . . .' Tess began. 'It's a question of priorities and I genuinely did think it wouldn't take long to find Louis – but all things being equal, allowing for administration difficulties and intergovernmental authorities' communication . . .'

'It's all right, you can cut all the social-worker speak. You don't have to look for Louis flipping Gregory,' Sophie said, enjoying her moment.

'I don't?' Tess said, blinking.

'No you don't, because I've found him. Or rather a private detective I hired did. It took two weeks. It was easy, actually.' Sophie found that she had to press her lips together in order to prevent herself from sticking her tongue out and going 'na-na-na-na' at Tess, Izzy-style. 'He's coming back to "get his girls" apparently.' Sophie did a passable

211

impression of his deep and slightly gruff voice. 'As if he owned them or something.'

'Oh,' Tess said again, feeling horribly shamed by the younger woman. 'Well, that does change things.'

'Yes it does a bit, doesn't it? So, do you want to tell me now why you lied about finding Louis or shall we save it for another time? Perhaps for a formal complaints hearing?' Sophie said icily. 'Because I don't mind telling you I thought you were supposed to tell the truth. I thought it was in your job description.'

Tess screwed up her mouth into a tight knot. 'I did tell you the truth, mostly. Look, they needed a place to stay and you seemed to think it was important that Louis might be back on the scene soon – so I let you draw your own conclusions. The point is . . .'

'My own conclusions!' Sophie raised her voice and then, remembering the children in the next room, took a deep breath and lowered it again. 'You lied to me. That's misconduct, probably.'

Tess paused before answering. 'The point is, I did what I thought was best for Izzy and Bella. And I didn't lie. Not exactly.' She smiled tentatively at Sophie. 'I know you want what's best for those children as much as I do. Don't you?'

Sophie considered the question and found that she did. 'Of course I do,' she said, glancing out of the kitchen window and over the row upon row of rooftops and TV antennae that made up the cluttered horizon. She looked back at Tess and gave her a conciliatory half-smile. 'OK,' she said. 'Let's forget that – for now. What is important is that you do your job.'

'Of course it is,' Tess said, determined not to be offended.

'You have to vet Louis, make sure that he's fit to be a father to those girls. You have to check and double-check everything he's been up to for the past three years.'

'Of course,' Tess said. 'It goes without saying.'

'And what if they don't like him – what then?'

Tess didn't waver. 'We have to try our best to reconcile them; we will reconcile them.'

Sophie nodded. There it was again – that absence of a decent Option B.

'And I thought it would be better coming from you,' Sophie said quickly, breaking eye contact with Tess.

'What would?' Tess asked her.

'The news – you know, about Louis coming home.' Sophie glanced sideways at her. 'You're trained to do that kind of thing, aren't you? Explain stuff like absent fathers and all that.'

Tess sighed, realising it was the least she could do. 'Right,' she said. 'Will you be there too?'

Sophie rolled her eyes. 'Obviously.' Admittedly, it had only just become obvious to her. A strange thing had happened to her in the last twenty-four hours, something she hadn't expected. When she thought about the girls and about what the future might hold for them, her stomach churned and she felt a deep sense of unease, as if the world she had once stood on so firmly was tilting and swaying. She wondered if for the first time in her life she was having an actual gut feeling about Louis Gregory. Perhaps her rarely utilised feminine intuition did indeed exist deep within her after all, and now it was kicking in and telling her to be cautious.

So before Tess arrived Sophie had sat on the loo for a long time (just in case it was indigestion) and concentrated on the feeling. It had, she realised, taken her an amazingly short time to feel totally responsible for Carrie's children. She concluded that the churning of her stomach was genuine fear. She knew that somehow she would have an impact on how they were going to live the rest of their lives and that it would be down to her, at least partially, whether or not they were happy. Sophie closed her eyes and tried to make a picture of Carrie the last time she had seen her, boarding that train at Paddington station, until she could see her smiling at her – sitting on the loo with her eyes shut, Sophie smiled back.

She couldn't say that she loved the girls, because she wasn't exactly sure what that felt like. But she realised that gradually she had begun to feel something for them, an almost new emotion that she had only ever experienced once before when she saw Artemis alone in a pen at the shelter. It was a strong and immovable impulse to protect them from anything harmful. She knew then she had to guarantee they were going to be OK, that she would have to do whatever it took to ensure their happiness.

'Look,' Tess said. 'I promise you absolutely that I won't let you or the girls down. I'll put Louis through every mill going and until then . . .'

'Until then,' Sophie said, almost casually as she redirected her gaze at the urban horizon, 'those girls aren't going anywhere.'

CHAPTER 13

'I need a couple of minutes,' Sophie told Tess, patting her red-hot cheeks which she knew had flared up during their conversation.

'OK, you go and take some deep breaths, and then – well, we'd better tell them, hadn't we?' Tess said, biting hard on her lip.

Sophie nodded and slipped past the girls, who had lost interest in the *EastEnders* omnibus and were in the process of making a camp out of the sofa and chair and Sophie's full-length leather coat. They both paused, standing stock-still like a couple of meerkats expecting to be pounced on at any second by an enraged predator, but Sophie barely glanced at her coat and offered them an absent smile as she headed to her bedroom.

'Right, now all we need is some tent pegs,' she vaguely heard Bella say as she shut her bedroom door. She sat on her bed and stared across at the dressing-table mirror. She thought about using her red-patches-green-cover-up-stick-thing but it had disappeared recently, quite probably another casualty of Izzy's apocalyptic attack on her make-up bag. Instead she picked up a spray can of deodorant and held its cool, smooth surface against first one cheek and then the other.

As she sat on the bed Sophie noticed a corner of pale pink material peeping out of her tightly shut wardrobe. She opened the door, still clutching the deodorant to her face, and pulled the trapped garment free. It was a new dress that she had bought just after Christmas in the no-man's-land between then and New Year. She had bought it at the full price of £359, even though she knew that less than a week later it would inevitably be half the price, because she had fallen in love with it instantly and because there was only one in her size. She'd made a mental note not to go back to that shop until at least April in case she saw how much the reduction was. Sophie didn't normally spend so much on dresses – although to be fair she needed party dresses a lot more than most people – but for some reason that dress, with its Twenties-style soft pink chiffon shift sliding over its deep-pink silk underslip, had appealed to the closet romantic in her. She loved the four tiny velvet-covered buttons at the scoop neck and the extravagant beadwork, hundreds of them radiating out from the princess-line waist and flaring into a handkerchief hemline. It was the kind of dress girls wore in musicals when dancing with their true love for the first time under the light of the silvery moon. And it was very flattering around the hips and bum.

Sophie had been secretly looking forward to

wearing it this week at the Madison Corporation's New Year's party that she had been so painstakingly organising for Jake, and before Jake had announced quite plainly that he was attracted to her she had been looking forward to him seeing her wearing it, and wondering whether it would make him notice her as a *woman*.

Unlike most corporate seasonal parties the Madison bash didn't fall on or as near to the actual holiday as possible, when nobody would really want to come anyway, but had been scheduled, rather cleverly Sophie thought mainly because it was her idea, at almost the end of January. Jake wanted it to be extravagant, a flagship event, and Sophie had made sure that it was going to be just that. It was Cal, though, who had found a venue which could make that requirement literally come true: a full-on, top-class ocean liner that was docked at Tower Bridge for a week every two months, with a full-scale ballroom and superlative catering staff who were occasionally available for hire at the right price. Guests could even book a berth to stay in for the night.

Ever since Cal had discovered it they had both been waiting for the right client with the right budget to book it, too afraid to tell anyone in case someone else took the credit. The Madison Corporation was that client, and it was going to be magical. It was the first party in ages that Sophie had actually been excited about.

Unconsciously she marked out the passing of

218

time by the events she organised, and by what she wore to them. That dress had been hanging in her wardrobe, silently ticking like a kind of alarm clock, counting down the humdrum routine days until something different and mildly thrilling happened.

Now, she realised, the bright pinnacle in her diary for weeks and weeks didn't really matter any more. It might boost her promotion chances, Jake would still be impressed by her looking blonde and lightly fake-tanned in dusty pink. But the excitement of wearing a floaty dress and matching satin shoes had faded. Sophie fingered the edge of the material and took a breath as she hung the dress back in her wardrobe.

'Never mind,' she told herself, patting her considerably cooled cheeks. 'It won't be long before frocks and parties are the highlight of your life again.' Except that as she padded back to the living room where she heard Tess and the girls laughing, she had to admit she wasn't exactly sure if she wanted that to be true.

Tess had positioned the girls side by side in Artemis's armchair, wriggling and elbowing each other reflexively. As Sophie had left her bedroom Artemis appeared through the open window and slunk past her, taking up her new favourite position on the arm of the chair by Bella's side. She ducked and tilted her head for Bella, who scratched behind her ears obligingly, and gave Sophie her usual glare.

'Well, here we are,' Tess said, beaming at the girls.

It was exactly the same smile that she had given Sophie just before announcing Carrie's death. Tess really had to work on her delivering-important-news face, Sophie thought. She made it look like you were about to find out that you'd somehow won the lottery even though you never played, not that your world was about to be tipped upside down – again. Bella knows, Sophie thought, watching the girl narrow her dark eyes at Tess. She recognises that smile.

'You two have had a lot to cope with, haven't you, in the last few months?' Tess's smile widened.

'Yes we have!' Izzy sang in agreement, assuming her grown-up face.

Bella nodded and crossed her arms.

Sophie looked at each girl's expression and felt the now more familiar tightening in her chest.

'I know you've been moved about a lot, one place to another, and I know that . . .' Tess paused and rubbed her knees with the palms of her hands, making a rasping noise over her tights. 'I know that you must miss Mummy very much.'

'I do,' Izzy said sadly, her narrow shoulders slumping. 'But she can't come back, because Aunty Sophie said she was in the sky which is very far.'

Bella put her spare arm around Izzy's shoulders, pushing her slightly deeper into the cushion of the chair with the weight of her embrace.

'And you have both been very brave and very

good. Aunty Sophie has told me how *especially* good you've been since you came to stay with her.'

Sophie, Bella and Izzy all looked at Tess with open-mouthed disbelief.

'Well, mainly good, anyway,' Tess said, hurrying along. 'And you like it here, don't you?'

'I like the telly,' Izzy said, brightening a little. 'And I used to like chicken nuggets but I don't any more. I think I'd like fish fingers next and carrots. We used to have carrots, didn't we, Bella?' Bella nodded again. 'Orange food is my favourite, actually,' Izzy finished.

'Tess,' Sophie said, under her breath, 'just get to the point.'

'So girls,' Tess said, reinstating her beam. 'Do you remember your daddy?'

'No,' Bella said quickly. 'We don't.'

'I don't,' Izzy agreed. 'I haven't got a daddy, have I?' she asked with genuine curiosity. 'Or a grandpa? Or . . . a dog?'

'Well, actually, Izzy, you have – got a daddy I mean.'

Izzy's face transformed into a picture of pure delight and surprise which would have moved Sophie, if she hadn't seen her use exactly the same expression when confronted with a pair of her damp pants that she'd cunningly slipped behind one of the remaining sofa cushions the last time she hadn't quite made it to the loo.

'Oooh Bella – we're getting a daddy!' she said, drumming her heels against the base of the armchair.

'No we're not, Iz. Our dad's not around any

more. He left home when *she* was a baby,' Bella said carefully to Tess, jerking her head sideways at her sister.

'Well, yes, I know, darling,' Tess said. 'But guess what? Your daddy is coming back to see you! And *maybe* if you want it, girls, you might go and live with your daddy!' Tess clapped her hands together and Izzy jumped off the armchair and began spinning.

'Hoo-*ray*! Hoo-*ray*! Hooo-*ray*!' she shouted as she pirouetted.

'NO HE IS NOT!' Bella stood up and shouted over her sister so that the younger girl stopped and stood stock-still. 'HE IS NOT COMING BACK HERE AND I DON'T WANT TO SEE HIM AND SHE DOESN'T WANT TO SEE HIM AND WE DON'T WANT HIM SO IF HE COMES HERE YOU CAN JUST TELL HIM TO GO AWAY AGAIN BECAUSE NOBODY LIKES HIM OR WANTS HIM!' She ran out of the room, slamming first the living-room and then the flat door behind her.

'Oh fuck,' Sophie said, leaping over the back of the sofa after her with an athleticism she hadn't known she possessed.

Tess looked at Izzy, who returned her gaze anxiously, still standing perfectly still. After a moment she unfroze herself and crossed over to Tess, putting her hands on Tess's knees.

'She's not supposed to say fuck in front of us, is she?'

Mercifully Bella had not opened the main front door onto the street and run under a bus, as Sophie had momentarily feared. She breathed a sigh of relief when she saw her huddled at the bottom of the stairs, and walked slowly down to join her.

'Are you OK?' she asked.

'Yes,' Bella lied badly, her voice slightly muffled by a layer of purple fleece.

Sophie brushed a lock of Bella's black hair away from her cheek and tucked it behind her ear.

'I'm sorry, I knew it would be a shock and every-thing but I thought you'd be pleased . . .' This was true. She had just assumed the girls would leap into Louis's arms, whether or not he was decent father material. It had never occurred to her that they might not want him.

'I'm not pleased,' Bella said, turning her face a little so that Sophie could see one eye and half of her mouth.

Hesitantly Sophie reached out and rubbed Bella's back. 'I can see that,' she said with a half-smile. 'But well, do you remember your dad at all, Bella?'

Bella sat up and brushed her hair out of her face a few times. 'Yes,' she said darkly. 'I was a bit older than Izzy when he . . . he just went.'

Sophie tried to frame the million or so ques-tions she had into one that was manageable for a girl of six and a bit.

'Well, was he unkind to you or to Mummy, was

he mean? Did he ever . . . hurt you?' Sophie asked carefully, not exactly knowing or wanting to know just what she was asking. To her huge relief Bella shook her head.

'No, but he went away, didn't he? He left us all alone. He didn't come back. He didn't even say goodbye to me and I thought . . . I thought he was my friend. He used to say I was his best friend. After that Mum said we didn't need him, we didn't need any man to look after us because we looked after each other – we were the three musketeers.' Bella stared at her knees.

Sophie tried again. 'I know that this must be hard, Bella, but, well . . . he is coming all this way to see you – that must mean something. And when I told him . . .'

'*You* told him?' Bella said quickly, looking up at Sophie.

'Yes,' Sophie confessed. 'When I told him what had happened he said he'd come straight away.' She pushed her own misapprehensions to one side. 'So he must care about you to do that, mustn't he?' Bella didn't move so Sophie continued. 'And well, you are going to need a proper place to live soon and I just thought it would be better if it was with . . .'

'We've got a proper place.' Bella stared at Sophie, a deep furrow slotted between her brows.

Sophie blinked at her and winced internally. She hadn't expected this.

'We live here, don't we?' Bella asked quietly.

'With you? You said at that childminder's we could stay with you.'

Sophie took her hand away from Bella's shoulder and dropped her head. It hadn't occurred to her that Bella might have thought her stay in the flat was anything other than temporary, and that her promise at the childminder's was more general than specific.

'Aren't we staying here with you?' Bella said, looking worried. 'Have we done something wrong again? I know we're naughty sometimes but it's usually by accident and—'

Sophie shook her head, and felt her chest tighten again.

'It's not because you're naughty,' she told Bella gently. 'Look, Bella, right now I don't know what's going to happen next because so much has happened already that I never expected. But you have to know that when you came here it was only supposed to be for a week or two . . .' She stopped. 'You're not supposed to live with me for ever. You wouldn't want to live in my silly little flat with no garden now, would you?'

'I wouldn't mind. Will we have to move again?' Bella's voice dwindled away to almost nothing.

Sophie looked at her tiny frame, so stiff and resilient, and she wanted to say something, anything to make her feel happier and more secure. But she couldn't lie to her, not now. She and Izzy deserved the truth.

'Yes,' Sophie said softly. 'I'm sorry, Bella.'

'With who then?' Bella's face was ashen under the bright hall lighting, her voice small and feather light. 'With Dad? Strangers like the childminder?'

Sophie cursed herself inwardly. Just when she thought she was getting the hang of communicating with Bella she went and put her foot in it. She felt her total ineptitude all too keenly.

'All you've been through – it must be so hard for you, Bella,' she said eventually, sidestepping her question. 'I think you're amazing – you cope so well when you must miss your mum so much.'

'I don't miss her,' Bella said. 'I can't miss her. I haven't got time you see, because everything keeps changing and just when I think it's going to be OK it changes again and I have to get used to all new things and be in charge of worrying about what's going to happen to us. Mummy told me that I was in charge when she wasn't around, of looking after Izzy, I mean. I think . . .' Bella paused for a long moment. 'If I start thinking about her and missing her I'm afraid I won't be in charge any more – I'll be too sad and then I'll forget to do anything else.'

Sophie pulled Bella to her, impulsively wishing that she could physically draw all the pain out of her small body and absorb it. It was the first time she had hugged her god-daughter.

'I do see,' she said, thinking about the first months after her dad had died. 'I really do. But you know what? You don't have to be in charge. I know you feel like you do – but you don't. You've got Tess and Grandma and me, even Artemis, to do all the worrying and the looking after for you and Izzy. If you want to be sad you won't be letting anyone down. Your mum wouldn't think so, not for a second.' Sophie paused for a moment and thought very carefully about what she was about to say. 'I don't know your dad, Bella, I don't know why he went and I don't know why he didn't keep in touch with you, but I do think you sort of have to give him a chance. Because he is your dad and you said he used to be your friend.'

'But what if he's horrible to us?'

'Well, if he is then you don't have to live with him. You don't have to do anything you and Izzy aren't happy with, OK? Everyone is here to make sure that you and Izzy are happy and safe.'

Bella looked up at Sophie, her dry eyes burning. 'But what will we do then?' She fixed Sophie with a stare. 'If we can't stay here?'

There had to be a moment like this, Sophie thought, in everyone's life when the very next thing you said could change you and the world as you knew it for ever. Sophie felt her stomach dip and churn as if she had just run headlong at a cliff edge, and had brought herself to a stop at its very brink.

'Then we'll work out what's best,' she said, feeling like a coward, unable to deliver the promise that Bella wanted.

'What's best?' Bella said dimly, staring down at her feet again.

'Yes.'

Bella sat up a little and lifted her chin to look at Sophie.

'OK,' she said with a look of weary resignation that should never have visited her young face. 'OK, Aunty Sophie.'

There had to be something, Sophie thought, some promise she could make to Bella and to Izzy that she absolutely knew she could keep. Some promise that could give the children something solid to rely on.

'Bella, I've been flaky, I know I have,' she said with a sigh. 'Dragging you to the office and back. Making you watch TV all day long, not knowing what to feed you and then just feeding you one thing, but please believe me when I say I want you to have the best and happiest life you can, I really, really do. And you just wouldn't have that with me – would you?' Bella blinked at her and said nothing. 'But I promise you – whatever happens I'll be on your side. I'll stick by you and Izzy. I'll never let you down. I promise – always, for ever, whatever.' Sophie said the three words on an impulse and sat back a little as Bella's eyes widened.

'How did you know?' she asked, resting her cheek against Sophie's arm with a sudden touching display of affection that Sophie had not expected. She felt Bella's breath on her skin and kissed the top of her head, and for a moment it seemed there was something physical connecting them, a new closeness created on this bottom stair. Sophie had never known how to kiss Bella before that moment, but suddenly it seemed perfectly natural.

'Know what?' Sophie said to the top of Bella's head.

'That's Mummy's special proper promise to us. Whenever she said "always, for ever, whatever" we knew – we knew that things were really, *really* true.'

'Well, then you know that you can trust me,' Sophie said, and Bella tightened their embrace.

It happened then, like a slow turning circle finally completing itself. Sophie now knew for certain that she was beginning to care more about what happened to Bella and Izzy than she cared about what happened to herself.

CHAPTER 14

'What, nothing at all?' Tess said, attempting to stir some life into her forlorn cup of machine coffee as she sat at her desk. 'Nothing. Not a word,' Sophie told her over the phone, sitting on what used to be her bed, looking at her reflection in the mirror and wondering if that was facial hair shadowing her top lip or just a trick of the light. 'I mean, it's been . . .' She unfurled a finger for each day since she had spoken to Louis. 'Saturday, Sunday, Monday, Tuesday – Wednesday. Five days if you count today. It doesn't take five days to get anywhere any more unless you're walking. I mean, it's not as if he was in deepest darkest Per— Well anyway it doesn't take five days, does it?'

Tess sat back in her chair and twirled it from left to right. 'No, I wouldn't have thought so,' she said. 'But I suppose there are other considerations. Maybe he had to give notice at the charity—' Sophie barked a short laugh at the word charity. Tess waited a moment before continuing. '*Maybe* he couldn't get a flight or the money for a flight – have you thought about calling him again?'

Sophie glossed over that rather obvious idea.

She didn't want to dial the number that had cost her £55 an hour plus VAT and talk to him because that would mean that he was still in deepest darkest Peru, which had implications she was aware of but not quite ready to think about fully yet.

'He said he was coming right away. He made it sound like he was going to leave that minute and get on a plane. And the girls are all on edge. Bella is really upset about the whole thing and Izzy goes mental every time the phone rings or the doorbell goes. It's been a nightmare keeping them occupied.'

Tess sank the lukewarm distant relative of caffeine in one gulp and grimaced. 'Well, TV does wear a bit thin after a while,' she said.

'We haven't just been watching TV, actually,' Sophie said resentfully. 'We've been to the park twice, the corner shop, Grandma Stiles *and* we sat in the car with the doors open and played CDs for a couple of hours.'

'And Izzy too?' Tess asked, genuinely impressed.

'Yes,' Sophie said with more than a hint of pride. 'Next time we're shutting Phoebe's doors and the time after that I might turn the engine on. We'll be on road trips before you know it.'

'Phoebe?' Tess enquired.

'Yes, Phoebe – that's the car's name,' Sophie said a little sheepishly.

'That's a really good idea,' Tess told her with naked astonishment.

'Thanks for your unwavering belief,' Sophie said wryly, neglecting to mention she got the idea out of the dog book. 'And they really like shopping so we've done quite a lot of that. We even went to the supermarket.'

'And I bet it was better than last time,' Tess said.

'No, it was a God-awful nightmare, but at least this time I knew what to expect so it wasn't so bad,' Sophie explained seriously. 'I think I'm building up a resistance to the horror. It's sort of like when you become an alcoholic and after a while it doesn't matter how much vodka you drink, it doesn't make you drunk any more.' Tess decided to leave that part out of her next report. 'All in all,' Sophie concluded, 'we've had a pretty good time.'

'That's really great,' Tess said. 'But listen . . .'

Sophie leaned a little closer to her dressing-table mirror and ran a finger along her top lip. Yes, it was definitely regrowth. A few more weeks of this and she'd qualify as a primate.

'Sophie?' Tess had been talking to her.

'Er . . . what did you say?' Sophie asked awkwardly.

'I *said*,' Tess sounded a little irritated, 'that we have to give the man every chance to do the right thing. I mean, that was big news you gave him. He might have needed a day or two to come to terms with it.'

'Oh, what – like I got, you mean?' Sophie said sulkily.

'You weren't married to Carrie,' Tess admonished her.

'No and neither was he for very long!' Sophie snapped.

Just at that moment the door buzzer vibrated through the flat with its insistent electronic rattle.

'It's the door, it's the door, it's the DOOR, IT'S THE DOOR!' Izzy's cries grew louder as she made her way from one side of the flat to the other.

'Oh shit, I've got to go. Izzy, don't open the flat door!' The sound of the flat door banging hard into the hall wall echoed in Tess's ears. 'I said don't you dare open the front door!' Tess heard Sophie call out.

'If it's him, ring me,' Tess said, but she realised she was talking to a dialling tone.

'Oh, it's you,' Izzy said, looking up at Cal.

Sophie arrived 0.01 seconds later, streaking past Bella who stalked into the bedroom and shut the door firmly behind her.

'What did I say about opening the front door?' Sophie asked Izzy, ignoring Cal for a moment.

'You said don't open the front door,' Izzy replied, looking up at her sweetly.

'And what have you just done?'

'I opened the front door!' Izzy said, slowly and carefully, as if it was obvious.

'But I said not to!' Sophie said, raising her voice a little and stamping her foot.

'I know! But it's not him anyway it's just *him*.' And Izzy flopped face down onto the doormat in one fluid movement and lay there perfectly still in – mercifully silent – protest.

Sophie, who had become used to this particular manoeuvre and had stopped worrying that Izzy was suffering from blackouts, looked up at Cal. 'Aren't you supposed to be individually testing thirty-eight thousand fairy lights for the Madison party?' she asked with a tight smile.

'Couldn't be arsed,' Cal said dryly. He looked down at Izzy. 'I have to say, Izzy, I thought you'd be more pleased to see a man with an Animal Park Play Set.' Izzy did not move.

'Animal Park doesn't match up to her daddy,' Sophie told him, worrying about how much the three-year-old had invested in the appearance of her father. She had thought Izzy might just forget about it once it was mentioned. But she didn't – the arrival of Louis seemed to be the subject of her every thought and question. 'But why are you here, Cal? You really should be at the ship, you know – marching about with your clipboard giving all the workmen a hard time!'

Cal looked sceptical. 'I've already done that,' he said. 'Even though it's not in my job description. I need you to check some final details with me and sign off some invoices. I'm not authorised.'

Sophie nodded. 'Come on then, Iz, ups-a-daisy.'

'I wanted it to be the daddy man not the flowery-smelling man!' Izzy wailed, deciding silent protest wasn't getting her anywhere. Sophie scooped her up and flung her over one shoulder and began staggering up the stairs.

'I feel strangely rejected,' Cal mused as Sophie deposited Izzy on the armchair and looked at her. She wasn't really crying; it was the other type of crying she did – a sort of dry, repetitive whinge – usually when there was a remote danger that she might not be the centre of the universe for five seconds.

'How about you take a chocolate biscuit to Bella to cheer her up?' Sophie suggested.

Izzy's face instantly transformed into a radiant smile. 'And me as well? Can I take me one too?'

Sophie nodded and handed Izzy two cookies. 'Go on then, and don't eat Bella's on the way!'

Izzy giggled and ran out of the room. Sophie looked at the packet of biscuits and then at Cal. She took one out and put it in her mouth, whole.

'Blow? Mots fer moblem?' she asked him through a haze of crumbs.

'If only Jake could see you now,' Cal said, observing her with some distaste. 'If you had a sex life, you know, you wouldn't be bulimic. Anyway, there are no problems. I just wanted to check a few details with you, like have you confirmed the menus with the caterers?'

'Check,' Sophie said breezily.

'Have you OK'd the pyrotechnics with the Health and Safety chaps?'

'Check . . .' Sophie said, as if there would be anything that she, the Queen of Perfection, would overlook.

'Have you arranged a babysitter who won't send the girls into hysterics?'

'Che— Oh fuck,' Sophie cursed and took another biscuit from the packet.

'I knew it. Well, you have to be there. All the big cheeses will be there, including Gillian. The Madison do is possibly the biggest party McCarthy Hughes has ever thrown this side of the Atlantic. It's going to be fabulous and you'll be there in the spotlight, everybody looking at you and thinking how wonderful you are.'

'I know!' Sophie wailed. 'But the girls don't like anyone but you! Will you do it?'

'I'm not doing it,' Cal said. 'I've worked my butt off for this party. I'm going there to enjoy myself.'

Cal was the master of making sure people were mixing and trouble-shooting any incipient problems, and after all the help he had given her he was the one who deserved the credit most of all.

'Right,' Sophie said.

'So . . . ?' Cal waited.

'Well, I mean that's it, isn't it? I can't go,' she said, nodding in the general direction of the bedroom. 'I can't take those two to a grown-up party. There are too many choking hazards for one thing – plus practically everything is flammable. Imagine the insurance costs if we sank it!'

'There's got to be someone,' Cal said, thinking furiously. 'Someone that they know you won't leave them with for ever. Someone strange enough for them to feel at home with . . .'

'Thanks,' Sophie said.

Cal clicked his fingers. 'How about their grandma?' he suggested.

'Nope, she'd never get up these stairs.'

'No, their other grandma – your mum, I mean,' Cal said, as if it were obvious.

'Well, technically she's not their grandma *but . . .*' Sophie considered the prospect of her mum in charge of Bella and Izzy for a couple of hours. She had not heard from her since the night she had come round with the dog book, not unless you counted one phone message which consisted entirely of yapping dogs and that was probably more to do with Scooby messing with the speed-dial button than her mum trying to call her. Anybody else's mother would have been round here helping out, taking an interest, interfering at the very least. Still, it did seem like her mum was the last, no, only, resort.

'Would they like her, do you think?' Sophie asked him.

'They'll love her. She's bonkers. Plus she can come here and they'll feel safe.'

'What the hell.' Sophie picked up the phone and dialled her mum's number. After the usual dog-related pauses Iris eventually came to the phone.

'Hello?' she said.

'Mum, it's me. Listen, I've got a favour to ask you and I really need you to do this for me, no arguments.'

Sophie kissed Izzy and then Bella on the tops of their heads.

'Those pyjamas are fab,' she told them. 'Total princess jammies.'

Izzy giggled. 'You look like a *real* princess,' she

237

said. 'All sparkly and lovely and you don't smell. I quite love you when you look nice.'

Sophie glanced down at herself. Thanks to her mum's early arrival she hadn't scrubbed up too badly. She'd even managed to shave her legs and wax her top lip as well as shower and wash her hair. She hadn't had time to straighten it, though, so it just sort of wafted about like a yellow cloud of gold, as Bella had poetically put it. Like a flyaway mass of static, more like, Sophie thought, but she preferred Bella's description.

'It's not bad, this dress, is it?' she said, delighted that after mountains of oven chips it still fitted her.

'You do look pretty,' Bella said solemnly. 'But you are coming back, aren't you?'

'Of course!' Sophie exclaimed, crouching down with some difficulty in her heels. 'Now you two be good for my mum, OK? Go to bed when she tells you to.'

Izzy nodded. 'You'll definitely come in our room and see us when you get in, won't you?' Bella insisted.

'Yes, I definitely will.' Sophie stood up, using Izzy's head to steady herself. 'Right, I'll be off then.'

She walked carefully down the steps to the street door with her mum.

'Now you know what to do, don't you?' she asked her.

'Yes. Watch telly and get drunk.'

'Mum!' Sophie protested. 'I'm serious!'

'So am I, darling. Don't let them play with

matches, don't give them any sharp objects and don't let them run under a bus.' Iris recited the list of concerns that Sophie had given her verbatim. 'Look, you've been doing this for a little under two weeks. I've been doing it for thirty-five years.'

'Mum, I'm twenty-nine!' Sophie said, appalled. 'And I'm not joking about the bus thing – the latch on the door downstairs is well dodgy . . .'

'They'll be fine. I've got your mobile number. I'm just glad you asked me to help you at last.'

'What do you mean – I was waiting for you to offer to help me!' Sophie exclaimed.

'Oh no, dear,' her mum said mildly. 'I learnt a long time ago never to offer to help you. It just annoys you because you usually know best. I've been waiting years for you to need me for anything. Now, off you go and have a good time.' Iris gave Sophie a look of approval and Sophie smiled warmly at her.

'You've really helped me out here, you know,' she said.

'I knew I was good for something,' her mum told her. 'And you look lovely. I'm sure you could get a boyfriend if you tried.'

'Yes, but do I want one?' Sophie mumbled as her taxi pulled up outside, thinking of Jake waiting for her aboard the ship.

CHAPTER 15

'It looks incredible, doesn't it?' Cal said with quiet pride, leaning next to Sophie as they looked over the golden balustrade encircling the ball room. 'Exactly like *Titanic*.'

Sophie nodded and sipped her martini.

'Yes it does,' she said. 'But hopefully without all the sinking and drowning and Celine Dion.'

Cal gave her a disapproving look.

'Don't diss Dion,' he told her. 'She gives me hope that somewhere out there I might one day find my very own Leonardo to float about on a piece of wood with and then watch freeze to death.'

Sophie looked surprised.

'Really?' she said. 'One day you want to get that committed to someone?'

Cal thought about the prospect for a moment and then shrugged.

'No,' he said. 'Probably not. At least not with any of that lot down there.' He sighed and flicked his imaginary hair out of his eyes. 'I don't know – why are all the sexy men either married or straight?' he asked woefully.

Sophie looked bemused. 'You *are* joking aren't you?' she said, looking at the motley crew of suited doppelgängers dancing like their dads below.

'Of *course* I'm joking,' Cal said. 'God, considering you're my boss you're pretty dim sometimes.'

Sophie watched a parade of waiting staff emerge from the kitchen in perfect unison with tray after tray of canapés and spread out amongst the ravenous crowd. It was rather like watching feeding time in an incredibly well-dressed tank of piranhas.

'Actually Cal, I've been thinking,' she began. 'You know, when you came around this morning I had this sort of revelation . . .'

Cal finished his martini and looked at the empty glass regretfully.

'Oh God, not another lipstick lesbian – it's like a plague!' he said. 'Still, I always suspected.'

Sophie ignored him. 'I was thinking that you've more or less organised this party by yourself and, well, I wondered why it was you never pushed me to promote you. I mean, you've been my PA for years – a brilliant one. You've never asked to have a shot at organising your own event, and yet, when the chance is thrust upon you – well, you're brilliant at it.'

'I know,' Cal said. 'Look, I like working for you, my salary goes up every year and I get a good bonus. My job is seriously easy and I'm only twenty-five. I like coming into work at nine, swanning around until five and then going out to blow my wages. It does get to be a bit of a drag when your boss's dead best friend's kids turn up and then suddenly that bit in your contract about performing extra hours as and when necessary becomes all too real. But, well, don't let this go to your head – but you're a good boss.'

Sophie glowed with pleasure. She'd always *thought* she was.

'Cal, I want to promote you,' She said.

'Oh God.' It wasn't quite the reaction that Sophie had been expecting.

'It's just that I realised today exactly what it is you do. You're right, you do much, much more than your job description.'

Cal rolled his eyes. 'I could have told *you* that,' he said.

'Well,' Sophie persisted, 'if you want it you've got it.'

Cal blinked and looked at her. 'Got what?' he said, carefully bemused.

'The promotion!' Sophie exclaimed. 'I've talked to Gillian about it already and she thinks it's a great idea. We both think that you'd make a fantastic account manager. You are brilliant at your job, Cal, God knows how considering you spend most of the day surfing the Internet for vintage Galliano – it's only fair you get recognised for it.'

Sophie watched the ever-changing disco colours light and relight the halo of Cal's profile with pink, then blue and then gold. A small, sweet smile turned up the corners of his mouth.

'Really?' he said, his habitual urban guard slipping just a little. 'I don't know, Sophie, it's hard work isn't it? And I'm not keen on change, I'm a Cancerian.'

Sophie laughed. 'I just think you can do more in the company,' She said. 'I'm offering you a chance. If this was the other way round you'd tell me to get out of my rut of insecurities and paranoia and start living my life for once, and anyway you're practically doing all of it already. You'd only notice the change in your pay packet.'

Cal glanced at her. 'That's my kind of change.' He looked at Sophie for a moment longer. 'All right then. As you're begging me – I accept.'

Sophie offered him her hand and they shook on it.

'I want more money of course,' he said. 'And I still won't sleep with you – you realise that, don't you?'

Sophie sighed. 'That is definitely not in the job description,' she said emphatically.

Sophie wondered how she could look at her watch without offending Jake, who had found her forty minutes ago and had had her pinned in one corner ever since.

'My God,' he'd said, looking her up and down with naked intensity the first moment he'd seen her. 'You look stunning.' And he had continued to stare at her, making Sophie squirm a little.

'Sorry,' Jake had said. 'It's just – well, you look

incredible.' He had smiled and it was a sweet, boyish smile that had made Sophie smile and blush too.

And she had enjoyed standing here in Jake's company. He'd listened with real interest to the latest news about the children and her concerns and hopes about finding Louis. He'd laughed at Sophie's smiling and oddly proud tales of Izzy's antics, and looked genuinely touched when she'd told him about her and Bella's heart-to-heart.

'You really care about those kids, don't you?' Jake had said to her a few minutes ago.

'Well,' Sophie had replied, 'I suppose I do – in a way.'

Jake had looked at her with a renewed intensity that made her take a step back.

'You'd make an incredible mother,' he said now, smouldering at her.

'No I wouldn't,' Sophie said reactively, scared by the comment.

'You would,' Jake asserted.

'I wouldn't,' Sophie insisted and then she clamped her mouth shut, realising that the exchange was dangerously close to sounding like a playground spat.

Jake cast an embarrassed glance at his toes before looking at her again. 'I scare you, don't I?' he said.

'You don't,' Sophie lied.

'Why do I scare you?' Jake asked himself more than Sophie. 'I think it's because I wear my heart on my sleeve. I'm too full on and should be more mysterious and cool, right?' Sophie shrugged. 'I apologise, Sophie.'

He looked so sad that impulsively she closed the space between them and put her hand on his arm.

'Don't be sorry,' she said. 'I'm just a bit rusty, that's all. I haven't done this for a while and I'm English, you know. Reserved and all that.'

Jake's smile faded as he looked into her eyes, and Sophie felt sure that at any moment she would be swept away by his sexual magnetism and charisma. If she wasn't, then seriously, she had to be clinically dead.

But to her amazement, even as Jake's soft firm lips closed in on her in the shadows she found herself worrying that she should be mingling more, networking, exchanging business cards and building contacts. She should have checked that the second wave of canapés was ready to go and that the drinks were still flowing, and most importantly that the pyrotechnics people had everything ready for the fake New Year countdown that was due to take place at 10.30 – well it was a school night.

Jake's fingers were entwined in the hair at the nape of her neck and his hand pressed firmly into the small of her back until, finally nudged out of her detached reverie, Sophie kissed him back. She felt Jake's reaction to her kiss with a hard physical jolt. She broke off the kiss and took a step back.

'You're incredible.' Jake's voice was dark with longing. 'Let's get out of here. I've got a room on board tonight.'

Sophie looked at him uncertainly. In the last few moments of that embrace she had wanted to kiss him, she had wanted his hands on her, or at least her body had.

'I don't know,' she said. 'I mean the canapés and the fireworks . . .'

'Come on,' Jake said, brushing aside her protests as he took her hand and started to lead her through the crowd and towards the cabins. Sophie let him lead her because part of her wanted to go, part of her wanted to know what it would be like to be undressed by Jake in the state cabin of a luxury cruise liner. But a much bigger part of her knew with some relief that it wasn't going to happen. Not here, not tonight anyway, and especially not with her brothel-pink pants on.

'Jake.' Sophie pulled him to a stop and then let go of his hand. She lifted her chin and took a step back, conscious of the crowd around them.

'I can't,' she said, shaking her head. 'I'm at work here! Gillian would kill me.'

She laughed awkwardly. Jake looked disappointed. He sighed.

'I'm sorry,' he said. 'A little too much good champagne and not enough of beautiful you. It's made me a little crazy. Of course you're right.'

Sophie smiled at him gratefully. 'I have to go,' she said, gesturing at the party that was simmering all around her. 'I've got to check the last lot of arrange-ments and then I've got to get back to the girls before they burn the house down or something.'

Jake grinned and shrugged. 'One day I'll get you to myself.'

'You will,' Sophie said, wanting to give him something.

'I could take you home?' Jake offered hopefully.

'No. This is your party! Stay and have a good time.'

Sophie turned on her heel and walked quickly into the crowd without looking back, knowing that Jake would be watching her.

'God, you are shit,' Eve said, appearing at her elbow with barely a rustle of her long, extremely clingy green dress. Sophie thought she looked like the snake in the Garden of Eden.

'Thanks,' Sophie said dryly. 'And how are you?'

'I mean with Jake there – the poor bloke's been trying to shag you all night.' Eve stared at a shocked-looking Sophie. 'Can you really not tell or is it all an elaborate hoax to make you more elusive and alluring?'

Sophie shook her head. 'There is nothing going on between me and Jake,' she said firmly. It would be disastrous if any gossip found its way onto the office grapevine. Not that Eve needed any hard facts to spread a story, but in this case Sophie's reputation as an oblivious ice queen seemed to be standing her in good stead.

'Good God, woman,' Eve said. 'He's so hot for

you that they practically had to raise Tower Bridge to accommodate his hard-on!'

Sophie shrugged. 'It's been lovely chatting to you, Eve, but I've got a few more details to sort out for *my* party.'

'Bitch,' Eve said as Sophie glided off towards the kitchen and Sophie knew that on that occasion, even though Eve had had the last word, *she* had won. The event had won for her. It was truly brilliant.

And somewhere out there in the crowd Gillian would be thinking exactly the same thing.

The tramp sitting on her doorstep rather took the edge off Sophie's triumphant glow. When she saw him she sighed and considered walking past and lurking around the corner for a bit, in the hope that he would get bored of her doorstep and move on. She watched him for a second from behind a plane tree. He was a hulking great bloke with one of those seriously suspect beards that look as if they might harbour a mini ecosystem all their own. He was leaning back, resting his elbows on the steps, looking for all the world as if he were enjoying the view from his balcony across the Italian Alps.

It wasn't that Sophie didn't have sympathy for the homeless; she did. After all, she gave £5.99 a month to Shelter and ticked the box about the tax refund, so she knew that she cared. She just didn't care for one of them being on her doorstep.

But as he looked like he was there indefinitely, there was nothing else for it: she'd just have to go over and ask him very politely to move and hope he wasn't of the care in the community variety. She scooped up the loose change in her coat pocket that she had retrieved from the taxi driver.

'Here's three twenty-eight,' she said, holding out the money. She was alarmed to see that she'd made the tramp jump, which could never be a good tactic. 'Move on please, my husband's a policeman. He'll be home any minute.'

The tramp looked her up and down with a distinct air of bewilderment.

'Fuck,' he said, half-laughing. 'You really made me jump. Anyway you're here now, thank God. I'm freezing.'

Shit, Sophie thought, he *is* care in the community. 'Look,' she said, wondering if he looked yellowish because of the streetlight or if he was in fact yellow. 'I understand that it must be hard being mental and everything, but . . .'

The tramp stood up abruptly, causing Sophie to stumble backwards down the step and lose her balance momentarily. She felt the man's arm encircle her waist and steady her before withdrawing to a respectable distance. It was then that she realised he smelt rather nice for a tramp. She squinted hard at the vagrant in the glow of the street lamp.

'Oh,' she said bluntly. 'It's you. Hello, Louis.'

He looked older than Sophie remembered, which was down to the beard and, of course, partly down to the fact that he was older, six years older, as was she.

'Your mum wouldn't let me in,' Louis said amiably, as they stood together in the shared hallway. 'She said you'd kill her if she did and that I'd better come back tomorrow to talk to you. But I've waited so long, I couldn't wait until then. So I waited for you to come back. At least it's warm in here. It's freezing outside.' He looked Sophie up and down once again with the benefit of electricity.

Sophie blinked at him in the bright hallway. The lights in this communal part of the converted house were timed to stay on for only five minutes or so. In two or three minutes they would blink out and she found herself hoping that when she turned them back on he'd be gone. Now she could see him clearly it was obvious that he wasn't a tramp, he was just rather travel-worn and scruffy. He had a sort of quilted red parka on over a thick jumper and, until he had taken it off a moment ago, one of those so-called beanie hats pulled down over thick, longish black hair. And his beard wasn't as bushy as Sophie had at first thought – at least a third of it was just the fringes of his black scarf tucked up under his chin against the cold.

'I didn't think you were coming,' Sophie said, glancing up the stairs to the front door of her flat and suddenly wishing that she was on the other side of it. 'I mean, you said you were coming right away – about a week ago.'

It seemed unreal to be standing here with Louis. She had almost stopped believing that he was real at all, but now that he was here she found she didn't know what to say. She had totally and uncharacteristically failed to prepare. Besides, she was irritated with him for being so relaxed. Sophie unwound her own pink beaded scarf from her neck and slipped off her faux fur coat. She suddenly felt very hot.

'Wow,' Louis said, and then seeing Sophie's expression added, 'really nice dress I mean. I like pink.'

Sophie raised an eyebrow, gratified to see Louis unsettled at last by the oddness of their situation.

'So what now?' she asked him, sweeping her hair back over her shoulders, a haughty gesture Carrie used to tease her about endlessly.

'Well,' Louis said, showing a great deal of interest in the cornicing. 'You know let's . . . get on with it?' He clapped his hands and rubbed them together like a classic silent-movie villain. 'Look, I'm sorry I didn't get here right away, but I couldn't leave the school totally in the lurch. I had things to sort out. I had to get money together for a flight. Luckily I already had most of it saved up. I know I hung up on you – that was stupid and rude. I don't think I really knew where my head was at just then, if you know what I mean?'

Sophie supposed that she did. 'Anyway I'm sorry about that and sorry it took me so long to get here. I've had a nightmare getting here, believe me.' If Louis expected any kind of sympathy from Sophie he was disappointed. 'So like I say, I couldn't just leave people in the lurch,' he finished.

'Couldn't you?' Sophie heard herself say, her voice crisp with frost. 'I rather thought that was your forte.'

Louis's open, friendly smile froze and wilted.

'Look, I'm here now,' he said, biting his lip, 'and I want to see my girls. My daughters. I've come a very long way and all I've been thinking about is this moment. Let me see them, please.'

Sophie studied Louis, standing casually in her hallway. He looked perfectly comfortable with the situation. He didn't look anything like a man whose ex-wife had recently died, leaving his abandoned children virtual orphans. Sophie had not expected him at all right at that moment, but as he was here she felt he should be nervous, full of regrets and remorse and sort of guilty-looking. He was none of those things, and it made her furious.

'The girls are asleep,' she told him briskly, stepping up onto the bottom stair so that she was almost level with him. 'Surely you must realise that you can't just walk back into their lives, wake them up and say, "Hey girls, Daddy's back!" after three years!' Sophie searched for something, anything to shake his almost indecent composure. 'Besides – Izzy doesn't really know who you are,' she said bluntly. 'And Bella doesn't even want to see you.'

Louis's face did not move a muscle as he returned her direct look.

'Listen,' he said in measured tones. 'You're the one who found me. I thought you'd be glad to see me. And anyway – they are *my* children. And if I want to I can go up those stairs and take them out of here tonight. You can't stop me.'

Sophie moved up another step. She knew that he was right: she had been the one to find him and should be glad to see him, but still she had to will her simmering fury to stay internal and not visually manifest itself by igniting her skin. She didn't know why she was reacting to his arrival the way she was, but she felt that *somebody* should be angry with Louis Gregory for leaving his family behind, and as she didn't see anybody else available to do so, it might as well be her.

'Actually no, you can't take the children,' she said, moving one step at a time away from him. 'And yes I can stop you. I have been granted a residency order *and* in the eyes of the law I'm their legal guardian. You'll need a court order to take them anywhere.' Sophie stretched the truth slightly, gambling that Louis knew as little about the legalities as she did.

'But I'm their father!' Louis looked crestfallen and Sophie realised that he was not as bullish and confident as he had at first appeared. She took a breath and evened out the tone of her voice.

She realised she wanted something rather complicated from Louis. She wanted him to show the level of remorse she thought appropriate for his crime. But she didn't want to scare him off completely; she couldn't risk him leaving and never coming back. She had to push her own emotional reaction to him to the back of the queue and remember the girls.

'Louis,' she said, 'this is what I suggest you do. I suggest you go away and find a place to stay. And in the morning, when you look less like an escaped convict, you can come back.' Sophie reached the top of stairs and looked down on him. 'I'll tell the girls you're here in the morning. We'll take it from there, OK?'

Louis stood stock-still, his eyes locked on Sophie's for a moment, and then shrugged. 'I don't have much choice, do I?' he said, heading for the door. 'I'll be back first thing.'

Just at that moment the lights blinked out. Sophie stood in the darkness and held her breath. But when the light returned Louis was still by the front door. Sophie watched as he unlatched it and zipped up his parka against the cold.

'Oh by the way,' she said, 'the girls are coping really well, considering they've lost their mother. Thanks so much for asking.'

Louis's face flushed with anger as he slammed the front door behind him.

Sophie took a deep breath and found she was shaking. Not once while she had been waiting, hoping for Louis to turn up, had she considered that her reaction to him might be so physical, so visceral. Bright red blotches had already begun to blossom under the thin material of her dress and her blood was ringing in her ears. She knew that speaking to him the way she just had wouldn't solve anything. But the moment he had stood in the hallway, his presence filling every corner, it was as if he had lit a touchpaper in her. She couldn't just stand by and make this homecoming easy for him. She had to stand up to him for Carrie and her children.

Sophie let herself into the flat and found her mother standing in the hallway.

'Has he gone?' she asked in a whisper.

'Yes Mum, thanks for making him wait,' Sophie replied, following her back into the living room.

'How did it go?' Iris asked her. 'He seemed like a very nice young man. He was disappointed when I said he couldn't come in but he didn't make a fuss.'

Sophie thought carefully about her five minutes with Louis.

'I don't really know,' she said. 'But you're right – he seems normal, nice.'

And then Sophie realised. That was it. That was the reason he had made her so angry.

If he was so normal and nice then why did he run away?

CHAPTER 16

Izzy had chosen to wear her new fairy dress to meet her father, over an orange jersey top with her favourite green and black striped tights that had once belonged to a Halloween outfit. She was sitting on the edge of Artemis's chair drumming her heels against the leather-clad base with infuriating regularity, utterly unaware of the murderous looks she was incurring from the cat, which was balanced on the back of the chair just above her left shoulder. If it had been anybody else – apart from Bella – Artemis would have dealt with them by now with her usual violent efficiency.

'Is it time NOW?' Izzy asked exactly thirty seconds after the last time she had asked when the Man Who Is Her Daddy was coming.

Tess, who had arrived over an hour earlier, shook the silver bangles on her wrist until she could get a clear look at her watch. 'No, darling – we'll just have to wait a bit longer.' She raised an eyebrow at Sophie, who was standing in the small kitchen cradling a cup of coffee more for comfort than for its contents.

'OK, Bella?' Sophie asked the girl, who was lying

256

on the floor staring blankly at the ceiling. She nodded and blew out a puff of air, fanning out her thick fringe momentarily. Somehow she had managed to dress herself entirely in black, quite a feat considering that black wasn't exactly the main choice of colour in most six-year-olds' wardrobes. Of course, when Sophie looked closely she noticed that Bella had committed the cardinal sin of going into her wardrobe without permission. She had adapted a black shirt, black sweater and a black belt into a sort of dress, a pair of Sophie's black woolly tights wrinkling around her ankles. Bella must have judged, correctly, that the gravitas of the occasion would mean that Sophie would not be cross with her. In any case it was hard to be cross with someone who had shown such initiative and managed to look so funny when they were trying their utmost to look foreboding and cross. Perhaps it was the one small detail Bella hadn't succeeded in covering that made her so sweet instead of surly – her boots were still pink.

'We're not going anywhere with him are we, though?' Bella asked after a while, her voice anxious despite her defiance.

'No,' Tess said, giving her a pat on the shoulder. 'Not today.'

Sophie put her mug down on the kitchen counter and walked into the living room. She knelt down on the floor next to Bella and looked at her. Bella returned the look with her much practised scowl.

'Are you going to be OK?' Sophie asked her again.

'I said I was, didn't I?' Bella told her.

It was true, Bella had said that at just after three in the early hours of the morning. About half an hour earlier than that she had padded into the living room and kneeling by the side of the sofa had stared at Sophie until finally her sluggish and underused sixth sense had kicked in and she had opened her eyes.

'Oh good,' Bella had said. 'You are awake.'

It turned out, probably inevitably Sophie concluded, that she was not going to have to break the news of Louis's imminent arrival, not to Bella at least because Bella already knew. She had 'overheard' Sophie talking about him to her mum last night and had heard her saying that he would be back in the morning. Bella had tried to go to sleep and pretend she didn't know about Louis, like she had to at Christmas when she pretended she didn't know that it was Grandma who put the presents at the bottom of their beds and not Father Christmas, because obviously it wasn't Father Christmas as no-one had told him where they had moved to and as she knew for a fact that Grandma didn't post their letters to him because Bella had found them in her knitting basket.

'But then,' Bella had told Sophie gravely, 'I realised that I had only pretended about Christmas so that Izzy wouldn't find out and get upset but as Izzy is going to know about HIM in the morning anyway I thought it would be better to get up and come and see if you were awake than to worry about it all by myself.'

Sophie didn't know whether to be touched or terrified but she had somehow made room for Bella, who had clambered over her and tucked her feet under Sophie's duvet.

'What worries you the most?' Sophie had asked her, hoping that getting Bella to talk about her worries would help.

'Everything I can think of.' Bella had lifted Sophie's arm up so that she could wriggle under it. 'We don't have to go anywhere with him, do we?' she had asked Sophie when she was positioned comfortably.

'No,' Sophie had said, adjusting to the warmth and weight of Bella's small body against hers. She had expected to feel tense and awkward as the child snuggled closer to her, but instead she felt a new kind of still calm. 'Not at all. I don't think anything much will happen tomorrow. You'll all just say hello, get to know each other again.' Sophie had moved her neck to an obtuse angle in order to look at Bella. 'I know how you feel, being worried about your dad coming back. It must be huge, not having seen him for so long – but there are some things that no matter how much we worry about them we just have to face, and most of the time they turn out not to be nearly as bad as we thought they would be. And *sometimes* they turn out to be wonderful.'

Bella had yawned, nestling into Sophie's body, and they had watched the headlights of the relentlessly passing traffic beam momentarily across the ceiling, minute after minute.

'We could hear the sea in my old house, sometimes,' Bella had said after a while. 'We couldn't see it because it was sort of on the side, but in the summer when the windows were open we used to be able to hear it. *Woosh, woosh, woosh.*' Bella had swept her fingers in and out to mimic the motion of the waves. 'A bit like the cars going by outside your house.'

Sophie had listened for a moment longer. 'Yes, a little bit. Look, you'll be all right tomorrow, won't you?' Sophie had asked Bella, when she should have been reassuring her. Selfishly, she wanted her to say yes.

'I will be,' Bella had said, her answer distorted by a lengthy yawn. 'Because I have to be, don't I? Like you said.'

Sophie had fretted for a few minutes, worrying about what she had said exactly. Had she actually told a six-year-old to stop worrying and pull her socks up? That was how Bella had made it sound, but it wasn't what she had meant to say.

'Listen, Bella?' Sophie had wanted to try again. 'Bella?'

But somehow despite her anxieties Bella was sound asleep, something that Sophie did not quite manage to achieve for the rest of the night.

★   ★   ★

Which was why, on the following morning, she had a shooting pain that ran from the top of her head down her neck and stabbed its way into her left arm. Sharing the short two-seater sofa with Bella had given her a very painful crick in her neck. Either that or she was having a heart attack. At that moment the latter option seemed entirely possible.

Tess jangled her bangles again and squinted at her watch. 'He definitely said this morning?' she asked Sophie.

'Yep,' Sophie replied. And he had seemed so adamant that Sophie had assumed he meant first thing, which was why she had called Tess on her mobile at just after seven and got her over to the flat for eight. It was now almost ten. That was three hours of Izzy racing around like a demented tree fairy. Three hours of Bella sulking like a kindergarten beatnik and two hours of Tess jangling her bangles and squinting at her watch. Obviously Louis Gregory's concept of time was entirely different to the rest of the world's. He seemed to think that 'coming now' meant tipping up five days later and that 'in the morning' could be any old time before midday.

'In my experience,' Tess said, 'it's a good idea to get a set time so that everyone knows exactly where they are. I have several other cases I need to attend to. I really can't stay much longer.'

Sophie was just about to complain that it was no good lecturing *her* when the flat buzzer sounded and all four females jumped.

261

'He's here!' Izzy shouted, scrambling off Artemis's chair and shooting out into the hallway, sending the cat flying in the opposite direction.

'IZZY!' Sophie yelled in hot pursuit. 'Don't you dare open—' The flat door slammed open, further deepening the new Izzy-manufactured dent on the corresponding wall. 'Izzy, wait there! I mean it!' Sophie shouted. She wanted to close her eyes as she watched Izzy half scramble, half tumble down the communal stairs, but she was too busy chasing her. Izzy made it to the front door and jumped up to open the old-fashioned and never-replaced latch, which was located halfway down the door and easily within her reach. It swung open, and sure enough, Louis stood on the other side of the door looking down at her. Sophie reached them a second later.

'Is that him?' Izzy said, looking ever upwards, open-mouthed, until she reached Louis's lofty head. Sophie put her hand on Izzy's shoulder. It was unfair, she knew, but she wished the three-year-old was a bit less awe-inspired by her admittedly very tall, and objectively speaking rather handsome, long-lost father.

'Yes,' Sophie said. 'Izzy, this is Louis. Louis is your daddy.'

Father and daughter regarded each other with equal hesitation until Louis held out a hand and, turning on her ballet-shoed heel, Izzy flew back up the stairs with the same haphazard technique and at the same breakneck speed as she had descended them. A moment later the flat door slammed shut.

Sophie looked awkwardly at Louis and shrugged. At least he had rid himself of the last vestiges of tramp-hood. His hair, though still touching his shoulders, was washed and pushed back from his face and he had shaved off his beard, revealing a clean, smooth jawline and generous mouth, his children's mouth. Without the hat, the scarf and the facial hair he looked a lot less irritating and much better, Sophie admitted with oblique regret.

'So you finally made it then?' She was struggling not to sound bitchy but somehow she just did. She stepped aside and gestured for Louis to enter.

'Yes, finally,' Louis said, his tone carefully measured. Sophie shut the door behind him and he took a breath. 'Can we start again? I'm really sorry about last night. You were right, I was bang out of order. I don't know if it was the jet lag or the shock, but I just didn't want to wait. I didn't even think I'd have to. But I was stupid coming over. I'm sorry, I didn't want to piss *you* off.' He smiled at her. 'Definitely not part of my plan after everything you've done for the girls and for me . . .'

Sophie was not surprised by the charm of his follow-up smile, nor its effect on her. It made her want to like him, which in turn made her feel cross again. She couldn't go around liking people willy-nilly, not Louis anyway. Not when there were questions to be asked and arrangements to be made. Was he serious about being a dad again? Was he suitable? Instead of smiling back she nodded stiffly.

'And I know,' Louis continued after a moment, 'I know I should have been here earlier, a lot earlier but I, oh fuck – to be honest I've just been walking up and down outside for about an hour. I'm shitting myself . . .'

'Look,' Sophie said, lowering her voice, 'if you're going to freak out, now is not the time to do it.' She sighed with exasperation. '*You* are the grown-up here. All *you* have to do is get up those stairs and say hello to your daughters. *Apparently* you've been working with children for years. You must know *something* about how to talk to them by now,' she told him with open sarcasm, neglecting to mention that her own experience was limited to just a couple of weeks. 'And anyway, how can *you*,' Sophie looked up at Louis and guessed he was about six feet four, 'be scared of that small girl and her slightly bigger sister?' She also conveniently forgot her own very real five-foot-six-inch terror of Izzy that still reared its ugly head whenever the early-warning tantrum signs went off.

Louis swallowed and nodded purposefully. 'You're right,' he said. 'You're right.'

'Obviously I am,' Sophie said, slightly imperiously, which for some reason made Louis smile his irritatingly nice smile again.

Tess was the only person directly visible when

Sophie showed Louis into the living room. She stood up and smiled broadly at him, delivering her extra-special all-purpose disaster/celebration smile with her usual warmth.

'Hello, I'm Tess Andrew,' she said, extending her hand. 'The children's social worker.'

Louis's already hesitant smile faltered, but he shook her hand anyway with reasonable firmness and looked around the room. Like Sophie, who was leaning in the door frame, he spotted Izzy's special fairy scrunchie, which was just visible over the back of Artemis's chair.

'Oh dear,' Louis said loudly. 'It looks like that fairy must have made herself invisible.'

Sophie and Tess exchanged looks behind his back. Sophie rolled her eyes and Tess dimpled and twinkled. So much for her being objective – she looked like she was in love already.

'That clever fairy must have made herself invisible and flown all the way back to fairyland,' Louis continued. 'What a very clever fairy.'

'I *am* a clever fairy!' Izzy jumped out from behind the chair, a mass of various glittery substances. 'Here I am!' she cried.

'Oh my!' Louis said, clasping his hand to his chest and sitting down on the sofa abruptly. 'You gave me quite a shock!'

Izzy giggled and hopped over to him. Louis's long and large frame seemed to fill the small room the way that two girls, a woman and a social worker didn't. 'I'm a fairy because I've got my fairy dress on haven't I? And yesterday I went to the shops and the café with Aunty Sophie and also there's my cat over there except she's gone now because she doesn't like you but she doesn't like anyone much except for me and Bella, me the most, and I was in the car and a big van made it go BANG and I don't like cars now do I?' Izzy paused for breath. 'Except for Phoebe who I don't mind and sometimes Phoebe gets lonely so we sing to her.' Louis's smile did not waver as Izzy related the story of her life in twenty seconds, but Sophie thought she had seen something in his eyes when Izzy described the car crash, some fleeting shadow perhaps.

Sophie had formulated a theory that Izzy's seemingly flippant recounting of the accident that killed her mother didn't mean that she didn't understand it or that she wasn't hurt and afraid by it. She had to talk about it to everybody she could, because somehow saying it out loud made it real for her. She hoped that Louis would see some of that in Izzy, that he'd understand she was still fragile despite her resolute chirpiness.

'You are a very, very brave little girl, aren't you?' Louis told Izzy gently. She hopped one step nearer to him.

'Yes I am,' she said. '*And* I can do ballet, because it's easy, you just go round and round and do pointing. Are you my daddy?'

Louis bit his lip and nodded. 'Yes,' he said, as if the fact was somehow news to him. 'I am.

266

I'm your daddy and I'm very, *very* pleased to meet you.'

Izzy cocked her head to one side and examined him. 'Do I like you?' she asked him, spreading the palms of her hands upwards, her habitual expression of a question.

'I don't think you know yet. I think you'll decide when you're ready. But I like you very much already.'

Izzy nodded. Tess beamed and Sophie resisted the urge to shove two fingers down her throat.

'I am lovely,' Izzy agreed. 'I'll make you a cup of tea for now.' And she raced off at top speed into the bedroom where her plastic tea set was stored under Sophie's bed. Bella was no doubt languishing on top of it. Sophie wondered if she should go and prise her out from underneath the duvet, but decided against it.

This of all things Bella had to do at her own pace, and if she felt anything like Sophie did at that moment, it would be as if she had just stepped off a tall building and the world was rushing up to meet her. Sophie couldn't help but feel that after what seemed a lifetime of wanting this to happen, now that it had, it was too soon. She wasn't ready.

'She really looks like me, doesn't she?' Louis said to Tess. 'Don't you think?'

Vain and a megalomaniac, Sophie thought to herself as she retreated into the kitchen to make real cups of tea.

'They both look like you,' Tess said pleasantly. 'Of course, I never had the pleasure of meeting Carrie but I've seen photos of her. She was always laughing. It's easy to see where the girls get their spirit from. But as for their dark good looks, definitely you.' Tess actually giggled, which Sophie considered to be most unseemly at her age.

Sophie emerged from the kitchen and handed Louis a mug of a tea.

'Oh right, thanks,' he said. He set the tea carefully down on a coaster on the coffee table, ironic considering the coaster was directly positioned above one of Izzy's permanent marker-pen masterpieces. There was a moment's silence.

'Is Bella here?' Louis said. 'I mean – will I see her today too?'

Before Sophie could say anything Izzy flew into the living room at full pelt and threw a plastic teacup into Louis's lap.

'There you go!' she shouted, out of breath and excited. 'Drink it, drink it up!'

Louis retrieved the cup from between his legs and took a long, noisy sip. 'Ahhh,' he said, before handing the cup back to Izzy. 'Deee-licious. But mind the real hot drinks, won't you. You don't want to get burnt.'

'OK,' Izzy said. 'Would you like more tea?' Louis nodded and Izzy edged her way carefully past the coffee table on her way out, beaming at Louis as she went.

Typical, Sophie thought, if I'd told her that it

would have been third-degree burns all round by now. She glanced at the doorway. Bella was standing on the threshold of the room. Sophie caught Louis's eye and nodded at the door. He turned round and saw his elder daughter.

'Bellarina!' he said, holding out his arms. For a second Bella did not move and then she walked around the sofa and stood beside Sophie. Louis dropped his arms but his smile remained steady.

'It's so good to see you,' he said, shaking his head as he took in the sight of her. 'You've grown into a big grown-up girl.' For some reason the natural ease with which he had engaged Izzy seemed to vanish. For a moment Sophie could not understand why, and then she realised. He had never met Izzy before. They had no history or past, their relationship started with a clean slate. But he had been a father – a wonderful father, according to Carrie – to Bella for three years.

A few weeks ago Sophie would not have believed that Bella would still carry around the memories and the feelings of her three-year-old self, but then until a couple of weeks ago she would have thought that young children didn't really feel or think anything, that their emotional sensitivity and intellect didn't really kick in until they were at least thirteen and properly human. But now Sophie knew Izzy and Bella, she knew otherwise, and she knew absolutely that the three-year-old girl that Louis had left behind along with his wife was still there, still part of Bella, still furious, frustrated, hurt and confused.

Louis leaned forward in his chair and looked at Bella, who looked at her toes. 'I'm so sorry, Bella, about Mummy, I really am. I really wish that I had known about it sooner so that I could have come and been with you. When I found out I came as quickly as I could and—' Louis studied Bella's face for a moment. 'You're angry with me. It's OK, you should be. I have a lot to explain to you. A lot of things to say I should have said before, but please believe me when I say I really have missed you. I've thought about you every single day.'

Sophie sensed the tense lines of Bella's body, and noticed her hands clenched into fists at her side.

'I came to see what you looked like,' Bella said. 'You look the same.' She glanced up at Sophie. 'I'm very tired. I think I'll have a nap.' Sophie nodded.

'I don't have to talk to you,' Bella told Louis. 'Aunty Sophie said.'

Louis pressed his lips together. 'No,' he said. 'You don't . . .'

'I know. Goodbye.'

'Goodbye darling.' But Bella walked out of the room without looking back.

'Are you OK?' Tess asked Louis gently.

'Shouldn't you be asking Bella that?' Sophie said scathingly, as if Louis weren't present at all.

'I will,' Tess said. 'But as my job is about reuniting the family as a whole, I have to consider the feelings of all parties. The girls have got you fighting their corner. Louis has no-one.'

Sophie was about to voice her protest when, ignoring her completely, Tess turned to Louis and asked him again, 'Are you OK?'

'I suppose I should have expected that,' he replied, glancing warily at Sophie as if she might pounce on him the moment he opened his mouth. 'But to be honest I've been thinking about seeing her for so long that I didn't think about what would happen when I actually did.'

Sophie sat down in Artemis's chair and crossed her legs. Why, she wondered, wasn't the social worker grilling him like she was supposed to? She stared meaningfully at Tess.

'These times are always difficult, dear,' Tess told Louis. 'There are many adjustments to be made, many hurdles to be overcome. Think of what the girls have been through recently, losing their mother at such a young age when they needed her the most. Moved around from one place to another. Their little lives have been a real roller-coaster for the last six months. There's been no security or stability. That's why it was such a godsend when we found Sophie. They've blossomed here.' Sophie's head snapped up at that comment. Had they? she wondered. 'They are different children and that's why for the foreseeable future we don't want to give them any more

271

upheaval than is necessary, do we? That's why it would be better for them to stay with Sophie while you are all getting to know each other.'

Louis looked up sharply. 'But they're *my* girls,' he said, stubbornly. 'I'm their dad. I can take them now if I want to – you can't stop me.'

Tess shook her head. 'I think Sophie already explained that I can. Look, Louis – we didn't know if you were definitely coming back until a few days ago. We have yet to take any further decisions on what would be the next step for the girls. We certainly won't be changing their current situation until a few things have been clarified.'

Finally, Sophie thought, she's playing hard ball. She felt relieved by Tess's statement, relieved to know that the girls wouldn't suddenly just be gone.

Louis looked dumbstruck. 'What sort of things?' he asked Tess, who smiled at him reassuringly.

'Well, why don't you come to my office and see me this afternoon and we can talk over the details,' she said, reaching out and patting his knee. 'It's nothing to worry about, but I'm sure you would want us to check and double-check anyone who the girls might live with one day. Even you,' Tess went on before Louis could respond. 'Now, how about two – can you make that?'

Louis's shoulders dropped but he didn't argue.

'I suppose so,' he said, taking the card that Tess held out to him.

'Excellent.' Tess jangled as she rose to her feet. 'Well, I'll be off now but can I suggest that we

272

agree a visiting strategy? Firstly it's very important that you agree a time and stick to it so that the girls know they can rely on you. Secondly I suggest you extend each visit a little bit. Don't try to rush it. These things take time. I'll see you later.' She grinned at Sophie. 'Don't worry, I'll see myself out.'

But Sophie followed Tess down the stairs anyway. 'Um, excuse me,' she said, 'but you can't just leave him here with me. What if he goes all mental, ties me up and runs off with the girls? What if he's a loony psycho killer?'

Tess smiled her triple-chin smile. 'When you've been in my job as long as I have you know when someone is the loony psycho-killer type or not. There's a lot we have to find out about our Mr Gregory. But I'm fairly sure that is not one of them.'

Sophie rolled her eyes. 'Yeah, well, that's what they said about Ted Bundy,' she said scathingly. 'Anyway, let's not forget that it was *you* who was fairly sure it would be OK to leave two small children in *my* care, shall we?' Sophie frowned, confused by how she had managed to insult herself when Tess had been her target.

'Exactly.' Tess reached out and caught Sophie's hand. 'You're really good at this, you know. Much better than I thought you'd be.'

'Right,' Sophie said crossly. She didn't know whether to be touched by the compliment or to give in to an urge to beat Tess about the head with the nearest blunt instrument for manipulating her so successfully. Still, she supposed that probably made *her* the nearest thing to a loony psycho killer in the flat right now.

Sophie paused as she closed the flat door behind her. She looked at the entrance to the living room and at the back of Louis's bowed head. Neither girl seemed to be in there, so Sophie took a detour via her bedroom and stuck her head around the door. Bella was lying on the bed playing with Artemis and what had once been a pair of Sophie's control-top satin sheer tights.

'OK?' Sophie said. She had long ago given up wasting energy mourning the gradual demise of her wardrobe. Bella nodded.

'Where's Izzy?' Sophie frowned – she couldn't see her in the bedroom.

'Baking,' Bella said, pointing downwards. 'At least she was, but it all went a bit quiet a few minutes ago.'

Sophie walked around the bed where, sure enough, Izzy's lower half was protruding out from under it. The excitement of the morning must have overcome her – she was fast asleep. Carefully Sophie fished her out and laid her on top of the bed, as far away from Artemis as possible.

'Do you think she's got narcolepsy?' Sophie asked Bella.

'No,' Bella said, as if she had the first clue what narcolepsy was. 'I think she's three.'

'Of course,' Sophie said with a smile. 'Silly me.

Well, look, I think Louis will be off soon. Do you want to say goodbye?'

'He never said goodbye to me,' Bella said, bluntly. She laid her head down on the pillow and ran the palm of her hand along Artemis's back. 'Besides, I'm having a nap anyway.'

Sophie nodded and, closing the door quietly behind her, she returned to the living room.

'They're both asleep,' she told Louis. 'Izzy's funny like that. One minute she's all go and the next she's snoring like a pro.'

Louis smiled.

'Bella used to be just the same.'

He and Sophie looked at each other for a moment, neither one knowing exactly what to say next.

'Right,' Louis said, standing up abruptly. 'I'll be off. What time do you want me tomorrow?'

Sophie felt herself blush inexplicably and cursed her unpredictable complexion.

'Well, early's good. They get up at six. So – eight?'

'OK, eight it is.' And Louis was gone as suddenly as he had arrived, leaving her small flat feeling positively palatial in his absence.

Sophie sat down in the unusually quiet living room and rubbed her eyes as she thought about Louis. He didn't seem like an ogre, or a thoughtless womaniser with a string of kids stretching around the world. He seemed truly delighted to see Izzy and Bella again and anxious that they would like him. But none of those things fitted with the picture she had built up from the bits and pieces of information she had gleaned about him. If he had just callously run out on Carrie, why would she have kept his absence a virtual secret from Sophie? If he was so concerned about his children why did he go as far away from them as he possibly could? If he was such a good father, the kind of father that had a cute pet name for his elder daughter, and if he was such a good person, this selfless charity worker, then why did Mrs Stiles hate him with a passion? And why was Bella still angry with him?

Somewhere in between all this lay the truth about Louis Gregory. Sophie knew that it was up to her to find it.

She was still trying to puzzle it out when Jake phoned.

'I called you at the office. I was sure you'd be there enjoying your success,' he told her. 'You should have about a hundred people calling the office today all wanting the same thing!'

Sophie grimaced and tapped her forehead with the heel of her palm. She had really been looking forward to going in today, to taking all the glory and capitalising on her success. But the moment Louis turned up she had completely forgotten about all of it. She hadn't even called Gillian, which meant that she had let slip a crucial moment to consolidate her position. She swore silently.

'Louis was here when I got back last night,' she told Jake by way of explanation.

'Ah, the prodigal father. How'd that go?'

'Hard to tell really. I don't know how to be with him. Whether I should be angry and cross and protect the girls from him. Or whether I should be nice and helpful and try to get them to like him. I mean, he got Carrie pregnant and ditched her. Maybe he's not the sort of man who'd make a decent dad.'

'Oh, I don't know,' Jake said reasonably, 'you don't know what happened between him and Carrie. Maybe you shouldn't cast him as the bad guy until you know all the facts.'

'That's just it,' Sophie said. 'I don't know, and I wish I did.'

'Then ask him,' Jake told her as if it were obvious.

'I can't ask him!' Sophie said, sounding horrified.

'Why not?' It was a good question.

'I hardly know him.' Sophie knew her answer was inadequate.

'But you've been caring for his kids,' Jake pointed out. 'You were once close to his wife.'

'I just . . . I can't ask him outright.'

Jake laughed. 'Then be nice to him, let him trust you. Soon enough he'll relax and tell you what you want to know.'

Sophie nodded.

'That *is* a good idea,' she said hesitantly. 'I know I should try to do that but when I think about what's he's done I just want to thump him.'

277

'Don't do that,' Jake advised. 'Play the long game, it works every time. Or at least I hope it does.'

Sophie smiled. 'I'd better call the office. Check everything's OK. At least Gillian will be glad to know that Louis's back, although I'll have to take a few days out completely now until the girls get used to him, if they ever do.'

'I shouldn't worry about Gillian,' Jake told her, a smile in his voice. 'I spoke to her this morning. I told her that I was thrilled with the job you'd done and that I would be signing a long-term contract with McCarthy Hughes based largely on you.'

Sophie took a moment to absorb this piece of information.

'Jake . . .' She began uncertainly. She supposed she ought to be pleased. After all, the seal of approval from her biggest client could only help show Gillian how well she had dealt with work under the circumstances – that in fact she had excelled herself even when the going was tough. But somehow Jake talking directly to Gillian made her feel uncomfortable. After all, they weren't exactly discreet last night. Anybody could have seen them kissing. And what would Gillian think if she heard about that?

'Jake, thank you – but I don't want people to think that you're putting a word in for me because of – us,' Sophie said uneasily.

Jake laughed but Sophie could tell she had somehow wounded him.

'Sophie.' Jake's voice hardened. 'You might remember that before I started mooning around you like a love-sick schoolboy I ran the UK operation of the Madison Corporation, the world's third biggest private asset management corporation. I know my business and I promise you no matter how much I want you, I would *never* compromise my position just to impress a woman . . .'

'Of course you wouldn't,' Sophie said hurriedly. 'I know that. Oh Jake, I'm sorry . . .'

'You're good at your job, Sophie,' Jake interrupted her. 'And I'll be sticking with McCarthy Hughes for our event management because of that and that alone – whether or not anything happens between us.'

'I'm sorry, Jake. I'm just a bit tired and there's so much going on . . .'

'You know what?' Jake said, clearly not wanting to hear Sophie say that line again. 'You need to take some time out from work completely and perhaps you should take some time out from me too. Try to figure out what you want and call me when you do, OK?'

'I will call you,' Sophie said, suddenly feeling anxious that he was withdrawing from her so abruptly. 'Jake, you've been great these last few weeks. Thank you.'

'It's no big deal,' Jake said, his voice melting a little.

'And I'm so sorry about last night,' Sophie said.

'Oh baby,' Jake said warmly. 'Not as sorry as me.'

CHAPTER 17

By the next morning Sophie had formulated a plan which she considered to be a work of Machiavellian genius to rival any of Eve's concoctions.

She was going to take Jake's advice and be nice to Louis. It was a simple plan but one that invariably worked when she was hooking a difficult client. She would be perfectly pleasant and non-confrontational, and gradually he'd let his guard down. When he was relaxed with her and trusted her, then she'd find out exactly what he was about and exactly who he was. And when the time was right she'd be able finally to ask him – what did happen between him and Carrie?

Sophie had thought she didn't know anything very much about Carrie's relationship with Louis or her feelings for him, other than the brief descriptions of general contentment that Carrie had given in passing during their rare conversations over the years – even, it seemed, after he had left. But the more she thought about it the more she realised that she knew more than she thought, that there were tiny clues slotted inside memories that Sophie had rarely, if ever, accessed until now. And now another piece of the puzzle had come back to her as she was formulating her plan.

Carrie had sent her some photos after the wedding. Sophie remembered that the camera must have been rarely used, because the photos showed Carrie throughout the developing stages of her early relationship with Louis right up until the so-called honeymoon when she sat on the beach at St Ives looking, according to Carrie who had inscribed the back of each picture, 'Like a big fat whale'.

Sophie reached over and switched on the light next to the sofa. She looked at the video clock. It was nearly seven thirty, a virtual lie-in when Bella and Izzy were in your life; the excitement and drama of yesterday must have worn them out. It didn't take her long to find the photos, she knew exactly where they were – in a shoebox on top of one of the kitchen units. Sophie retrieved the box and sat down on the edge of the sofa, praying that the girls would stay in bed for a few moments longer. She didn't want Carrie's photos to upset them.

The first four or five were all taken on the same beach. It must have been right at the start of the relationship. Carrie was smiling and radiant, her brown curls blown about by the breeze coming off the sea. She and Louis had taken photos of each other. In Carrie's her arms were outstretched as if begging for an embrace, and in another she was blowing a kiss right at the photographer. Louis looked less comfortable in his, his hands shoved in his pockets, a shy smile on his face and his shoulders shrugged against the cold. But in one image Carrie had caught him unawares, staring out at the horizon, looking relaxed and, yes, quite attractive in a scruffy and unkempt kind of way. Sophie turned the photo over and smiled. 'Mine all mine!' Carrie had written triumphantly. The last photo of this set was of them both. Carrie must have held the camera at arm's length to get them both in, because it was blurred and out of focus. It was easy, however, to make out the broad width of their smiles, even though Carrie's hair had blown over most of Louis's face in the second that the film was exposed.

There were a few landscapes of the Cornish countryside, each inscribed with the location, time and date, and after those came two photos of what eventually had become Carrie's house. A tiny two-up, two-down terrace seemed to perch precariously on one of the steep lanes that led up from the beach. Virgin Street it was called. Carrie had laughed and laughed when she told Sophie her new address, delighted that she of all people was going to be living on such a chaste road. The house had cost much more than they could afford and Carrie had had to swallow her pride and beg her mum for a deposit, Louis taking on a second job to make the mortgage repayments. But Carrie had known from the moment she set eyes on the run-down little house that she had to have it, and she got it. That, Sophie reflected, was just like Carrie – she always got what she wanted in the end.

Then came the wedding photos. Clearly whoever had taken these was more than a little worse for wear at the time, as the subject of each print was tilted and skewed, as if the wedding had taken place during an earthquake. They were mainly of Carrie and Louis, holding hands and laughing. Louis was flushed and Sophie remembered that he had been quite drunk and had stumbled through the vows. Carrie, who was very pregnant by then, looked so happy, almost victorious. And then Sophie saw herself – or at least half of herself – her face obscured by her hair. Carrie had reached out a hand to her and pulled her close and as Sophie looked at the photo she suddenly recalled what Carrie had whispered in her ear in that moment, so vividly that she could almost feel her breath on her neck. 'I've finally done it, Sophie. I've got everything I wanted. I'm free.'

Sophie remembered thinking that being married to a drunk surfer and saddled with a baby at not quite twenty-three was the very last thing she would call free, but Carrie had seemed to believe it. Then she came to the final photos: Carrie on the beach, in a big, loose, white cotton shirt, propped up on her elbows, a plate of sandwiches balanced on her bump. In the background Sophie saw something that she hadn't remembered. She had always assumed that Louis had taken these last few photos which Carrie had captioned 'The Gregorys honeymooning at home', but he couldn't have because he was in them. Not in the foreground but much further back, just above Carrie's left shoulder.

Sophie peered at the photo – yes, it was definitely Louis messing around with someone else, another girl. A slender blonde. He had his arms around her waist and she had her head tipped back and was smiling up at him. Sophie bit her lip. If she had been about to give birth and was sitting on a beach with her brand new husband frolicking with some hussy a few feet away she would have been livid. But would Carrie? Probably not, Sophie concluded. Carrie had an amazing self-confidence and self-belief. She would never have believed that Louis would do any more than flirt with the girl because he absolutely loved her. Carrie had told Sophie that often enough in the years before Izzy. It must have been devastating for her when he left – she would have been totally unprepared. It must have hurt her pride just as much as her heart. Maybe that was why she hadn't told Sophie about it.

Sophie ran her thumb along the edge of Carrie's face and was surprised to feel a rush of tears build up behind her eyes. She closed them and took a deep breath. She hadn't cried for Carrie yet, she hadn't had time to, and in all the chaos and confusion she had almost forgotten that she had loved her once. Despite their distance she knew that if she had walked into a room and found Carrie there, not only would she have been delighted to see her but they would never have stopped talking and laughing until it was time to go. Sophie had taken their friendship for granted, and now she realised she would never again walk into a room and see Carrie there.

'Mummy!' Sophie jerked her head up and saw Izzy peering over the side of the sofa.

'That's Mummy!' Izzy said, delightedly pointing at the photos that were laid out on the sofa. She ran round and sat next to Sophie, who gathered the photos up into a loose pile. She looked down at Izzy's expectant face and, although she was uncertain that she was doing the right thing, she handed her the first photo on the pile, Carrie blowing a kiss.

'Oh Mummy,' Izzy said, chuckling fondly, and she planted a kiss on the photo.

Silently Sophie handed her photo after photo and each one seemed to thrill her even more.

'That's that man who is my daddy there!' she exclaimed at the first image of Louis. 'With my mummy!' She seemed to think that it was incredible they should be together, and Sophie realised that Izzy probably didn't understand that they had once known each other. She cooed over the wedding pictures and laughed at Mummy with the sandwiches balanced on her tummy.

'Mummy.' And just as Sophie had done she ran

her finger gently along the side of Carrie's face. 'Mummy,' she said, more softly this time.

Sophie put her arm around Izzy and held her own reactions tightly in her chest. 'You can keep these if you like,' she said. 'And then you can look at Mummy whenever you want.'

Izzy nodded, and gathering up the photos she held them close.

'Where is Mummy again?' she asked after a while.

'She's in the sky, Izzy, and the stars and the sun,' Sophie said, carefully making sure her own voice stayed steady.

'And in the moon and the trees and the lamp-posts and the, and the – houses?'

'Yes, Mummy's all around you. Watching over you and loving you and keeping you safe.' More than anything Sophie wanted to believe her own words, she wanted to recapture some of the childish faith Izzy had.

'But I want to see Mummy, properly,' Izzy said, her voice very small now and her eyes welling with tears. 'I want to cuddle her up.'

At that moment Bella, already washed and dressed, appeared on the other side of the sofa and, pulling herself onto the seat she put her arm around Izzy too so that it criss-crossed over Sophie's.

'See that bump,' she said, pointing at the photo. Izzy nodded, her bottom lip still quivering. 'That's me in there, that is.'

'That's not you in there,' Izzy said with a the glimmer of a smile. 'You couldn't get in there!'

'I could when I was a tiny, tiny baby and not even born yet.'

Izzy examined the photo again. 'Where's me?' she demanded, but with a fraction of her usual imperiousness. 'Where's me in a bump – I had a bump too, didn't I?' Fortunately Sophie did have a photo that Carrie had sent her just before Izzy was born. It had arrived in an envelope with only a brief message scrawled on the back: 'Thought you'd like to see how fat I'm getting!'

Sophie quickly flicked through the remaining contents of the shoebox and took the photo out. Carrie was smiling, although she looked a little thinner in the face and paler in that photo and, now Sophie compared the two, Carrie's initial radiance was entirely gone. Still, she handed it to Izzy.

'Here,' Sophie said. 'That bump is you.'

Izzy laughed again even as the tears dried on her cheeks, and as Sophie relaxed she discovered that she had been holding her breath. She glanced up at Bella, who was looking at the last photo of Carrie, her lips pressed into a thin line, her hands folded in her lap.

'Are you OK, Bella?' Sophie said. It was a question she found herself asking routinely, never receiving a satisfactory answer. Where Izzy was beautifully transparent her sister could be like a tightly closed book.

Bella nodded and hopped off the sofa. 'I'm getting

Cheerios,' she said, and she trundled into the kitchen.

'And me, and me as well!' Izzy shouted, scooting after her, leaving the photos scattered across the sofa. Sophie gathered them up and put them back in the wallet.

'I'll leave these on the table,' she called out to the girls, who were doing their best to attract vermin by scattering cereal all over the floor. 'Better get a move on because Louis will be here any minute.' And just then the buzzer sounded through the flat. Sophie looked at the clock. It was right on the dot of eight.

If there was one thing that Sophie decided she was never, *ever* going to do ever, *ever* again it would be to answer the door to a handsome man in her cartoon pyjamas.

'You did say eight, didn't you?' were Louis's first words to her as she ushered him up the stairs, hoping that the length of her hair would somehow be enough to prevent him from getting the full-on Snoopy effect of her nightwear combined with her blazing hot cheeks.

'Yes, yes, I did,' she said, trying to keep the brisk tone out of her voice and to remember Plan Nice. 'We found some old photos, and we got held up looking at them.'

Louis waited for Sophie to go into her flat first. 'Suits you,' he said dryly, with a smile. 'Snoopy style, I mean.'

'Ha, ha,' Sophie said without mirth, narrowing her eyes at him. When she walked into the living room Bella was ensconced on Artemis's chair eating her Cheerios and watching GMTV, and Izzy was on the floor doing the same thing only a lot less tidily.

'Hello, the man who is my daddy!' Izzy said, waving her spoon at Louis. 'I saw you today!'

Bella said nothing, only glancing at Louis who loomed awkwardly in the corner of the room.

'Look,' Sophie said. 'Make yourself a drink if you want one. I need to get dressed.'

Louis smiled again.

'What?' Sophie demanded.

'It's just that – well, you're a lot less scary in pyjamas,' he said quickly and headed for the refuge of the kitchen.

Swallowing her irritation, Sophie looked from Bella to Izzy. 'Be good,' she said. 'I'll be ten minutes.' But she took at least twice that time because she felt compelled to have a shower and give her hair a quick wash as well, applying extra concealer and mascara to make up for the pyjama incident. While it obviously didn't matter at all what Louis thought of her, her Snoopy pyjamas did not put her in the best light, and if he thought of her as the kind of person who wore cartoon characters to bed, then it would be much harder for her to get him to take her seriously. And she didn't like the way he had seemed to relax in the situation before she had. Yes, it would make implementing Plan Nice much easier, but why should Louis – the one who was utterly in the wrong – have the way made so smooth for him that he could easily forget he had at least some part in creating this tragedy? The thought of it made Sophie edgy and defensive.

When she returned at last to the living room, her damp hair preparing to frizz around her shoulders, Louis handed her a cup of coffee.

'You look great,' he said, quite naturally and easily.

'Er, thanks,' Sophie said, thrown off kilter once again by his casual cunning.

She looked at the children. Bella seemed engrossed by a woman's account of a botched hysterectomy, while Izzy had abandoned her cereal and was showing Louis the photos. He looked at them exactly as Bella had done, all expression carefully folded away.

'And that is *you*!' Izzy told him, pointing him out in case he didn't realise.

'Yes,' Louis said, producing a smile as Izzy looked up at him. 'It is.' He turned to Sophie. 'I thought I could take them to London zoo, it's quite mild out and dry.' He opened the contents of the plastic bag he had been carrying and brought out two hat, scarf and glove sets, a pink one with proper gloves attached to the hat and a lilac one with mittens. 'I got them these just in case it was a bit cold.'

'Mittens and kittens!' Izzy said, grabbing the lilac set and trying to put it on despite the fact that all the bits were still attached to each other with plastic tags.

Sophie hadn't thought about actually taking the girls out, but remembered her plan and Tess's assessment of Louis as not the child-snatching type. This was backed up by a long phone conversation she had had with Tess late yesterday afternoon. She had told Sophie that Louis was co-operating fully with her and that he seemed to be genuine about his commitment to his daughters. Sophie decided that it would be good for the girls to get out and it might be easier for all of them when they weren't in such a confined space.

'OK, but, um, well, can I come too?' she said, remembering Tess's stipulation.

Louis seemed slightly taken aback. 'Why? I mean – that's great, I'd like you to come along – but I'm not planning to smuggle them abroad or anything.'

Sophie nodded. 'I know that, but they don't know you, do they?' She shrugged. 'Look, I'm sorry but Tess told me I should stay with them for the first few visits. If you don't like it you'd better call her.'

Louis sighed. 'No, no, if that's what Tess wants. Right then.' He winked at Izzy. 'Want to go to the zoo, Izzy?'

'Yes I do, I do want to go to the zoo! I want to see the penguins and the spiders,' Izzy shouted, her new hat jammed on her head, the mittens flailing off the side like demented antlers. Louis and Izzy laughed together, their dark eyes dancing.

'I'm not going,' Bella said flatly, without taking her eyes off the TV.

Louis sat quietly, watching Bella anxiously.

'You are going,' Izzy said. 'You're coming with me to see penguins and spiders, aren't you?'

Bella shook her head and glared at Izzy. 'I am not,' she said emphatically.

Sophie saw Izzy's lip begin to quiver and quickly knelt beside her. 'It's OK, darling,' she said, putting an arm around her. 'Hang on a minute.' She gave Izzy a squeeze and walked the short distance over to Bella on her knees. 'Bella, I know this is hard for you but please don't make it hard for Izzy too. She wants to go to the zoo. And I bet you do too, really, don't you? I'll be there, and if you don't go none of us will.' Bella blanked her.

Izzy came over and put her hand on Bella's knee. She was sobbing: deep, dry, ragged breaths that sounded painful. 'Please, Bella,' she begged. 'Be happy!'

'Come on, Bella,' Sophie said. 'Show Izzy what a grown-up big sister you can be.'

Bella sighed and looked at Sophie. 'I *am* only six you know,' she said glumly and Sophie felt terrible.

'I know,' she said. 'I keep forgetting you're such a little girl because you're so clever.'

'OK, I'll come to the zoo I suppose – but I shan't enjoy it,' Bella said reluctantly.

CHAPTER 18

There was a debate about how to get there. Probably in an attempt to scupper the whole expedition Bella refused to go on the bus because 'buses smelt', and although at first Izzy seemed quite happy to go in Phoebe – partly because of Sophie's 'therapy' but especially because she had bought a booster car seat for Izzy and cat-shaped sunscreens for both girls' windows, despite the now total absence of any sun – as soon as they reached the end of the road and turned left instead of right, and she realised that taking their usual route around the block would not get them to the zoo, she started crying and quickly became hysterical.

'No NO NO NO NO NO NO!' she screamed. 'GET OUT GET OUT GET OUT!'

'My God,' Louis said, alarmed, twisting around in his seat. 'Shhh Izzy, it's OK, it's OK. Stop the car,' he ordered Sophie. 'She needs to get out.'

'Hang on,' Sophie said. 'Just wait a minute. Bella, let's sing.'

Louis stared at her.

'Sing? Look, she's really upset so just stop the car—'

But Sophie and Bella had already begun to sing their new and constantly revised version of 'Motorcycle Loneliness'. Louis watched as Izzy's screams gradually subsided into sobs and as he vaguely recognised the song he sat back in his seat, staring straight ahead at the road. Sophie glanced at him. It was hard to tell what he was thinking but he suddenly looked like he was miles away. By the time she had turned the car back into her road Izzy was calm again.

'It's all right now, Izzy,' Bella said, helping her clamber out of the car onto the pavement before engulfing her in a hug.

'I hadn't realised, I didn't know; she was in the car too, wasn't she?' Louis asked Sophie quietly, who quickly filled him in on the details of the accident as the girls hugged each other.

'It's really frightened her, hasn't it?'

Sophie nodded but clapped her hands as Izzy and Bella came over.

'But we're making progress, aren't we, Izzy? We went quite far then and nothing bad happened, did it?' Izzy shook her head and wiped her new mittens across her nose, leaving a trail of mucus shimmering across her cheeks. Sophie took one of the tissues that she had begun always to keep some-where on her person and mopped Izzy's face. 'We go a little bit further every day but I think that today was just a bit too far all at once,' Sophie explained to Louis.

'That's a really good idea,' Louis told her.

She smiled at him. 'Thanks. I read about in a dog-training book.'

Louis blinked at her. 'Right,' he said, raising his eyebrows. 'Well, I'll say one thing for you, you're full of surprises. Excellent. So what's the new plan?'

'Well, as Bella is dead set against the bus, there's only one plan left. We'll take the Tube.'

It was an interesting journey, to say the least. Izzy became convinced that the Tube trains were fire-breathing dragons. Bella, who refused to sit anywhere near Louis, took a seat as far away as possible from him and Sophie, who was concerned that a six-year-old girl should not appear to be alone on the London Underground, sat next to her. At this point Izzy insisted on sitting on Sophie's lap. So they made the whole trip without exchanging a single word with Louis, although Izzy did occasionally throw him a cheery mittened wave.

And when they emerged at Camden Town, because Regent's Park station was closed, it was raining. Louis had thought about hats but neither he nor Sophie had considered the possibility of rain, probably rather foolishly as the first half of February was making up for the year's early brightness by becoming the second wettest month in recorded history.

'Let's run!' Louis shouted, grabbing Izzy's hand

and heading in the direction indicated by the tourist signpost.

'Um, hang on—' Sophie called out to him in vain. She had been about to point out that it was actually rather far from Camden Town station to the zoo, but it was too late. She looked at Bella, and taking her hand they ran after him. It took them twenty minutes to get to the zoo. By then it had stopped raining, but they were all wet through and out of breath.

'That was pretty far,' Louis said to Sophie. 'You should have said.'

She bit her tongue and said nothing as he generously offered to pay the entrance fee.

'Two adults and two kids, please,' he told the girl in the booth.

'You save eight pounds with a family ticket, sir,' she said, fluttering her lashes at him, dimpling prettily. Louis's brow furrowed and Sophie worried for a moment that he might be about to point out that they weren't *exactly* a family. But then the girl asked him for forty-two pounds for a family ticket and he went a shade paler under his Peruvian tan.

'Right, OK,' he said. 'Um, do you take traveller's cheques?'

Sophie knew that she could and possibly should have stepped in with her credit card, but she decided if Louis was serious about being a dad he needed to know about things like how much it cost to go to the zoo.

'I only wanted to visit the zoo,' he muttered to

Sophie as they filed through the turnstiles, 'not to buy it.'

Sophie smiled at him. 'A bit different from Peru, hey?'

'I'll say.'

Sophie looked at the bedraggled girls. 'Let's get a warm drink and then we can stand under a hand-dryer for a few minutes to dry out a bit before we look at the animals. What do you reckon?' Sophie looked up at the sky. 'There's some blue up there now, look.'

Izzy nodded. 'Mummy made it,' she said.

Sophie thought that it was only fair that she should pay for the three hot chocolates and a coffee, so Louis and Izzy picked which one of the many empty tables they wanted to sit at in the Pelican Café, and Bella came to the till with Sophie.

'See,' Sophie said. 'It's not so bad is it?'

Bella said nothing but looked across the café to where Izzy was screaming and giggling as Louis tickled her with her discarded mittens.

'It's good to see Izzy laughing, isn't it?' Sophie tried again as she carefully guided Bella and the tray of hot drinks across the café.

This time Bella shrugged and mumbled, '*She's* always laughing.'

Sophie set the tray down on the table and hung up the girls' coats on the back of their chairs.

After their drinks had warmed them all up a

little, Sophie said, 'Come on girls, let's see if we can dry off a bit.'

Izzy was chattering happily about penguins as she sat on the loo and Sophie ruffled Bella's hair under the hand-dryer until it was nearly dry.

As Izzy hopped off the loo and made rather a meal of pulling up her tights, she giggled at Bella and said, 'It's good to have a daddy, isn't it Bella? Cos now Mummy's gone Daddy can look after us instead!'

Sophie was completely unprepared for what happened next.

Emitting what Sophie could only describe as a growl, Bella flew at Izzy and pushed her violently. The smaller girl jerked back and fell hard against the toilet wall, banging her head with an audible crack.

'Don't you dare say that!' Bella shouted at Izzy. 'I hate him! I hate him! I HATE HIM!'

Izzy was screaming, hurt and frightened tears streaming down her bright red face. Realising that Bella was about to attack Izzy again, Sophie grabbed her, putting her arms around her so that her embrace encircled the child's flailing arms.

'BELLA!' she found herself shouting. 'Calm down, NOW.' But Bella did not calm down. Izzy sat screaming on the floor, her arms outstretched to Sophie, desperate to be comforted, and Bella struggled furiously, attempting to break free. For what seemed like the longest time Sophie thought she would be stuck in the ladies' loo at London zoo for ever, caught between the two of them, unable to reach out and comfort Izzy, unable to calm Bella down. Then the door opened and Louis stuck his head round.

'Everything all right in here? I thought I heard . . .' Seeing immediately that it wasn't, he came in. 'What happened?' he asked.

Sophie shook her head, indicating that now was not the time to go into details.

'Just take Izzy outside. She banged the back of her head, quite hard I think. You'd better make sure it's not cut,' Sophie said over Bella, who was now bright red and sobbing.

Louis reached Izzy in two long strides and scooped her up, but instead of taking her out as Sophie had requested he paused by Bella.

'Bella, darling, please—' he began.

'I hate you!' Bella screamed at him. 'Go away, go away, go away!'

Louis froze for a moment and looked at Sophie.

'I think you'd better go,' Sophie said, desperately nodding at the door.

At last Louis relented and carried Izzy, sobbing into his chest, back to the café.

Hours seemed to pass in the few minutes that Sophie stood there, her arms securing Bella to her body as she waited for her to calm down. Finally she felt her rigid muscles soften, her racing heart slow and her ragged breaths begin to even out. At last Sophie was able to let her go, and she turned Bella around to face her, her hands on her shoulders.

'Why did you do that to Izzy?' she asked Bella evenly. She had never seen the girls have a fight more serious than a squabble over who got the baby doll and who got the felt-tips. And even those they usually resolved between themselves after a while. To see placid, self-contained Bella so furious and out of control was more than a shock to Sophie. It had frightened her.

'I don't know,' Bella said. 'And anyway, she doesn't know anything. They can't make me live with him if I don't want to, can they?'

'No, they can't make you, Bella, but it's really important that you give him a chance.'

'Because you don't want us?' Bella said accusingly.

'No! Not because of that, and anyway, it's not that I don't want you—' Sophie stopped herself before she said too much.

'But you said I didn't have to like him,' Bella insisted.

'I know what I said. But don't stop yourself liking him, either. I don't think Mummy would have wanted you to hate him, would she?'

'No, she wouldn't,' Bella said reluctantly.

'So why can't you give him a chance and get to know him again? He might be all right.' In fact, Sophie thought, so far he had seemed very much all right.

Bella shook her head. '*She* doesn't know anything,' she said, referring to Izzy again. 'She is just a baby who wants a nice new daddy. She doesn't even understand what happened!'

Sophie dropped her head. 'That's not true, Bella. Izzy misses your mum just as much as you do.' She was almost at a loss as to what to say next. 'I thought you understood that.'

Bella screwed her fists into her eyes, rubbing them vigorously. For once she was looking and acting the age she was. Sophie crouched down and hugged her.

'Izzy doesn't know him,' Bella said. 'She doesn't remember him going. *I* do. And it's not right, it's not right for her to be all happy about him coming back when Mummy can't.'

Sophie's mind went blank, all the advice and words of wisdom she seemed to have been plucking out of nowhere recently deserting her. And then in the back of her dark, blank mind she saw a tiny flame of a memory, which she thought she had smothered long ago, begin to flicker and burn brightly.

'My dad died when I was quite young,' Sophie told Bella. 'I was older than you. I was thirteen, but it was almost the same as it was for you. It wasn't expected. I said goodbye to him one morning as he left for work. By the time I got home from school he had gone.' Bella watched her, her dry, dark eyes hot with the absence of tears. 'I missed him so much, Bella, I didn't want to feel that pain. The only person who made me able to bear it was Carrie, your mum. I couldn't go to my mum because she was as upset as me. And I didn't have any brothers and sisters. Your mummy was always there for me, to help me through it. Always, for ever, whatever – remember?'

Bella nodded. Feeling cramp bite into her thighs, Sophie sat down on the toilet floor, grateful that the bad weather had kept the convenience empty so far. Bella sat down with her. 'Your mum helped me – not to forget, but to control it.' Sophie hesitated. She wasn't sure that this was a memory she wanted to revive. But, she reasoned, look at where burying her pain and memories had got her, a lone, cold fish. Bella was only six – you shouldn't have to do that when you were only six.

'Christmas came,' Sophie went on. 'It was about three months after Dad had died. We went to stay with some cousins of Mum's in Suffolk. She thought it would be for the best, that it would be better than her and me looking at each other across the Christmas table on our own. I hated it. I didn't want to go and stay with loads of people I hardly knew. I didn't want to do anything. If I couldn't be with my dad I wanted to be at home on my own and forget Christmas.'

'That's what I wanted too but we weren't allowed to stay at home either,' Bella said.

Sophie nodded. 'I know,' she said. 'But it turned out that when we got there Mum was right. It was good to have some cousins to hang around with, some other things to look at and listen to. I didn't stop missing Dad or hurting, but it helped me to turn it down. Like when you turn the volume down on the telly, do you understand what I mean?' Bella nodded. 'And then on Christmas Day we were all pulling crackers and my mum got a joke in hers, and she read it out loud – I can't even remember what joke it was now – but it made her laugh.' Sophie paused as she remembered the moment. 'I hadn't seen her smile in three months but there she was laughing and laughing, for what seemed like for ever. I was *so* angry. I got up and I shouted at her. I said how could you? I ran out of the room and into the garden so fast that I kicked my chair over and my drink too. I was so angry with her, Bella, because I thought her laughing meant that she had already forgotten Dad.' Sophie bit her lip and, reaching out, brushed a strand of Bella's hair behind her ear. 'Mum came and found me. She knew why I was so cross, and she told me that sometimes you have to practise being happy, even when you're not, because otherwise you might forget how altogether. She said that Dad would want me to be happy whenever I could, that he'd never want me to miss a single chance to laugh because of him.' Sophie found herself smiling as she thought of her mum. She had taught her something after all, perhaps more than she realised, even if it was only now that she finally understood.

'It's easier than you think to let being happy go for ever, and once it's gone it's hard to get it back again,' Sophie said. 'I don't want that to happen to you. Mummy wouldn't want it, and believe it or not neither would your daddy. Is that why you pushed Izzy? Were you angry with her for being happy?'

Bella regarded her for a long moment and then she put her arms around Sophie's neck and kissed her softly on the cheek.

'Yes,' she said. She took a breath. 'I know really that Izzy misses Mummy as much as me. I just hate him. He makes me so angry and I took it out on Izzy. I'm sorry.'

Sophie clambered to her feet. It was pointless to press her any further, especially when she felt Bella had just begun to really trust her. And Sophie found that having her trust was an achievement that gave her more satisfaction than anything she had done in the office. Because getting Bella to trust her was far, far more difficult than going to work and jumping through hoops to impress Gillian every day.

'I think you'd better tell Izzy that, don't you?' Sophie said, holding a hand out to help Bella up.

They emerged at last from the ladies' and Sophie gratefully took a breath of air that was not tinged with disinfectant or another scent that she chose not to dwell on. Bella and Izzy saw each other across the café, and Izzy climbed off Louis's lap and made her way towards Bella. They met halfway and hugged each other tightly.

Sophie stayed a few feet away and looked at

Louis over their heads, but he wasn't looking at her. He was looking at his daughters, his face wrought with sorrow.

'We could still go and see the spiders,' Sophie said as the girls broke their embrace.

'I want to go home,' Izzy said, looking at Bella. 'I don't like the zoo any more. It's stupid, like you said.'

'Maybe that would be best,' Louis said, looking suddenly tired and careworn as he joined the small group with the girls' coats over his arm. 'Maybe it was too much, too soon. Come on, let's go back.'

Back at the flat, a little over two hours after they had left it that morning, Bella helped Sophie empty three tins of tomato soup into three bowls and put them in the microwave one by one.

'Right then.' Louis appeared in the doorway. 'I'll be off.'

'Hang on a minute,' Sophie said, gesturing that she wanted a word. 'Bella, don't touch the microwave when it beeps, OK?'

Bella nodded, studiously ignoring her father.

'So,' Louis said as Sophie followed him to the flat door. 'Same time tomorrow then?'

Sophie felt every exhausted muscle in her body ache at the very thought of another morning like the one she had just had, and longed for simpler times when the girls would watch TV and she would hover around trying to avert calamity at every turn.

'You're sure you're up to it then?' she asked.

Louis shrugged and opened the door. 'I have to be, don't I? If I want to make it work. And I really do want to make it work.' He looked at Sophie closely. 'I really appreciate the way you've handled this. A lot of people wouldn't have got involved at all. But you took the girls on, you kept them from going into care and you made sure I found out what had happened. When we first met I was worried that you hated me.' He smiled and Sophie felt all her careful methodical plans fly out of the window as she was drawn into the depths of Louis's dark eyes. Those dark eyes had charmed Carrie into giving up everything for him, Sophie reminded herself.

'You might not care either way,' Louis told her, 'but what you've done means an awful lot me.'

Sophie felt suddenly panicked – honesty seemed like the best policy. 'I'm not doing it for you,' she said. 'And I did hate you a bit.' She nipped her lip with her teeth. 'Look, Louis, there's something I don't understand. And it's worrying me—' Louis waited for her to continue. 'I don't understand why you did what you did. Why you ran out on Carrie and Bella. Why did you just go and never come back or keep in touch?'

Louis's head jerked up and he took a step back. 'That's none of your business,' he said, the contours of his jaw hardening as he spoke.

'Isn't it?' Sophie asked him. 'While I have guardianship over your children I think it is, whether you like it or not.'

Louis's face darkened further. 'Look,' he said. 'You were Carrie's closest friend but she didn't tell you what happened.' That point did rather hoist her by her own petard. 'If she didn't want you to know then why should I tell you? Anyway, that was the past, things were done and said that caused a lot of hurt and pain. But none of that matters *now*,' Louis insisted. 'Now my children are all that matters.'

'It matters to Bella,' Sophie said, with simple emphasis. 'She's furious with you, Louis – can't you see that?'

Louis's gaze dropped. 'I know,' he said quietly. 'She has a right to be. But what happened between me and Carrie has nothing to do with her, it's in the past.'

'Oh don't be so naïve,' Sophie snapped. 'It has everything to do with her – and Izzy. If you want either of them to really trust you, you will *have* to face it sooner or later.'

Louis's face was very still. 'I know I have a lot of bridges to build. A future to build, but this is my chance to do the right thing by my daughters. I want you to know that.'

Sophie's next words sprang out of her mouth before she had a moment to consider them. 'It's a shame you had to wait for their mother to die before you made the effort.'

The moment she had said it she regretted it, but she lifted her chin and held his gaze. Louis looked at her as if reassessing his opinion of her, and said nothing for a moment. Then he released the latch on the flat door and pulled it open an inch.

'I'll be back at the same time tomorrow,' he said, his tone perfectly even. 'I'll see you then.'

Louis pulled the door shut behind him, and Sophie stood for a second or two looking at its smooth surface.

'Should have stuck to Plan Nice,' she told herself. She knew that Plan Nice would have worked eventually, but for some reason at that moment when she had looked into his eyes she'd felt like she could ask him anything and that he'd tell her the truth. But whatever she had felt then, she must have been wrong.

She blamed Carrie's children. Ever since they had arrived in her life she had been slowly but surely losing any sense of decorum and composure.

CHAPTER 19

Sophie had taken the girls to see Tess at her office for a change, because she had to get out of the flat and Louis had said he would come in the afternoon for once – he had things to sort.

The last eight days of constant heavy rain and electric light during the day had finally got to her and filled her head with cotton wool that was scarcely improved by the frantic visits she had managed to make to the office. She knew she should be gearing up for the next big event, but where work was concerned she couldn't seem to get out of neutral. It was just as well that the success of the ship party was still carrying her high for now.

She'd had eight days of Louis filling the flat with his presence to such an extent that Sophie thought it must actually be shrinking, or else he was growing even taller, Alice-in-Wonderland-style. Eight days of Bella often secluded in the bedroom, alone except for Artemis and her felt-tips, producing drawing after drawing of a sea filled with mermaids. And eight mornings of Louis's perfect politeness, his initial attempt at a warmer friendliness seemingly abandoned.

There had been one occasion when Sophie thought that perhaps there could have been a thaw in relations between them.

On the sixth day a beam of sunlight had fought its way through the clouds and there had been a break in the relentless wet weather. Louis and Sophie had simultaneously come to the decision that they should take an immediate trip to the park without even having to confer. Sophie had gone into the bedroom and grabbed the girls' wellies from under the bed just as Louis had been finding coats and hats. They had bumped into each other in the hallway.

'I thought we could—' Sophie had begun.

'Take them to the park,' Louis had concluded. They had laughed awkwardly and set about rousing the girls from their fifth viewing of *The Little Mermaid* that week.

They had taken the short trip to the park in a truncated column of two by two. Louis and Izzy had led the party, with Izzy skipping, hopping and swinging on Louis's hand and Bella and Sophie bringing up the rear in almost complete silence.

'You must have seen it a hundred times,' Sophie had said, trying to placate Bella's annoyance at having her favourite movie cut short.

'I wanted to see the end,' Bella had said petulantly.

'You can see it when we get back. Look, Bella

why don't you try doing something radical – like enjoying yourself?'

Bella had looked up at her and sighed deeply. 'I'm trying,' she had said. 'It's all these days inside in my head making me cross. I'm sorry.'

Sophie had smiled at her and picked up her hand. 'I know how you feel. Come on,' she had said as they entered the park. 'Let's see how high we can swing on the swings!'

Sophie had been pushing Bella as high as she possibly could when Izzy fell off the slide. She didn't fall very far or very hard, but as she had put out her hands to break her landing she had grazed her palms quite badly. Sophie had had to resist the urge to run to her in a way that had become an everyday reaction in the last few weeks, especially as Izzy was an expert in getting into the kind of scrape that usually resulted in minor injury. She had watched Louis pick her up and hold her tightly, but still she cried.

'So— So— Sophie,' she had wailed and stretched out her arms. Louis had brought her over to the swings straight away, and as Sophie sat down on one he lifted Izzy onto her lap.

'Let me see,' Sophie had said, examining the grazed palms very carefully. 'Ohhh that must sting ever so.' She kissed each palm gently. 'Is that a bit better?'

'A bit,' Izzy had confirmed bravely with a noisy sniff. Sophie reached into her pocket and pulled out a tissue to gently blot Izzy's face, and a tube of Savlon that had evicted her lipgloss from its usual home. In the meantime Louis had crouched down in front of the swing, his hands either side of Sophie, holding the swing chains steady. It felt odd to have this virtual stranger in such close proximity. It gave Sophie a curious, tilted feeling, almost like being drunk in the daytime.

Bella had peered over Sophie's shoulder. 'Hardly anything there!' she had scoffed as Sophie smoothed antiseptic cream on Izzy's wounds.

Sophie had shot Bella a warning look. 'Don't worry, this magic cream will make it all better, OK?' she had said.

''kay,' Izzy had sniffed again. 'But you carry me though.' And the small group had returned to the confines of the flat. This time Louis had walked on his own a few paces behind the slow and lumbering girls, and Sophie was sure she had developed a hernia.

When Louis had left, a little while later, Sophie had followed him downstairs, hoping there'd be some post for her to collect that wasn't a credit-card bill.

'She wanted you, didn't she?' Louis had said as he opened the door. 'Wanted you to comfort her, I mean. Kiss it better.' He had dropped his chin. 'I suppose I shouldn't be surprised, I mean she's known you longer than she's known me, but it made me realise that even with Izzy, getting her to trust me isn't as easy as just turning up and making her laugh. She still wanted you.' It was the first time in days Louis had said anything to Sophie that wasn't strictly necessary, and for a moment she didn't know how to respond.

She had taken a step closer to him. 'It will take time,' she had said eventually and inadequately. 'But you have to be prepared for it to take as long as the girls think it should take.' Sophie had decided to share with him one of the many things she had learnt about children just recently. 'You can't rush a way a person is feeling, even little people. They feel emotions too. Properly and really, I mean,' she had said, nodding with emphasis.

Louis's mouth had twitched in a smile.

'What now?' she had said, fighting her impulse to return the smile. 'Look, you might think I'm funny but I've only been doing this a couple of weeks. I've only just realised that children are humans!'

Louis had laughed and Sophie couldn't help but join in then. 'I don't know what Carrie was thinking when she made me the girls' guardian,' she had said wryly.

'You're doing amazingly well, Sophie. You were so good with Izzy today. It must be amazing to be three and really believe in magic, that someone's kisses can take away all the pain.' Louis's smile had dimmed fractionally. 'I wish they had wanted me.'

Without thinking Sophie had stretched out a hand and rested it on his arm.

'One day they will, I'm sure,' she had said, knowing that it was probably true and feeling a little jealous of the time when she wouldn't mean so much to the children. When she would just be distant 'Aunty Sophie' again and not someone who was vital and important.

'You should go now,' she had said, a little abruptly.

'Same time tomorrow?'

Sophie had considered the prospect with resignation. 'No chance of a break, is there?' she'd asked him on impulse.

Louis's face had darkened. 'A break? I thought you understood how much time I've got to make up. A break for who? For you? Because this isn't about you.'

'I know that,' Sophie had snapped at him angrily. 'I sort of guessed that when my normal life went totally to pot just so I could babysit your children!' She caught the rise in her voice and forcibly subdued it. 'I thought for the girls,' she lied shamelessly. 'A break for them to clear their heads, a chance to relax a bit without you . . . being . . . everywhere they look.'

Louis's face had been perfectly still for a moment and then he'd shaken his head. 'Sophie, I'm sorry you don't like me but, like I said, this isn't about you. Same time tomorrow.'

The thaw was definitely over.

Tess was trying to explain Louis's position to Sophie, who was only half-listening as she watched the girls run up and down the corridor outside Tess's office like a pair of Muppets. Occasionally a flash of pink and purple sped by, preceded a second earlier by demented giggles. 'He was married to Carrie you see, which means he is automatically granted parental responsibility . . .'

'Yes, but every dad has that; it doesn't mean every dad deserves it,' Sophie said tartly.

'Well, no, actually if they hadn't been married he would have no automatic rights at all, not according to the law. But anyway, by leaving the family home, by not contacting the girls or making formal arrangements to support them financially or emotionally, he has contravened the terms of parental responsibility and so if the court considers it proper they could forfeit his rights. Ultimately it's up to a judge to decide whether or not he should have parental responsibility re-instated, and whether or not he should be granted a residency order and with it full custody of the children.'

Sophie blinked at her. 'And?' she said. 'What are they going to decide?'

Tess shrugged and took a sip of her coffee. It was still disgusting even at room temperature and with four sachets of Sweet'n Low emptied into it.

'I'd say it was almost clear-cut. Louis has come out of his background checks extremely well. Not a blemish on his record in this country, and did you know that when he was in Peru he helped a charity that took homeless and abandoned disabled children off the streets of Lima? These kids were given a chance at education and a life other than trying to scrape an existence picking over rubbish tips. He was quite literally giving them a chance to grow up.'

Tess was going all misty-eyed, so Sophie tutted loudly. 'Yes, well,' she said. 'That whole St Francis of Assisi thing would play a lot better with me if he hadn't actually abandoned his own children.'

Tess had to admit that Sophie had a point. 'Yes, it is a dilemma, but the court makes a point of accepting that good people make bad mistakes. It doesn't like to split up a family unless it absolutely has to.' Tess more or less quoted from the book on family law she had been reading the night before to make sure she was absolutely clear on all the proceedings that were even now under way. Louis had come back from Peru without much money, but what little he did have he had invested in a respectable B&B and a good solicitor, and although the legal side was strictly speaking down to the authority's legal team, Tess prided herself on knowing what she was talking about. 'And, of course, what the girls want has an awful lot to do with it. That and my recommendations. I have to file my report by the end of this week.'

Another flash of colour whizzed by the open door. Tess examined Sophie's profile as she watched the girls at play, an unconscious smile lightening the edges of her mouth. Tess leaned forward on her desk. 'What interests me most at the moment, Sophie,' she said, 'is what you think. What do you want to happen?'

Sophie jerked her head round to look at Tess. 'How do you mean?' she asked.

'Well, I more or less press-ganged you into taking the girls, didn't I?'

Sophie nodded, pursed her lips and crossed her arms just to show that she still hadn't entirely forgiven Tess for that.

'Well, then it either meant you took them or they were taken into care. I had to rush through the temporary residency order because I was so scared you'd change your mind. That was twenty-odd years of collecting favours gone in two days.' Sophie raised her eyebrows. She hadn't realised. 'When you were looking for Louis, you were doing so in order to provide an alternative to you. So that it would be between Louis and going into care. So you could get back to your life and not feel guilty.'

Sophie looked a bit sheepish. 'Ah well – see, that's not *exactly* true . . .'

But Tess waved away her feeble protest. 'It is,' she said. 'But that's not my point. My point is, if I understand what's happening here, you're not just prepared to keep the girls indefinitely until they go somewhere else to live. I think if it came down to it you would actually have them for keeps.'

Sophie expected herself to scoff but the scoff

did not arrive. Instead she examined the very last remnants of her nail varnish and let a nagging and terrifying thought that had been plaguing the back of her mind since her conversation on the stairs with Bella, finally form itself.

'I don't know,' she said carefully. 'But if it really wasn't going to work out with Louis then, well – do you think that I could do it? Give them a good home?'

Tess looked at her. 'Actually I think you could,' she said seriously. 'But Louis is here now. Something would have to go badly wrong for that situation to arise. You understand that, don't you?'

'I know,' Sophie said. 'It's stupid to even think about it really. It would never work. I have my career and . . .' She couldn't think of anything else to say.

Tess shifted in her seat. 'Well, the girls have a natural parent alive, present and correct and prepared to take them,' she said, 'and he is doing his best to make himself viable. He's lined up an interview with the NSPCC, and he should have a job and a permanent place to stay soon. He's been asking about when Bella will be found a temporary school place. He's worried she's missed too much already, and she has.'

'It's the Christmas holidays,' Sophie said, as if she knew what she was talking about.

'Sophie, it's February! Anyway, Louis's been in touch with Bella's old school and they are holding a place for her; apparently she was their star pupil. And Izzy's nursery would be delighted to have her back.'

Sophie cursed herself. The reason she didn't know about any of this was because she had rashly abandoned Plan Nice. She'd pushed Louis too far and now he didn't seem to like her much, a consequence she found disturbing, because if – as Tess said – it was inevitable that they returned to him, she didn't want to lose the children completely from her life.

Then she thought about exactly what Tess had just said. 'Their old schools in St Ives?'

Tess leant back in her chair. 'Yes. They won't be going anywhere until this is all settled and the supervision order is lifted, but I ought to tell you that it will be settled soon, Sophie, it could even be in the next couple of weeks. All being well, I think the girls will go back home to Cornwall with their father. And I think that will be the best thing for them.'

Sophie tried to imagine what it would be like to have her old, peaceful, ordered life back again. 'But Bella hates him.' She decided not to imagine such a restoration to civilisation just then. 'She really hates him, and you said it matters what the children want.'

Tess nodded. 'It does,' she said, carefully. 'It does matter what the children want but I don't think Bella hates him, not really. She's hurt and angry and worried and confused. But she doesn't hate him.' Tess smiled, and reaching over the desk she placed her warm and heavy hand over Sophie's light and cold one, squeezing it for a moment. 'I think what you've done for the girls so far has been wonderful; much, much more than I ever expected. You've brought Bella out of her shell and I know that Izzy's taking short trips in the car now. All that means so much. But there's one thing you have to do, the only thing you can do really – you have to help Bella come to terms with what has happened. You have to help her make friends with her dad and then Izzy won't have to worry about who to be loyal to all the time. And while you're at it perhaps you could make friends with Louis yourself. It would be so much easier for the girls,' Tess added cautiously.

The shouts from outside grew louder and suddenly Tess's office was filled with noise as Bella and Izzy crash-landed into Sophie, giggling and laughing. Sophie grinned at them.

'Ready, steady – go!' she shouted and they were off again. She turned back to Tess, her smile vanishing instantly.

'But, I mean, what about the reasons why Louis and Carrie split up? What about why he didn't stay in touch with the girls? Doesn't that matter at all?'

'It matters to you, I can see that – but families drift apart for all the wrong reasons every day. It's a tragic fact. It's up to people like me to try to make sure it doesn't happen in the first place, or to try to repair the damage when it does. We have a really good chance to repair a family here, Sophie – to repair lives. And I have to admit that it's largely thanks to you. Louis is not a criminal, or an abuser. The kind of man he is now is what is important. The past doesn't really matter any more,' Tess said, echoing Louis's words. 'If I could just see that Bella and Louis were making progress together I'd feel so much better. Then this terrible time of their lives would be over at last, and they'd be able to start again. Will you help them? Because, I'll be honest, I think that you're the only person who really can.'

Sophie paused for a moment, feeling as if the pit of her stomach was filling with heavy black stones. There really was only one thing she could say. 'Of course I'll help her. I'll help them both, I just want them to be happy.'

It was curious, Sophie thought, as she hurried the girls back to the flat in time to meet Louis, that *she* didn't feel happier. Elated, even. Somehow, through all the chaos, she had managed to pull off quite a coup. She'd rescued the girls from care and kept a promise to Carrie, made her boss love her and possibly even secured herself a promotion in the process. She had located the apparently perfect father more or less single-handedly and was now helping to restore the girls to family life, a family life in the place that they loved and called home. She should feel triumphant.

In less than a month she'd have her bed back, she'd hopefully have a major promotion and much more shoe money than she could ever need – well, perhaps not *that* much. She'd have peace and quiet and all the time in the world to pluck her eyebrows and wax her legs and watch films featuring scenes of a sexual and violent nature. She could even start smoking properly again. She should feel ecstatic.

But she didn't, she didn't feel that way at all.

'Maybe,' Sophie thought reluctantly as she let the girls into the flat, 'it's because I'm afraid of what I will feel when my "perfect" life is fully re-instated. Perhaps I'm afraid of being something I have always been, but never allowed myself to think about before the girls came. Perhaps it's because I'm afraid of being alone – again.'

This was probably why she called Jake, even although she had barely thought of him since the last time they had spoken. He had told her to call him when she figured out what she wanted. Well, she knew one thing, she didn't want her life to go back to the empty impersonal routine it had been. She was loath to admit that her mother could be right about anything, but maybe she was right about this – she did need someone in her life.

'I thought I wasn't going to hear from you again,' Jake said, his voice neutrally pleasant. 'I thought I'd blown it. I'm glad you called, Sophie, unless it's to tell me it's over, that is!' He chuckled nervously.

'We haven't even begun yet, Jake,' Sophie said tentatively.

322

'Are we going to?'

'You know,' Sophie said with a smile, 'you really should ask me what I think about the weather first and then something else general and meaningless before you plunge into all this important stuff.'

Jake laughed. 'I just want to see you,' he said.

Sophie pushed the threatening echoes of loneliness firmly out of her mind and thought about the handsome, kind, considerate man who really did seem to care about her. She was sure he would fill the gap that would be left when the girls were gone. She was sure if she put her mind to it she could really care about him.

'I want to see you too,' she said.

'When?' Jake asked her, all trace of neutrality gone.

'This evening?' Sophie said, suddenly wanting to see him quite badly.

'I'll be there.'

'Three tickets to see . . .' Louis drew out the suspense to such an extent that Sophie thought Izzy might actually pop, '. . . *The Little Mermaid on Ice* – this afternoon!' he finished.

Izzy screamed and danced around the coffee table. He grinned at Sophie, so pleased with himself that he forgot to be frosty. 'Although I've got to say it sounds like animal cruelty to me, but still . . .'

Sophie found herself laughing and stopped when she caught Bella's expression. Bella glared at her and then looked down at the three tickets that Louis had fanned out on the coffee table.

'No thank you,' she said.

Sophie bent down a little and put an arm around her shoulders. 'But it's *The Little Mermaid*, you love *The Little Mermaid*!'

'There's only three tickets,' Bella said.

Louis caught Izzy as she danced by and hoisted her onto his hip in one fluid movement.

'Ah, yes,' he said. 'Look Bella, I'm sorry – I didn't want to leave Sophie out, it's just, well, there were only three tickets left . . .'

Bella stared at him. 'I'm not going unless Sophie can come.'

Sophie sighed and remembered what Tess had told her. 'Well, perhaps I could buy another ticket on the door?' she suggested. Louis's face fell and she realised that he had hoped that if he suggested something he knew Bella would love, she might actually want to go with him and Izzy. But mainly him – without Sophie. He had been trying to move out of what he must see as an implacable stalemate.

'You won't, it's sold out now – I got those three from a tout. Can you believe there are *touts* selling tickets to see *The Little Mermaid on Ice* – what kind of world are we living in?' he said glumly. He sat down heavily on the sofa and Izzy landed on his lap with a giggle. 'Look, you three take them and go, I'll see you all tomorrow.'

Before Bella could react Izzy launched her

protest. 'Noooooooooo,' she wailed. 'I want to go with Daddy not Sophie! Bella *please* come with us! *Please!*'

Bella looked at the tickets again, and at her sister in Louis's arms. 'I'm sorry,' she said quietly. 'I can't.' She turned on her heel and walked steadily out of the room.

Sophie sat down on the sofa next to Louis. 'She really wants to go, you know,' she said. '*The Little Mermaid* is her favourite.'

'I know,' Louis said, clearly uncertain where Sophie was coming from. 'Just not with me.'

'I don't know. I think she wants to go with you, but there's something stopping her. It's like she said, she just can't.'

Izzy climbed off Louis's lap and fluffed her fairy skirt. 'I need a poo,' she told them matter-of-factly, and skipped out of the room.

Sophie thought for a moment and then looked at Louis. 'I saw Tess today,' she said. 'She told me you're more or less up for father of the year.'

Louis looked surprised, delighted and then wary in turn. 'You mean . . . ?'

Sophie nodded. 'She says she thinks things will go your way as long as her report supports you. And as I'm fairly sure she's in love with you I don't think you're going to have to worry on that score.' Sophie thought of Tess's advice. 'Look, Louis – we have to clear the air between us. Carrie was my best friend. I loved her and I suppose I've been trying to defend her, which means sometimes

I've been a bit out of order with you. I wanted to know what went wrong and why she didn't tell me.' Louis began to talk but Sophie stopped him. 'I wanted to know for Carrie's sake, and Bella's, but mainly for me. I thought I was her best friend, but when it came to the crunch she didn't talk to me, she didn't tell me anything. Maybe just because I didn't ask her and because I didn't care enough to notice. I want to be a friend to the girls and . . . and you. I'm sorry I was so prickly to begin with. I've been feeling bad myself, but I'm trying to look at the big picture now. So,' Sophie offered him a tentative smile. 'Can we start again?'

Louis's face relaxed and opened into a smile. 'Of course,' he said, with a rush of warmth. 'God I'd love that.' There was a moment's silence as each of them tried to work out how to adjust their tenuous relationship to a more friendly one.

'I miss her too, you know,' Louis said after a while, and it took Sophie a second to realise he was talking about Carrie. 'I can't believe that she's dead. She was so . . .' He paused, struggling to find the right words. 'She was such a force of nature, she seemed invincible. And I still cared about her, I still hoped she finally got what she wanted, that everything worked out as she planned.' He looked down. 'I really wish she was here now.'

Sophie looked at him and for the first time she got an inkling that perhaps it wasn't Louis who had walked out on Carrie. Perhaps, just perhaps, Carrie had sent him away. But why, when she had told Sophie often enough that he was the love of her life? There were so many questions Sophie wanted to ask him, but she had no intention of making the same mistake again. Instead, she would let her truce with Louis hold and gradually strengthen. Besides, there were other more important things to think about now.

'You go to *The Little Mermaid*,' Sophie told Louis. 'Go and take Izzy with you. I'll stay with Bella. Perhaps I can try to talk her round.'

'Aren't you afraid I might kidnap Izzy or something? What about having to stay with us?' Louis said, looking up at her with that effortlessly intense gaze he managed so well.

It took Sophie a moment to find her voice. 'No,' she said, finally managing to speak. 'If you'd been taking both of them I might have worried, but I know you wouldn't go without Bella.'

'You're right,' he said, 'I wouldn't leave my Bellarina – not again, anyway.' He gave a mirthless laugh and glanced out of the window at the afternoon sky glowering darkly over the rooftops. 'I used to take her for walks every day after work. I worked earlies at the printers so I'd be home by five. Every day we'd go for a walk, unless it was snowing or really cold. When she was a tiny baby it was to give Carrie a break, and then as she got bigger just because we wanted to.

'In the summer I'd wheel her in her pram along

the cliff walk and we'd look at the birds and the sun on the sea. In the winter I'd take her past the beach up the hill opposite the town, and we'd watch the lights glittering against the sky and try to count the stars. When we got back she'd draw what we'd seen for Carrie while I made her tea. She never got to bed till well past seven but Carrie said it didn't matter, it was more important that we had our special time together, that we had a chance to be friends.' Louis paused and swallowed. 'Bella was my best friend. We learned something new together every day.' He slumped back in the sofa. 'I blew it, didn't I? I didn't really stop to think about anyone else but myself, I know that now. I've known it for a long time. I just wish I could make her understand how much I've missed her. How sorry I am.'

Sophie nodded. 'I know.'

'Really?'

'I think I'm beginning to,' she said.

They watched each other for a moment in the half-light of the dark damp day, and Sophie wondered if Louis was seeing her in the same way she was seeing him. As someone she had really only just met about four or five minutes ago.

'Right.' Izzy reappeared with her mac on over her fairy dress. 'I've finished my poo and I did *most* of it in the toilet!'

CHAPTER 20

After they had gone Sophie sat in the shadows and listened to the silence of her home. It was a sound she had grown used to in her years in the flat, the sound of her private life, her very own bubble – a contented background hum. But somewhere lost in that silence was Bella, and suddenly Sophie wished with all her heart for noise and plenty of it.

She thought about Louis describing his daily walks with Bella, their exploration around the coast of St Ives, the ideas and the stories they would have created as they walked. Either he was an excellent actor and a consummate conman *or* Tess was right – he was basically a good man who'd done some very stupid things. But how did you explain that to a girl who had once idolised her father and had found out far too soon that he was only human?

It seemed as if Bella was holding too tightly to herself and to her sister to be able to consider letting anyone else in, even her father. She was trying, with all her might, to hold onto Carrie and to love her in exactly the same way that she had when she had been dropped off for school on the day that Carrie had died. No-one knew better than Sophie how hard that was, and how such an effort could wear you out.

Poking out from under the corner of Artemis's chair was one of Bella's prolific drawings. Sophie bent over and scooped it up. As usual it was a picture of the sea, drawn with bold swirls of grey, green and blue, leaving intentional gaps of white paper that made it look as if it really was a body of water rising and falling with the tide. In the midst of the sea were the mermaids, ten or so little curly-haired girls garlanded with flowers, laughing and playing. They reminded Sophie of someone – of Carrie, of course. In the background Bella had drawn the shore, always the same in each picture, a hill rising out of the sea with little box-shaped houses on its crest, carefully coloured around so that they remained white.

Sophie looked at the drawing for a long time and then she realised. The houses weren't a fantasy, another construct of Bella's fertile imagination – they were the houses in St Ives. Bella had been drawing home.

Sophie put the drawing on the coffee table and looked at her watch as she made her way to the bedroom. It was just after two – they had plenty of time before Izzy and Louis would be back from the show. Time to show Bella something that, for some reason, Sophie thought might just be really important.

She walked into the bedroom and switched on the overhead light. 'We're going out,' she said, throwing Bella's coat at her. Offended by the sudden glare, Artemis scampered out of the window with an angry yowl and Bella sat up, rubbing her eyes as her vision adjusted to the brightness.

'I don't want to go out,' she said bluntly.

'Yes you do. Come on, no arguments, just you and me. I'm taking you to see something really special.' Sophie did her best to make it sound enticing and keep her own apprehension out of her voice.

'I'm not going to *The Little Mermaid*, am I?' Bella asked with a heartbreaking mixture of belligerence and hope.

Sophie shook her head. 'No. This trip is just for you and me. Come on.'

Bella's second Tube journey was much less eventful than the first, and much quieter. She sat next to Sophie, her hand, still in its glove, slotted into Sophie's. As Sophie counted the stops as they went by, Bella made it her business to stare at everyone else on the train with open curiosity until they coughed and raised their book a little higher. They changed twice and finally got off at Blackfriars.

'Where are we going?' Bella asked again as Sophie marched her briskly through the wet streets, the shiny pavements streaked with reflections of coloured light.

'We're going to see a painting,' Sophie told her, taking a corner at such a high speed that Bella's feet almost didn't touch the ground as she struggled to keep up.

'A painting?' Bella said, clearly disappointed that it wasn't a musical extravaganza on ice. 'Where?'

Sophie stopped at the slope that led down to the entrance of Tate Modern. 'Here,' she said.

Bella looked up at the huge bulk of the converted power station standing stalwart against the silvered sky. 'Wow.'

'Exactly. Come on. We're going in.'

They were lucky. The rain, the season, the day of the week and the hour had all conspired to keep the gallery relatively unclogged, so that for once a visitor could enjoy the functional majesty of the building as well as the exhibits it contained.

'Ooooh,' Bella exclaimed, gawping at the huge sculpture that filled the foyer. 'It's gigantic!'

Sophie paused and looked up at Anthony Gormley's work.

'It is,' she agreed, flicking open the folded map. 'According to this, I think the painting I want to show you is quite far up the escalators. Let's go and look at it first, and then we can have a look at anything else you want to, OK?'

Bella hopped readily onto the escalator next to Sophie. Sophie felt a knot in the pit of her stomach. She had no idea if what she was about to show Bella would have any benefit for her at all, if it would even mean anything to the child.

But she also worried that it just might mean too much and if it did, Sophie realised, she didn't know what she would do next. But she knew, whatever happened, she had to go forward because there was nowhere else to go. And anyway she had a feeling it would turn out all right, a feeling her mother would call intuition.

With another quick look at the map, Sophie led Bella to the modern British painters wing, and then to a small room at the back of a network of galleries which overlooked the river. She pointed at a sign on the left of the entrance to the room. 'What does that say?' she asked Bella.

Bella looked at the sign for a moment and smiled. 'The St Ives School of Art!' she exclaimed. 'Are Mrs Benson's sunflower paintings in there?' she demanded, hopping towards the door in anticipation.

'No,' Sophie said. 'At least I don't think so. I think these paintings are a bit older.'

As they entered Sophie scanned the room, hoping and praying that the canvas she was looking for was here, that it hadn't got put into storage when the collection was moved from Tate Britain some years ago. And then she saw it, smaller than a painting should be, she had always thought, and almost inconsequential. In fact, when Carrie had brought her to see it in its old home across the river, her first words had been, 'A child could do better than that. *I* could do better than *that!*' But then Sophie's appreciation of art had always been much less sophisticated than Carrie's.

She took Bella over and showed her the painting.

'*St Ives, Version Two 1940*,' Sophie read out the label as Bella studied the painting closely. 'It's by a man called Ben—'

'Nicholson,' Bella finished. 'I know. Mum used to take us to Tate St Ives all the time. Some of his pictures are there too.' She looked again at the painting that Sophie remembered thinking should have been entitled *Mug and Possibly Spanner* and took a step closer.

'Home,' she said, pointing to the top right-hand corner, where Nicholson had painted the beach and part of the town of St Ives.

Sophie stood behind her and rested her hands lightly on her shoulders. She took a deep breath and began to say what she had brought Bella all this way to hear.

'They had this big exhibition of St Ives artists years and years ago, when your mum still lived near me in London. We were doing our A levels at the time. We were supposed to be revising – practising – for our exam. But your mum didn't really like practising. She said we needed to get out, get some sunshine and fresh air before we went bonkers.' Bella smiled. 'She brought me to see this painting. Well, not just this painting, she made me see the whole exhibition. But it was this painting especially that really got to her. I don't know why, but the minute she saw it she loved it.'

Sophie paused and moistened her dry lips, realising she was nervous. Bella stood perfectly still, looking at the picture, but Sophie sensed she was listening very closely.

'To be honest with you,' Sophie said, 'I never really got it. I think your pictures are better than this one – but your mum said it was called . . . um, abstract constructivism or something ism anyway.' Sophie hurriedly glossed over the parts she didn't understand. 'She said – now let me think – she said that it was powerful and emotional, that the painter had caught a moment in time and trapped it with light on the canvas for ever.' Sophie smiled as the conversation came back to her sentence by sentence. 'I said it looks like a painting of a mug to me, and she said there was no point in her practising for her art exam any more because she'd never be that good. Well, I thought she had gone bonkers, but anyway, she sat and looked at this painting for a long long time. I mooched around waiting for her until eventually I had to drag her away. I think I wanted to go to the café and have cake. Carrie looked at me and she said,

'"I'm going there, one day."

'"What? Where?" I asked her, or something like that.

'"There, St Ives," she said. "I want to sit exactly where he was when he made that, I want to see that view and feel that light on my face. It's like someone's finally shown me where my home is.

And I'm going there as soon as I can. To live and fall in love and have my children and paint. Then I'll be free of this dirty old city and free of my . . ."' Sophie stopped herself saying 'my mother' and instead inserted, '"Free of school and I'll be happy. I just know I will," she said.' Sophie told the top of Bella's head, in Carrie's own words, '"I don't know why, I just know that when I'm there I'll be so happy. This painting told me so." ' Sophie knelt down beside Bella so their heads were level.

'And she was happy, wasn't she? Because she had the sea, and the light, and Izzy and you. And she loved you both so much, Bella.'

On the last word Bella crumbled onto the floor and buried her face in her hands. For a split second Sophie watched her, watched her shoulders shudder and shake and realised that, probably for the first time since her mother had died, Bella was crying.

'It's OK,' Sophie said. 'It's OK darling, it's OK.' She put her arms around Bella, who turned into her embrace.

'Mummy,' she said, through her sobs. 'I just want Mummy back.'

Sophie was glad that the people who happened into the small gallery took one look at the distraught child on the floor, turned around and walked right out again. They sat there for a long time until Sophie felt the damp of Bella's tears pervade her jacket, until Bella's shoulders stilled except for the occasional long and deep shuddering breath and at last she was quiet. It was then that Sophie realised she had been rocking her. She stopped and brushed the damp hair from Bella's face.

'I'm sorry,' Sophie said. 'I didn't want to make you sad.'

'But I'm sad anyway,' Bella said softly. 'All the time.'

Sophie nodded. 'I know.'

'Because it was just like a normal day,' Bella said and Sophie held herself perfectly still, as if any sudden movement might frighten Bella back into silence. 'We'd stopped on the corner so that I could walk into school with Lucy like always and she rolled down the window for a kiss. It always stuck halfway so I had to stand on my toes to kiss her. And then I ran off and never thought about her again until – I never looked back or waved goodbye or anything.'

Sophie stayed silent.

'One of our gerbils died, before. He was the only person I'd ever known who died and Mummy got us another one that looked just the same and after a while Izzy forgot it was a different hamster. I don't want her to forget Mummy and just remember him. *I* don't want to forget Mummy. I keep expecting her to come and collect us. I keep wishing she would just *come*. But she won't.'

'No,' Sophie agreed gently. 'She won't. But listen, Bella, you and Izzy, you're not alone in the world. You have me, and Grandma and Tess and you have Louis. You have your dad.'

'I don't want him,' Bella said, but without anger.

Sophie kissed the top of her head. 'Don't you?' she asked quietly. 'Are you sure? You must remember how much you loved him once, otherwise you wouldn't hate him so much now.'

'He just went too,' Bella said. 'He didn't say goodbye to me like I didn't say goodbye to Mum. He can't just come back and be all happy when Mum can't. He just *can't*, it's not fair.'

Sophie understood Bella's logic perfectly and she knew that in some ways she was right. It wasn't fair.

'I don't think he thinks that he can,' she said. 'I think he just wants to make friends with you again. He said he wishes you'd never fallen out and I believe him.' Sophie thought about everything Tess had said to her that morning. 'Look, when he first came I was angry with him too, but I don't think he did what he did to hurt you. I think he sort of did it to hurt himself.' Bella looked up at Sophie with a furrowed brow. 'What I mean is, I think he's a good person and that you should give him a chance.'

Bella did not look convinced.

'OK,' Sophie tried again. 'I loved your mum and your mum loved me, I think – what do you think?'

Bella smiled. 'Yes, she used to tell us about you. You made her laugh a lot.'

'Well, before all this happened I hadn't seen your mum for ages, for years actually. But I still loved her. I still knew that when we saw each other the next time things would be like they always were between us, because I still loved her. And when – when I realised that I'd missed my chance to see her again I was very angry with myself. I still am. But I let you and Izzy come and stay with me, even though you are noisy, messy *brats*.' Bella smiled and nodded in agreement. 'I didn't do it because I loved you, you pair of hooligans. I did it because I still loved your mum. Even after all those years and even though she was dead I still wanted to be a friend to her. It is possible to still care about a person even when you're miles away. Even when you don't see them all the time.'

Bella studied Sophie's face as she thought about what she'd said. 'Do you like us now?' she asked Sophie after a beat. 'Me and Izzy, I mean.'

Sophie laughed. 'Of course I do, I *love* you now!' She realised it was true as she said it.

'Good.' Bella clambered to her feet. 'Because I suppose I love you too.'

She held out a hand and Sophie let her think she was hauling her up.

'Thank you, Aunty Sophie,' Bella said, as Sophie stamped her numb foot down a few times.

'For what?'

'For bringing me here to see the painting. I don't know why. But I feel better now I've seen it. I feel sort of – lighter.'

'I'm glad,' Sophie said, with palpable relief. 'I truly am. Come on, let's go to the gift shop.'

'Oooh,' Bella said. 'Are we going to buy a rubber?'

There were no posters of Ben Nicholson's painting, and no postcards either. The only reproduction that Sophie could find was in a huge yellow book about him, with a cost that she assumed was calculated in direct proportion to its enormous weight and bulk.

'That's a lot of money for one picture, especially considering that I'm planning to rip it out,' she told the young man behind the counter, who watched her consider the purchase, the book open at the painting.

'Not a huge Nicholson fan then?' he said, giving Sophie his best cute smile as she glanced up at him.

'I am,' Bella said, standing on her tiptoes so that she could peer over the counter. 'But I've only got fifty-seven pee.'

The man nodded at her. 'Cool,' he said to Sophie. 'Cool kid – yours?' He looked back up at Sophie, who was slightly flushed by her time at the Tate, her hair tousled and a little wild.

'Er, no,' she said, considering the question a rather personal one.

'Ah, so you're sort of a mentor. Cool,' the young man, probably a student, said again. He glanced around the near-empty shop. 'Look, hang on a minute.' And he took the book and vanished.

In his absence two tourists joined the queue

and after a minute or so one began tapping her foot.

'He'll be back soon,' Bella told her quite sternly. The tourist stopped tapping.

At last the young man returned and handed Sophie a tube. 'Colour photocopies of your painting,' he told her, leaning over the counter so that his cheek was close to hers. 'Pretty good quality too and I enlarged them. They're on me.' He sat up again and looked down at Bella. 'You can start saving for the book, I reckon you'll be able to afford it by 2010.' He winked at Sophie. 'Don't tell anyone, OK? I'll get shot and then I'll never finish college.'

Sophie smiled warmly at him and noticed that he was a kindred spirit in the skin department at least, as both his cheeks flushed a deep red in an instant.

'Thank you so much,' she said. 'That's really kind.'

'Not that kind,' the man said. 'I made you two copies. My phone number's on the back of one. Maybe you'll call me sometime?'

'Er, thank you,' Sophie said one last time before they left the building. That was very nice of him, she thought as she steered Bella towards the exit. But quite honestly she just couldn't think of a reason why she would ever call him.

'He liked you,' Bella told her as they emerged into the chill of the dark afternoon.

Sophie laughed. 'Don't be silly,' she said.

'Oh, Aunty Sophie,' Bella said pityingly. 'No wonder you haven't got a boyfriend. Lots of men like you and you don't seem to notice!'

Sophie stopped and looked down at her. 'What are you on about?' she asked her.

'That Jake. Anyone could tell he was in love with you, following you around, helping us home when we'd been shopping that time.'

Sophie smiled and felt a gush of warmth towards Jake. 'Yes,' she said. 'That was nice, wasn't it.'

'And most men look at you when we're out, even *he* thinks you're pretty.'

'Who?'

Bella looked up at Sophie and shrugged. 'Even Louis thinks you're pretty – it's obvious.'

Sophie laughed and shook her head. 'And why do you think that?' she asked her, only because if Bella was clearly so delusional about Louis there was a chance she could be wrong about Jake.

'Because,' Bella said, 'whenever you're not looking at him he looks at you and when you do look at him he has to try really hard not to look away.'

'Oh,' Sophie said. 'Really? I mean nonsense!'

It was foolish, but for some reason that piece of information had started a flutter in the pit of her stomach.

'I'm not saying he loves you or anything, like Jake does,' Bella said bluntly. 'In fact he probably thinks you're quite bossy and rude. But he definitely must think you're really pretty, else he wouldn't look at you and not look at you.'

'We're going to be late,' Sophie said hurriedly, taking Bella's hand and heading towards the Tube station. She didn't want to think the thoughts that Bella's offhand comment had stirred up. She wanted to think about Jake carrying all their bags home on the bus instead.

When they got in Sophie unrolled the two coloured photocopies of the painting, separated one and smoothed it out on the table.

'When things have settled a bit,' she said, 'I'll put this in a frame for you. But for now—' Bella followed Sophie into the bedroom where she Blu-Tacked the picture onto the wardrobe opposite the end of the bed. 'Now you'll be able to look at the painting whenever you like. And you'll be able to think about your mum. You can be sad when you think about her and you can be happy. Both are allowed.'

Bella sat on the edge of the bed. 'I think I'll do a drawing,' she said, and Sophie breathed a sigh of relief. It seemed as if she had done the right thing after all.

She was engaged in the new-to-her art of preparing fresh vegetables when Louis and Izzy came back. She had expected to hear Izzy's hollering long before she arrived, but instead Louis appeared behind her in the kitchen doorway, making her jump. Izzy was fast asleep in his arms.

'The downstairs door wasn't shut properly, and your flat door was on the latch,' he said by way of explanation, looking wary of making her cross again. 'Shall I put her in the bedroom?'

'No, just put her on the sofa for now,' she whispered.

He deposited the child carefully and came back into the kitchen where Sophie was peering at the never previously used cookery book. She was attempting lamb stew. It was difficult already, but Louis's presence in the tiny room was making it near impossible. She shut the book with a snap and turned around to look at him.

'How did it go?' she asked quickly, feeling the need to breathe in to maintain the foot or so distance between them.

'Great,' Louis said, a slow smile spreading across his face as he reflected on the day. 'Really great, but my God, she's a real live wire isn't she?' he chuckled. 'I thought we were going to get thrown out at one point.'

Sophie smiled at him. 'Yeah, been there,' she told him. 'Frequently.'

'But she loved it. She thought it was magic, I mean real magic. It must be great to still truly believe in magical things. It's a shame really that one day she'll have to find out it's not true.'

Sophie shrugged. 'I don't know, Carrie always believed in the magical, she even saw it in all the mundane things around her. I think Izzy will prob-ably be just the same.'

They smiled at each for a moment, and Sophie

realised belatedly that she was still holding her sharp knife rather aggressively.

'I'll get off,' Louis said, looking slightly uncomfortable as Sophie stared at the potential weapon in her hand with some surprise.

'Oh, OK – right. Well, bye then,' she said.

'If you like you could have tea here.' It was Bella.

She stood in the doorway and looked up at Louis.

'Really?' he said cautiously. 'With you, you mean?'

'And Izzy and Sophie too,' Bella said. 'Obviously. Although I don't think we'll all fit on the kitchen floor.'

'Er – thank you.'

'That's OK,' Bella said. And she went back into the living room and turned on the TV. Her slumbering sister didn't even stir.

'You might not want to stay for tea actually,' Sophie said, feeling foolish and suddenly nervous.

Louis's face fell. 'Oh, right, well, if you think it's a terrible idea – too soon and all that, I suppose . . .' he began.

'Oh no,' Sophie said, smiling at him. 'I think it's a great idea. It's just that – well, I really can't cook.'

'Well, that's lucky then, because I can. Move over.'

For the first time ever Louis got Izzy ready for bed, and although she still didn't allow him to do anything for her, Bella let him read Izzy a bedtime story in the bedroom as she sat on the sofa and finally finished her fairy pony story for Sophie.

'The end,' Bella said, looking very satisfied.

'That was wonderful,' Sophie said, sincerely.

'I know,' Bella said. As Louis came into the living room she went out, pausing to say a formal good-night on the way. He sat down on the sofa next to Sophie uninvited, and much more relaxed than this morning.

She edged away from him, suddenly feeling self-conscious for some reason.

'I don't know how to thank you,' Louis told her. 'I just owe you so much and I hardly even know you.' Sophie shrugged. 'Except I feel as if I've always known you, through Carrie I mean,' he added hurriedly.

'Oh well, you know . . .' she said awkwardly, willing the blotches to stay dormant.

Sophie remembered Tess telling her how important it was to stay friends with Louis, but somehow the more she liked him the harder that seemed to be. And ever since Bella had told her that Louis must think she was pretty that had made things worse, shifted whatever kind of fledgling relationship that she might have with Louis, so that she felt nervous and unsettled.

As if sensing her discomfort, Louis stood up and went to look out of the window at the traffic rushing by.

'There's two weeks until Tess files her report and

the court makes a decision. It seems like too long and not long enough at the same time, do you know what I mean?'

Sophie nodded. She knew exactly what he meant.

'I don't know what to do next,' Louis confessed. 'I thought it would be easy, like it was with the kids in Lima, but although I cared about those kids, a lot, I didn't love them, they weren't part of me. I'm so frightened of messing up this chance with Bella that I keep thinking I'll do or say something stupid every time I see her.' He looked at Sophie and smiled. 'It's bit like falling in love.'

'Well,' Sophie said, taking a deep breath. 'I did have an idea today, one that would have to involve all of us to work. But I think there is a way we can finally get Bella to completely relax and open up. And a way of settling Izzy too.' Louis turned in his seat and studied Sophie's face carefully. It was the last straw as far as her complexion was concerned, the blotches were definitely coming.

'Really?' he asked her. 'Tell me.'

'Well,' Sophie paused. 'I think we should use these two weeks to take the girls back to St Ives for a visit.' She could scarcely believe her own ears. 'I mean, you have to go down there anyway, don't you, to find a place to live and a job, so I think we should all go, a sort of a halfway visit. I think you and I should take them home.'

They were still discussing how and when, when Jake arrived.

347

'Jake!' Sophie beamed her best hostess smile at him as she led him up the stairs.

'You hadn't forgotten I was coming, had you?' Jake joked.

'Don't be silly,' Sophie said, guiltily enough to make Jake look at her sharply.

She led him into the living room, where Louis was standing with his jacket in his hand. If Louis seemed to fill up the small room, having two men in it made Sophie feel like she could only hover in the doorway. Jake and Louis looked at each other.

'You're the father,' Jake said pleasantly, leaning forward and offering a hand accompanied by his all-American smile.

'Louis Gregory,' Louis said. He raised an eyebrow at Sophie, who at that precise moment had been somewhat distracted by the sight of two very good-looking men standing next to her sofa.

'Oh – er, sorry – Louis, this is Jake, my . . . friend,' she said with a neutrally apologetic shrug. The men shook hands quickly and then withdrew, each taking a pace back. A bit like pistols at dawn, Sophie thought.

Louis stood up straighter so that he edged above Jake by a couple of inches. Jake broadened his shoulders and puffed himself out like Artemis when she was cross.

There was a long moment of silence when nobody moved. Somehow a casual meeting that should have been brief and meaningless seemed charged with tension. Jake was the first to move. He held out a carrier bag to Sophie.

'I picked us up a couple of bottles of Pinot Grigio,' he said, with slight emphasis on the word 'us'.

'I love Italian wine,' Louis said.

Sophie looked at him. 'Oh? Well – do you want to stay and have a glass?' she asked him, compulsively well-mannered.

Louis seemed to consider the offer seriously as he looked from her to Jake and then at his feet. 'I'd better go,' he said at last, and the tension, real or imagined, seemed instantly to drain out of the room.

'I'll let you out,' Sophie said, deciding she needed the minute or so it would take to get back up the stairs to her flat to figure out what had just happened.

'I didn't know you had a boyfriend,' Louis said as they reached the main door. 'I don't know why – I mean it's obvious *you* would have.'

'Is it?' Sophie said.

'Well yeah. I mean you're, you know – great-looking and generally . . . great. Of course you would.'

Sophie felt a rush of pleasure at his words. She didn't think she'd ever felt so flattered in her life. Certainly other men including Jake had said things that were far more flowery and much more romantic, but for some reason none of those words had ever sounded as completely honest as Louis's did.

'Gosh,' Sophie said, and then, 'did I just say gosh?'

Louis laughed. 'You did, but I like it. Look, it must have made things difficult for you with Jake, having the girls. I hope your relationship hasn't suffered because of it?'

'Oh no,' Sophie said. 'Jake's been great but actually he's not quite my boyfriend. He's more of a sort of date thing. Except we haven't been on any dates yet.' She wondered why she was sharing this information so inexpertly with a man whose business it certainly was not.

Was it because she wanted him to know she was single? Did she want her dead best friend's husband to know that she was single? She refused to think about what that meant on the grounds of taste and decency. But the more she'd got to know him, the more she was warming towards him, which wasn't what she wanted at all. Now was not the time to develop an inappropriate crush.

'Right,' Louis said. 'So, I'll see you in the morning and we'll plan the big trip.'

'We will,' Sophie said. They smiled at each other as she held the door open, letting the chill of the night air cool her cheeks.

'Goodnight, Sophie,' Louis said. And for a long moment after she had closed the door she stood and thought about what it had felt like to be standing next to him. It had to be wrong to feel like she had in that moment. It had to be.

There was only one thing for it. She'd have to go upstairs and kiss Jake.

'I was starting to think you'd gone with him,' Jake said, holding out a glass of wine.

'Don't be silly.' Sophie sat down on the sofa next to him. She looked at his lovely mouth and gorgeous blue eyes and took a large gulp of wine.

'He's younger than I thought he would be,' Jake said. 'He's younger than me, I think. Don't you?'

'Um, he's my age I suppose,' Sophie said, diligently admiring Jake's chiselled nose. 'So a bit, I guess.'

'And really tall,' Jake said.

Sophie laughed. 'Anyone would think it was *you* who fancied him,' she joked, before she realised exactly what she'd said.

'Me as opposed to who?' Jake said carefully.

'No-one!' Sophie replied hurriedly. 'That's not what I meant, I just meant . . .' She looked into her wine glass for inspiration. 'I meant you sounded very interested in him.'

'I'm always interested in my competition,' Jake said, his tone cooling as each second passed.

'Jake!' Sophie exclaimed. 'Louis is my dead best friend's ex-husband! He's not competition!'

'Are you sure about that?' Jake asked her.

'I'm sure.' And as if to prove it, Sophie did something she had never previously done in her entire life. She lunged at Jake and kissed him.

For a moment he was immobile with shock, for a second or two longer he kissed her back and then slowly and reluctantly he pushed her away.

351

'You're really screwing with my head,' he said.

'I'm not,' Sophie contradicted. 'That's why I asked you to come over tonight. So we could move things on. You and me – a couple if you want.'

Jake sat up and looked hard at her. 'Something in you has changed since the party,' he said. 'You look less reserved, less detached. Actually that's wrong, you don't look at *all* reserved or detached. You look like someone turned you loose in the world and you're enjoying living and breathing in the middle of it, instead of just looking on from the edges.'

'Yes,' Sophie agreed, even though she didn't quite get what he meant. 'I am. I mean I'm doing those things that you said because of you. *You've set me free!*'

'Nope,' Jake said. 'It's not me.'

'It is!' Sophie insisted, sounding, she realised, a little too desperate for it to be true.

'Sophie,' Jake looked sad as he said her name. 'It might be that the new challenges that life has thrown at you have woken you up. Or maybe it's realising when you found out Carrie had died that life is too short to sleepwalk through it. Maybe it's even those two girls and their father.' Jake looked grim. 'Maybe it's him.'

'Him!'

Jake cut off Sophie's protest with a wave of his hand. 'Whatever it is, it isn't me,' he told her firmly. 'And I'm not the kind of man to take second best. I thought you'd wake up one day and see what a charming, good-looking catch I am and that you'd want me as much as I want you. But, as sorry as I am, I don't think that's going to happen.'

'I have,' Sophie said. 'It is.' But even she wasn't convinced.

'I think I'd better go,' Jake said.

'I don't want you to go,' Sophie said, her voice small.

'I know you don't, but I think you want me to stay as a safety net to catch you if all this high-wire balancing you're doing doesn't pay off. But I can't be that to you, Sophie, as tempting as it is. I can't be your safe option. Whatever you need to make you happy right now – it isn't me.'

Jake set his wine down on the table and leaned over and kissed Sophie's cheek. 'I'll call you when you're back in the office. We'll schedule a meeting.'

'Jake, I . . .' Sophie didn't know what she wanted to say.

'It's OK, honey, I know,' he said as he headed for the flat door. 'You've got a lot of other things to think about right now.'

CHAPTER 21

There had been longer journeys in terms of distance and even importance, Sophie knew that. Like Edmund Hillary reaching the summit of Everest or Neil Armstrong playing golf on the moon. Those were, she knew, difficult, almost impossible and world-changing, humanity-inspiring journeys. However, she was also entirely convinced that never in the history of mankind had anyone taken a journey as tiring, depressing and remorselessly irritating as the journey she was taking to Cornwall on that cold and rainy day.

A real test of human endurance, Sophie thought, was a six-hour car journey with a car-phobic three-year-old, a know-it-all-often-annoyingly-correct six-year-old and their long-lost, emotionally confused, irritatingly attractive father. And she had come to that conclusion only forty-five minutes into the trip.

It was dusk when they drove into St Ives. The optimistically anticipated six-hour trip had stretched into an excruciating eight, and at last, for these final few minutes of the journey, the car was quiet. Izzy had finally fallen asleep about twenty minutes earlier, and Louis and Bella had fallen silent for an entirely different reason, Sophie guessed. As they descended into the heart of the town, past hotel after hotel and a brace of B&Bs, all garnished with a procession of forlorn-looking palms bending in the wind, she glanced at Louis's profile, occasionally highlighted by the beams of passing cars, and in the rear-view mirror at Bella, who stared fixedly out of the glass. Both of them wore exactly the same expression, that of someone watching the life they had once known and loved slip silently past their windows like a lost dream. Sophie knew all too well what Bella had lost, and as she watched Louis's face she realised his sense of loss was almost identical. He must have loved Carrie very much, she realised sharply. He probably still did.

'Louis,' Sophie asked, feeling awkward for breaking into his thoughts. 'Have you got the directions to the B&B?' She had to repeat the question before Louis heard and blinked at her.

'The directions? Oh right – yes, of course. Sorry, miles away.' He fished about in the plastic bag between his feet and pulled them out. 'Right, it's on Porthminster Terrace, so left up Albert Road, that's the next left and then left again.'

Sophie nodded, and glancing to her right saw the sea moving darkly in the gloom. 'Oooh look!' she exclaimed, from force of childhood habit. 'There's the sea!'

Izzy did not stir and both Louis and Bella

blinked blankly at the view. 'Mmm,' they said with identical laconic cadence. And then the car was silent once more.

Sophie looked around at the family room she was sharing with the girls. It wasn't a bad room; it was clean and once you got past the pinkness, the rose-patterned wallpaper with contrasting border and the lurid magenta candlewick bedspreads it was quite pleasant.

'We're less of a B&B and more of a boutique hotel,' Mrs Alexander, the proprietor, had assured them as she'd shown them this room and Louis's single next door.

'Oh?' Louis had said, looking around him with genuine interest. 'What's the difference then?'

Mrs Alexander had seemed to purse her entire body from the lips down. 'Well, I would have thought *that* was obvious,' she'd said.

Miraculously Izzy had not woken as she was transferred from the car and onto the double bed. She didn't even stir as Sophie gingerly undressed her and exchanged her pants for a pull-up nappy, deciding it was better to be safe than sorry with other people's bedlinen.

'Strictly speaking,' she murmured to the slumbering child, 'you've weed so much today that I shouldn't think you'll need to go again for about two years, but anyway, we wouldn't want to upset Mrs Alexander.' She carefully tucked her into one side of the bed and looked up at Bella as she returned from the en suite bathroom already in her pyjamas.

'You haven't even eaten yet,' Sophie reminded her, glancing at her watch. It was only just six.

'But I had all those Pringles in the car,' Bella said. 'Anyway, I'm tired. You don't mind, do you?'

Sophie now considered herself experienced enough in childcare to know that a tube of salt and vinegar Pringles did not constitute what Tess would call a balanced meal, but she also knew that there was no point in forcing a tired child to stay up and eat broccoli.

'Of course not,' she said, pulling back the covers so that Bella could hop into bed, leaving the single free for her. She didn't mind Bella's early night exactly, but whilst having an actual bed to sleep in was a definite improvement, she had not fore-seen the disadvantage of the enforced early bedtime brought about by sharing with two children under seven.

'Do you want a story?' she asked hopefully. Bella shook her head and yawned.

'Night,' she said and she was instantly gone, as if she could not wait to escape to the refuge of sleep.

Sophie listened to Bella's rhythmic breathing, complemented by Izzy's squeaky snore, as she sat on her single bed in the dark and looked at the thin sliver of light that ran along the bottom of the bedroom door. She could either stay here and stare at what she supposed to be the ceiling for hours on end until she fell asleep, or she could go and see Louis next door. It wasn't as if there was anything wrong with that, or that if she did go it would have any special meaning. It was just that the idea of visiting him in his bedroom in a B&B in St Ives felt rather strange. This was mainly because until very recently he had been the arch-villain in everybody's life, including his own, but also because once in his room Sophie had no idea what on earth they would do for an entire evening, if it wasn't to talk intensely and earnestly about the girls or Carrie. And Sophie knew that she, for one, didn't have the energy to do that. But considering the alternative, there was nothing else for it. With her hand on the doorknob she paused, and then she turned around and crept into the small en suite bathroom where she brushed her teeth and hair in the twilight, and risked the haphazard application of some clear lipgloss.

Louis seemed to have been expecting her, as he smiled when he opened the door and stepped aside to let her into the narrow room. Sophie glanced around. His single bed was positioned against the wall that divided their bedrooms. Her bed, she realised, was in exactly the same position on the other side of the wall, which, for some reason that she didn't want to dwell on, disconcerted her.

'Just in time.' Louis gestured at a tray of sandwiches and a pot of tea that balanced on a narrow dressing table. 'I ordered us food. Apparently providing food in the evening is what makes the difference between a B&B and a boutique hotel.'

'Obviously,' Sophie said smiling, partly to cover her surprise that Louis had not only been expecting her but had also ordered her sandwiches. She found the plate of white triangular shapes with the crusts cut off curiously touching.

'I thought both the girls would be exhausted,' Louis said, repositioning the tray on his bed and pouring out two cups of tea. 'But I ordered extra sandwiches just in case. Bella asleep too?'

'Out like a light. Full up with junk food.'

'I felt a bit guilty not being in there helping you, but, well, I don't expect Bella would have wanted me barging in, would she?' He couldn't help but let a hopeful note creep in, so Sophie just said, 'She was really tired. Couldn't get two words out of her. I know how she feels.' She laughed weakly, hoping he'd take the hint. Louis nodded and sat down on the bed, the tray beside him. Sophie took this as an invitation to sit on the other side of the food. He held out a cup of tea for her, which she took with both hands and sipped. Louis nodded at the TV that was positioned on a shelf on a wall opposite the bed.

'There's quite a good film on,' he said as he helped himself to a tuna sandwich.

In the end it turned out that Sophie didn't have to worry about what they would talk about because they didn't talk at all really, except to make the odd comment on the film, the sandwiches or the rather pungent plug-in air freshener that Louis finally banished to the hallway when the tuna started to taste of petunias. Instead of the intense and earnest discussions that she had feared, time slipped by and their conversation rose and fell as easily and as naturally as the tide against the shore.

The music to the ten o'clock news woke Sophie and she realised that she must have nodded off, propped up against the wall on Louis's bed, and had probably snored and possibly dribbled.

'Fuck,' she said, sitting bolt upright and surreptitiously wiping her chin just to be on the safe side. 'Sorry.'

Louis smiled but did not take his eyes off the TV. 'It's cool,' he said. 'Although I was wondering how we'd both fit into the bed if you didn't wake up.' It was a casual remark but it was enough to make Sophie feel the heat prickle on her skin as she got a fleeting impression of what it *would* be like for her and Louis to be closely entwined in that bed . . . She wondered if he'd made the comment deliberately to rattle her, and then dismissed the thought immediately. Of course he hadn't, she told herself. He had no clue that she was finding it increasingly difficult to be around him, he was just making conversation. She was the one blowing it all out of proportion.

It was classic behaviour, Cal would say. *Cal* would say she was again fixating on a man she could never have, precisely because she could never have him. Because she preferred to torture herself with hopeless fantasies rather than risk anything messy and physical and real. Well, Cal might be right but if he knew how frightening it felt to be this close to the object of her attraction, he would understand. It was simply better not to let it get out of hand.

'Utterly inappropriate,' Sophie accidentally said out loud.

Louis looked at her with a furrowed brow. 'Pardon?'

'Oh nothing.' She stood up, smoothing her tousled hair behind her shoulders and pulling her shirt down over her jeans. 'Just that I should go to bed. I'll see you in the morning then – we're sticking to Plan A, are we?'

Louis nodded, but he looked hesitant, un-surprisingly considering what constituted Plan A.

'Louis, are you OK?' Sophie suddenly felt compelled to ask him, despite his obvious reluctance to talk about any of the reasons they were here. He shrugged and stood up, switching off the TV. The small room was filled with him.

'I'm all right,' he said, looking down at Sophie. 'Like you said, I have to be, don't I? I'm the grown-up here and—' In the silent seconds of his pause it seemed as if they simultaneously closed the gap between their bodies, just by the tiniest fraction. 'And, well, I'm glad you're here,' Louis finished. 'Listen, are you bored of me thanking you yet?' His mouth formed half a smile.

'Bored? Never,' Sophie said with fragile lightness.

'I love gratitude. Bring it on.' Louis's smile completed and Sophie was sure that the oxygen levels in the room depleted.

'Well, then. Thank you again,' he said, and then without warning he breached the remaining space between them in one swift move, and left the remnants of a soft warm kiss on her cheek almost before she knew what had happened.

'Right then,' Sophie said, her voice a decibel higher than usual. 'Bedtime for me, see you in the morning. Night then!' And she had closed Louis's door behind her before she had finished the last word.

She stood for a moment in the hallway and studied the endlessly swirling pattern of the carpeted floor as she considered the phenomena she had just experienced. Taking a brief audit of her sexual history, Sophie worked out that she had had three lovers in her lifetime, one a boyfriend with whom she had had the most sex to date. She was fairly certain she had been in love with him, which automatically made sex better according to popular belief. She and Alex had had all kinds of sex, all over her flat *and* his, which meant it must have been good sex because everybody knows that sex that's not in a bed is good sex. They had done at least three positions, and there had been orgasms. Alex had not always been there, but nevertheless orgasms had been had whilst she had been seeing him. Whenever Eve joked about her near-virginal frigidity, Sophie had confidently scoffed, remembering those orgasms. And as for Carrie's schoolgirl-crude declarations of what it meant to be truly turned on, Sophie had just laughingly agreed and secretly decided that that degree of sexual pleasure was just fictional, the sort of thing women's magazines and slushy novels bang on about all the time but which nobody really ever experiences. And nothing, not even Alex in his thong (*especially* not Alex in his thong), had ever led her to change her opinion on that subject.

Until about two minutes ago, when her dead best friend's ex-husband kissed her innocently on the cheek and for the first time in her life Sophie had felt something that she could only describe as her knickers. Fizzing.

'Fucking Nora,' Sophie said and then, 'bollocks.'

She crept back into the room she was sharing with Louis's daughters and, undressing quickly, climbed into her single bed without even bothering to clean her teeth. 'Arses,' Sophie cursed once more under her breath and yanked the bedspread over her head. She had been really looking forward to a good night's sleep in an actual bed, and now when she finally had the prospect of one, she wouldn't have time to do any sleeping. It looked like the way Louis made her feel was more than just one of her usual safe, unrequited crushes. It was hot, intense and very real.

No, she wouldn't get any sleep tonight. She'd spend all night lying awake worrying.

CHAPTER 22

'We have all been on a long journey,' Izzy said, with a fair amount of mysticism considering her age. 'Haven't we?'

'Yes we have,' Sophie said abstractedly. She smiled and nodded as Izzy chattered, and fiddled anxiously with her napkin. The three of them had been in the breakfast room since seven, and would have been there a good hour earlier if only they could have got away with it. Izzy had revelled in the cereal selection and Bella had picked at the edges of fried egg on toast for almost forty minutes. Louis had still not come down, and Sophie did not know whether to be relieved or annoyed. It struck her as highly ironic that *she* was the one up at five o' clock with the children, while their natural father slumbered blissfully unaware, just a few inches of brick and some insulating material away. And yet she wasn't sure she'd ever be ready to face him again.

Sophie swore at herself. She had to be the only woman since the demise of the great Victorian novel to get so flustered over a totally lame, not remotely special or sexy kiss on the cheek. Maybe if Louis had grabbed her in his arms and flung her onto the bed and ravished her, maybe *then* her total flakiness would be understandable. But he hadn't – the thought had never crossed his mind. Furthermore, she would never have allowed herself to get heated over Carrie's husband – ex or not – whilst Carrie had been alive, so how could such feelings be permitted now she was dead? Well, put it this way, if Sophie's Catholicism had not lapsed and she'd happened to mention some of last night's wilder thoughts in confession, she was fairly sure that no amount of Hail Marys would have saved her from a specially reserved spot in Hell. But instead of hightailing it to church in search of redemption, she told herself it was all nonsense and silliness and just a figment of her wrung-out imagination. When she'd finally had a decent night's sleep and all this emotional wrangling was over and she had her normal life back, she'd realise that she hadn't had 'fizzy knickers' at all. It was probably cystitis.

'Daddy's fab-li-us, isn't he?' Izzy said.

'Yes he is,' Sophie agreed absently just as Louis appeared in the doorway, still damp from the shower and clean-shaven.

'Thanks,' he said to Sophie, with a broad grin. 'You're pretty wonderful yourself. I'm sorry I took so long coming down, I thought I'd better shower and shave before people started mistaking me for a stinky old tramp again.' He winked at Bella, who looked studiously unimpressed. 'I thought that later on you could have a couple of hours to your-self while I did a solo shift?'

Sophie looked at him. 'Lovely,' she said, wondering if Mrs Alexander had any cranberry juice – wasn't that supposed to be good for cystitis?

'What are we doing here?' Bella demanded, pushing her plate away. She fixed her gaze on Sophie. 'Are you going to leave us here with him?'

Sophie looked at her pale, pinched face. She and Louis had told the girls the day before yesterday that they were bringing them down to St Ives for a visit. She had expected them to be thrilled, but instead Izzy had questioned her relentlessly about the mode of transport and how long it would take to get there, and Bella, seeing yet another upheaval in her already tumultuous life, had said nothing at all.

The night she had tucked the girls in before they left, Sophie had knelt beside the bed and brushed Bella's fringe out of her eyes, whispering, 'Aren't you glad to be going back home? I thought you missed it?'

Bella had turned onto her side, so that most of her face fell into shadow. 'It won't be going home though, will it? Because Mummy's not there. And going back now means the end of living here with you and the beginning of living with him, doesn't it?'

Sophie searched the shadows of Bella's face, fixing onto the tiny points of reflected light in her eyes. 'Yes it does,' she said simply, knowing that any lie, even a white one, would not help Bella. 'But I thought you were starting to feel better about that? Better about your dad?'

She had expected more questions from Bella, but instead the two points of light blinked out for a moment and then Bella had whispered, 'I'm going to sleep now.'

She hadn't questioned the trip further until this moment. Sophie looked at Louis, who reached into his pocket and pulled out a set of keys which he laid on the table. Bella and Izzy looked at them. Two Yale, two mortise, tied together on a faded bit of multicoloured ribbon to which was also attached a faded pink troll, its hair matted and sticky.

Bella looked up at Sophie. 'Mummy's keys,' she said quietly. 'He's got Mummy's keys.'

'Trollee!' Izzy cried, picking up the keyring and kissing the creature attached to it. 'But I mustn't lose you, must I? 'Cos Mummy will be very cross.' She said the words like an automatic mantra, before furrowing her brow and placing the keys back down on the table. 'But Mummy's not here, so I'd better not play with you.'

All four of them stared at the keys as if they were some kind of talisman, or the way to unlock a secret door to the past. Quickly, before the moment could be filled with any more meaning, Sophie picked up the keys and jangled them, as if she could shake all of the significance out of them.

'We're going to look at the house,' she said briskly, as Louis seemed unable to explain. 'Things happened very quickly when you first went to stay with your gran, so we're going back there to get any of your things you might want. And to check that the house is OK, before . . .'

Bella frowned. 'Before what?' she said.

'Well . . .' Sophie began, out of habit, but Louis interrupted her.

'When Mummy died she gave us the house. It belongs to us now, all three of us,' he said.

'Mummy gave the house to you?' Bella sounded incredulous and Louis realised his mistake. She was not the sort of child to fall for adult half-truths.

'Well, half of the house belonged to me to begin with, from when I lived there with you, Bella, and then when Mummy died the other half became mine because Mummy and I were still married.'

'You weren't married,' Bella said. 'Married people live together.'

Louis reached out for her hand, which she withdrew and held under the table, gripping it tightly.

'Yes, I know,' Louis said, resting his hand on the flowery tablecloth instead. 'But in the eyes of the law we were still married and . . . anyway, the house belongs to all of us now, you me and Izzy. We're going to look at it and decide what we want to do with it.'

Bella released one hand and snaked it through Sophie's arm. 'What do you mean, do with it?' she said uncertainly.

'Well, we could sell it,' Louis said carefully. 'Or we could live it in it. You, me and Izzy.'

Carrie's house was in the middle of Virgin Street. It was a narrow, whitewashed house, its two front window frames and door painted bright blue. As they had walked down the steep road Sophie had been able to pick it out without needing to look at the numbers. It was the only one to have a roof glittering with frost in the bright, cold morning. A cold, empty house at the heart of a row of warm, busy lives, slotted side by side around the place that had once been Carrie's pride and joy. It hadn't been completely neglected. A neighbour checked in on it regularly. Turned lights on and off, picked up the junk mail that continued to arrive long after any meaningful correspondence had dried up, and made sure it didn't get so cold that the water pipes burst. When Louis had spoken to the solicitor who had posted him the house keys he discovered that there was something else the neighbour had been doing too, but he wanted to keep that a secret for now.

The four of them stood opposite the house and looked at it.

'Is Mummy in there too?' Izzy said, and it was hard to shake the sensation that she might be. That at any moment Carrie might open the front door and ask them where on earth they had all been. 'Shall I ring the bell?' she asked, pulling at Sophie's sleeve. 'For Mummy to let us in?'

'Mummy's not in there, stupid,' Bella said, rather harshly. It was the first thing she had said since Louis's announcement at the breakfast table.

Izzy's bottom lip began to wobble. 'I'm not stupid,' she protested softly. 'Mummy's in the sky and the stars and the sea and the trees, isn't she, Aunty Sophie?' Sophie nodded, wincing internally as she realised where Izzy's train of thought was going. 'So she could be in the house too, couldn't she?'

It was her fault for agreeing with Izzy every time she asked her is Mummy in the lamppost, roundabout or rain. The constant reassurances she had been giving Izzy suddenly seemed like a terrible mistake.

'Um, the thing is . . .' Sophie began, before Louis interrupted her, kneeling beside Izzy and hooking an arm around her shoulders.

'Mummy is sort of in the house,' he said, trying to hide the strain in his voice. 'Memories of Mummy will be there, things that remind us of her and make us think about her. But Mummy won't be there. She's gone, Izzy.'

Izzy buried her face in Louis's jacket and Sophie saw Bella watching them intently, emotions racing across her heart-shaped face like clouds across the sun.

After a moment Bella reached out and put a hand on Izzy's shoulder. 'It's all right, baby,' she said, using the word as an endearment instead of her usual insult, with Carrie's warmth and intonation in every syllable. 'Don't be upset.'

Izzy emerged from Louis's embrace and took Bella's gloved hand.

'Right,' Louis said, straightening up, one hand still on Izzy's shoulder. 'Let's get out of this cold.'

For a minute or so nobody said anything as they looked around the small front room that led into a galley kitchen, and a ground-floor bathroom beyond that. After a while Louis turned on the lights and, going to the foot of the stairs, turned up the heating thermostat. There was an audible click, and the radiator under the window sill began to creak.

'Everything's still working,' he said, glancing around the room. 'Nothing's really changed.'

For a second Sophie had wanted to ask him what on earth *could* have changed in a vacant house over six months, but then she realised: this was the first time Louis had set foot in the house in over three years. Under what circumstances he left it, only he and possibly Bella knew. He continued to look around and then, in one quick stride, he crossed the room and picked up a framed photo from the mantelpiece. It was a picture of him and Carrie on their wedding day.

As Louis studied the photo, his profile hidden by his hair, Sophie felt herself take a deep, sharp, reflexive breath and in that moment she realised: Carrie really was gone.

It was being here, so nearly close to her, almost engulfed by the space her absence made.

She really was dead, because if she wasn't here

in this house – in this life that Sophie had subconsciously imagined for her even when she didn't give it a second thought from day to day – then she wasn't anywhere. Sophie felt her eyes sting.

'I'll just . . .' she said, as she hurried through the kitchen to the bathroom, hopeful that everyone else was so lost in their own thoughts that they hadn't really heard or noticed her. She pulled open the sliding door that concealed the apricot bathroom suite which had come with the house. It had always made Carrie laugh because it came complete with a bidet.

Sophie closed the toilet lid and sat on it. She took deep and steady breaths and tried to focus her mind, but the tears came, slow and hot. Her shoulders shook and her breath juddered, and she felt Carrie's death keenly in the centre of her chest, as if a small but vital part of herself had been ripped out.

'Don't you dare cry,' she whispered to herself. 'Not now.' Furiously she brushed away her tears with the heel of her hand, repeating the process after every blink – but still they did not stop. Somehow, as if crying had improved her vision, she saw everything in the bathroom with startling clarity. A pair of gold hoop earrings gleaming in the soap dish, an opened box of Tampax half-concealed by the side of the lavatory. A bra, once hand-washed and long ago hung across the shower-curtain rail to drip dry, now stiff and dusty. Sophie wept even harder.

She hadn't anticipated this. She had expected to be the strong one, there to support the children and even Louis too if he needed it. But here she was weeping, crying like she never had before, even when her father had died. Sophie had begun to believe that she would never grieve for her friend. But instead she had picked the worst time of all to crumble and be weak – crying for Carrie but also crying for herself.

Sophie cried because she missed her, but she also cried for all the things she had lost before Carrie's death. Her father, her childhood. Her friendship with her mother. Her sense of self. Her courage and adventurous spirit. The things that losing Carrie had somehow given back to her, one by one.

She had fallen in love with two children who should never have been hers to love. Somehow this complicated whirlpool of events had woken her up, and now she wanted what Carrie had had and would never have again. And that made Sophie cry all the harder, because if that was true, wasn't she trying to steal Carrie's life? And if she was, she knew she would be hopeless at living it. She could never have a tenth of the energy, audacity and verve that Carrie had brought to every day. That was the woman Louis and his daughters loved and missed so much. Just as Sophie feared she might never pull herself together there was a knock on the bathroom door.

'Aunty Sophie?' It was Izzy. 'I need a wee. You've been ages, are you doing a poo? Does it smell?'

Sophie took a deep breath, dried her face with her palms and arranged her mouth into a smile before pulling open the door. 'No, no,' she said, ushering Izzy in. 'You're OK, it doesn't smell.'

Izzy pulled down her trousers and pants, and lifting the toilet lid edged her way onto the seat. She examined Sophie's face as she passed water.

'Your eyes have gone all black,' she said. She cocked her head to one side, stretched out both her arms and said, 'Don't worry, baby. Don't be upset.'

If just over a month ago anyone had told Sophie that very soon she would be openly weeping in the embrace of a three-year-old girl who comforted her as she sat on the loo, Sophie would have laughed in their face. But now, Izzy's arms around her neck, her hot breath on her cheek, were exactly the sensations she needed to feel calm again. Izzy patted her on the back several times as Sophie knelt before her, and after a while Sophie broke the embrace, cupped Izzy's face in one hand and kissed her forehead.

'You're a lovely little girl,' she said, realising she wasn't going to cry any more.

At last she felt connected to the world again for the first time since that freezing day at the crematorium. She stood up, knowing that the first tears she had shed for Carrie wouldn't be her last but for now, at least, she felt lighter and stronger.

Strong enough to give the support that she had intended. As Izzy concentrated on her business Sophie looked into the bathroom-cabinet mirror and washed her face in cold water until all traces of tears and make-up were gone. Her skin remained burnished but her eyes seemed fairly clear as long as no-one looked into them too deeply.

The toilet flushed behind her and Izzy pulled up her trousers, a trail of toilet paper poking from the back of them like a tail. Sophie plucked it out and put it down the loo. She was about to lift Izzy up to the sink to wash her hands when the little girl picked up a three-legged stool that had been left by the bath and carried it to the sink.

'Do you like coming back here?' Sophie asked her as she washed her hands with the kind of enthusiasm that was bad for the environment.

'I do like it,' Izzy said thoughtfully, 'and partly I don't like it, because, well, it's funny and a bit sad.'

Sophie watched her hop off the stool, pull open the door and head back towards the living room. Sometimes she couldn't tell if Izzy was being curiously insightful or if she was just mimicking the conversation of grown-ups. But on that occasion she felt certain the three-year-old had said exactly what she meant.

When they returned to the front room Louis was sitting on the sofa, with a photo album open on his lap. His expression was unreadable, hidden by the forward sweep of his long hair, but Sophie thought she could see the tension and sadness in every line of his body.

'Whassat?' Izzy asked, climbing up and kneeling beside him.

'It's you,' Louis said brightly for her sake. It was strange, Sophie thought ruefully, how all four of them were pretending to be stronger than they were for the sake of the other three. 'It's your baby book. I found it with Bella's. I took all the photos of Bella. I think your mum must have taken most of these.' She's only in one of them. I've missed so much.' He sighed.

Izzy traced the outline of her own baby footprint in the book and giggled.

'Is Bella upstairs?' Sophie said, looking up the narrow staircase.

'Yes,' Louis said. 'She wanted to go and find some things. I offered to go with her, but she said "no thank you" very politely.'

Sophie nodded. The atmosphere of the house was so full of Carrie that it seemed easier to be apart from him, to disperse somehow the intensity of emotions.

'That's my girl,' she said, before calling up the stairs. 'Bella? Are you all right up there?'

'Come up!' Bella called in response. Sophie glanced at Louis but he didn't look up from the baby book.

Sophie felt foolishly apprehensive as she climbed the stairs. She had never imagined herself to be the sort of person with an overactive imagination, but in this house it was easy to let thoughts run wild. And after the last few weeks, especially since Louis had arrived in her life, she wasn't at all sure what sort of person she was any more. She wouldn't have been surprised to find Carrie at the top of the stairs waiting to ask her just what she thought she was playing at, falling for her husband.

'Hello?' Sophie called out, annoying herself with the note of tension in her voice.

'In here!' Sophie followed Bella's voice to the small second bedroom, expecting it to be a child's room. But as she entered she realised immediately it was Carrie's room. Her grandmother's art deco wardrobe that she had loved so much dominated the small space, and there was just enough room remaining for a single bed and an ex-dining chair on which a pile of folded laundry still waited to be put away. Bella was sitting on the bed, her head peeking out of a huge red mohair jumper. She rolled the sleeves up until her hands appeared.

'This was Mum's favourite jumper,' she said to Sophie, smiling. 'It still smells like her a bit. Smell!' She thrust out a sleeve towards Sophie, who sat down beside her and sniffed the garment. It did have a faint aroma of Carrie's favourite rose oil, and Sophie wondered how – out of all of them – Bella seemed to be so relaxed here, and happy. For the first time since Sophie had met Bella again at her grandmother's house, all the lines of tension that had characterised her slight body seemed to have melted away. Sophie looked at Bella and realised she was six and a half years old again, not some small noble adult carrying the weight of the world around on her shoulders.

Bella knelt up and picked a black leatherette jewellery box off a shelf over the bed. Taking it down carefully, she tipped it up and turned the handle of the clockwork mechanism before gently lifting the lid, holding the box at eye level. As the red felt interior of the box was revealed and the tiny plastic ballerina within began to twirl and pirouette, Sophie smiled in recognition.

'Carrie got that for her fourteenth birthday,' she told Bella, who was watching the tiny dancer. 'She said she *hated* it and wished she could burn it – that all she wanted was money for clothes and records and that your gran had got her this just to pi— to annoy her. But she never did throw it away. She always kept her jewellery in it, even when she was grown-up.' Sophie listened as the tinny rendition of 'The Blue Danube' began to slow. 'Maybe your gran knew her better than she thought she did, after all. You'll have to tell her about the box. She'd really like to know.'

Bella set the box down on the bed and pulled out a couple of strings of glass beads, dropping them over her head. She took out some earrings and looked at them in the palm of her hand for a moment before putting them back into the box and taking out a butterfly brooch. Sophie pinned it on the jumper for her.

'Can I take this?' she asked Sophie, shutting the lid of the box, before tugging at the jumper. 'And this?'

Sophie nodded. 'Of course you can,' she said, and she impulsively hooked her arm around Bella's neck and planted a kiss on her forehead. Unwittingly Bella was making this visit to Carrie's house easier for her, when really it should have been the other way round. 'You seem happy to be here, Bella. Do you think you'd be happy living back here with your dad?'

Bella stared at the faded and rubbed gold border that decorated the box's lid for a moment.

'This is my home, mine and Izzy's,' she said. 'Not his.'

Sophie was prepared for that response. 'But darling, you know you will have to live with your dad eventually and . . .'

'I know I have to live with Dad,' Bella said with less venom than Sophie had expected, and using the word Dad instead of him. 'But I want to live *here*, Aunty Sophie. I want to come back home to St Ives and school and my friends. Where I can nearly touch Mummy. It's like I left one morning and I didn't even know that I wasn't coming back. But I didn't. I didn't ever come back until now. And it seems right to come back even if – even if not all of us *can* come back.'

Sophie nodded and kissed Bella again.

'I don't know if Izzy feels the same way,' she said, releasing Bella from her hug. 'And as far as your dad is concerned – well, it's hard to know what he's thinking, but I think you're right.' Sophie looked around the room. Despite the cold outside, the back of the house seemed to trap the morning sun and it was bathed in glowing warmth.

'Do you feel OK about living with Louis now?' she asked Bella.

'Well . . . I'm prepared to discuss it with him, if it means I can come home.'

Sophie nodded, trying not to smile at the small girl's formality. She felt – something she had no right to feel – a sense of rejection.

Suddenly Izzy's scream reverberated through the small house.

Sophie, who was getting used to Izzy screaming the place down over nothing in particular, wondered what they would find as she and Bella went downstairs. But any residual apprehension she might have had dissipated the moment she saw the three-year-old.

Izzy was standing in the middle of the living room, her face rapturous as she almost strangled the life out of a huge ginger tomcat.

'It's Tango!' she cried joyously. 'Tango! Tango!'

'Tango!' Bella leapt the last two stairs and joined the group hug of which Tango was the remarkably compliant centre.

'OK, guys,' Louis said, laughing, 'you'll scare him.'

'Nothing scares Tango,' Bella said, hefting the giant cat out of Izzy's grasp and lumbering with him to the sofa. 'He's the toughest cat in St Ives!'

Louis took Tango from Bella as she climbed up and sat beside him, and then plonked the animal back in her outstretched arms.

Sophie, who was not used to seeing cats handled so roughly without the kind of protest that resulted in at least the loss of an eye, looked on in awe. Tango must have been twice the size of Artemis, had half an ear missing and a little bare patch over one eye. He looked like a real bruiser, but there he was purring like a, well, like a pussy cat, in Bella's arms, as she scratched him behind one ear.

'How can he be here?' Bella asked. 'He went to a cats' home!'

'I know, I was going to tell you but I was worried he might not show up. Leslie from next door, the lady who was coming in every day,' Louis added for Sophie's benefit, 'said she found him here one morning about four months ago. She called the cats' home and they told her he had been rehomed in Mousehole; ironic or what? Anyway he can't have liked it, because he left his new home the first chance he got and came back here. She didn't know how he'd made it so far in one piece or how long he'd been living off scraps before she found him. The cats' home phoned his new family and they took him back, but he came back again. So everyone agreed it was best to just let him live here. Leslie's been feeding him. I think he divides his time between here and next door now. They've become quite good friends.'

'Tango,' Izzy said softly as she knelt at Bella's

feet. 'Can we take him home too?' she asked Sophie. In a moment of confusion Sophie tried to work out the logistics of fitting two children and two cats – one psychotic, one freakishly huge – into her small flat before realising that her flat was no longer home, at least not for Bella and Izzy.

'It's not up to me,' Sophie said, nodding at Louis as she tried to suppress an unexpected pang of loss. She sat down on a chair.

Louis reached out and scratched Tango under the chin. 'All right, old mate,' he said with fond familiarity before saying to the girls, 'Well, it's not up to me either.' He looked at Bella. 'Izzy told me she'd like to live in a new house, when we come back.'

'With my own bedroom,' Izzy said firmly.

'Well, maybe,' Louis said, cautiously. 'But anyway, Bella – what about you?'

'I want to live here,' Bella said into Tango's neck. She glanced up at Louis and pressed her lips together, stubborn and resolute.

Louis looked around the small front room, with good and bad memories stuffed into every corner. This was the last place he wanted to come back to, Sophie could see. But she could also see that he desperately didn't want to let Bella down.

'It's just I thought a fresh start maybe . . .' he said tentatively, 'for us all.'

'*This* is home!' Bella insisted, her voice heavy with the threat of tears. She pointed at Louis. 'You can't just take us away from here and make us forget Mummy. You can't just pretend that we've always been happy and that *nothing* happened. *You* left us here! Here at *home!*'

As Tango twisted anxiously out of Bella's arms and scooted behind the sofa, Izzy stuck her thumb in her mouth and climbed into Sophie's lap.

'I'm not pretending,' Louis said carefully to Bella, as if the wrong intonation could blow everything. 'I know I was wrong to leave you the way I did, Bella. I'm so sorry . . .'

'But why did you, why?' Bella shouted, standing up, running at Louis and bringing her fists down on his legs.

Izzy buried her face in Sophie's hair and tightened her arms around her neck. Sophie squeezed her back.

Louis leant forward and put his arms around Bella's stiff shoulders.

'I don't know,' he said softly. 'I was stupid and selfish and wrong. And I've regretted it and missed you all every minute since. And most of all I wish I'd spoken to your mum again and told her how sorry I was. Because I am sorry, Bella. I'm sorry, Izzy. I am so sorry.'

Izzy slid wordlessly out of Sophie's lap and crossed to Louis, flinging her arms around both her father and sister and drawing them together in a hug.

'Don't make us live somewhere we don't know again,' Bella said.

'I won't make you do anything,' Louis said, but Sophie could see the stricken look on his face.

She knew that coming back to this house would be unbearable for him. A permanent reminder of what he'd lost, of what it seemed he'd thrown away.

'Why don't you all have a think about it,' Sophie suggested quietly, afraid to intrude on this moment, noticing how Bella had relaxed into the embrace of her family and buried her head in Louis's shoulder. 'It's been a very difficult day for you all. Coming back here is a very big step and perhaps you need to talk and think a bit more before you decide anything. What do you think, Bella?'

Bella's face emerged from Louis's hair and she roughly wiped the back of her hands across her face.

'I need to ask you more things before I know what to do,' she told her father.

Louis's tense and stricken face visibly lightened at words which anybody else might have found intimidating. It was clear that he wasn't afraid any more of what might happen between him and Bella. He was just glad that some kind of relationship had started at last.

'And we need to ask Tango where he wants to live too,' Izzy added solemnly, fishing the cat out from his refuge and squeezing him hard, and as Sophie looked at Tango, she felt certain he'd want to live wherever Bella and Izzy lived.

'We've got a lot to talk about,' Louis said to both girls. 'But I think we'll work it out.' He said it so hopefully it made Sophie's heart hurt.

'Yes,' Bella said. 'I think we will.'

CHAPTER 23

Sophie stood in shadow and waited on the far side of the narrow street as she watched Louis, Izzy and Bella chatting to their next-door neighbour, who occasionally interrupted the conversation with rapid-fire kisses and bear hugs for the children. The three were gradually becoming a family again, the bonds between them slowly tightening and knitting. Bonds which did not include her. She wished she could at least take some credit but she felt that it would have happened sooner or later anyway, even if the girls had never crash-landed into her life. Even if she'd gone on blissfully unaware, organising corporate parties on the eighth floor of her very own ivory tower, ironing her hair every weekday morning, wearing her pyjamas all weekend. Even without me, she thought, they would have found each other.

As for her, she'd soon be going back to that life and everything would be exactly the same as it had been before. Well, not exactly the same, Sophie decided. *She* wouldn't be the same.

She thought about her job, her flat and her tiny

insular social life that she barely managed to maintain, and the same question that people were always asking her came into her head: why? What was all that hardwork and near-solitude for?

Sophie didn't know the answer, but she realised – standing watching Louis, Bella and Izzy talking to their old neighbour – that she had *never* known.

The three across the road said their goodbyes and crossed over to join Sophie.

'She seems nice,' Sophie said, automatically holding out a hand which Izzy took as she hopped up onto the kerb.

'She is,' Louis said. 'She was really pleased to see me.' He sounded so surprised that he must have had his own reservations about coming back to a town that had a small enough community of locals for everyone to know everyone else's business. He must have wondered if he would be thought of as a returning hero or unwelcome villain. The fact that at least one old friend had been glad to see him must have come as a relief.

'I've got an appointment with the solicitor after lunch.' He glanced at Sophie. 'Would you come with me? I could do with a bit of moral support.'

Sophie was touched that Louis had asked her. 'And the girls?' she asked.

'If you were all just outside or in the foyer it would really help,' Louis told her levelly.

'Oh, well, OK then.'

She felt a little glow of pleasure that Louis wanted her to 'just be there,' a glow she quickly put out. She had to curtail this crush, she really had to, because unlike her previous imaginary dalliances she sensed that this one could hurt her badly.

'And then,' Louis continued, entirely oblivious to her inner turmoil, 'I suppose we should visit estate agents, and employment agencies.' He sighed. 'It'll be weird being a wage slave again. Still, got to be done—' He looked up the sky, which was clear blue above their heads although rain clouds were gathering over the sea and it was quite breezy. 'Anyway, let's go for a walk on Porthmeor Beach while the weather's good, shall we?'

'Yes!' the girls chorused, and Izzy swung Sophie's hand as they headed down to the sea.

Izzy raced off as soon as they got there, instantly tumbling over and rolling around in the damp sand.

'She'll be wet through!' Sophie worried, but Louis only smiled.

'She's three and she's having fun – a bit of wet won't hurt her,' he said, chuckling indulgently at his daughter's high spirits.

'I'm going swimming!' Izzy called out to them, her voice almost carried away by the wind as she rushed towards the choppy sea, still dotted with surfers. Unable to employ the kind of laissez-faire that Louis displayed, Sophie instinctively raced after Izzy, a fact that thrilled her more as she squealed and dodged Sophie's attempts to catch her. Woman and child chased each other recklessly a few short feet from the edge of the surf until finally, all her fears forgotten, Sophie grabbed Izzy around the waist and fell backwards onto the sand. Izzy turned in Sophie's arms to face her, the rising wind whipping Sophie's hair between their faces, tickling Izzy's nose and making her laugh even more.

'We'll have fun, won't we?' she said, her eyes bright with laughter. 'When we all live here in our new house. You and me can do chasing all the days!'

Sophie extracted a hand from underneath Izzy's body and held her rebellious hair back from her face, fighting that pang of loss again.

'Well . . .' she began, but just at that moment the tide rushed in one inch higher and bathed the left side of her body in an icy caress.

'Bananas!' Sophie said, remembering for once not to swear. Izzy squealed with delight as Sophie picked her up and they ran out of the reach of the incoming tide. Once they were at a safe distance Sophie set Izzy down and looked at the soaking strip that ran the length of her jeans.

'We'll have to go back and get changed,' she told Izzy, who was running around her in a circle and didn't seem as bothered about being wet and cold as she was. Sophie looked at the clouds that had gathered in size and darkened. 'It's going to rain. Come on, Izzy, let's catch Daddy and Bella up.'

'No!' Izzy said, disagreeing automatically. 'I'm going paddling!'

'Don't be mad,' Sophie said, scanning the beach for Bella and Louis. 'In this weather?' Eventually she spotted a pair of figures, surprisingly small in the distance. It looked as if Bella was walking a step or two ahead of her father and Louis was talking, Sophie could tell, because he always used his hands just as much as language to express himself.

For a moment the wind dropped and a beam of sunlight broke through the clouds as Sophie watched the two distant figures, wishing she could work out what they were saying to each other just by looking at them. And then Bella stopped walking suddenly and in one stride Louis caught up with her. There was another beat, perhaps a few more words exchanged, and then, without looking, Bella began to walk on again. This time she held out her hand, and Louis took it.

And then the wind rose again, bringing with it something else.

Izzy was screaming again. Sighing, Sophie looked round, expecting to see her in proud possession of a not-so-dead crab or bunch of seaweed.

But Izzy was not on the beach.

'IZZY!' Sophie screamed; a cold drench of fear flooded her chest. Dimly aware of Bella and Louis stopping in their tracks and turning round, Sophie shouted again, 'IZZY!' And then she saw her, or rather her red anorak, billowing and blooming as it was buffeted by waves, and her heart clenched in dread.

Izzy was in the water.

Sophie did not know what she was going to do or how she was going to do it, but she absolutely *knew* that she had to be there in the water with Izzy. She must not lose sight of her, must not let her head disappear beneath the waves again before she was at her side. Sophie ran into the surf without feeling the shock of cold water as it rose to her thighs and then to just above her waist. She was only aware of the resistance of the water, slowing her run to a frustrating wade. Somehow Izzy was still afloat and managing to hold her head out of the water. As she got closer Sophie could see the terror in her face and then suddenly the tide washed Izzy right into her arms. Sophie held onto the child, who was screaming and struggling, as tightly as she was able against the pull of the retreating tide. She didn't know how fast the tide might come in, but she knew she had to get out of the water as quickly as possible before she was forced to try and swim instead of walk ashore. It struck her in a moment of clarity that there was a real chance that if the tide was strong enough and the wind cruel enough everything might go horribly wrong for both of them. She felt a fear sharper than anything she had ever felt before, a fear that made her weak, her legs buckling beneath her. And then she remembered Izzy in her arms and she tightened her grip on her and steadied her legs.

'I've got you,' she said out loud as she tried to turn back towards the beach.

Then Louis was in the water with her, lifting Izzy out of her arms and propelling them back onto the land at last. Bella ran into their legs as they emerged from the water and flung her arms around the sodden group, and two or three surfers and some passing dog-walkers gathered round them.

'You all right?' she heard a woman say kindly.

'Do you want an ambulance?' another asked.

Sophie shook her head. 'Bella, careful,' she heard herself say to the girl clinging onto her legs, her voice remarkably calm. 'You'll get all wet!'

'I don't care!' Bella said and the four stood together, arms around each other for a moment, Izzy still crying hysterically, unable to believe that she was finally safe.

'Dude, take this.' A young surfer, his suit still wet from the sea, offered them a huge beach towel.

'Thanks, mate.' Louis said gratefully, taking it and the other towels that were offered. 'Come on,' he said, his voice shaking. 'We've got to get dry.'

Louis came into their room carrying a tray of steaming hot drinks. 'Four hot chocolates courtesy of Mrs Alexander,' he said, setting the tray down on the dressing table.

Sophie, Izzy and Bella were huddled under the covers on the double bed, all of them in their pyjamas and Sophie with one arm around each child's shoulders. Sophie had found some children's programme on the TV to take Izzy's mind off things and she watched it intently, sucking her thumb, a finger twirling her hair round and round relentlessly. Bella's dark eyes were fixed on Izzy as if even in the safety of the double bed she had to keep watching her, just in case.

Louis smiled for the benefit of the group, but his face was flushed from the cold and Sophie could see he was still shaken.

'What kind people on the beach,' she said, 'helping us to get dry, and that lady who brought us tea from the café.'

'Yeah.' Louis smiled. 'That's what I love about humanity. Just when you start thinking the whole world's full of selfish, cruel individuals, you realise that actually given the chance all we want to do is to be nice to one another and help each other.'

'Way deep, dude,' Sophie said wryly, but she knew what he meant. She'd learned so much in the last few weeks.

'Anyway, how are you girls feeling?' he asked the threesome, sitting down on the edge of the bed. Two of them ignored him and Sophie just shrugged. She wasn't sure how to answer.

'I'm fine,' she said to Louis, with a small smile. 'I think I'm getting the feeling back in my toes. It might not be frostbite after all.'

He nodded, clasping his hands together as if he didn't know what to do with them. 'Mrs Alexander's called out a doctor just to be on the safe side. She'll be here in about twenty minutes. It's amazing that Izzy didn't swallow more water,' he said, looking at the transfixed girl. 'It's incredible that she stayed afloat. I think her anorak must have acted like a sort of temporary water wing, trapping air underneath it.'

'Maybe. I mean, really, it was all over so quickly, wasn't it? I suppose it wasn't that serious at all really?'

Louis looked at her. 'It was serious enough for a three-year-old,' he said, heartfelt.

'I'm sorry, Louis,' Sophie said, feeling un-expectedly emotional at the thought of what might have happened. She shivered. 'I'm really sorry. I just took my eyes off her for a moment . . .'

Seeing she was distressed, Louis reached out and touched her shoulder. 'Don't be sorry.' I was the one who said a little bit of wet wouldn't hurt her. Kids get into scrapes. But you were there to help her. That's what counts. So thank you.'

'I didn't do anything much,' Sophie said, feeling her skin flare and ignite under his intense scrutiny. She sat up a little so that Izzy's head rested on her stomach. Bella shifted out of the embrace and turned onto her side. She appeared to have fallen asleep. 'I just waded in . . .'

'You were really brave,' Louis insisted.

'Not that brave,' Sophie said, feeling abashed. 'A bit stupid really – I can't swim.'

Louis blinked at her and the colour drained from his cheeks. 'Right.'

Izzy finally broke eye contact with Barney the dinosaur and reached out a hand to him. 'Daddy,' she said. 'Cuddle too.'

Louis took her hand and moving to the head of the bed put his arms around Izzy, stretching one leg out on the bed, the other still planted firmly on the floor.

'She said she wanted to go paddling!' Sophie whispered, as Izzy settled back into her programme. 'I didn't think she meant it. I should have remembered – when a three-year-old says she is going to do something, she really means it. I only took my eyes off her for a second – I'm so sorry, Louis. I mean what if—' The now familiar wave of panic surged through her again.

Louis shifted slightly and, reaching around Izzy, he picked up Sophie's hand. 'I said don't be sorry.' He tightened his fingers around hers. 'Not you.'

Sophie was sure the only thing that saved her from spontaneous combustion was Izzy, rejoining the conversation once again.

'Mummy *is* in the sea, Sophie,' she said, conversationally.

Sophie looked down at the little girl with surprise. Instead of the nervous wreck that she had expected, with a newly acquired phobia of water to add to her long list of terrors, the child seemed amazingly serene.

'Is she?' Sophie asked.

'Yes.' Izzy lifted her head and looked from Louis to Sophie. 'It was Mummy who pushed me back to you wasn't it?'

Sophie thought about the swell of the tide that had carried Izzy almost directly into her arms.

She rested her palm against Izzy's cheek and smiled down at her. 'You know what,' she said, feeling suddenly comforted by childish logic. 'I think you're right.'

Louis tried half-heartedly to persuade Sophie that they didn't have to come with him to the solicitors.

She pointed out, as she clambered out of bed, that the doctor had said they were fine and that a trip out would take their minds off it all.

It had been interesting to watch Louis's face as he had struggled with not wanting to go alone but wanting to do the right thing.

'Honestly, it's fine,' Sophie said, finding a clean, dry top. She had undone the top two buttons on her pyjamas before she realised what she was doing and dropped the T-shirt like a hot brick, nodding in the direction of the door. 'We'll meet you downstairs.'

Louis seemed just as embarrassed as she was by her sudden carefree impulse to undress in front of him and needed no further prompting to leave, but just before he shut the bedroom door behind him he turned around and said, 'You're sure you want to come?'

'We're sure,' Bella said. 'Because if you're going to look at houses shops then so are me and Izzy. You said we'd decide everything together, remember?'

Both Louis and Sophie sensed that Bella was testing him.

'Of course. Of course the three of us will decide together.'

Once the door was shut Sophie dressed herself and the girls quickly in three new pairs of jeans purchased especially for the trip and three brand new pairs of trainers.

'I look like you!' Izzy said pointing at Sophie, clearly delighted. 'Only I don't have a wobbly tummy.'

'Oh Izzy,' Sophie said as she picked up her bag, 'you really know how to pay a compliment.'

As Izzy and Sophie bustled out of the room she noticed that Bella was hanging back, picking at the fringe of her mum's red mohair jumper.

'Bella? Come on,' Sophie prompted her.

'He really likes you,' Bella said her eyes dark. 'Doesn't he?'

'A bit, I think,' Sophie said. 'And I like him too – a bit.'

'Does he like you the way he liked Mummy?' Bella questioned her closely. Worried that somehow Bella had seen through her exterior to spot her feeling for Louis, Sophie reacted strongly.

'God no!' she exclaimed. 'I mean no. Not at all.'

Bella bit her lip and looked long and hard at Sophie before she picked up her coat and walked out of the room.

'Good,' she said as she passed Sophie.

CHAPTER 24

'Are you sure?' Sophie asked Mrs Alexander again as they stood in the foyer of the B&B Mrs Alexander nodded vigorously. 'Yes, dear,' she repeated. 'Those two little mites are out like lights, the pub's only down the road and if they wake up I'll phone you on this number.' She brandished the Post-it note with Sophie's mobile number. 'I don't usually do babysitting, but we're quiet and these are extenuating circumstances. Go on – the pair of you, you look like you need a drink.'

Louis smiled warmly at their hostess – if she had been a bird he would have charmed her from the nearest tree.

'Exactly the kind of service you get from a boutique hotel,' he said, flirting shamelessly with the middle-aged woman. This was something of an uncomfortable revelation for Sophie, who had yet to see him overtly flirt. He was exceptionally good at it.

'Exactly,' Mrs Alexander agreed, fluttering her lashes coquettishly.

A cold gust of wind enveloped them as they

stepped out onto the street, and Sophie pulled her jacket tightly around her. Without comment, Louis dropped the weight of his arm around her shoulders and pulled her into the shelter of his body. Silently they crossed the road and walked into the pub.

'What do you want?' he said, leaning against the bar.

'I don't know, I just don't know!' Sophie found herself wanting to cry out in despair but instead she asked him for a brandy. 'Make it a large one,' she told him. 'For the shock.' She didn't tell him that it was the shock of having his arm around her that she needed it for, and not the near-drowning episode.

As Louis ordered, Sophie looked around the pub, which wasn't very full. Two old men sat in one corner and a group of rather rowdy locals in another. She made her way to a third corner and found a table. As she waited for Louis to deliver the brandy she considered the way he had put his arm around her so easily.

It could mean one of three things: either he now considered them to be such close friends that he felt as comfortable with casual embraces as Cal often was. In this case he was definitely gay, because Sophie had never yet known a straight man who did hugging just to be friendly. Or it could mean that he knew she secretly fancied him, which she did not anyway because that would be in extremely bad taste, but for some reason he *thought* she did and reckoned he was in with a chance. This made him an amoral philanderer – a description which until recently Sophie had thought fitted him perfectly, but which Louis had inconsiderately messed up with his irritating bouts of sensitivity and heroism. Or most likely, being a man, he probably didn't anxiously overanalyse every single gesture that he made and worry endlessly about the repercussions. Probably, Sophie concluded with regret, it meant nothing at all except that her crush, which she was determined to will into nothing, was getting out of hand.

'Good God,' she mumbled to herself as Louis approached the table. 'I seriously need to get back to work. I'm starting to turn into Lisa.' And for a moment she missed the emotionally flat and tranquil landscape that her life had been a few short weeks ago.

Louis set the drinks down on the table and out of the four seats around it chose the one opposite her, proving conclusively that the arm thing meant nothing.

'So,' Sophie began, determined not to let her overtired and overly emotional brain do any more unauthorised thinking. 'How did it go at the solicitors?'

She had to ask him because even though she, Bella and Izzy had waited in reception giving him rather loud and boisterous moral support, when he had come out of his appointment he hadn't said a word. He'd just looked at the children with the expression of a man who had had a serious reality check.

'Let's go,' had been all he'd said, and fearing that he'd just been landed with debt, repossession or worse, Sophie had decided not to question him further in front of the girls.

Louis looked at the top of his pint for a moment. 'Weird,' he said. 'It turns out that the girls and I have got quite a lot of money.'

Sophie had not been expecting that. 'Really?' she said in surprise.

'Yeah, I know,' Louis said, looking equally amazed. 'When we first took out the mortgage, we took out an insurance policy as well, to cover the cost of the loan and a bit more besides if one of us died. The financial advisor talked us into it. Funny really, Carrie and I weren't exactly known for forward planning – but I think it was the baby coming. We suddenly realised we were grown-ups. But I've got to admit I didn't really know what the policy meant, I just kept paying into it even though sometimes when money was tight we were tempted to cancel it . . . it's not like we ever thought . . . but for some reason we never got round to doing it.'

Sophie listened to him talking about his life with Carrie, as a couple, a unit and a 'we', as if from a distance. Because she had not really known them as a couple it was hard to think of them that way, even when Louis talked about their domestic arrangements. It was like there were three sets of alternate realities that had nothing to do with each other: Carrie and Louis living life quietly with their two children on the coast, (Sophie's absent vision of her friend's existence); Carrie on her own struggling to bring up her kids after Louis abandoned her for the other side of the world; and Louis now – this half-known version of the man to whom Sophie was gradually becoming more drawn, at exactly the moment when she should be holding back.

Three parallel universes, and somehow Sophie had to make sense of them and draw them together without driving herself completely mad.

'Anyway,' Louis continued. 'While I was away I kept paying any money I earned from a few part-time jobs into our joint account. I knew Carrie didn't want my help but I couldn't not do anything, so I kept paying in what I had and the payment didn't get returned, so it made me feel better about things, I suppose.'

Sophie watched him carefully, talking about his abandonment of Carrie so casually. And yet she knew he was not a callous, careless person, she was sure of it. She said nothing and just kept on listening.

'The joint account doesn't amount to much,' he went on. 'Just a few grand. The solicitor told me Carrie never touched it at all after I left. But the direct debit for the insurance policy went out of that account. The mortgage on the house will be cleared and – there's nearly a hundred-thousand-pound lump sum too.'

Sophie blinked. 'Fuck,' she said simply.

'I know, and that's why I feel weird. When I found out about Carrie I was ready to come back here and fight for my girls. I was ready to buckle down and get a job and I knew I'd have to struggle to pay the mortgage on my own, but I was determined to do it because this was my chance to make things right, to do the grown-up thing.' He paused. 'A big part of this was selfishness, you know, to make me feel better about myself. And then almost as soon as I got back I realised that the way I felt wasn't important. It was all about my children, my two children. When I saw Bella's face I realised how I'd damaged her through my own weakness, I couldn't bear to let her down again. But I expected it to be hard. I wanted it to be. Somehow having all that cash handed to me on a plate like this seems wrong, it seems really wrong to profit from Carrie's death.' Louis struggled to say the last word, and shifted in his seat. 'So perhaps I should just give it to charity and start again. What do you think?'

Sophie blinked at him again.

'I wish you'd stop blinking and start talking,' Louis exclaimed. 'It's freaking me out.'

'Sorry.' Sophie took a breath. 'I just can't believe what I'm hearing. Louis, don't be mad! You can't give away the money. You and Carrie took out an insurance policy on each other's lives. That's all.

402

And now Carrie's gone you're entitled, more importantly the *children* are entitled, to the payout. It still would have paid out if you'd fallen down a volcano in Lima . . .'

'There aren't any volcanoes in Lima,' Louis interrupted.

'Whatever—' Sophie held up her hand to prevent further interruptions. 'My point is you kept up the repayments and you and the children are bene-fiting because of that. That's just the facts. But more importantly, this is exactly what Carrie would want for her children. She'd *want* them to have some security. She'd *want* you to have some breathing space. I mean, think about it, now you won't have to rush into a job you'd hate, like the one at the printers – you can spend more time with the girls, getting to know them. Maybe you can even buy a decent camera and start taking photos again.'

Louis looked up from the table top and stared at her.

'What?' Sophie asked him, feeling disconcerted.

'How did you know I wanted to get back into photography?'

'Well, you used to run your own business, didn't you, before Bella came and you needed a more regular income? Obvious really, no-one would do a crappy job they hated if they had the chance to do something they loved.' Sophie watched Louis's expression darken as he broke eye contact with her.

'Is that why you went, Louis?' She found the question rushing out of her mouth before she could censor it. 'Because you felt trapped into something you didn't want? Because you got married and had a baby before you knew it. Is that why?'

'No!' His voice rose in protest, and the other customers all looked over at them. 'No,' he said again more quietly. He picked up his empty glass and stood. 'I suppose it's about time we talked about this. I know it still bothers you and I want you to know the truth.' He swallowed. 'You've been a really good . . . friend to me. So I'll tell you if you really want to know.'

Sophie looked at him. Did she want to know? she asked herself. Because knowing would bring an end at last to this bubble that she had been living in, kidding herself that she was somehow vital to this fragile, budding family. But she knew that could not be true. In reality she needed to know exactly why Louis had left Carrie, so that she could put an end to her crush on him and move on, alone.

'I want to know,' she said.

'OK. But I need another drink first.'

CHAPTER 25

'Actually, I was happy,' Louis told her, after taking a long draught of his pint. 'I was really happy before it all fell apart. I didn't see it coming and when it did, it knocked me completely sideways. I couldn't handle it.

'Everyone said we were doomed to failure, Carrie's mum – obviously – but all our mates too, even if they were only joking. I don't think you were that impressed either, were you, from what Carrie said?'

Sophie considered denying it, but she just shrugged. 'It did happen very fast,' she said.

'I know, but I thought then – and I still feel, even after everything that happened – that just because something happens very fast, it doesn't automatically mean that it's wrong. Sometimes spontaneity is good.' Louis waited for a moment, as if he expected her to offer an opinion. When she remained silent he began talking again.

'We did get together quickly and Carrie was a force of nature that was hard to resist – but I didn't want to resist her! When a beautiful, funny, talented woman says she wants you, you don't stop to think about how fast it's going and where it might lead, not when it all feels so good.'

Sophie shrugged again. It seemed an appropriately comprehensive reaction, when she was so unsure of how she really felt.

'And it did feel good – as far as I was concerned it *was* love. And when Carrie fell pregnant I was incredibly pleased. I never knew my dad, and mum – well, she wasn't exactly the perfect mother. My nan brought me up. And she was wonderful, really wonderful – but I missed all that other family stuff that my mates had. Anyway, Nan died when I was seventeen and from then on, although I had a lot of good friends, I had no family. Until I met Carrie and then she and our baby became my family. Carrie didn't trap me. There was this one night on the beach when . . .' Louis trailed off, a faint smile on his face, lost in his memories.

Sophie sat quietly, feeling sick with jealousy and guilt.

'I loved Carrie,' Louis continued, 'she was my first love. I would have married her with or without the baby. I was going to ask her anyway when we'd been together for a year. I'd more or less decided that I would the day after I first met her. But when she told me about Bella it just came out. I proposed and she said yes and that was it. When I think about that now, I do wonder if, if Bella hadn't happened, another six or seven months down the line we would have still been so in love. But Bella did happen and I'm glad she did. I don't regret anything. It was a truly happy time.'

Sophie thought of the photo of Carrie on the beach with Louis in the background, his arms about another woman, probably flirting with her the way he had with Mrs Alexander earlier.

'Louis, can I ask you something?' she said.

He nodded, lifting his chin a little as if he expected she might want to punch it.

'Were you seeing other women after you were married?' Sophie asked, delivering her blow with swift efficiency.

Louis did not flinch. He held her gaze and shook his head. 'No,' he said, and he smiled to himself. 'Carrie used to say that I was a terrible flirt, but honestly I couldn't see it. I'm just nice to people and if that's flirting then I flirt with everyone, men included.'

Sophie thought about this for a moment. No-one could say she was a world expert on the matter, but she was more or less certain he had never flirted with her.

'Except for a person I'm really attracted to,' Louis said, 'then I sort of clam up.' He stopped himself and an uncomfortable silence hung between them for a beat.

Again Sophie sensed he was expecting her to say something. Not only could she not think of any response apart from shrieking hysterically, 'You've never flirted with me!' – she was also sure that even if she tried to speak, her mouth would not open. She was scared rigid. Too scared to think about what he might or might not be about to tell her. What he might be trying to say.

'I never cheated on Carrie,' Louis continued. 'Why would I? Carrie was radiant, the most beautiful thing I'd ever seen. Even more when she was pregnant and after Bella was born. She was like a sunrise that got more spectacular every morning. I loved her, Sophie, probably too much. When I look back on it I think it was almost adolescent. I'd never had a proper girlfriend before Carrie.'

'You must have!' Sophie blurted out, incredulously, her rebellious tongue probably loosened by an unpleasant tide of jealousy that rose in her chest as he talked about Carrie.

Louis arched an eyebrow, and a hint of a smile hovered around his lips.

'Why?' he asked her, inevitably.

'Well, you were twenty-three, twenty-four when you met Carrie,' Sophie said, conveniently forgetting that she herself had only ever had one proper boyfriend, and that hadn't been until she was pushing twenty-seven.

'There were girls,' Louis said, 'but no-one I connected with emotionally. That's why when it happened I think I poured so much into it. Maybe too much. You know, I actually think it was my commitment that scared Carrie. All I could see in my future was her and Bella – our family. All she could see was the same thing, and I think seeing that blotted out all the hopes and possibilities that she'd cherished for so long. I think in the end she felt she'd rushed into it.'

Sophie let that piece of information sink in. 'Are you saying Carrie ended the marriage?' she asked in disbelief. 'But she always said you were so happy, even after you'd split up she told me you were happy!'

Louis shrugged. 'Well, Carrie really hated to be wrong,' he said.

Sophie wondered if her friend's stubborn streak and dread of people crowing 'I told you so!' at her was a good enough reason for her not to mention the split to her. And then another thought occurred to her. Perhaps their friendship hadn't just drifted after the christening. Perhaps Carrie had deliberately begun to cut the ties. Something that would have been easy to do, as Sophie had hardly bothered to maintain them herself. Perhaps she hadn't ever been a really good friend to Carrie. And what use was it, she wondered, being loyal and steadfast to a friend who had gone for ever? Sophie had just started to allow herself to feel proud of her rescue job on this family, but if she had still been the kind of friend who exchanged vows and promises before Carrie had been killed, then Louis wouldn't be sitting here telling her everything now. She would have already known.

Sophie dropped her head in shame. She had let her friend down in life and now she was secretly lusting after her husband, who clearly still loved Carrie despite all the years that had passed.

'That's it,' Sophie told herself silently. 'The stupidity ends here.'

'So,' she said stiffly to Louis. 'What went wrong?'

He scrutinised her for a moment, probably taking her change in attitude as disapproval, which Sophie didn't mind at all.

'We didn't have much money,' he continued. 'And both of us working meant that Bella was in nursery full-time. Neither of us got to spend as much time with her as we wanted. Carrie had stopped painting. I hadn't been near my camera in months. I could see the daily routine was wearing her down. So I decided to take more shifts at the printers. Carrie gave up her shop job. She started painting again and we cut Bella's hours down at the nursery so she and Carrie could be together more. Don't get me wrong, it didn't seem like a sacrifice. I thought I was doing the right thing for my family and that made me feel pretty good.

'But Carrie and I hardly saw each other, and when we did I was almost always exhausted. Day by day we lost a little piece of the intimacy that had bonded us together.'

Louis paused and took a deep draught of his beer. Sophie followed suit with her brandy, feeling it burn the back of her throat. She wanted to know everything, but the thought of knowing terrified her. She took another sip.

'Then I got in one night, after about two months of working late, and she was waiting up for me.

She said she had some great news that might mean she'd be earning again. This new artist's studio and gallery was opening in the town, for local artists only. He was Welsh, and he was looking for two or three other artists to work there too. She'd met him at a friend's house. He was called Tony something. He really liked her work, wanted her to paint in the gallery. She was thrilled, really thrilled, she was so happy and – it was only when I saw her standing there glowing that I realised she hadn't been happy for months. And then she got pregnant again.' A shadow of pain passed across Louis's face, and Sophie's chest tightened.

'At first I couldn't understand, when she told me, why she was so . . . reserved. She couldn't look at me. I thought that maybe she was worried we couldn't afford a new baby so I tried to re-assure her, told her we'd manage somehow and she just burst into tears.

'"I'm so sorry, Louis," she said. "I'm so sorry." And then she said, "I don't think I love you any more."' Louis was no longer looking at Sophie, instead he seemed to be watching the swirling pattern of the pub carpet as he recounted the memory.

'She said she'd fallen in love with this other man, with this Tony. She said they'd been sleeping together for a couple of months. That it was really special. She said she didn't think the baby could be mine because there'd only been this one time in weeks.'

'She didn't tell me any of this,' Sophie said, shocked. 'I used to think that we were so close. That's why I took the girls, because of how close we'd been – always, for ever, whatever. That was what we always said. But I was wrong. Carrie must have felt that our friendship was over.'

Louis shook his head. 'I don't think so, Carrie used to talk about you all the time. She was always wishing we had the time and money to see you more. If things had worked out with Tony she'd have told you, I'm sure she would. But they didn't. And Carrie's dreams were so important to her, living them for real even more so. It was a matter of pride. I don't think she could bear to see them go wrong but she would especially hate other people to see them fall apart.'

Sophie's eyes met Louis's and part of her wished fervently that he was lying, that he was making all this up to look good, so she could hate him and that would be that. But she could see that he wasn't. Not even the most accomplished con-artist could lie with his entire body. Every muscle, every angle of Louis's body, each successive expression on his face indicated that he was telling the truth, a truth that was clearly painful for him and for her.

'So, she kicked you out?' she said. 'But then how do you know about what happened with this Tony?'

Louis took a deep breath and finished the last of his pint. 'No, she didn't kick me out. Like I said, the way I loved her was so fierce. I'd invested all my longing for a proper stable family into her. The way I reacted was pathetic – childish. I should have stayed, I should have tried to talk things through but I just went blind with hurt and rage. I went upstairs, I took my passport, my credit card, shoved some clothes into a carrier bag and I left with no idea where I was going.' Louis paused, the corners of his mouth pulled taut. He passed the back of his hand roughly across his eyes. 'The shouting had woken Bella up. She was crying in her bed, calling out to me, asking me to pick her up. I just walked straight past her. If there's one thing that I still wish I could change, it would be that moment. Over and over again I've woken up wishing that I had gone back to her. That I had picked her up and held her. It's the biggest regret of my life.'

Sophie wanted to reach out and put a hand on his arm, but before she could do so he seemed to physically pull himself together, withdrawing his hands from the table and sitting upright in his chair.

'Carrie didn't want me to go. She wanted me to stay and talk but I had to get out of there. I felt that my perfect life, everything I'd worked so hard to create, was ruined. I was like a child who wants to throw away a broken toy. I couldn't even look at her. I just walked out. I didn't even kiss Bella goodbye. The next twenty-four hours were like a nightmare; I can hardly remember them.

But I got a train to London and another to Heathrow. And I got the first standby flight to the States I could get on. Malibu!' Louis's laugh was empty of any pleasure. 'It was ironic because I'd always wanted to go there, before I met Carrie.'

He studied Sophie's face. 'What are you thinking?' he asked her. 'Do you hate me again?'

Sophie shook her head slowly, wishing desperately that she did because it would make her life so much easier. 'I can understand you walking out, but leaving behind the whole of your life? That's pretty hard to get my head round,' she told him honestly.

'She *was* my life, the whole of my life. I felt that if I didn't have her I didn't have anything. And before you ask, I didn't even think about Bella at that point. I didn't think about much at all except Carrie with the other man and . . . I think I wanted to show her I could be as selfish as she could. I wanted to shock her into wanting me back.'

Louis took a deep breath. 'I was an idiot,' he said, and it was his turn to shrug. 'I lived off my credit card for a while, got drunk a lot.' He grimaced. 'Generally acted like an idiot.'

Sophie guessed she was only now about to find out the extent of his folly.

'And then about a month after I arrived I woke up one morning, somehow sober, and I realised what I'd done to myself and to Bella. By trying to punish Carrie I'd punished myself and my little girl. I'd got it all wrong.

'I decided to call Carrie. I wanted to tell her I was coming home and that whatever happened between us I'd be there for my child. I had just enough left on my card to make the call and for a return flight.' Louis's face darkened. 'Only Carrie didn't answer the phone. Tony did. I should have asked to speak to Carrie, but I still loved her then. Hearing his voice was like twisting the knife in my gut so I just hung up.'

He sighed. 'Again I reacted like a spoilt child. I should have got that flight home anyway, worked things out with Carrie for Bella's sake. But the thought of doing that hurt too much, of being near her but not being with her. I decided it would be better to let Carrie build her life with her new family. I told myself that Bella would forget me soon enough and that would be for the best.' He shook his head bitterly. 'What bollocks. What a fucking idiot.'

Sophie watched his profile as he looked out of the window, trying to find the words to continue his story. It was as if everything he had told her was about a different man entirely from the one sitting opposite her now. Could anyone have changed that much in the space of three years? Was it possible that someone as impulsive and rash as the man Louis had described could become someone capable of bringing up a family on his own, someone solid and reliable? Could a person change so completely just by growing up? Something tightened again in Sophie's chest as she watched him, and sensing her looking at him he turned towards her and smiled.

'Shall I go on?' he said.

Sophie nodded, not quite able to return his smile, which faded when she did not respond.

He took a deep breath and began again. 'So, anyway, I got a flight to Brazil instead. I decided I was never going home. I was going to travel around South and Central America. But when I got to Peru, I stayed there. It's such a beautiful place, and so different from, well, here.' Louis gestured around him. 'It felt like I was finally far enough away for it to stop hurting. I'd been in Lima for about six months, volunteering for the kids' charity, by the time I realised that Carrie would have had her baby. I'd never had myself down as the worthy, charity type, but it was good working there. Like being part of a big family. They helped me get a visa, gave me a place to live and food.' Louis smiled. 'I worked with street children, incredibly brave and resourceful children. The foundation gave them a place to come to where they could feel safe for a night, eat a meal and learn something if they wanted. *Play* if they wanted.

'And at the evenings and weekends I worked in a tourist bar in town, so I was never still. I never had time to think. And then one day it hit me. The baby would have been born.

'It took me a long time to get up the courage to make the phone call, but I did. This time I was prepared for Tony to answer, but I knew I had to talk to Carrie, find out how she was, how Bella was. And the baby.'

Sophie realised she was sitting on the edge of her seat.

'But Tony didn't answer the phone. Carrie did and she seemed really pleased to hear from me. She told me she had had a beautiful little girl and that they were doing fine. I said I was glad things were working out for her, and then she seemed to think for a moment before telling me Tony had left and that she was glad he had. But that the three of them were happy.'

Sophie could picture Carrie saying those words. She always believed in living with the consequences of her choices, no matter what they were. Mrs Stiles said once that she wore her mistakes like badges of honour, and Carrie said that was the nicest thing her mother had ever said about her. But that was the difference between Sophie and Carrie. Carrie made choices decisively and rode them out no matter what happened. Sophie never chose what happened in her life – she let fate choose for her and never questioned how different things could be.

'Instantly I offered to come back on the next flight.' Louis was talking again. 'I said that she'd hurt me badly but I still loved her. I'd come back and we'd work things out. There was this long silence and I could almost taste the hope in my mouth.

'"I don't want you back, Louis," she said. "What happened with Tony is over but I still don't love you any more. I know I should, and I did once – so much. But I don't now. It's just gone. There's no point in you coming back for me, I want you to know that. But if you want to see the girls, I'll never stand in your way."

'We said goodbye and then she added one more thing. "There's something else you should know," she said. "Your daughter's name is Izzy."' Louis stopped talking. He rubbed his thumb over his eyes.

Sophie chewed her lip. She didn't know what to think about everything Louis had told her. She felt an urge to defend Carrie, but how could she when she had known nothing about any of this? She closed her eyes for a moment and thought about the last time she had seen Carrie, playing the scene back in her head. There had been a moment after the christening when Sophie had thought that Carrie wanted to talk about something else. But she had hesitated and then changed the subject. Maybe she was going to tell her all this. But if she was and then decided not to, it meant that even though Carrie had asked her to be the girls' godmother and guardian she had not felt able to tell her the truth about what had happened. She must have felt very lonely, Sophie realised.

'Why didn't you come back for Bella and Izzy? Carrie wouldn't have stopped you seeing them.'

Louis was silent for a while before taking a deep breath. 'At first it was because I still loved Carrie so much. I couldn't bear the thought of going back there and not being with her. It was selfish and stupid and immature. But the grief sort of swamped me. The only way I could get through it was not to think about it. I had to make myself not feel it – do you know what I mean?'

'Yes, I do,' Sophie said, so emphatically that Louis paused momentarily.

'And then one morning I was working in the vegetable garden with some of the children,' he went on, 'and they were slinging mud around and laughing, and I laughed too, and it was the first time I had really laughed and *meant* it in nearly two years. It was like I suddenly dropped all this weight that had been dragging me down. And all that pain and hurt that had been crowding out every other feeling finally dissolved. For the first time I could see things clearly. I could see what I had done.' Louis shook his head, as if he were still perplexed by his own behaviour.

'From then on I planned to come back. I knew I wanted to see my *own* children laughing like that. But it wasn't as simple as hopping on a plane again. I had to get together money for a flight home which took a long time – almost a year. And during that time I was training new volunteers to replace me. I didn't want to leave the children in the lurch. They were like a second family to me. I wanted to come back to England and I knew

I had to, but it was still hard to leave. People had been really good to me there and I was waiting until I felt I didn't love Carrie any more, because I thought it would be easier to be around her if I didn't love her.' Louis levelled his gaze at Sophie. 'I'd been ready to come back for months, but when you called I still hadn't quite got the money for the flight together.'

It took a moment for Sophie to let that last piece of information sink in. 'Did you still want to get back with Carrie?' she asked him, careful not to let any emotion colour her voice.

Louis shook his head. 'I wanted to see her, I wanted to apologise to her for behaving the way I did. I wanted to mend fences and make things right, for the girls' sake as well as my own. I had no idea how I would feel when I saw her. Now I'll never know. I left it too late.' He swallowed. 'It makes me very sad that I can't do that, and I really wish she were still here, I really do. But I didn't love her any more – not like that. All those feelings had been gone for a long time.'

Sophie let out a long breath. 'Did you have a lover in Lima?'

The look of surprise on his face matched her own at having asked the question. But instead of being offended, Louis shrugged.

'I had a couple of girlfriends,' he said. 'Not at the same time!' he added hastily. 'But it was never anything – special.' Amazingly, he didn't seem to have a problem with explaining himself to Sophie,

420

so she decided to ask him just one more impertinent question that had been in the back of her mind, before shutting up.

'When I called you that night, you thought I was someone else. You called me babe. Who did you think I was? One of your girlfriends?'

Louis furrowed his brow. 'No, I hadn't been seeing anyone for ages and . . .' Then he laughed. 'Maureen! It was Maureen.'

'Maureen?'

'She was my UK contact at the charity. Lovely woman, but always getting the time difference wrong. She was going to help me find a job and a flat to rent back in St Ives. When they told me an Englishwoman was calling at that time of the morning I thought it had to be her. I've never met her. I'll be seeing her next week, but she's got two children older than us so I don't *think* she'll be my type. She's lined me up with a local NSPCC charity for inner-city kids who need a break from city life.' Louis leaned back in his chair and regarded Sophie, the promise of a smile hiding somewhere around his lips.

'So after all that do you still think I'm a bastard?' he asked her quietly.

Sophie considered the question carefully. All this was too much for her to take in. Cal always said she had intimacy issues, and now she realised she had emotional issues too. She could not feel one more thing without imploding. She was feeling pain, loss, guilt and something else, something hopeful and yearning, all flowing recklessly over a strong undercurrent of attraction to the last man in the world she should feel that way about – her dead best friend's ex-husband. She realised Louis was waiting for an answer. She struggled to find some words that would sound normal. 'I think you were hurting and when people hurt they don't always do everything right.'

Louis bit his lip and nodded. 'I was hoping for a simple no,' he said wryly.

'But it isn't that simple, is it?' Sophie said, not exactly sure what she was talking about any more. 'It's seriously complicated.'

They watched each other across the table in silence for a moment.

'Yes,' Louis said, without taking his eyes off her. 'It is.'

'Anyway,' Sophie added hesitantly, 'it's just a matter of time before Tess calls you and tells you the children are yours. It doesn't matter what I think of you.'

Slowly Louis leaned forward, resting his elbows on the table as he closed the distance between them by a few inches.

'It does matter,' he said, his voice low. 'It matters to me.'

Sophie's mouth was dry and she found it difficult to swallow. She took a sip of her drink and moistened her lips.

'For what it's worth, Louis,' she said, still desperately trying to prise another meaning into this conversation, and yet terrified of what it might really mean. 'I think you'll be a great father. I think the three of you will be really happy. I've already told Tess that, too.'

Louis shook his head. 'Thanks, that means a lot – but that's not what I meant.'

Sophie felt as if every muscle in her body was rigid. She felt that it was entirely possible she might fossilise right there in the pub. They'd be able to slice her up and sell her in a local gift shop: 'Genuine Petrified Woman'.

'I didn't really remember you,' Louis said, 'before I came back, I mean. Carrie talked about you a lot and there was a photo in a frame. But I never really looked at it.' He paused, and bit his lip. 'So it came as a total shock to me to find out that you're so beautiful.' Sophie did not move. 'That first night I came to your flat and we were talking in the hallway and you took off your coat and – well, does it sound corny to say you took my breath away?' Sophie did not know what to say, but luckily Louis didn't wait for an answer. 'It does, doesn't it? It sounds like a line. But believe me, although at that moment I might have thought you were seriously hot, I never dreamt I'd start to think about you the way I am now. I was so angry when I left that night, with myself and with you. So I thought I'd just put the fact that you're so beautiful to one side. It was easy at first. I was there for my children and nothing else. You hated me and to top it off you were my dead, estranged wife's best friend. Not exactly the perfect girl to fancy.' Louis smiled. 'Actually I thought you were one of those women who care more about not chipping their nail varnish than anything else. And you were a bit of a bitch.'

Sophie had thought that she had been genuinely afraid for the first time in her life earlier that day when she had been up to her waist in seawater. But no, that had been a walk in the park compared to the pure fear and adrenalin that were coursing through her veins at that moment. What exactly was Louis saying?

'I'm seriously attracted to you, Sophie,' he said. 'Every sensible part of me is screaming at me to shut up. But there's something there – isn't there? Between us. I don't know what I'm thinking or feeling here, and I know it's insane for me to be saying all this to you, but I think I'll go insane if I don't.'

Louis picked up Sophie's hand and held her fingers lightly. 'Look, I know, if there was ever a wrong time, a wrong place or a wrong person to say this to, it's now, it's here and you're that person. But I have to say it, Sophie. For a while now, every time I look at you I want to touch you. Every time I touch you, I want to kiss you and if I could kiss you I don't think I'd be able to stop.' He waited for a moment and when Sophie didn't move he let go of her hand. 'In my head that last part sounded much less cheesy. I'm sorry. I just thought that maybe – I couldn't let us go back to our lives without saying out loud how much I'm drawn to you, that's all. Call me impulsive but life's too short.' Louis tried and failed to gauge Sophie's expression. He smiled weakly. 'You can slap me now, if you like.'

Sophie stood up so abruptly that her chair tipped over. She willed herself outside, dimly aware of people lifting their heads to watch her as she ran past. At last she was bathed in the cold night air and she felt her skin begin to cool. She crossed the street to the harbour front, leaned against the railings and watched the foam-topped waves shining in the moonlight as they raced inland. From the moment they had stepped into Carrie's house that morning, the whole day had seemed like a dream. She had experienced more emotion and turmoil in the space of the last few short hours than she had since the day her father had died. She heard the rush of the sea more clearly, smelt the salty chill in the air more sharply and saw each tiny reflection of light in the dark water perfectly. And she sensed Louis at her side a second before he reached her.

'I didn't know if you wanted me to follow you or not,' he said. 'So I thought I would, on the off chance.'

Sophie turned to face him. 'I'm glad you did.' Louis opened his mouth to speak but she stopped him. 'Look, if you want me to talk about other people's feelings then I can. I can do that all night. I'm a very good advice-giver. But I am not the sort of person who finds it very easy to talk about myself. I don't know what I'm feeling right now or what it means. I don't even understand it – but all of the things you said in there about me, I could say them back to you,' Sophie finished awkwardly.

'You mean you feel it too?' Louis said uncertainly.

'I do,' Sophie replied with difficulty. Louis smiled, but before he could say or do anything Sophie put her hand on his chest and halted him. 'But this isn't right, Louis. For us to do anything about it would be wrong. I think it might be really wrong—'

Louis nodded his smile fading slightly. 'You're probably right. But, well, would it matter . . . if we had just one night without thinking about anyone or anything else except for what's going on between us?'

Sophie studied him in the moonlight. That was all he was talking about. A one-night stand, a sort of therapeutic session to deal with the sexual tension. She felt simultaneously relieved, sad and excited. If that was all it would be, it didn't really count and there would be no consequences. It could be like stepping off the planet for a few hours and leaving it all behind. And for once Sophie wanted to do something completely foreign to her nature. Tonight she wanted to know what it felt like to be reckless and not care about tomorrow.

'I want to know,' she said. 'Which probably makes me an idiot.'

'That makes two of us.'

'Do you think so, because . . .' Sophie began, earnestly trying to rationalise what she was saying.

'Let's stop talking now,' Louis said, laying the tips of his fingers gently over her mouth. He watched in the moonlight, tracing the curves of her lips, and then at last he kissed her so that all she could feel for a wondrous few moments was the heat of his mouth warming every fibre of her being. Sophie broke off the kiss and found she was giggling.

'Not the response I was expecting,' he said, smiling as she buried her face in his jacket.

She caught her breath and looked up. 'I must be drunk. This isn't normal.'

'Well, don't back out on me now.' Remember what I said about thinking I might not be able to stop kissing you once I started? I was right.' Louis rested his hands on her shoulders, his fingers entwined in her hair. 'Sophie, stay with me tonight? Just tonight, please?' he asked her, touchingly nervous.

Sophie looked into his eyes and felt a heady rush of intoxication that she was sure had nothing to do with brandy.

'I guess we're going to find out how we both fit in that single bed after all,' she said, and she took a step into thin air and kept on walking.

CHAPTER 26

It was still dark when Sophie awoke.

For a moment she lay there waiting for her eyes to adjust, as the thin line of light around the door frame cast a sliver of light into the room. Still warmed and comforted by sleep, she stared at the door, trying to work out how it had moved from its previous position.

And then she remembered she was in Louis's room.

Sophie did not leap out of bed, partly because she did not want to wake Louis but also because she discovered that her limbs were so tangled in his it was impossible to move. She lay there listening to her heart thumping in her chest. Piece by piece everything that had happened came back to her in a series of jolting and shocking tableaux.

The moment they returned to the B&B. A second's hesitation before they crossed the doorstep. Their silent ascent to Louis's room, not looking at each other as they climbed the stairs, their fingers just touching on the handrail, Louis looking over his shoulder at her as he unlocked his door. Sophie standing perfectly still with her ear pressed to her and the children's door, looking at the pointed, scuffed toes of her pink, knee-high boots – now water-stained and dirty – as she waited, holding her breath, for a small voice to call out her name. Not knowing if she wanted to hear that voice or not.

Sophie felt again the knot of anticipation that had clenched her stomach into a fist as Louis had held out his hand and she'd taken it, and then . . .

She remembered his kisses all over her face and her neck, in her hair and across her shoulders. Their clothes somehow disintegrating, the heat his body gave off a moment before his skin met hers. The touch of his hands on her breasts, then his lips and teeth. Her own hands exploring the curve of his waist, the length of his thighs. Feeling him harden against the soft cushion of her belly. Feeling him shudder when she touched him and kissed him. Feeling him moving inside her, experiencing every tiny sensation, every part of him connected to her until she buried her face in his neck, her teeth catching the skin of his shoulder as she came and a moment later his voice whispering something softly in her ear, words she couldn't make out and didn't want to understand.

They were silent then and still, seeming to slot perfectly together in the narrow bed like a pair of puzzle pieces. And they must have fallen asleep soon afterwards, because that was exactly how they were still lying: Sophie folded inside Louis, his long arms and legs wrapped around her, holding her back against his chest. She edged herself onto her back and turned her head to look at him. Most of his face was in shadow, just the tiniest slice of light picking out one corner of his sleeping eye, the curve of his jaw and the corner of his mouth. His breathing was regular and deep, he was fast asleep.

Sophie was now wide awake and she could feel her blood pounding around her body. She felt breathless and anxious as the remnants of sleep slowly receded to reveal a sense of raw, wide-awake panic. It seemed as if all the reasons for this not happening, that they had hardly talked about and quickly dismissed last night, were solidifying into cold, hard realities all around her.

Sophie frantically tried to close herself off from the feelings that were surfacing with the early morning. Last night it had seemed so possible to do as Louis had said. To explore their attraction to each other free from the restraint of history or circumstance, and then go on with their lives as before. Louis had seduced her with his reasoning, his looks and his touches and she had let him. But she had been wrong when she thought there would be no consequences. If she had had a stupid unrequited crush on him last night, this morning it was much, much worse than that. Spending the night with him had brought all her dreams crashing into the real world where they could be trampled on and torn apart.

She had gone and fallen in love with him.

She could not do this. She could not be here with Louis. With Carrie's ex-husband, with Bella and Izzy's father. Being here was a betrayal, it was pointless and weak. She should have realised. He might have slept with her but he'd talked about Carrie with such warmth last night, how could he not still love her? And the place was so full of Carrie – everywhere she looked she felt her friend's presence – her friend who had always been there for her. How could she have even daydreamed about a life with Louis and the girls?

Reaching down to the side of the bed, she felt for her bag and was relieved when she found it almost straight away. She took out her mobile phone and checked the time.

It was just after five. She had to get back into her own bed before they noticed that she wasn't there. Immediately Sophie was gripped by panic as she began to grasp the implications of what she had done, and the reckless joy she had felt in Louis's arms seemed in another lifetime.

'Oh Christ,' she whispered to herself, feeling the prick of tears behind her eyes. 'Stupid, stupid, stupid.'

Carefully she began to ease herself out of Louis's embrace, but as soon as he sensed her moving his arms tightened reflexively. The thumb of his left hand ran lazily over her nipple as he kissed the back of her neck, burying his face in her hair. He shifted a little, moving his other arm out from underneath her, using it to prop himself up above her. Sophie felt him looking at her even though she could not see his face.

'Not a dream then,' he said softly, and Sophie felt the touch of fingertips run lightly across the contours of her face and neck, travelling over her breasts. For a heartbeat she allowed herself to remain still, closing her eyes even in the dark. And then she put her hand over his and stopped its exploration.

'I've got to go next door,' she whispered. 'They'll be awake soon.'

Louis flopped back onto the bed with a heart-felt sigh. 'It's still dark,' he protested his voice still warm with sleep.

'I know, but – still . . .' Sophie whispered. Louis didn't try to stop her as she swung her legs onto the floor and, sitting on the edge of the bed, bent over, searching for discarded items of clothing. Instead, as she found her knickers and pulled them over her ankles he transferred his caresses to the back of her neck and along her spine.

Abruptly, Sophie pulled her underwear up as she stood. 'I can't find anything,' she said irritably, feeling claustrophobic in the darkness.

'I'll turn on the lamp,' Louis said sleepily.

'No, don't—' Sophie said, too late to stop him.

Soft light filled the corners of the room and all sense of unreality was gone. He really was lying in his bed watching her. She really was standing before him, almost naked and feeling more exposed than she had ever done before.

'You are so amazing,' he said, his eyes running over her body. 'Come back here, please, just for a moment . . .' He smiled as he held a hand out to her.

Sophie saw her T-shirt lying inside out on the floor and picked it up and pulled it hastily over her head. She retrieved her jeans, lying in a crumpled heap at the foot of the bed, her fingers fumbling as she tried to pull one jean leg out the right way.

'I can't,' she said, her voice tight and nervous. 'If the children wake up and find I'm not there or even come in here . . .' Finally she slipped her legs into the cold denim and buttoned the jeans at the waist. 'And anyway, that's not what we said, is it?' Sophie made herself remind him, keeping her voice cool. 'It was just a one-off, remember?'

Louis sat up in bed.

'I didn't mean it literally. I meant . . .'

'What did you mean?' Sophie asked him, her anger surfacing protectively.

'I meant we could get the lust out of the way and then take it from there.' Louis looked at the expression on Sophie's face. 'I'm not very good at this bit,' he said quickly. 'At words and stuff. Look, I didn't expect this – I didn't expect to—' He faltered to a stop.

'To what?' Sophie hissed at him, conscious of the thin walls between them and the children. In fact, the whole room seemed to be closing in around her, the introduction of light making it seem smaller and closer, and she desperately wanted to get out of it. 'Get laid whilst you were sorting out your wife's estate? Must have been a real bonus for you.'

Louis sat up sharply and pulled on his trousers. 'Sophie, please. Why are you so angry?'

Sophie couldn't tell him; she couldn't tell him she was furious with herself for falling in love with him. It was better that he thought she was angry with him. Better than the alternative, the terrifying possibility that she might show him the reality of how she was feeling.

'I have to go now,' she said, gripping the door handle.

'Sophie, wait . . .'

She closed the door on him.

For a moment or two Sophie stood outside the room where Louis's two daughters were sleeping. She couldn't go in there, not yet, she realised. She was sure the moment that Bella looked at her, she would know something had happened with Louis, something that shouldn't have. Sophie didn't want Bella to know, the last thing she wanted was to wreck the fragile peace that Bella had found both with her father and within herself with one foolish, thoughtless act. Bella trusted her, loved her even. Sophie was determined to preserve that.

Uncertain of exactly what she was doing or where she was going, Sophie walked past her bedroom door and crept down the carpeted stairs. At the bottom she sat down and pulled on her boots. She paused and glanced back up the stairs for a moment as if she thought Louis might be there watching her, but the top of the stairs was empty so she opened the front door and stepped out into the dark morning.

The cold immediately raised an army of goose-bumps across her skin but Sophie welcomed the chill that numbed her burning cheeks. Her mother had said to her once that the darkest hour was always before the dawn. She meant it, Sophie knew, as an uplifting metaphor, a way to try to get Sophie through after the loss of her dad, when she couldn't see any hope, but as Sophie walked down through the near-empty town, still perfectly dark and still, she was certain that when the sun came up her troubles would really begin.

Sophie found her way back to Porthmeor Beach, the beach where she had run into the sea after Izzy.

She told herself it was a random destination at the end of a frantic walk, and that it was inevitable that she would end up staring at the sea, as it leaked into the dark horizon and washed the black out of the sky, but there were other routes to the sea closer to the B&B and Sophie knew she had come here deliberately. It was here that Louis had brought her and Izzy out of the water and here that the four of them had stood together, embracing each other. It was on this beach that Sophie had experienced the very last thing she had expected to feel.

A sense of belonging, to each of them. To Bella, to Izzy – and to Louis.

As she sat on the sand, Sophie was dimly aware of the hard, cold damp that began to seep through the seat of her jeans. She drew her knees up and hugged her legs close to her as she watched the magic and movement of the ocean gradually begin to reveal itself. Her heart rate slowed and the vice-like grip of fear that had pressed around her ribcage seemed to loosen a little.

'What am I doing here?' Sophie asked herself, a whispered question that was immediately lost on a gust of wind. 'How did this happen?'

It had started as an inconvenience, Sophie admitted to herself. That was the overriding feeling she had felt when Tess Andrew had walked into her office all those weeks ago. Above every-thing else, in that moment and for a long time afterwards, she had been irritated and inconveni-enced by Carrie's children forcing this hiatus into her busy and ordered life. It was only now she realised that life *before* Bella and Izzy had arrived was the hiatus, because nothing, nothing about Sophie had changed for years and years until that moment. She had let year after year of her life slip away without anything to mark them out as special or important, as her half-forgotten dreams and ambitions quietly stagnated.

Sophie wasn't sure exactly when it happened but she knew it was only after Bella and Izzy had come that she had started living inside of her own life again instead of passively watching it tick by without her. And now, because of Bella and Izzy she was in love, maybe for the first time, maybe even for ever, because they had kick-started her heart. It wouldn't have mattered if it was just the girls Sophie had fallen for. If it had just been Bella and Izzy things would have been perfect, joyous even – Sophie would have found a new kind of freedom to be happy.

The trouble was it wasn't just Carrie's children who she was in love with. It was Louis too. Sophie weighed the heavy, debilitating sense of longing that seemed to be pinning her down, and she found it hard to breathe.

She rested her chin in the groove between her knees, used the heel of her hand to wipe her eyes that were watering in the wind.

It was odd, she thought, and sad, that the very thing that had brought her so close to Carrie again – so close that she could almost feel her sitting beside her on the freezing sand – was loving the people that Carrie would never be able to hold and love again. Sophie felt but did not hear the sob that formed in her throat. She felt so guilty. She felt like a grave robber.

Of course, it was the thought of actually being with Louis that terrified her. The reality of actually being with a man that she wanted so much made the possibilities of it all going wrong horribly real. Cal joked about her intimacy issues and clumsiness when it came to relationships, but secretly, in some small, quiet part of herself, Sophie knew she kept her distance from love because she could not bear the thought of another man she loved leaving her.

Sophie screwed her fists into her eyes and knew it wasn't the cold that was making her eyes water now.

If there was anyone who might make her want to take that risk, then perhaps it was Louis, but Louis didn't come on his own. He came with a past that was full of Carrie and with his children.

Even if the children didn't exist there were hundreds of reasons not to let anything else happen with Louis. He had passionately loved another woman. One who Sophie knew for sure had been more beautiful and vibrant than she could ever be, and who Louis might still love, despite his protests. There had been a look in his eye when he had talked about Carrie that Sophie couldn't be sure wasn't love.

He had talked about other girlfriends since Carrie, that was true. Women he must have been attracted to in the same way he was attracted to her. Sophie couldn't exactly remember the way he had described those flings but she thought the phrase 'nothing special' had been used. The panic tightened in her chest again.

What if Louis felt that way about her? What if he wanted to change the one night they had agreed on into some more because all he was pursuing was his attraction? And everything he had said and whispered last night had been a succession of lines, part of a tried and tested seduction routine? The recently neglected, practical part of her reminded her that he was still mostly a stranger to her. That despite those last few weeks and the night they had just spent together she hardly knew him at all. And the part of her that hurt and hoped knew she couldn't bear to be another nameless encounter that he might one day refer to as 'nothing special'.

Amazingly Sophie felt herself laughing even as the tears froze on her cheeks. She was hilarious. She was insane. She was just as afraid of him loving her as she was of him not caring for her at all.

Sophie shook her head and tried to focus on a way to untangle this mess she had made for herself. She thought about Bella and Izzy and how she felt about them. She loved them too and she felt this fierce, overwhelming urge to protect them from anything that might hurt them. She found she wanted more than anything else in the world to know for sure that neither of them would ever be hurt again.

Sophie drew her arms tighter around her and watched the sea.

It was simple, really. She knew with a sudden clarity that there was no dilemma. All she had to do was what was best, for the children, for Carrie, for Louis and for herself. She had to do the only thing that would preserve each of them from suffering any more hurt.

She had to leave.

If she left now the girls would still think about her happily, they would still love and trust her, and she would always be someone they could turn to. Sophie felt that by going she would still be honouring the memory of Carrie, keeping her promise to her, always, for ever, whatever. She would be able to love her memory instead of spending every day trying to compete with her ghost.

And if she left then Louis's pride might be a little stung, he might even be sad, but it was better to make this break now, so that in time whatever it was that had happened between them would be so far in the distance that it would be impossible to see, impossible to know what might have been.

Sophie knew that if she went back to her old life, her own quiet life, eventually the same routine – of work and home and half-baked desires – would insulate her once again against the threat of love and loss that was looming over her now. She would have back the life she had treasured so dearly. A calm, cool, peaceful life.

It was a good life, Sophie told herself. Her career, her home, it was all something she had created for herself, and now it would truly be a haven. Once she'd shaken off her feelings for Louis, life would be better than ever. She could do whatever she wanted, when she wanted.

Knowing that comforted her, but at the same time it made her cry even harder.

'Are you all right?'

Sophie looked up sharply to find a young man in a wet suit looking down at her, frowning with concern.

'You're not thinking of topping yourself, are you?' he said, looking regretfully at the surf he might have to forego to look after this strange, demented woman he had found on the beach.

Sophie forced her frozen face into a smile, dragging the sleeve of her top across her face. She realised she must look awful, but she felt calm for the first time in weeks.

'No,' she sniffed, 'I'm not thinking of topping myself. I think I've sorted it all out now,' she managed to say through numb lips.

'Good,' the surfer said, holding a hand out and helping her to her feet, 'because seriously, things are never *that* bad.'

And, Sophie thought as she began to walk slowly and stiffly back to the B&B, the darkest hour really was before the dawn.

CHAPTER 27

The road ahead was clear, so Sophie put her foot down and floored it, watching the speedometer climb steadily towards ninety. It was the first time she had speeded since Izzy had arrived in her life. She had expected to find the freedom of having her car to herself as just a machine – the child seat removed, the Manic Street Preachers silenced at last and cat sunscreens stuffed in the glove compartment – much more exhilarating than she did. But driving as fast as she could get away with, nothing but the sound of the car's engine quietly humming, had somehow lost its joy.

A mountain of black cloud was building on the horizon ahead and she knew that sometime in the near future it would be raining very hard, but she kept her foot down all the same, heading towards the bad weather with steady determination. She had told herself that once she was back in London, back in Highbury and back in her flat, she would be able to hear herself think again. She could start to make sense of the way her life had suddenly turned itself inside out and upside down without giving her any warning. Better still, she decided not to think about it at all. Not to think about everything that had happened with Louis last night. Not to think about the way she had left the children that morning. Not to think about everything that had happened to lead up to that parting, because she was sure that as soon as she got home everything would be all right.

But home was a few hundred miles away and Sophie kept playing back the events of the last two days, again and again in her head, like someone trying to make sense of a foreign-language film without the subtitles.

After returning to her room that morning, she had showered and redressed herself in clean clothes and then helped the girls as much as they wanted her to as they chattered and giggled and chose each other their usual rainbow collection of colours to wear. Sophie looked on, relieved that Izzy seemed to be over the trauma of her watery experience and was now just enjoying the excitement of it, building the adventure with every rhythmic retelling.

The hour and a half that she had had to wait between joining Louis for breakfast and it being nine o'clock seemed like an eternity. As she sat across the table from him Sophie felt almost visibly smothered in the vividly persistent memories of the night, as if his mouth and hands had left marks on her skin, revealing where each kiss and each caress had been.

She had poked at her breakfast with a fork and sipped her coffee, smiling dimly at the girls as they made plans for the day. It was almost exactly as it had been the previous morning, except that Sophie did not speak directly to Louis and he didn't talk to her. It was clear to her that he was just as certain as she was that this had all been a foolish mistake.

When nine a.m. finally came and normal office hours resumed Sophie had excused herself from the table and returned to her room, only to find that her mobile had gone flat. Self-consciously she had slowly descended the stairs, waving at the girls as she fed the payphone with coins and dialled Tess's number.

'Gosh, I haven't even got my coffee yet!' Tess had exclaimed breezily as she picked up the phone. 'How's it going down there? Any progress?'

Sophie had watched the family of three at the breakfast table, talking and laughing.

'Yes,' she'd said with mechanical honesty, 'it's going really well. Things sort of came to a head yesterday. Bella and Louis had a talk – they're deciding where to live. Bella wanted to stay in the old house at first. But they haven't made up their minds yet.' Sophie had paused, realising that she still didn't know exactly what the two of them had said to one another on the beach. So many things had happened that she hadn't had a moment to draw breath, let alone talk properly to Bella. 'They seem much more relaxed together now. Both the children seem to be looking forward to staying down here permanently. I think everything's going to work out how you wanted, Tess.'

Louis had looked up at that point and caught Sophie's eye. She had immediately turned her back on his gaze, although she thought she could still feel it touching her.

'. . . excellent.' Tess was finishing a sentence.

'The thing is . . .' Sophie had begun. 'Something's come up at work. They really need me back in the office, like yesterday. And I know Louis still has a lot to do down here, what with having to find a house, solicitors, sorting out the girls' school and nursery and stuff. So I was wondering, how long will it be before everything's finalised?' She'd taken a deep breath. 'What I'm trying to say is, can I leave the girls with him now? Down here?'

Tess had not answered straight away. 'Sophie,' she'd said after a moment, her voice weighted with concern. 'What's wrong?'

'Nothing,' Sophie had reassured her, far too quickly to be credible. 'Everything's really fine!'

Again there had been a moment's uncertain silence as Tess had tried to read her voice.

'Do you need to bring the girls back with you, take them away from Louis? You can tell me if there is *anything* to be concerned about,' Tess had pressed her.

'No! God, no, not at all, Tess. He's been fantastic, really. I truly believe he will be a great dad.' She had told Tess the truth, even though every word hurt her. 'It's just . . . I don't think they really need me now, and work does. And I really need to be there. And then there's Artemis – she hates it when I'm away, even with Mum looking in on her – so I thought that if it was all right, I could leave them here. Is that OK?'

'This seems a bit abrupt,' Tess had said, still fishing. 'Look, Sophie, if you've had another falling-out with Louis then I'd really like to know . . .'

'There's nothing wrong, Tess, I promise,' Sophie had said firmly. 'The girls will be fine with him. More than that, they'll be happy.'

'And there's no way you could stay a little longer?' Tess had urged her. 'Listen, Sophie, are *you* sure you just want to go like this? Those children – especially Bella – have come to rely on you. This will be a hard enough transition for them, even if things are going well with Louis. I know it must be difficult, but if you could stay just a little longer I'm sure they would really appreciate it . . .' The payphone had beeped in Sophie's ear as she considered what Tess had said.

'Sophie?' Tess had questioned her.

'I'm out of money,' Sophie had lied. 'I have to go. Thanks for everything, Tess.'

'But what about the girls?' Tess had said hurriedly. 'Think about them, please.'

'I *am* thinking about them,' Sophie had said. 'I have to go back. I have to go back because of them.'

But the line had already gone dead.

When Sophie had turned around Louis was ushering the girls up the stairs.

'What did you say to Tess?' he had asked her tensely.

'I told her I have to go back to London today,' Sophie had said, unable to look at him.

'You're leaving today?' Louis had asked her, as if he hadn't quite heard her. Sophie had nodded.

'Don't worry,' Sophie had said bitterly. 'I didn't tell her anything.'

Louis had taken a step closer to Sophie.

'Sophie, don't leave just because of what happened last night, it was . . .'

Sophie had stepped back. She hadn't wanted him to say that it was nothing, it wasn't important.

'Look,' she had told him before he could complete his sentence, 'it's time for me to go. I should go now before . . .' She had glanced up at the ceiling. 'Before it all gets out of hand. It's for the best that I go.' Somehow she had managed to tell him three times that she was leaving, but he had still looked as if he didn't quite believe it. He had probably thought she was making a huge drama out of nothing.

There had been a long pause and Sophie had got the sense that Louis had been forming and reforming sentence after sentence in his head, searching for the appropriate thing to say.

'You don't have to say anything,' she had told him.

He had bowed his head for a second before looking back at her. 'Just don't lose touch with the girls,' he had said eventually. 'They really need you.'

Sophie had nodded abruptly.

'I know they do,' she'd said. And she'd walked back up the stairs, leaving Louis at the bottom, trying to work out exactly how she was going to say goodbye to Bella and Izzy.

The motorway was busy, but Sophie weaved confidently between lanes, overtaking truck after truck and, at one point, sitting on the tail of a Ford Mondeo until it moved over to let her speed by, the driver mouthing justifiable obscenities at her in her rear-view mirror. But she didn't care, she wanted to be home.

As Sophie had knelt to kiss the girls goodbye, Izzy had wound her arms around her neck and squeezed her tight for a long time.

After a while Sophie had tried to disengage herself from the embrace but Izzy had only held her more tightly.

'Darling,' Sophie had said softly. 'I'll see you really soon.'

'Will you?' Izzy had demanded, drawing back to scrutinise Sophie's face for any dishonesty.

'I will,' Sophie had promised solemnly, but she had sensed a promise was not enough. It would be a long time, she had guessed, before Izzy would really believe that the people she loved would always come back to her again.

'I'm cross of you,' Izzy had said, dropping her arms to her side. 'I don't want you to go.'

Sophie had caught Louis's look above his youngest daughter's head. 'I've got to go. I'm sorry,' she had said simply.

'Be careful in Phoebe,' Izzy had said, her frown relenting slightly.

'I will,' Sophie had promised her. It was a promise she had broken more or less immediately, and now she felt an irrational pang of guilt. Reluctantly she curtailed her speed and moved over to the slow lane. It meant it would take her longer to get home, but it was one less thing to feel bad about.

Before that final goodbye, Bella had accompanied Sophie on her stocking-up trip to the local Spar that morning. Sophie had wanted to buy some cans of Coke and chocolate for the journey, as she was determined to make it back to London without stopping once and didn't care if she required junk food to do so.

They had walked, hand in hand, down the steep hill that the B&B sat on, following the bend of the road into St Ives, cutting through the steps that led deeper down into the town.

As they reached the bottom of the steps, they paused and looked out to sea.

'It's a lovely day today,' Sophie had said. 'You can smell spring in the air, can't you?'

'Let's go and look at the waves,' Bella had said,

tugging her hand in the opposite direction to the Spar. Sophie had sensed that Bella wanted to say something, so she hadn't objected. They had walked towards the sea and Sophie had followed her down the harbour steps onto the beach, relieved to see that the tide was out and the sand was relatively dry.

'I wanted to make sure that you're OK with Louis now,' Sophie had said. 'I saw you talking, but I never asked you what he said.'

The breeze had whipped Bella's hair across her eyes, causing her to clamp her fringe back from her forehead. Sophie had looked into her brown eyes, hardly ever so visible. She was such a beautiful child.

'Will you stay if I say I'm not happy?' Bella had tested her.

Sophie had touched Bella's cheek. 'You know I would,' she had said honestly, despite how much it would cost her. 'But are you?'

Bella had released her hair, crouched down on the sand and begun to dig up half a shell. Sophie had knelt beside her and watched.

'He told me he was sorry for everything that had happened, that he'd been a rubbish dad and that things happened differently from the way he planned but he was here now and he loves us and would always do his best. He said he'd never let us down, not ever.'

Bella had begun to clean the shell with the hem of her T-shirt. 'Sometimes grown-ups do let you down, even when they say they won't. But it's still Daddy,' Bella had said as she cleaned. 'It's still Daddy under there. I remember him more now that I've met him properly. I've missed him. I'm glad we've made up.'

She had handed Sophie the shell – half a clam – rough and greying on the outside, but with a soft pink and gently luminous sheen on its smooth inner surface.

'Thank you,' Sophie had said, running her thumb over its contours. 'So, you are happy to stay here with him and Izzy then? What about the house?'

'I am,' Bella had said slowly. 'And we've decided to look at other houses and see if there are any that feel right for all of us. But I still don't want you to go.'

Sophie had bowed her head. 'I have to,' she'd said into the wind.

'You don't,' Bella had said quickly. 'I've been thinking – I know you have a job and everything, but people have parties in St Ives all the time. I'm sure you could easily get a job doing parties here. And Artemis could come and boss Tango around, he'd like that.' Bella had caught hold of Sophie's wrist and tugged it. 'Please don't go, Aunty Sophie, please don't.'

'It's not just work, Bella,' Sophie had said, forcing herself to be firm. 'I was only ever looking after you for a bit and—'

'But you do love us though, don't you?' Bella

had asked her anxiously. 'You said you did before.'

Sophie had put her arms around Bella and pulled her half onto her lap where she was kneeling in the sand.

'I do love you. That won't change just because I have to go back. I have my own life in London, just as you have yours here. We'll see each other often, and write, and you can send me pictures and phone me and . . .' She had paused, willing her tears not to fall, to be strong for Bella.

Then Sophie had lifted Bella off her lap and turned her round so that they faced each other, both kneeling on the sand, her hands on Bella's shoulder. 'Bella, I have to go back,' she had said as she pushed herself into a standing position. 'There are reasons that you can't understand . . .'

'What reasons?' Bella had demanded and, realising that none of them were anything she could tell the child, Sophie had brushed the sand off her jeans and begun walking back towards the steps that led up to the harbour.

Bella had caught up with her and hooked her arm through Sophie's. 'What reasons?' Bella had repeated.

'Adult reasons,' Sophie had said, hating herself for talking down to Bella. 'I have to pay my bills, feed Artemis, look after my mum. Hundreds of reasons. You and Izzy don't need me now.'

'But we do! We do still need you!'

Sophie had stopped in her tracks, hearing the

tears in Bella's voice. She looked down at the child, her cheeks were wet.

'Please Aunty Sophie, please, don't go back and leave us. We *do* need you,' Bella had pleaded.

Sophie had wound her arms around Bella and pulled her into a hug. 'I have to go,' she had said.

'You don't have to,' Bella had insisted. 'Not if you don't want to.'

'I do,' Sophie had replied, holding back her own tears. 'I do.'

Sophie reached London during the rush hour, rain teeming down. She sat in the tightly packed queue of traffic, fidgeting with the radio until eventually she turned it off. Home was less than a mile away, but God knew how long it would take to get there. She resisted the urge to rest her head on the steering wheel, or to get out of the car and walk the rest of the way. She bit down on her rising frustration and suddenly an image of Louis just before she left, silhouetted against a clear blue sky, flashed in front of her.

'Don't want to think about *you*,' she grumbled under her breath. 'Done that already.'

CHAPTER 28

The heavy scent of the lilies on Sophie's desk mingled with the spring breeze that drifted through her open office window – two perks of her new job: fresh flowers twice a week and windows that opened on demand. It was curious that even after a month she still didn't really feel like she belonged at this desk. But no matter what she had tried to do to settle herself back into her old and new life, nothing had quite done the trick so far.

She hadn't expected to walk back into a promotion; in fact, it was the last thing she had been thinking about when she went into work that day, just over a month ago. On that day, she had actually been thinking about why she had got out of bed in the middle of the night and gone to sleep on the sofa instead. And because it was a new sofa, one she had bought as soon as she got home, that was long enough to sleep on at full stretch and didn't smell of curry, she had been wondering why she had lain there for most of the night, wishing that it had been the cramped and stinky old one instead.

The most that Sophie had hoped for on that day was that there would be a large backlog of slow, complicated, distracting administration awaiting her attention which would enable her not to think about the new sofa, or any of its related issues.

So she had been genuinely surprised when Gillian had called her into her office and broken the good news.

'It must feel as if a weight has been lifted,' she'd said when Sophie had told her about the girls going back home.

'It does,' Sophie had said, even though the crushing burden of emotion that had almost over-whelmed her on Porthmeor Beach still seemed to envelope her. She had decided to treat it like a kind of delusion, the sort that if you ignore it hard enough it will just go away.

Gillian had sat her down and made a long speech about loyalty, strength of character and fortitude which had begun to swim over Sophie's head, until she heard the word promotion.

'Promotion?' She had said quickly.

'Yes,' Gillian had told her. 'The time has come for me to take a step back. It's been hard deciding between you and Eve, but I think you've shown how much you can do in difficult circumstances. I think that's what won me over in the end.' Gillian had stretched out her hand over the desk. 'Congratulations, Sophie, you've got the job.'

Sophie had imagined this moment for such a long time, dreamt about it, enacted how it would be to hear those words and to know that she had finally reached the pinnacle she had been striving for, and now that it had happened? Well, it wasn't quite as satisfying as she had imagined. It was Louis's fault of course. It was all his fault, him and his children throwing a spanner in the works and upsetting the beautifully oiled machine that had previously been her life.

'Thank you,' Sophie had told Gillian, smiling at her, although she felt as if her lips were as stiff and numb as if she had been sitting on a freezing beach for half an hour. 'I'm so happy.'

The thing to do, Sophie had decided on the way back to her office, was to get as drunk as she possibly could, because that's what people did when they were celebrating. Gillian had asked her to keep the news to herself until she could make a formal announcement across the whole company, so Sophie had only told Cal, which was more or less the same thing as making an informal announcement across the whole company. But she had to tell somebody, so that person could tell her how marvellous it was. She thought she'd believe it then.

'So tonight we have to go out and celebrate,' she had told Cal intently after he had congratulated her. 'We've got that accounting firm do, so we can start knocking back the fizz there and then – what do you think – a club? I know, I'll call some friends and we can make a night of it. Excellent.'

Cal had looked confused for a second. 'It's a Monday, Sophie,' he had said slowly, as if he was talking to a slightly senile old lady. 'I'm fairly sure most of the people you know – and by the way do you actually know any people? – don't go clubbing on a Monday.'

Sophie had thought for a moment. Cal was right, she hadn't seen any of her friends in months, let alone spoken to them on the phone. Now she was back and free again she was going to change all that, she was going to change everything. She was going to fill her life up with so many events and nights out and dinners with the girls that she wouldn't have time to think about . . . well, anything else.

'You're right,' she had said. 'We'll just go to that party and then you and I can go clubbing. I'll get the several hundred people I know out on Friday night. We can have two parties. Hooray!' Sophie had made two small fists and shook them with forced enthusiasm.

'Hooray,' Cal had said, looking very slightly frightened.

It hadn't really worked out how Sophie had planned.

By nine that evening Sophie had been too drunk to do anything very much other than sleep.

Fortunately she was not a noisy drunk, just a dedicated one. So when Cal had found her propped up at the accounting do bar, gazing miserably at the martini she was drinking as if it were a crystal ball, he was able to usher her quietly out of the kitchen door and into the back of a cab without any of her clients seeing her condition.

'What happened to our night of crazy fun?' he had asked her, after he had told the driver her address. 'You are such a lightweight, Sophie. I knew you'd never manage to stay up past ten. I'll come back with you,' he had sighed. 'You need a coffee or thirty.'

'No, no!' Sophie had flapped her arms in denial. 'You gotta stay sort out the . . . things . . . 'kay?' She had burped noisily and giggled.

Cal had rolled his eyes at the anxious-looking cab driver and climbed into the cab with her.

'I'll come straight back,' he had said. 'Once I've got you home.'

It was when they were at home and Sophie was stretched out on the comfortable and clean sofa that Cal had knelt down beside her and asked, 'What's up Sophie? This isn't like you. Something's happened – what is it?'

'It is like me – this is the new me!' Sophie had declared and then, rather morosely, added, 'I hate this sofa.'

Cal had sat back on his heels. 'Is it because now you've got the job you don't think you can do it?' he had asked her dutifully, feeling the burden of being the sensible one weighing heavily on him.

'Don't be dericiclous . . . relidiclous . . . mad,' Sophie had mumbled, deciding it was safer not to attempt any words longer than one syllable.

'Is it the girls?' Cal had asked, as if he had just experienced a revelation. 'You miss the little brats running around trashing the place, don't you? Your biological clock thing has sounded the alarm and you're panic-drinking! Is that it?'

Sophie had turned her face into the cushion.

'Sophie?' Cal had prompted her. 'Sophie? Come on, tell me that I'm right, because you don't need a man to get knocked up you know. All you need is a willing donor and a turkey baster. I knew these two women who . . . Sophie? Sophie?'

Gingerly he had leant forward and looked at her face. She had passed out.

Sophie had sat up with a brain-wrenching start several hours later. Cal had left all the lights on in her sitting room, her head was thrumming and her mouth was sticky and dry. It had taken her a second or two to work out how she had got there, but once she had remembered, she had flopped her head into her hot palms. 'Oh God,' she had moaned out loud.

Through her fingers she saw that Cal had left her note on the repolished coffee table.

'Have gone back to save your career. You were out of it. Think you need to get laid ASAP.'

'Ha!' Sophie had laughed mirthlessly. 'It was when I got laid that everything went pear-shaped. I should have been a nun. I have a lot in common with nuns. I would have been a natural nun. Plus I look great in black.'

For a second Sophie had caught a glimpse of

herself in the mirror, talking aloud to her empty flat. Once she had preferred her own company to anybody else's; now she had to talk to herself just to be sure that she was really there. It was all *his* fault.

'You have a great life,' she had told herself as she padded to the bathroom and splashed her face with cold water. 'You have your own space, some really good clothes, a great job, lots of friends. You did the right thing, you did the only thing you could do. So just get over it and move on.' After drying her face Sophie had gone into her bedroom and looked at the neatly made bed. With a sigh she had turned around and gone back to the sofa, switching lights off as she went.

Once in the semi-darkness of her living room, Sophie had slipped off her cocktail dress and draped it carefully over the back of the sofa before lying down on it and pulling the quilt that was still there from the previous night over herself.

For a long time in the half-light she had listened to the sounds of the traffic and watched the pattern of headlights flickering across the ceiling. But she hadn't slept: it was impossible with her hung-over brain fizzing and humming with a chaotic jumble of incoherent thoughts that she could neither make sense of or silence.

After a while she had heard Artemis come in.

'Night Artemis,' Sophie had said, wanly. 'Sleep well.'

But instead of Artemis climbing into her favourite

armchair she had done something she had never done before. She had leapt onto the sofa and sat on Sophie's stomach, looking at her with luminous eyes. Carefully Sophie had stretched out a hand and stroked her behind her ears. Artemis hadn't purred, but she hadn't tried to claw out Sophie eyes either. Sophie had sat up a little and squinted at the cat just to make sure it really was Artemis and not some randomly affectionate interloper. Artemis had stared back at her. The cat had never sought out attention from Sophie before; it disconcerted and upset her to think that all the upheaval had affected Artemis as well.

'Oh Artemis,' Sophie had said, 'you must miss them too.'

Artemis had drawn back from Sophie's strokes and turned her back on her before settling down to sleep.

'I understand.' And Sophie had leant her head back against her new faux fur cushions. 'I don't want to talk about it either.'

In her new, lily-scented office, Sophie closed her eyes for a moment to rid herself of the memory of that particular escapade and concentrated on the caress of the warm air on her cheek, carrying with it the promise of summer, before going back to work on her doodle: a mermaid whose tail had reached down the margin of her notebook and flared out across the few notes she had made on the meeting where she was now.

Oh shit, she was in a meeting.

Sophie looked up, and sure enough everyone sitting around the table had stopped talking and was looking at her expectantly.

'So what do you think about that idea then?' James Winter, one of her new executives, pressed her. 'I mean, everybody's done the London Transport Museum and the Aquarium, but you've got to agree that's a one-off venue idea, right?'

Sophie glanced at Cal, who was sitting on her right-hand side and who had scrawled in inch-high letters on his notepad, 'CONCORDE'.

'Well, yes, it's a good idea, James,' Sophie said, sitting up in her chair a little. 'But I think there are some issues that need clarification. Firstly, where's the nearest decommissioned Concorde – in London? Close enough to get a busload of people there? And secondly, aren't they a bit small inside? It might be like having a party in a really long, narrow, living room. Maybe if the venue was the hangar and the plane was like a sort of chill-out room . . . but anyway, have you even found out if it's possible to hire one for parties?' James looked sheepish. Sophie was not surprised – his ideas, though original, were often a bit pie in the sky. 'Look into it and get back to me. Anyone else got any ideas? No? So, let's catch up on new business leads – anything, anyone?'

She knew Cal had something to say, but before he could open his mouth Eve's chair slammed forward and she grinned at Sophie from the other end of the conference table.

'That'll be me then,' she said.

Eight pairs of eyes swivelled in Eve's direction.

Everyone had been surprised when Eve didn't hand in her notice immediately, back on the day that Gillian formally announced that Sophie was taking over from her. She had made the announcement in the open-plan part of the office, and the collective sigh of relief was almost audible. Gillian had talked briefly about logistics, asked Sophie to come and see her in an hour or so, and then turned on her heel and returned to her office with a spring in her step that Sophie had never seen before.

Pretty soon everyone else who was milling about and offering Sophie their congratulations had noticed that Eve had not moved a muscle, but was standing with her arms folded across her chest, staring dangerously hard at her rival. It was at that point that everyone had suddenly remembered jobs they had to do elsewhere in the building and scuttled away.

Eve had stalked purposefully over to where Sophie was waiting rather warily for her, feeling that she should have her gun hand twitching at her holster if only she had one.

'So you're fucked off you didn't get the promotion?' Sophie had felt someone had to say it.

'Yeah,' Eve had said evenly. 'But not surprised. I knew you'd get it. All that dead best friend's kids business really gave you the edge, you bitch.'

Sophie had considered the statement. Ironically it was true: being out of the office for weeks on end, looking after the girls but keeping her hand in at work, had boosted her in Gillian's estimation no end.

'So you're leaving?' Sophie had asked her flatly. Curiously, she discovered she didn't want Eve to go. Gillian had said it had been a hard choice to make between the two of them, and Sophie wanted Eve to stay and be her exit route. She wanted someone to take her place just in case she ever got up the courage to walk out of her job and go round the world or something. She didn't think she ever would; she had had her one moment of reckless courage and it hadn't ended well. But she liked the thought of it being an option.

'No,' Eve had replied, eyeing Sophie. 'I'm just going to work out some undetectable way of poisoning you.'

Sophie had laughed a little nervously. 'Believe it or not, I'm glad you're staying,' she had said

'It's mainly because I don't think you'll be here very long,' Eve had continued. 'You've gone even softer since you came back from nannying. I reckon you'll find some poor investment banker to marry you and get knocked up before the year's up, so I'm just biding my time really.'

Sophie had snorted in response. 'Trust me, that's so not going to happen,' she had said, knowing that she *really* didn't want to marry an investment banker.

'Anyway,' Eve had said, 'it's probably just as well you got the job and not me.'

'Why?' Sophie had asked her, genuinely intrigued.

'Well, you can't hang around wheelie bins smoking when you're the boss, can you?' Eve had said.

'No,' Sophie had replied, with more regret than she had expected. 'I suppose you can't.' But it wasn't the chance to skive off that had made her feel a sudden pang of regret. It was something else entirely that she wouldn't tell Eve or anyone. A quiet truth had been nagging at her from the moment she had returned to the office. Now that she had everything she had been working towards for the best part of her adult life, now she had the power and prestige and money, she had made a very depressing discovery. She didn't really want it.

The huge Friday-night event she had planned to celebrate her promotion had had to be put off for a week due to the lack of availability of willing guests at such short notice, and even then numbers had dwindled rather rapidly to the two or three people from the office, including Lisa, who weren't too scared to have a drink in front of the boss, Cal, before he went off to meet Mauro, and Christina, the only one of Sophie's friends not currently in the kind of relationship that monopolised Friday nights.

'Thank Christ you're back in town, Soph,'

Christina had told her as she set two glasses of wine down at their table. 'If it wasn't for you I'd have no-one to go on the pull with. I can't believe it, *everyone* is hooked up. It's so *dull* when everyone is happy.'

'Oh, I know,' Sophie had said enthusiastically, as she took a large gulp of her wine. 'Well, I'm not happy. Any time you want to go on the pull, count me in.'

'You're so funny,' Christina had said, laughing. 'I've quite missed you. So fill me in then – where *have* you been recently? I thought you'd emigrated or something. Didn't somebody die?'

Perhaps if Christina had known what was coming she wouldn't have bothered to ask, but when Sophie was only a mere twenty minutes into recounting her trials and tribulations of the last few weeks, Sophie had noticed that Christina wasn't really listening to her. Instead she was gazing rather obviously at someone just over Sophie's left shoulder.

'Chris!' Sophie had attempted to regain her friend's attention. 'I'm telling the story of my life here!'

Christina had jumped. 'God *sorry*. I just couldn't take my eyes off that man over there. He's *very* handsome. And he looks rich. Probably married of course or – Christina had sat back in her seat and dropped her palms onto her knees. 'Typical, he's talking to Cal . . . I should have known. The best ones are always married or gay.'

'Or widowers,' Sophie had added without thinking.

'Or what?' Christina had asked her.

'Nothing,' Sophie had said quickly. 'Anyway, that will be Mauro, Cal's been going on about him non-stop since I got back . . .'

Sophie had turned round to get a look at the man who had captured Cal's attention for longer than two minutes and as she saw him she caught her breath. It wasn't Mauro.

It was Jake Flynn.

'Oh God,' Sophie had said just as the music lulled for a moment.

Jake had looked up and smiled at her. Sophie had turned quickly back to Christina and downed her glass of wine.

'What?' Christina had demanded. 'Don't tell me he's yours? Seriously, if *you* get a boyfriend before I do I'm going to kill myself, because it officially means there is no hope for me.'

Sophie wasn't listening, she had picked up Christina's drink and sunk that too.

'Hey!' Christina had protested.

'I'll get you another, but I've got to go over and talk to him first. You know all that stuff that happened in Cornwall?' Christina had looked blank. Sophie had shaken her head in irritation. 'Well, a lot of stuff happened there, stuff I can't seem to move on from or stop thinking about *night* after *night* after . . . and, anyway, I don't know why I didn't think about it before. Jake is the solution, Jake will take my mind off things, he's totally into me or at least he was. And if he still is then I'm going to be totally into him. You said it – he's practically perfect.'

Luckily Sophie hadn't seen the expression on Christina's face as she headed determinedly towards the bar where Jake was standing. If she had the look of horror and disbelief might have put her off her stroke a little.

Sophie had planned to approach Jake with the kind of cool sophistication she knew he was attracted to. Unfortunately, she had tripped a little bit when she was only a step or two from him and ended up stumbling into his chest.

'Oh,' Sophie had said, righting herself. 'It's these new shoes. Impossible to walk in.' She had glanced down to see which of the ten or so pairs she had bought since she had been back she had put on. Annoyingly the ones she had randomly selected that morning didn't go at all with what she was wearing.

'Sophie.' Jake had smiled at her, his voice carefully neutral. 'Good to see you! I heard your news today and when I went by the office they said you'd be here. I wanted to buy you a drink, so you'd know I'm cool about everything and very happy for you, although I guess I'll be doing most of my business with Cal now – you'll be far too important to deal with me.'

'I'll always have time for you, Jake,' Sophie had said, tossing her hair as coquettishly as she knew how.

Cal had looked from Sophie to Jake. 'Good to see you, Jake. I'm off now,' he had told Sophie. 'Remember what I said.'

'What did you say?' Sophie had asked him.

'That you need to get laid ASAP,' Cal had replied, and then he had gone.

Sophie had covered her face with her hands and Jake had gently removed them and smiled at her, still holding her wrists.

'First rule of management, never let your staff see you're embarrassed.'

'Oh, I've blown that one about two hundred times already and I don't even start my new job until next week.' Sophie had laughed and noticed Jake had held her for a moment or two longer before he let go. Perhaps it wasn't too late after all.

'I sort of didn't expect you to come back.' Jake had handed her the glass of wine he had ordered for her.

'Didn't you?' Sophie had asked him with real curiosity. 'Why?'

'It looked to me like something was going on there. I didn't think you'd be able to leave them. Any of them.'

Sophie had sipped her drink and fought the rising tide of sadness that swelled in her chest.

'I missed you actually,' she had said, looking up at Jake. He had watched her for a moment as if he were trying to read her mind and in response she had tried to banish any thoughts of Louis that might be lurking in her eyes. She knew what she was doing was wrong but maybe Cal was right, maybe she did need to get laid. If she had another man in her bed, a man who cared for her and wanted her, then perhaps she'd be able to get the persistent memory of the last one out of her head for good.

'That's not why you came back,' Jake had said with a sad, wry smile.

'I'm sorry about the way I acted the last time I saw you, Jake. Throwing myself at you like that. You were right to say what you did, I was confused. I needed to go to Cornwall. But once I was there I realised how wrong it all was for me. How complicated.'

'Just because something's complicated it doesn't make it wrong,' Jake had said casually. 'It's worth pursuing something that will make you truly happy, even if it's difficult getting there.'

Sophie had resisted the urge to scowl. Jake wasn't being nearly as helpful as she had hoped he would be.

She had supposed she'd just have to seduce him and as she had no idea how to go about it she had decided to be as direct and as blunt as possible.

'Jake, I want you,' she had said, somehow holding his gaze and her nerve at the same time. 'Sexually.'

Jake had to raise his hand to his mouth to cover his smile and Sophie felt her skin instantly blotch.

'I'm sorry,' he said and his smile was gone in an instant, replaced by that compelling, blue gaze.

Finally, Sophie thought, he was taking her seriously.

'Why?' Jake had asked her.

'Why!' Sophie had raised her voice and a few people looked across at her. 'What do you mean why?' She had dropped her voice to a whisper. 'Isn't it enough that I do?'

Jake had set his glass down on the bar and led Sophie away from the busy bar to a quiet corner near the fire escape.

'You know I want you,' he had told her, his voice low and urgent. 'I've wanted you for a long time. I wanted you even after I told you I didn't.' Jake had given a brief, mirthless laugh. 'You know what? I don't really care if you are into someone else. If you want me to take you to bed just to help you forget that someone else then I will. That's how much I want you, Sophie. But answer me honestly, do you really want this? Do *you* really want *this*? Because I don't care if I get hurt – but I couldn't stand to see you hurt yourself any more.'

Sophie had looked in Jake's intense blue eyes and she had willed herself to say yes, she wanted him to take her to bed.

But she couldn't. She couldn't use Jake like some kind of medication because it wouldn't work and anyway he was right, she would only be hurting them both.

She had dropped her gaze to her feet. 'Oh Jake,' she had said softly. 'I'm sorry. I'm such a fool.'

Jake had swallowed and nodded stiffly. 'You probably are,' he had said. 'But not for the reasons you think.'

He had turned on his heel and walked out of the bar and Sophie had not heard from or seen him since. All she knew was that his people called her people whenever they needed anything done.

So, all the going out, all the cocktails and shopping and smoking and not even Jake had helped. From the moment she had come back she had tried, really tried, to fit herself back into her new and improved life but nothing she could do would change the most startling and frightening fact: despite her new, frantic, city life, she was desperately lonely. And there were only three people in the whole world who could take that loneliness away.

Three people who it was far too late to go back to now – even if she had the courage to make the trip.

The meeting broke up and Eve paused by Sophie's end of the desk to drop off some paperwork.

'OK?' she said generally, but Sophie knew she was referring to her vacant spell in the middle of the meeting she was supposed to be running.

'Fine, getting a cold or something,' Sophie said, with half a smile.

Eve raised an eyebrow before leaving.

Cal checked his watch. 'It's lunchtime,' he said. 'Come on, let's go out for a walk.'

Sophie looked at the pile of paperwork on her desk without enthusiasm. 'I can't, Cal, I have to catch up on all of this *and* read the minutes from the meeting – has Lisa finished her report on the last function she managed yet?'

'You're joking, aren't you?' Cal said, picking up the offending pile, arranging it neatly and dropping it in all its entirety into one of the deep drawers of Sophie's filing cabinet. 'There, that's filed. Lisa won't have finished that until this afternoon if we're lucky. She's out to lunch, in all senses of the word, with the new love of her life. A brickie called Micky. Cute, huh? Anyway, it's a beautiful spring morning out there and we're going for a walk to clear our heads. Come on! I'll buy you a Mars bar, although God knows you look like you've had enough already, judging by the fit of those trousers.'

A few minutes later they sat side by side on a bench in Finsbury Circus, looking at a bed of red tulips bobbing cheerfully in the breeze.

'Why is this called a circus?' Cal asked her. 'When it's square?'

Sophie shrugged. 'Don't care,' she said.

Cal sighed. 'Look. When you first came back and were a bit off-beam I thought it was exhaustion. All those weeks of wiping arses and noses, ugh! And when you went through your thankfully short period as a drunken lash I thought it was the stress of getting a job you probably couldn't really do. I put up with the constant hangovers, the nights out, spending *my* lunchtime taking *your* impulse buys back for you because you're too embarrassed to do it yourself. I thought, she's had a difficult time. It will take time to adjust. But you've been back for over a month now, Soph. You keep getting *more* vague and airy-fairy, not less. And I know for a fact you aren't enjoying any of this crazy merry-go-round you've got yourself stuck on; I've never seen a more miserable socialite. Which leads me to one conclusion. Unless you've developed a very boring addiction to heroin, which you haven't because you hate needles, you're depressed. So, I'm finally begging you to please tell me – why are you depressed?'

Sophie frowned at him, her exhaustion making it hard to follow him. 'I'm fine. Honestly!'

Cal sighed again and rolled his eyes. 'I preferred you when you were in love with Jake,' he said wistfully. 'It was much less complicated.'

Sophie managed to raise a small smile. 'I was never in love with Jake – I wish I had been and anyway I'll be fine,' she said. 'Like you said, I just need a bit of adjustment time, that's all.'

Cal looked at his watch again. 'A month not long enough? Look, I'd prefer you just to tell me, but as you're going to make me guess . . . You fell in love with the kids and then their good-looking mysterious dad and he toyed with your affections before cruelly spurning you – is that it? Hey, that's a bit like *Jane Eyre*; you could go round and burn their new house down, after evacuating the children first of course. That'll get his attention. No, hang on, I think that was the mad first wife in the attic.'

Sophie did not crack a smile, her gaze fixed on the tulips, but Cal persisted. 'You could see the girls, couldn't you?' he asked her. 'I bet Mr Mysterious would let you seem them, even if he doesn't fancy you. All you'd have to do is pick up the phone and ask.'

Sophie wondered if Cal had guessed how many times she had sat with her phone in her hand and thought of dialling the number that Louis had sent her along with a change of address card the girls had made shortly after she got back. He hadn't written anything in the card except for their details and underneath that Bella had written, 'We love you Aunty Sophie!'

Of course she couldn't 'just pick up the phone'. Of course she couldn't, because picking up the phone would mean talking to him and hearing his voice and before she knew she'd be right back to square one which would be difficult because she hadn't actually moved off square one since the day she'd left St Ives.

'I can't,' Sophie simply told Cal. 'I just . . . can't.'

'He must have really fucking spurned you,' Cal said, 'for you to be so down about it after all this time. If I didn't have such a pretty face to protect I'd go and beat him up for you.' He put an arm around Sophie's shoulder. 'Look, Sophie, you've got to give up this unrequited-love lark. It hurts now but I promise you it will get better eventually. Really.'

Sophie looked at him. 'He didn't spurn me,' she said on impulse. '*I* spurned *him*.' She paused and looked puzzled. 'Have you ever noticed when you say a word you don't use much a lot in one go its starts to sound weird? Spurn . . . spurn . . . spu—'

'Hold on a minute!' Cal's tone snapped her out of her reverie. '*You* spurned *him*! *Why?* I mean WHY have you been moping around here for weeks on end depressing us all with your miserable face when you could have been romping around the heather or whatever the fuck they have in Cornwall with Mr Mysterious the whole time?'

Sophie rubbed her eyes with the heels of her hands. It was more or less that very same question that had kept her awake every night since she'd got back.

On the beach, in the cold, in the hours before dawn everything had seemed perfectly clear. She had felt she knew exactly what she was doing up until the moment she had pulled up outside her flat in London. From that moment she had been running as fast as she possibly could to get away from the persistent, nagging doubt that she had made the worst mistake of her life. That Louis really wanted her as much as she wanted him and she had denied them both the chance to find out.

Sophie thought she must be the only person in the world who was actually capable of being almost terminally sensible. God knows, it felt like her decision was killing her very slowly and painfully.

'It's too late now,' she insisted, giving Cal the same answer she had given herself. 'I had this tiny, slim chance of making something happen and I ran away from it. I mean, of course I did. I'm me, aren't I? I missed my chance. It's just too complicated now.'

'Oh yes, it is,' Cal said with heavy sarcasm. 'It's deeply complicated. You fancy *him*, he fancies *you*. You both love his kids. That's a really tricky one, that is. Better ruin everyone's life, including mine, while you think about it for all eternity.' He glared at Sophie. 'How, pray, is it complicated?'

Sophie glared back at him. 'Because . . .' Sophie struggled to dredge up all of the beach reasons. 'He's Carrie's husband. Being with him would be like cheating on Carrie! And maybe he doesn't really like me, maybe he just wanted me for a fling and then if I fell for him and it all went wrong what would it do to the girls? Those children have been through enough and . . . and other reasons I forget just now, but which are very sensible, actually.'

Cal nearly choked on his Diet Coke. 'You are impossible,' he told her. 'He Is In Love With You.'

'How do you *know*?' Sophie wailed, flinging up her hands in despair.

'Because I know you, and I know the reason you ran away back here wasn't because of any of that crap you've just spouted. It was because you *know* he loves you too and you're scared shitless. Why else would you be in such a pathetic state.'

'I still can't go back, Cal. He's Carrie's husband.'

Cal raised both his beautifully shaped eyebrows skyward. 'That is not a real reason,' he said, with some frustration.

'It *is* a real reason,' she insisted. 'And it's a bloody good reason too, thank you very much.'

'Look, even I know that Carrie and Louis weren't together for years before you met him. You haven't told me the whole story, but I've worked out that whatever broke them up, it wasn't just that he was an evil genius. It was probably because, like the rest of us, they were both human. I mean, think about it, Soph – you were in love with Alex, weren't you?'

'I thought I was,' Sophie conceded, although she couldn't see the point of the question.

'Exactly – and that was over two years ago. So tell me, how do you – an alive person – feel about the fact that he's getting married in two weeks?'

'Is he?' Sophie said absently, 'that's nice.' Then her brow furrowed and she glanced at Cal. 'How do you know?'

'I don't.' I was just proving the point. If Carrie was here she wouldn't care about you and Louis being together. *She* would have moved on.'

Sophie nodded. 'I know,' she said. 'But she's not here to say it's OK and that makes it impossible.'

Cal gave her a scathing look. 'Tell me the real reason you're doing this to yourself.'

'What other reason would there possibly be?' Sophie said half-heartedly.

Cal gestured at the cloudless sky. 'If Carrie is up there right now she's probably shouting at you, "Go to him, you stupid cow!" Oh no, you're not joining a nunnery instead of marrying the captain and becoming Mrs Von Trapp, based on some misguided principle. Not even you are that stupid. You're doing it because you're terrified. Terrified of being in love, terrified of being happy, terrified of waking up and realising that the life you've lived for years on end was actually a shit one.' Sophie's eyes widened, but Cal didn't give her a moment to interrupt him. 'Yes, Sophie, your life to date has been boring and small and lonely and repetitive – join the club! But if you have a chance to change that, you don't have to just stick it out anyway, like some kind of self-inflicted punishment for being happy. That's just twisted!'

'That's not it!' Sophie said, her protest weakening by the second. 'Well, it is a bit. But it's more than that, Cal. Like I said, it's not just him, is it? It's a whole family, a family that's just starting out. What if it all went really wrong with Louis, what then for the girls? Wouldn't it be terrible if we broke up and they were in the middle of it? I couldn't do that to them.'

'No-one's saying you should run down there and marry him. Just be together, keep it casual, see how you feel. Keep the girls posted. Let them know you'll still love them, however it works out. For once in your life make a choice for yourself, Sophie Mills!'

Sophie considered the words she hadn't dared say to herself. 'Am I strong enough, though?' she asked Cal. 'What if it goes wrong?'

'You're strong enough,' Cal told her without reservation. 'You've proved how strong you are. And anyway, I've got a feeling that this is a choice you won't regret. I'm practically psychic, you know.'

'It's a long way to go for dinner on a Friday night,' Sophie said, throwing up the last obstacle for him to shoot down.

'Are you happy at work, Sophie?' Cal asked.

'No,' Sophie said honestly. 'Not any more.'

'Then leave,' Cal instructed her. 'Rent out your flat, find a place to stay down there. Oh yes, there will be a bit of a scandal here. Gillian will disapprove and Eve will be triumphant, but what do you care? You'll be milking a cow in the country, all blissed up and fat. Well, fatter.'

'But this is my job, my dream job,' Sophie protested weakly. 'I loved my job.'

'You said loved, past tense. And anyway it's not wrong for your dreams to change, you know. It's just wrong if you don't pursue them with every ounce of energy and determination that's got you this far. You've got money in the bank and anyway, I'm sure they have parties all the time in Cornwall. You could get in on that scene. Organise a pig-throwing festival or whatever it is they do down there.'

Sophie smiled. 'Someone else said that to me once,' she said. 'But it's a big risk, it's scary.'

'Taking risks is what life is all about, Sophie,' Cal said in exasperation. 'I thought you would have known that, wearing that shirt with that lipstick. Right out on a fashion limb.'

Sophie laughed and felt a sudden surge of adrenalin. 'I might just do it,' she said a little shakily.

'Not might, just do it.'

Sophie looked into Cal's steady blue eyes and picked up his hand.

'I'm going to do it,' she said, her eyes wide with excitement and terror. 'Fuck!'

'It will be wonderful,' Cal said, kissing her on the cheek.

'Oh but hang on.' Sophie gripped Cal's hand hard enough to make him wince. 'What if . . . what if Louis has gone off me?'

'Oh, shut the fuck up. As if!'

CHAPTER 29

I t had taken a while to find the cottage Louis and the girls were renting. It was set against the steep rise of the hill, about a mile out of town. A small, whitewashed building, it looked as if it had weathered a hundred storms and still stood strong.

As Sophie pulled up at the bottom of the drive she wondered again if this had all been a really bad idea. If she should have at least called first, checked out how Louis was feeling, or even if he had anything on that weekend. He might be out; he might be in with some Cornish beauty in his arms. The girls might have gone off her . . .

She suddenly wished that her mum had broken down when she had told her straight after work yesterday what she was planning, and begged her not to go. But instead she'd just hugged Sophie and said, 'You go, darling, you do what you have to do. And if it all works out for you, you never know, maybe I'll get my dog sanctuary down there after all.' And then she'd offered her a packet of biscuits for the journey, which Sophie had had to decline on the grounds that they were Bonios.

As Sophie sat in the car she wondered for the last time about what she was doing, about the chance she was taking and how it might all go dreadfully wrong or might even go wonderfully right. Knowing that, however her decision turned out, she had had to make it anyway. Sophie stopped her compulsive speculation and took a deep breath. It was a beautiful evening, the sun lighting up the foliage around the cottage with a fiery halo, gilding everything with its glow.

She got out of the car, opened the rear door and lifted a plastic carrying case carefully off the back seat where it had been secured with a seat belt. Biting her lips, she went to the front door, but before she could ring the bell she heard voices echoing in the air. Peering through the front window she saw that Louis, Bella and Izzy were all in the back garden. The girls were decked out in macs and wellies and it looked as if they were helping Louis with some planting, although from what Sophie could see it looked as if the gardening had recently deteriorated into an all-out mud fight and Bella and Izzy shrieked with laughter as Louis chased them around in circles, a sod of soil in each fist. For a moment Sophie looked on at the perfect picture that made her happier and more afraid than she had ever been in her entire life.

'Well, it's now or never,' she told the carrying case. The carrying case was still sulking.

Sophie did not know how to greet them, so for a long moment she just stood there, case in hand, watching them, her heart in her mouth. Then Izzy saw her.

'Aunty Sophieeeeeeeeeee!' she screamed, and hurled her dirt-covered self at Sophie, spraying mud everywhere. The carrying case yowled in annoyance, so Sophie set it down and, kneeling, wound her arms tightly around Izzy.

'You've grown so much,' she said, kissing the girl's earth-smeared cheeks several times.

'I know,' said Izzy proudly. 'I'm as tall as a giraffe nearly.'

Then Bella was there, her arms around Sophie's neck, kissing her cheeks one after the other.

'You're here again!' she said, delighted. 'I knew you'd come back! It is a long visit, isn't it?'

Sophie untangled the girls from around her and looked over their heads at Louis, who was watching her with astonishment, his hands on his hips.

'Well, maybe,' she said, looking at him steadily. 'If you want it to be.'

'We do, we do we do!' both girls sang in unison, dancing round her.

At last Louis spoke. 'Girls!' he said lightly. 'Come on, you're getting Sophie all muddy! Go in and get changed into something clean and dry, OK? It's nearly teatime anyway.'

'No!' Izzy protested. 'Don't want to!'

Bella looked from Sophie to her dad.

'Yes you do,' she said, grabbing Izzy by the arm and dragging her towards the house whilst tickling her so that her protest gradually morphed into a giggling fit.

'Oh, before you go.' Sophie remembered the carrying case. She picked it up and held it out to Bella. 'They don't accept cats at the B&B I'm booked into. Will you look after Artemis for me?'

The children squealed with delight and Bella returned to retrieve the case, carrying it carefully into the house. Amazingly it began to purr.

Sophie stood up and smoothed down her skirt.

'I'm a bit of a mess,' she said, laughing nervously, not quite brave enough to look at Louis.

'A bit,' he said, taking a step closer. 'Why are you here, Sophie?' he asked her gently, looking deep into her eyes. 'I need to know because I can't . . . why are you here?'

Sophie thought about the hundred or so reasons and excuses she had invented on the journey down to be near Louis without actually having to tell him why, from redundancy to a sudden allergy to cities. But when it came to it she realised she'd already wasted too much time. The truth had always been there, from the first night she had spent with Louis, but she had been too scared to see it. Even during her freezing vigil on the beach, she realised she hadn't been looking for the truth, not really. She had been looking for reasons to leave because she thought leaving would be easier than facing what she already knew, that Louis felt about her exactly the same way she felt about him. She couldn't have been more wrong.

'To be near you,' she said simply. 'To be close enough to where you are, to be able to go to dinner with you on a Friday night, or go for a walk on the beach with you and the girls every Sunday. To be able to be with you when there's nothing else to think about or feel except what it's like to be with you. To get to know you and see if I'm right about the way that you make me feel. To find out if I'm really as in love with you as I think I am.' Finally Sophie looked up at him. 'If that's OK with you.'

Louis closed the last two steps between them in one movement and held her tightly for a long time. He kissed the top of her head and then released her a little so that he could look at her face. 'It's definitely OK by me,' he said. 'It's more than OK.'